# STAR WARS
## —ADVENTURES—

# THE LIGHT AND THE DARK

Facebook: **facebook.com/idwpublishing**
Twitter: **@idwpublishing**
YouTube: **youtube.com/idwpublishing**
Instagram: **@idwpublishing**

ISBN: 978-1-68405-797-9          24  23  22  21      1 2 3 4

Cover Artist
**Nick Brokenshire**

Letterers
**Jake M. Wood** and
**Johanna Nattalie**

Series Assistant Editor
**Riley Farmer**

Series Editors
**Elizabeth Brei** and
**Heather Antos**

Collection Editors
**Alonzo Simon** and
**Zac Boone**

Managing Editor
**Lauren LePera**

Collection Designer
**Nathan Widick**

**Lucasfilm Credits:**

Senior Editor
**Robert Simpson**

Creative Director
**Michael Siglain**

Art Director
**Troy Alders**

Lucasfilm Art Department
**Phil Szostak**

Story Group
**Matt Martin, Pablo Hidalgo,**
and **Emily Shkoukani**

Originally published as STAR WARS ADVENTURES issues #1–6.

Nachie Marsham, Publisher
Blake Kobashigawa, VP of Sales
Tara McCrillis, VP Publishing Operations
John Barber, Editor-in-Chief
Mark Doyle, Editorial Director, Originals
Erika Turner, Executive Editor
Scott Dunbier, Director, Special Projects
Mark Irwin, Editorial Director, Consumer Products Mgr
Lauren LaPera, Managing Editor
Joe Hughes, Director, Talent Relations
Anna Morrow, Sr. Marketing Director
Alexandra Hargett, Book & Mass Market Sales Director
Keith Davidsen, Senior Manager, PR
Topher Alford, Sr Digital Marketing Manager
Shauna Monteforte, Sr. Director of Manufacturing Operations
Jamie Miller, Sr. Operations Manager
Nathan Widick, Sr. Art Director, Head of Design
Neil Uyetake, Sr. Art Director Design & Production
Shawn Lee, Art Director Design & Production
Jack Rivera, Art Director, Marketing

Ted Adams and Robbie Robbins, IDW Founders

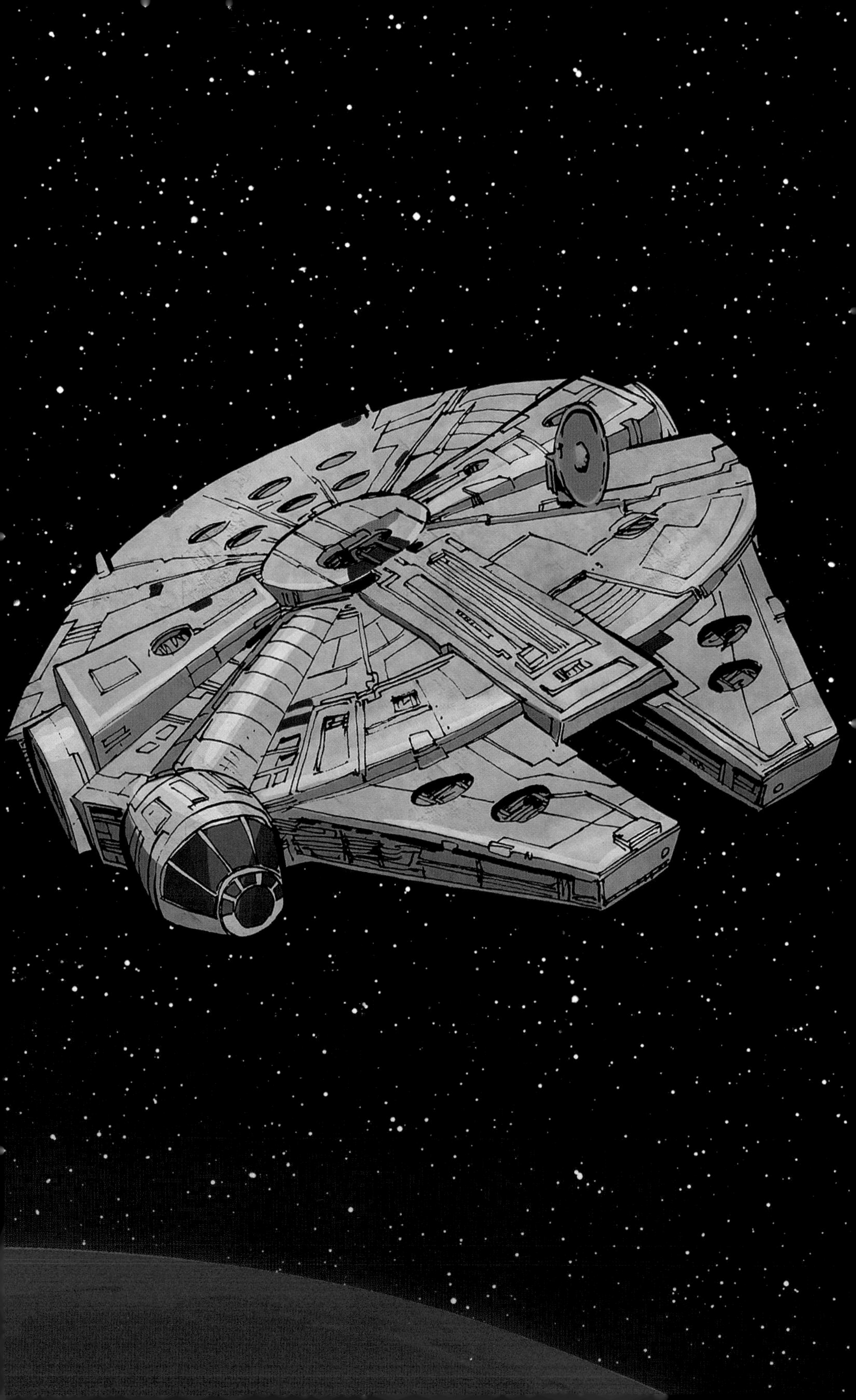

PAGE 7 THE OBSTACLE COURSE
WRITTEN BY MICHAEL MORECI
ART BY ILIAS KYRIAZIS
COLORS BY CHARLIE KIRCHOFF

PAGE 33 LIFE DAY
WRITTEN BY MICHAEL MORECI
ART BY MEGAN LEVENS
COLORS BY CHARLIE KIRCHOFF

PAGE 59 THE INCIDENT
WRITTEN BY KATIE COOK
ART BY CARA McGEE
COLORS BY BRITTANY PEER

PAGE 85 INVASION OF ECHO BASE
STORY & ART BY NICK BROKENSHIRE

PAGE 95 FOLLOW AND LEAD
WRITTEN BY SAM MAGGS
ART BY DAVIDE TINTO
COLORS BY REBECCA NALTY

PAGE 105 THE HOSTAGE
WRITTEN BY SHANE McCARTHY
ART BY MEGAN LEVENS
COLORS BY CHARLIE KIRCHOFF

PAGE 115 CREDITS
WRITTEN BY JORDAN CLARK
ART BY YAEL NATHAN

PAGE 125 THE SHORT GOODBYE
WRITTEN BY CASEY GILLY
ART BY BUTCH MAPA
COLORS BY CHARLIE KIRCHOFF

PAGE 135 THE GAZE ELECTRIC
WRITTEN BY DANIEL JOSÉ OLDER
ART BY NICK BROKENSHIRE

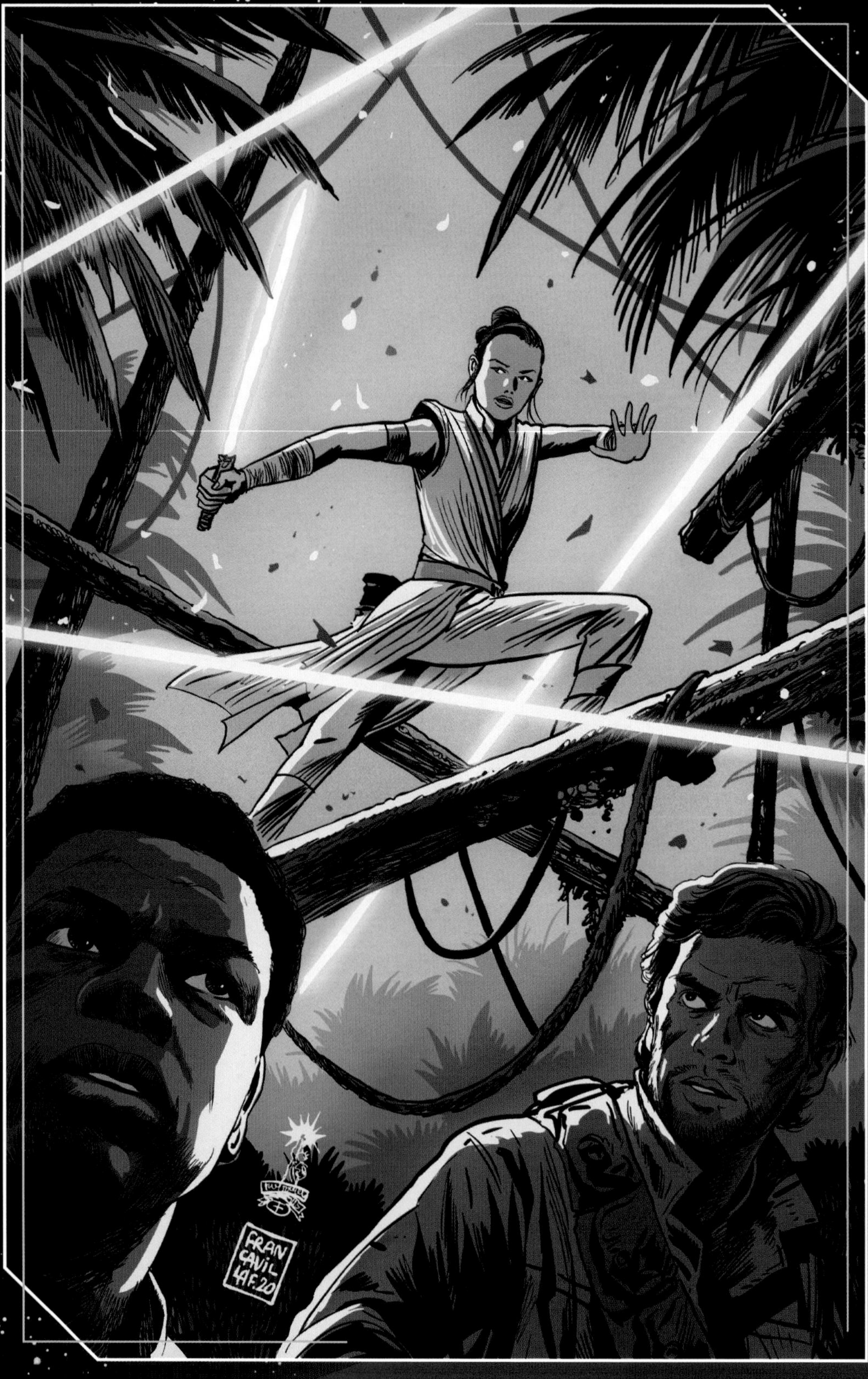

ART BY **FRANCESCO FRANCAVILLA**

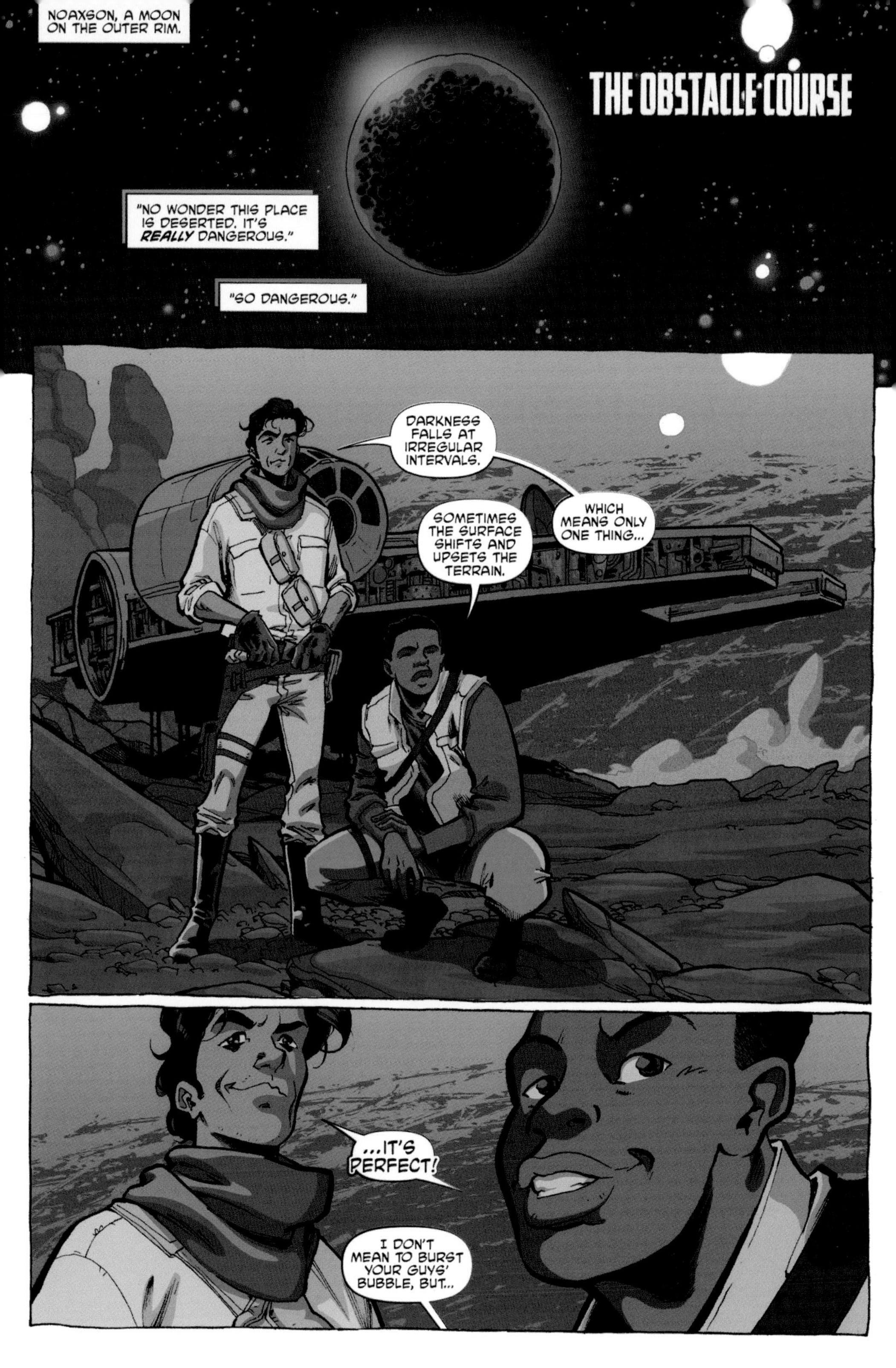
NOAXSON, A MOON ON THE OUTER RIM.
THE OBSTACLE COURSE
"NO WONDER THIS PLACE IS DESERTED. IT'S REALLY DANGEROUS."
"SO DANGEROUS."
DARKNESS FALLS AT IRREGULAR INTERVALS.
SOMETIMES THE SURFACE SHIFTS AND UPSETS THE TERRAIN.
WHICH MEANS ONLY ONE THING...
...IT'S PERFECT!
I DON'T MEAN TO BURST YOUR GUYS' BUBBLE, BUT...

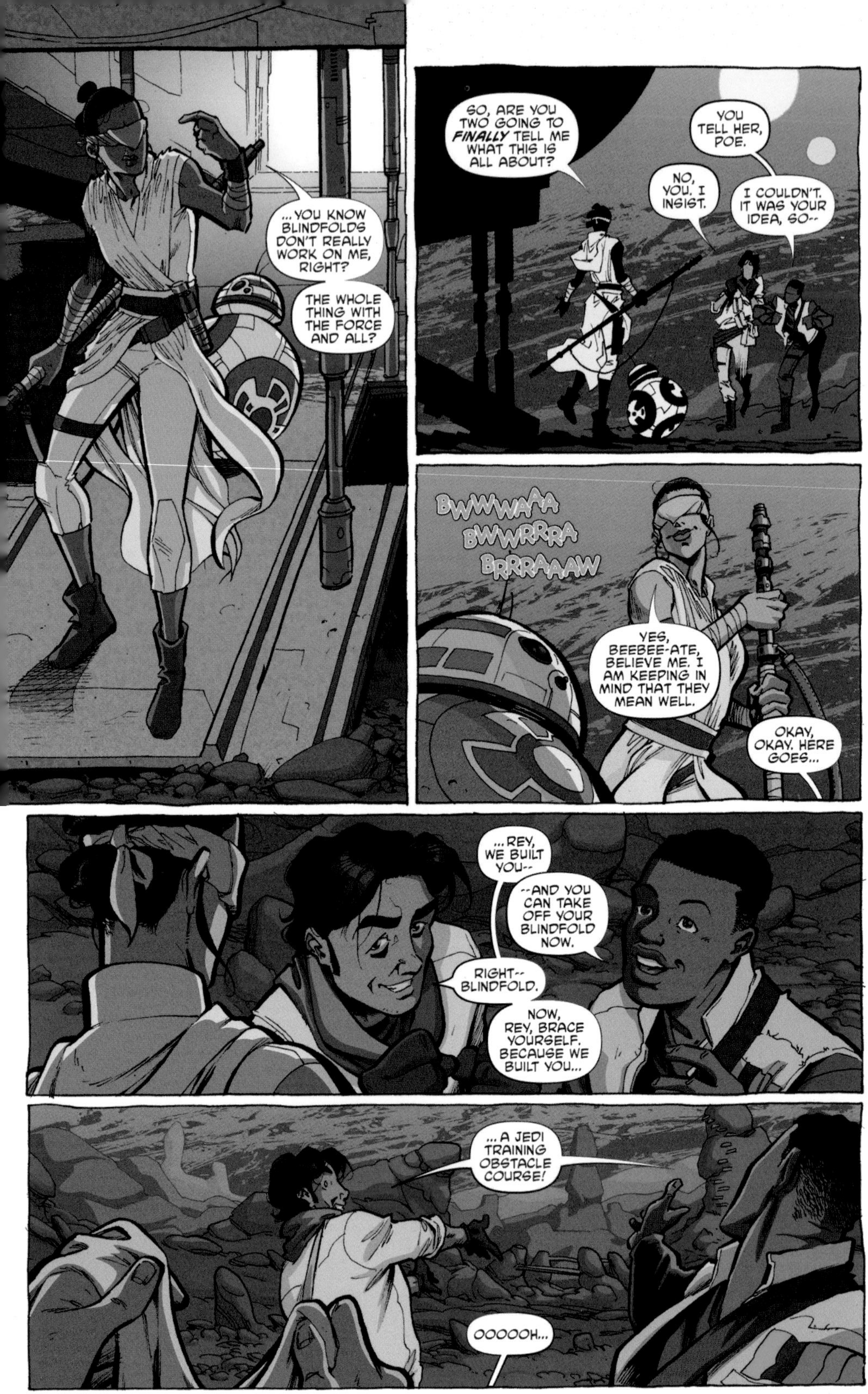
...YOU KNOW BLINDFOLDS DON'T REALLY WORK ON ME, RIGHT?
THE WHOLE THING WITH THE FORCE AND ALL?
SO, ARE YOU TWO GOING TO FINALLY TELL ME WHAT THIS IS ALL ABOUT?
YOU TELL HER, POE.
NO, YOU. I INSIST.
I COULDN'T. IT WAS YOUR IDEA, SO--
BWWWAAA
BWWRRRA
BRRRAAAW
YES, BEEBEE-ATE, BELIEVE ME. I AM KEEPING IN MIND THAT THEY MEAN WELL.
OKAY, OKAY. HERE GOES...
...REY, WE BUILT YOU--
--AND YOU CAN TAKE OFF YOUR BLINDFOLD NOW.
RIGHT-- BLINDFOLD.
NOW, REY, BRACE YOURSELF. BECAUSE WE BUILT YOU...
...A JEDI TRAINING OBSTACLE COURSE!
OOOOOH...

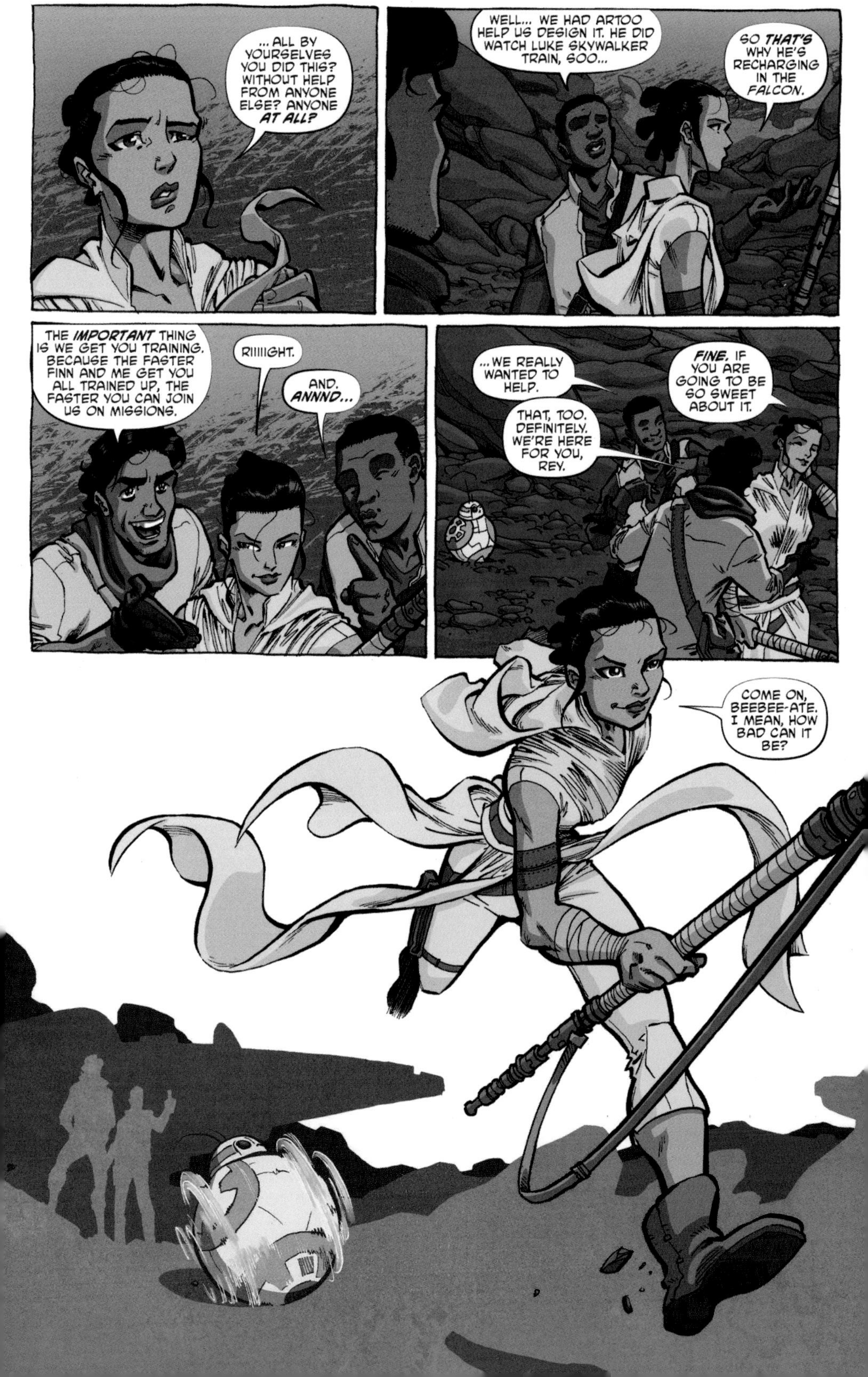

... ALL BY YOURSELVES YOU DID THIS? WITHOUT HELP FROM ANYONE ELSE? ANYONE AT ALL?
WELL... WE HAD ARTOO HELP US DESIGN IT. HE DID WATCH LUKE SKYWALKER TRAIN, SOO...
SO THAT'S WHY HE'S RECHARGING IN THE FALCON.
THE IMPORTANT THING IS WE GET YOU TRAINING. BECAUSE THE FASTER FINN AND ME GET YOU ALL TRAINED UP, THE FASTER YOU CAN JOIN US ON MISSIONS.
RIIIIIGHT.
AND. ANNND...
...WE REALLY WANTED TO HELP.
THAT, TOO. DEFINITELY. WE'RE HERE FOR YOU, REY.
FINE. IF YOU ARE GOING TO BE SO SWEET ABOUT IT.
COME ON, BEEBEE-ATE. I MEAN, HOW BAD CAN IT BE?

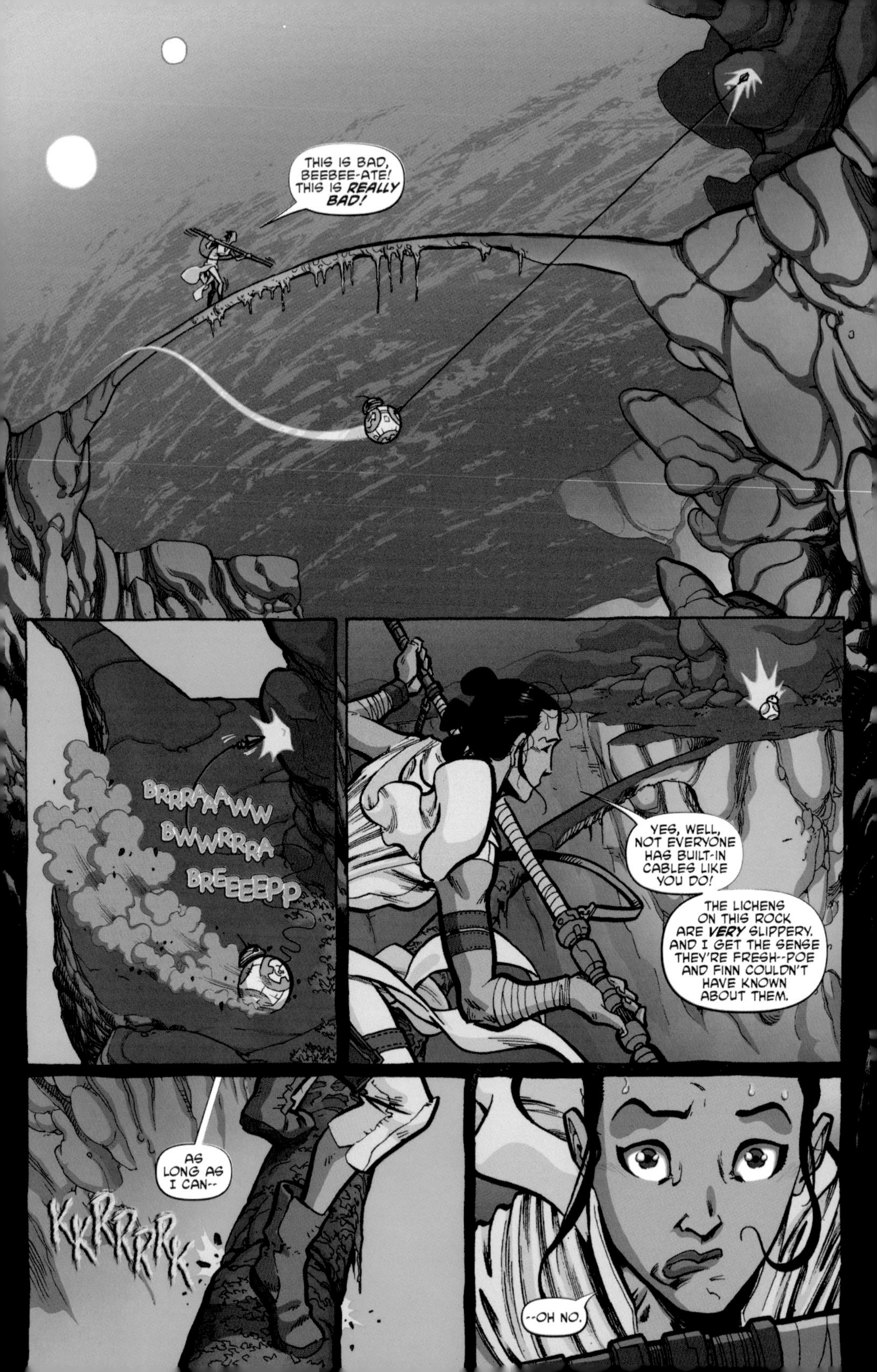
THIS IS BAD, BEEBEE-ATE! THIS IS REALLY BAD!
BRRRRAAAWW
BWWRRRA
BREEEEPP
YES, WELL, NOT EVERYONE HAS BUILT-IN CABLES LIKE YOU DO!
THE LICHENS ON THIS ROCK ARE VERY SLIPPERY. AND I GET THE SENSE THEY'RE FRESH--POE AND FINN COULDN'T HAVE KNOWN ABOUT THEM.
AS LONG AS I CAN--
KKRRRRK
--OH NO.

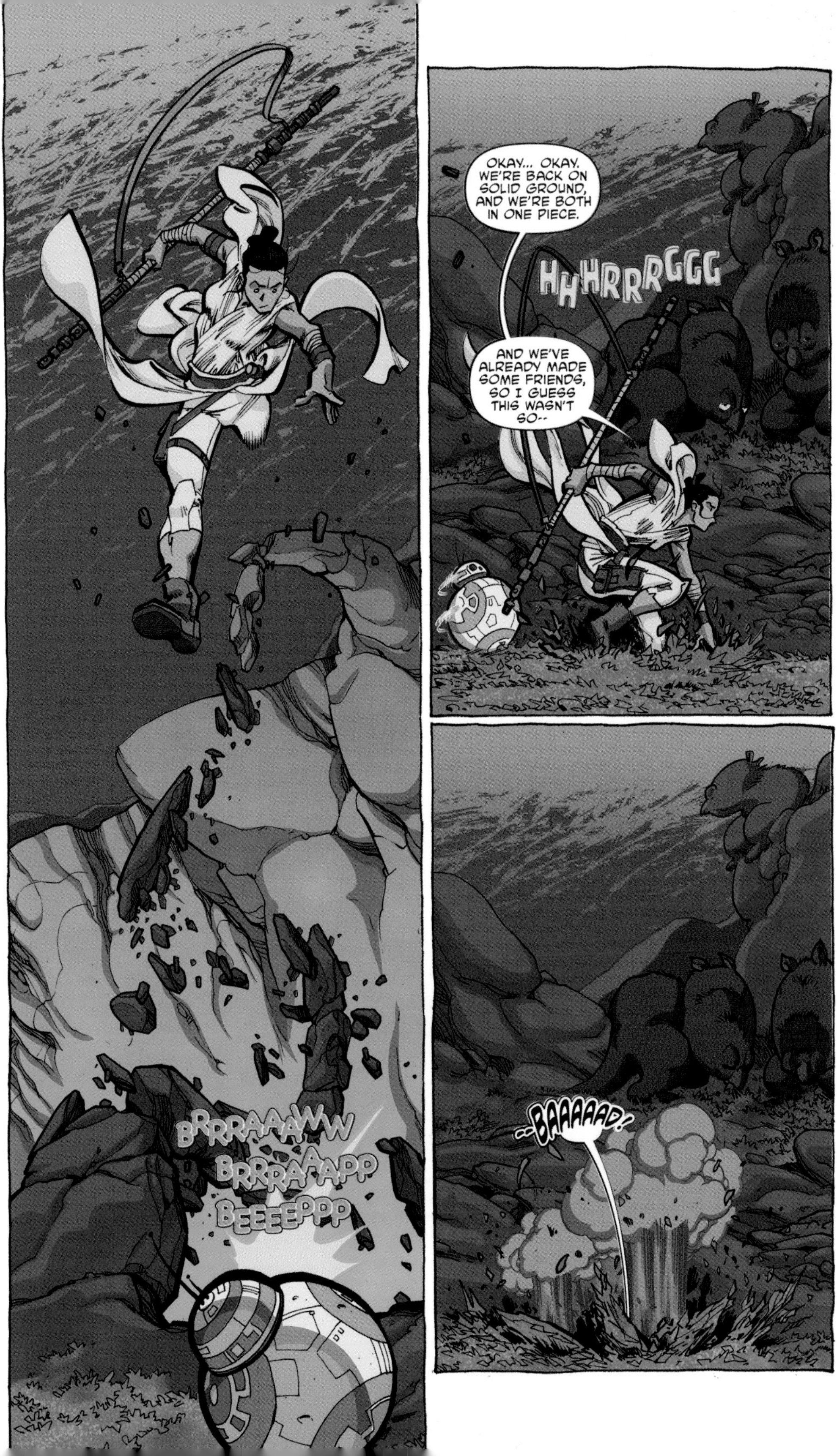
BRRRAAAWW
BRRRAAAPP
BEEEEPPP
OKAY... OKAY. WE'RE BACK ON SOLID GROUND, AND WE'RE BOTH IN ONE PIECE.
HHHRRRRGGG
AND WE'VE ALREADY MADE SOME FRIENDS, SO I GUESS THIS WASN'T SO--
--BAAAAAD!

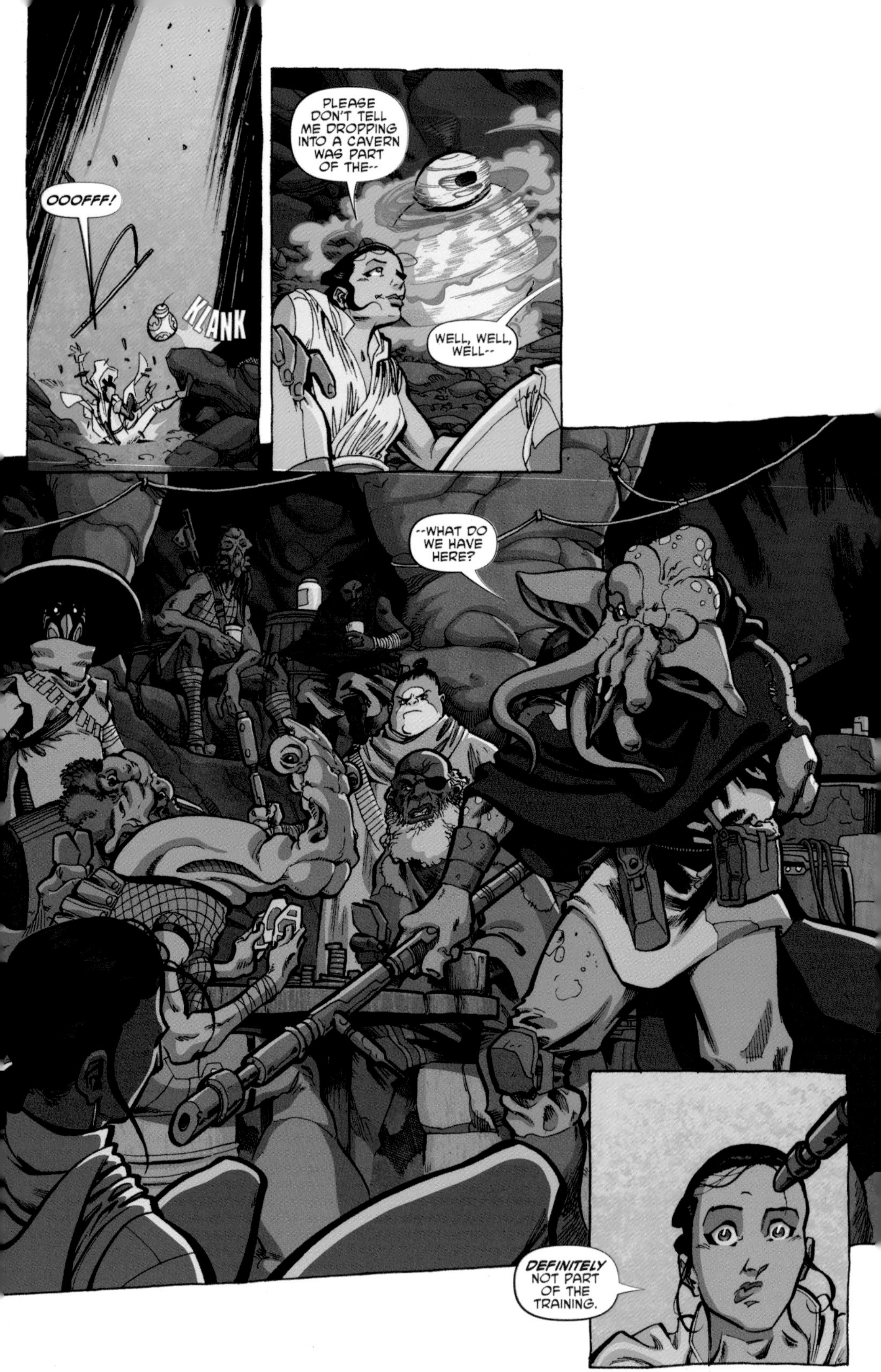
OOOFFF!
KLANK
PLEASE DON'T TELL ME DROPPING INTO A CAVERN WAS PART OF THE--
WELL, WELL, WELL--
--WHAT DO WE HAVE HERE?
*DEFINITELY* NOT PART OF THE TRAINING.

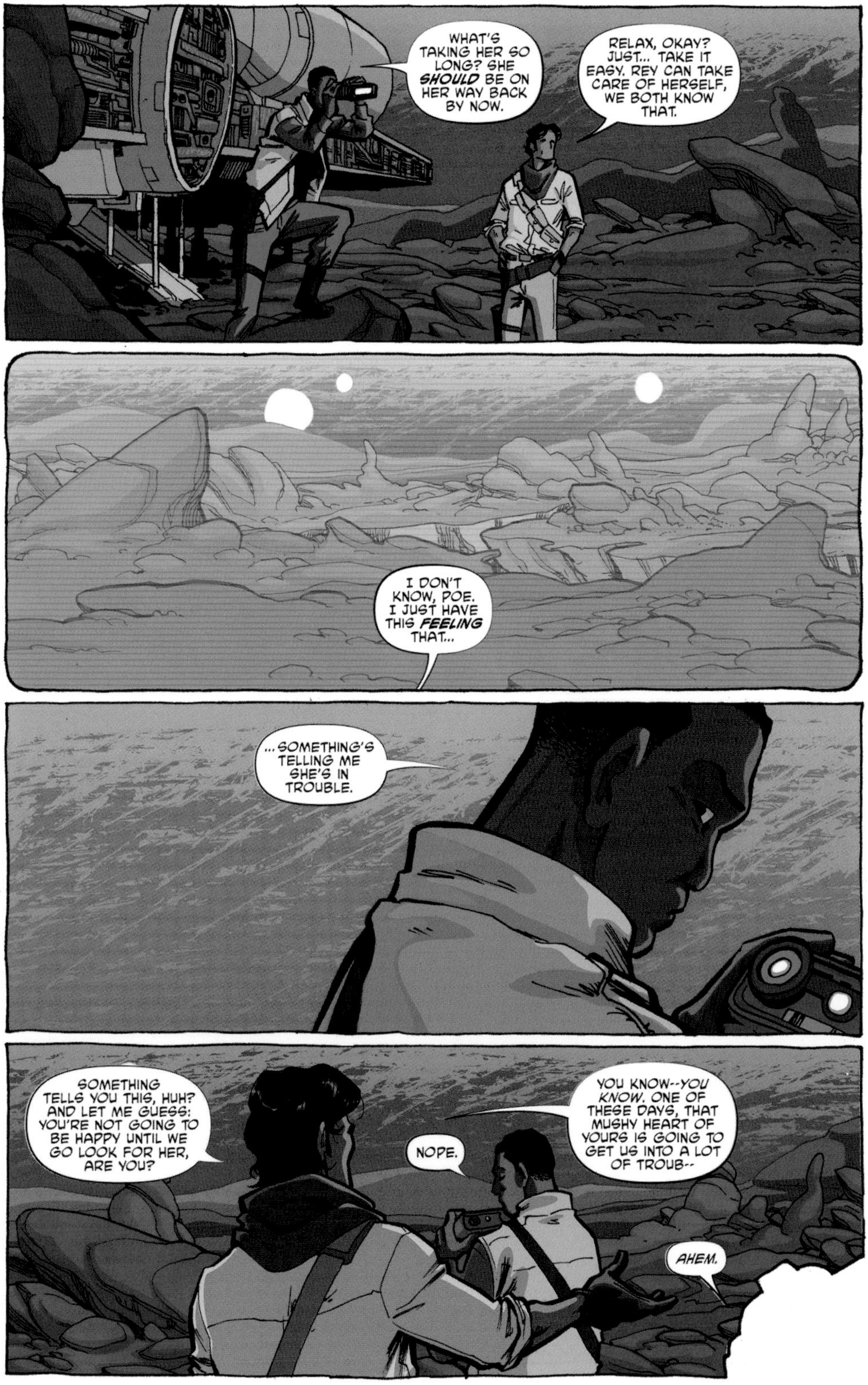
WHAT'S TAKING HER SO LONG? SHE *SHOULD* BE ON HER WAY BACK BY NOW.
RELAX, OKAY? JUST... TAKE IT EASY. REY CAN TAKE CARE OF HERSELF, WE BOTH KNOW THAT.
I DON'T KNOW, POE. I JUST HAVE THIS *FEELING* THAT...
...SOMETHING'S TELLING ME SHE'S IN TROUBLE.
SOMETHING TELLS YOU THIS, HUH? AND LET ME GUESS: YOU'RE NOT GOING TO BE HAPPY UNTIL WE GO LOOK FOR HER, ARE YOU?
NOPE.
YOU KNOW--*YOU KNOW*. ONE OF THESE DAYS, THAT MUSHY HEART OF YOURS IS GOING TO GET US INTO A LOT OF TROUB--
*AHEM.*

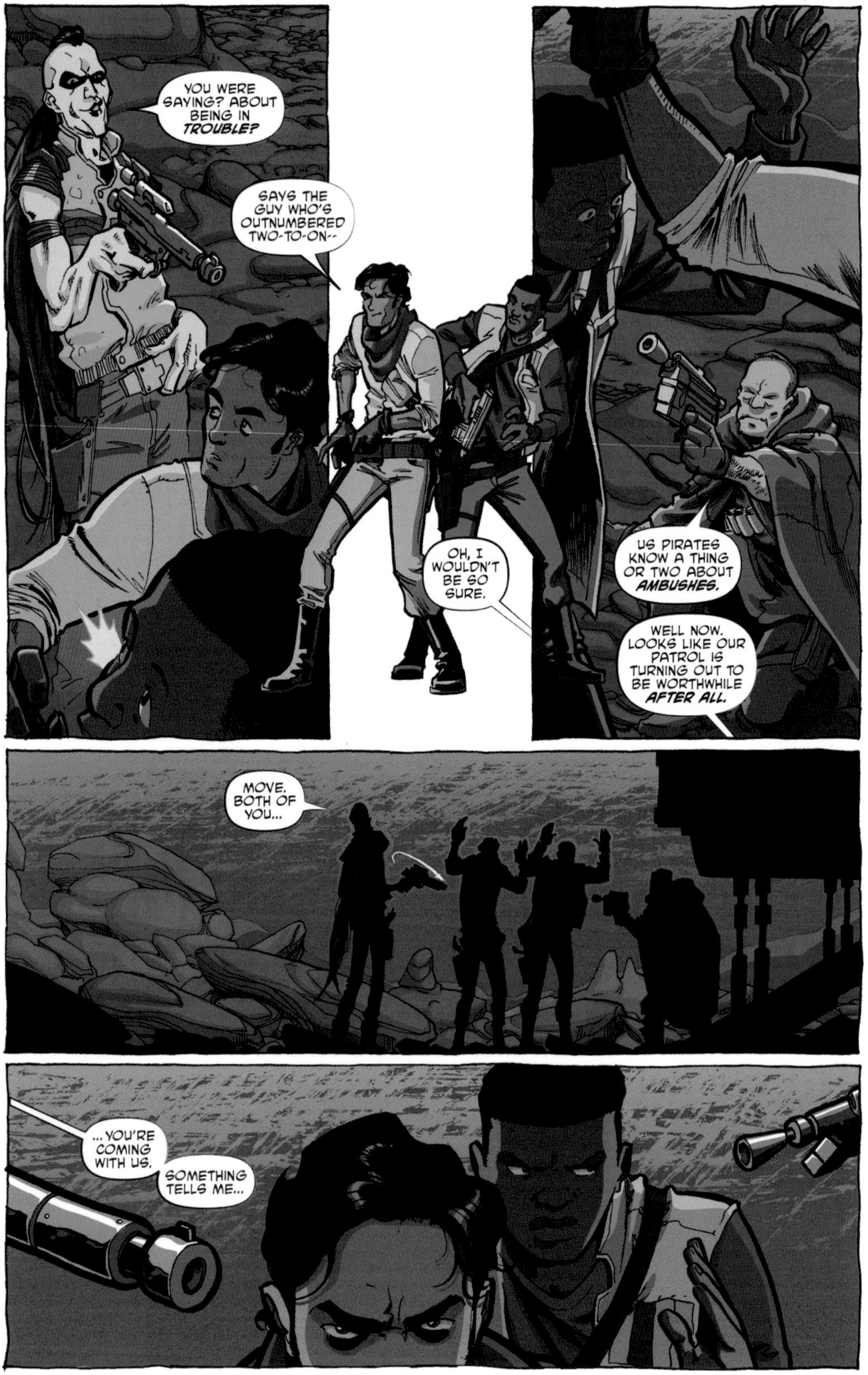
YOU WERE SAYING? ABOUT BEING IN *TROUBLE?*
SAYS THE GUY WHO'S OUTNUMBERED TWO-TO-ON--
OH, I WOULDN'T BE SO SURE.
US PIRATES KNOW A THING OR TWO ABOUT *AMBUSHES.*
WELL NOW. LOOKS LIKE OUR PATROL IS TURNING OUT TO BE WORTHWHILE *AFTER ALL.*
MOVE. BOTH OF YOU...
...YOU'RE COMING WITH US.
SOMETHING TELLS ME...

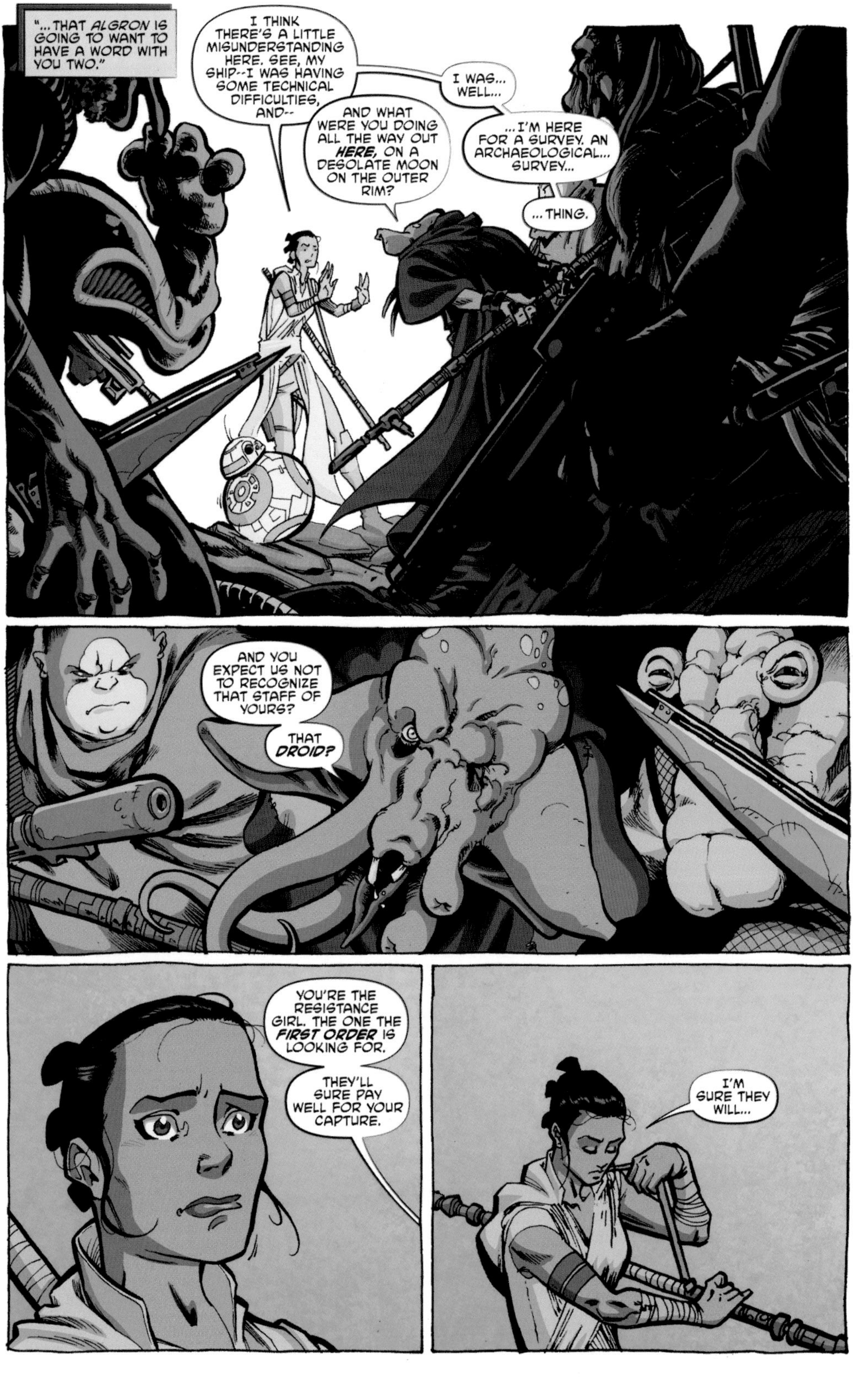
"...THAT *ALGRON* IS GOING TO WANT TO HAVE A WORD WITH YOU TWO."
I THINK THERE'S A LITTLE MISUNDERSTANDING HERE. SEE, MY SHIP--I WAS HAVING SOME TECHNICAL DIFFICULTIES, AND--
AND WHAT WERE YOU DOING ALL THE WAY OUT ***HERE,*** ON A DESOLATE MOON ON THE OUTER RIM?
I WAS... WELL...
...I'M HERE FOR A SURVEY. AN ARCHAEOLOGICAL... SURVEY...
...THING.
AND YOU EXPECT US NOT TO RECOGNIZE THAT STAFF OF YOURS?
THAT ***DROID?***
YOU'RE THE RESISTANCE GIRL. THE ONE THE ***FIRST ORDER*** IS LOOKING FOR.
THEY'LL SURE PAY WELL FOR YOUR CAPTURE.
I'M SURE THEY WILL...

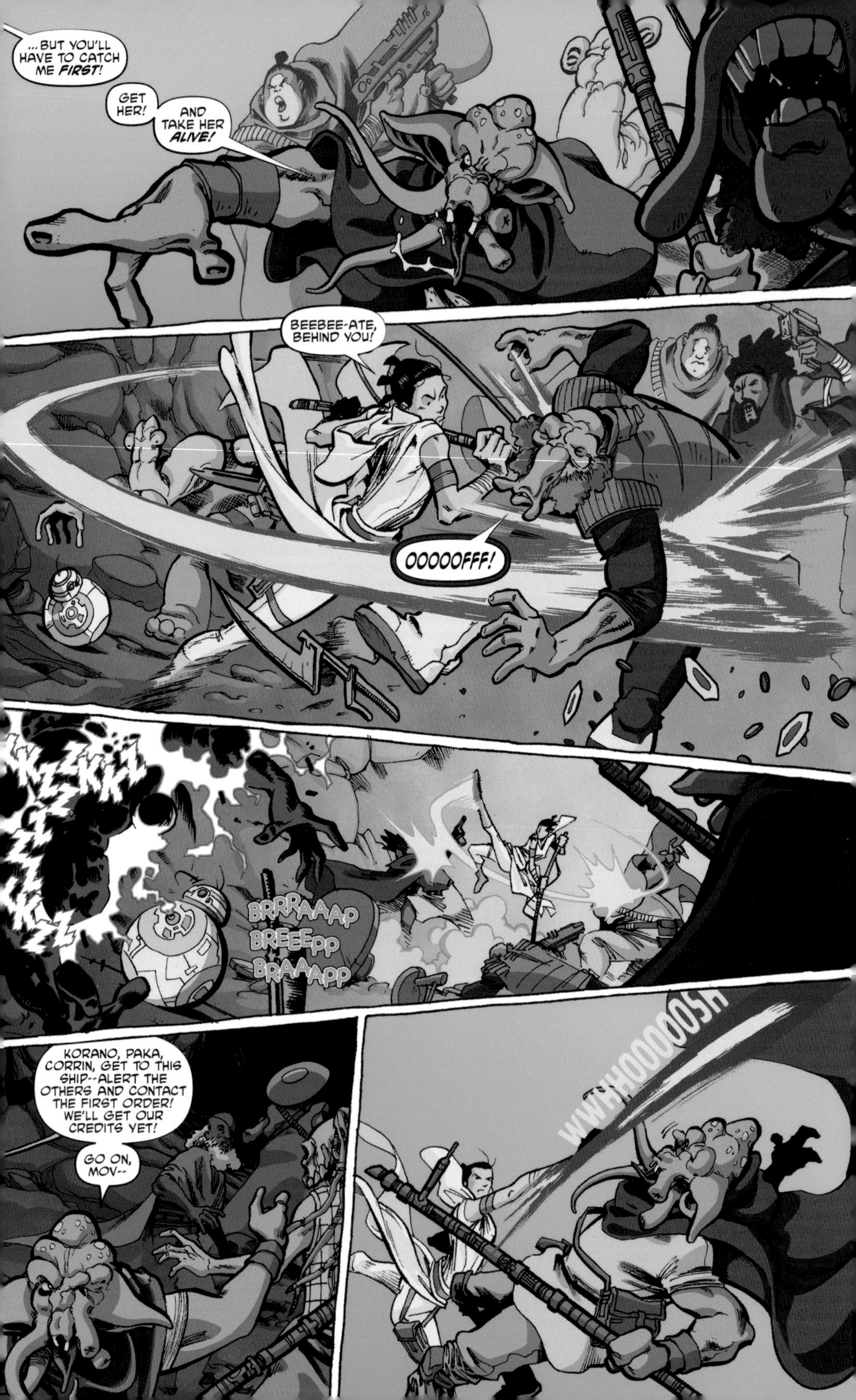
...BUT YOU'LL HAVE TO CATCH ME *FIRST*!
GET HER!
AND TAKE HER *ALIVE*!
BEEBEE-ATE, BEHIND YOU!
OOOOOFFF!
KZZZKKZZ
BRRRAAAAP
BREEEPP
BRAAAAPP
KORANO, PAKA, CORRIN, GET TO THIS SHIP--ALERT THE OTHERS AND CONTACT THE FIRST ORDER! WE'LL GET OUR CREDITS YET!
GO ON, MOV--
WWHOOOOOSH

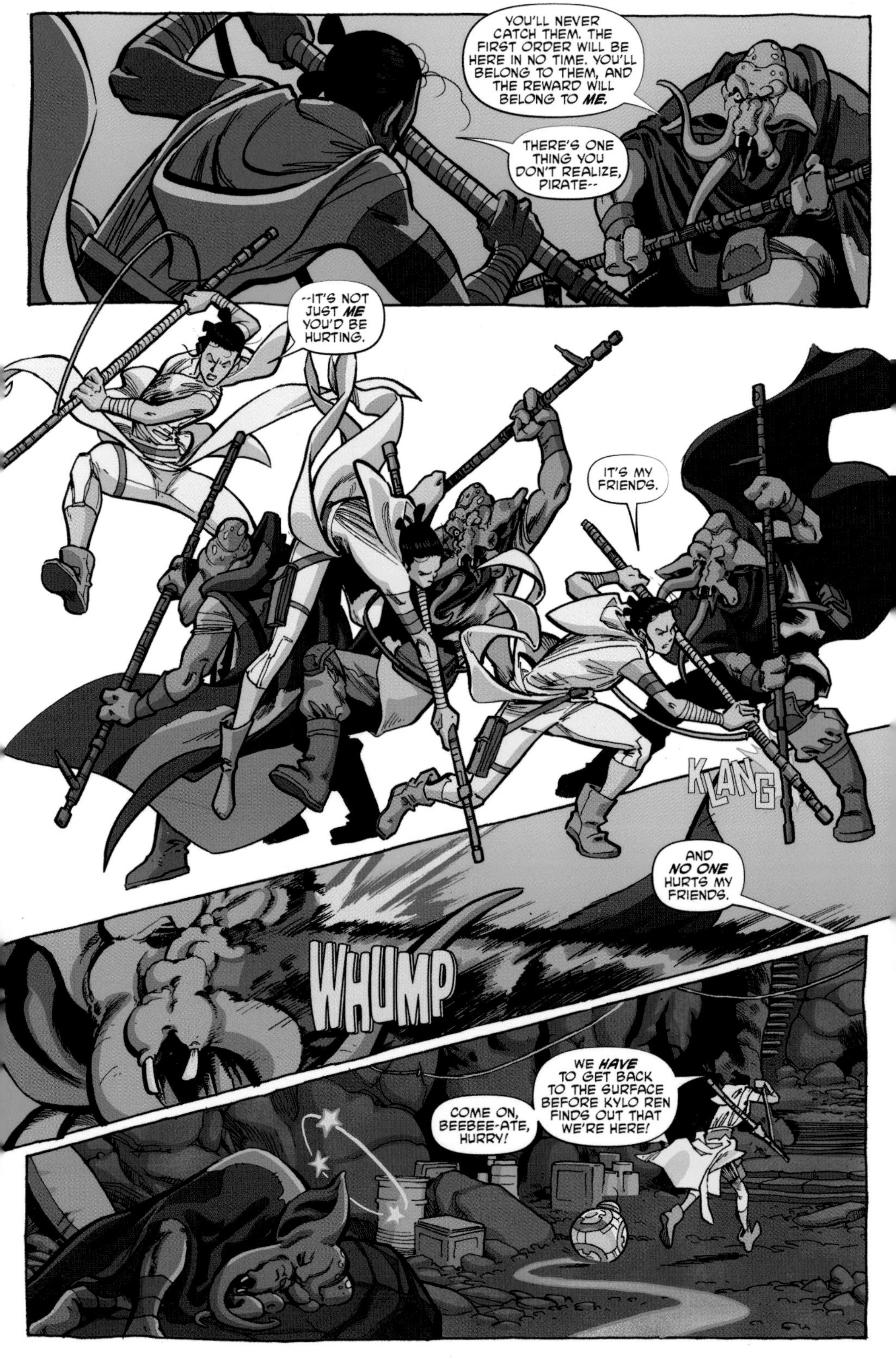
YOU'LL NEVER CATCH THEM. THE FIRST ORDER WILL BE HERE IN NO TIME. YOU'LL BELONG TO THEM, AND THE REWARD WILL BELONG TO *ME.*
THERE'S ONE THING YOU DON'T REALIZE, PIRATE--
--IT'S NOT JUST *ME* YOU'D BE HURTING.
IT'S MY FRIENDS.
KLANG
AND *NO ONE* HURTS MY FRIENDS.
WHUMP
WE *HAVE* TO GET BACK TO THE SURFACE BEFORE KYLO REN FINDS OUT THAT WE'RE HERE!
COME ON, BEEBEE-ATE, HURRY!

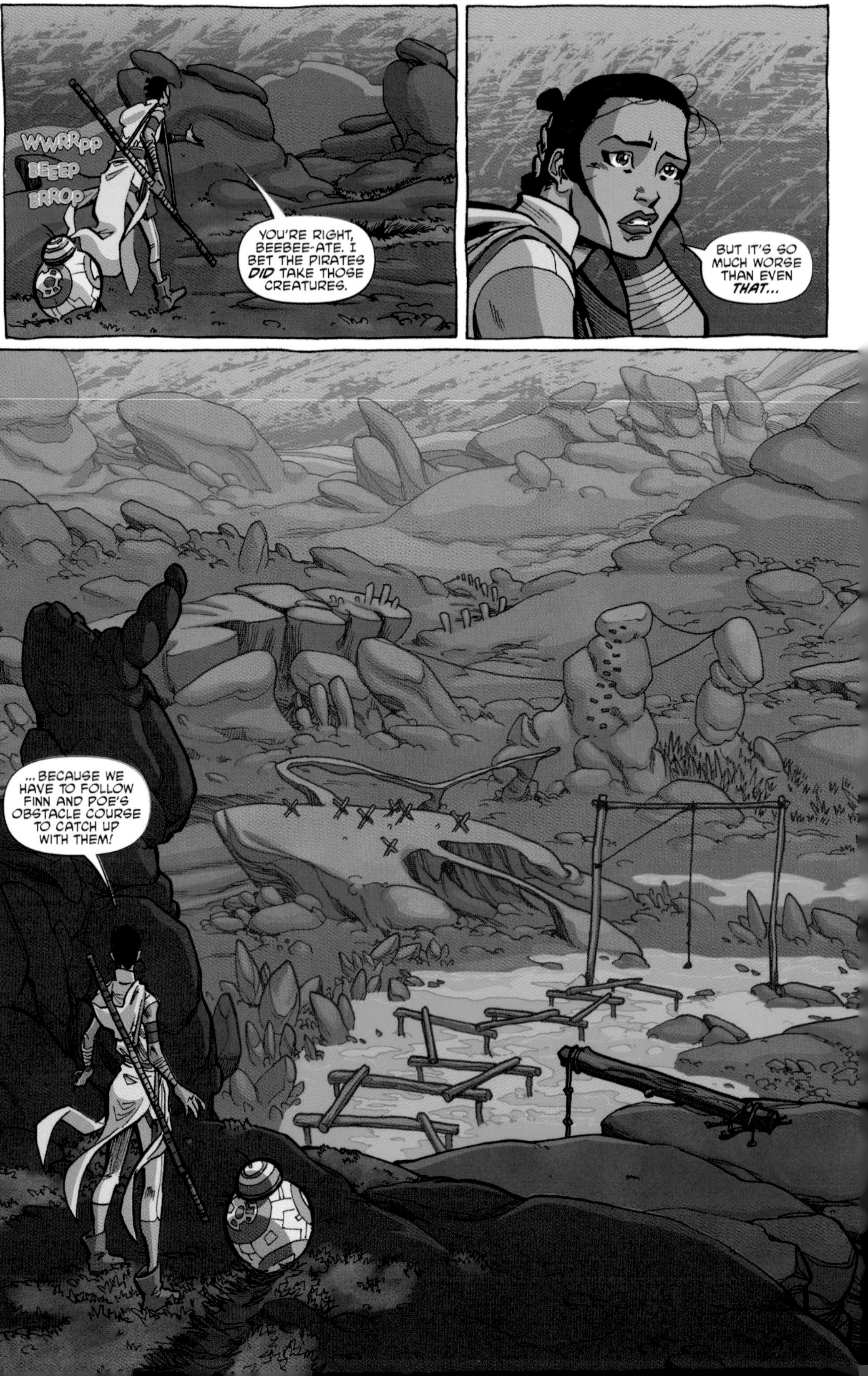
WWRRPP
BEEEP
BRROP
YOU'RE RIGHT, BEEBEE-ATE. I BET THE PIRATES *DID* TAKE THOSE CREATURES.
BUT IT'S SO MUCH WORSE THAN EVEN *THAT*...
... BECAUSE WE HAVE TO FOLLOW FINN AND POE'S OBSTACLE COURSE TO CATCH UP WITH THEM!

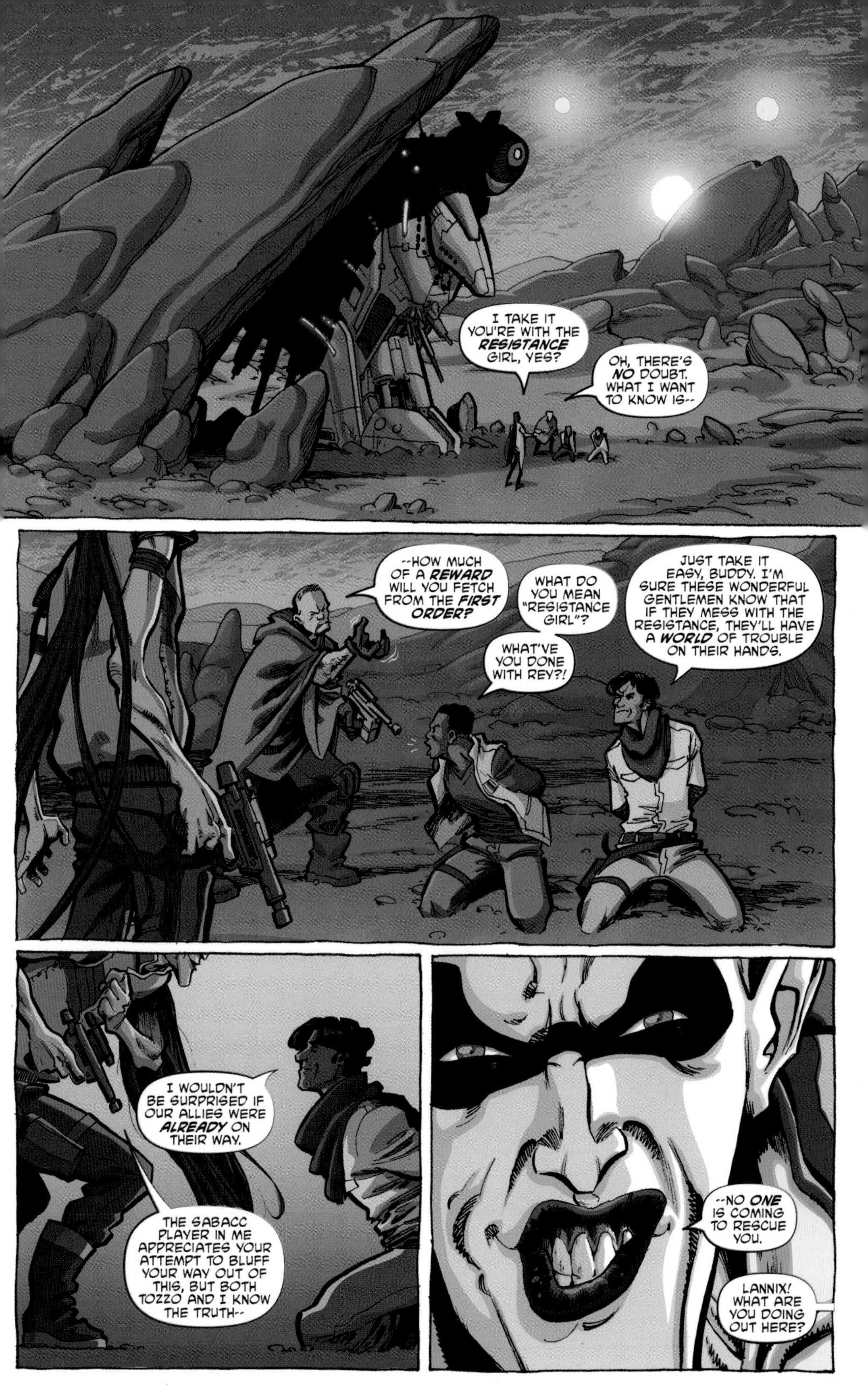
I TAKE IT YOU'RE WITH THE RESISTANCE GIRL, YES?
OH, THERE'S NO DOUBT. WHAT I WANT TO KNOW IS--
--HOW MUCH OF A REWARD WILL YOU FETCH FROM THE FIRST ORDER?
WHAT DO YOU MEAN "RESISTANCE GIRL"?
WHAT'VE YOU DONE WITH REY?!
JUST TAKE IT EASY, BUDDY. I'M SURE THESE WONDERFUL GENTLEMEN KNOW THAT IF THEY MESS WITH THE RESISTANCE, THEY'LL HAVE A WORLD OF TROUBLE ON THEIR HANDS.
I WOULDN'T BE SURPRISED IF OUR ALLIES WERE ALREADY ON THEIR WAY.
THE SABACC PLAYER IN ME APPRECIATES YOUR ATTEMPT TO BLUFF YOUR WAY OUT OF THIS, BUT BOTH TOZZO AND I KNOW THE TRUTH--
--NO ONE IS COMING TO RESCUE YOU.
LANNIX! WHAT ARE YOU DOING OUT HERE?

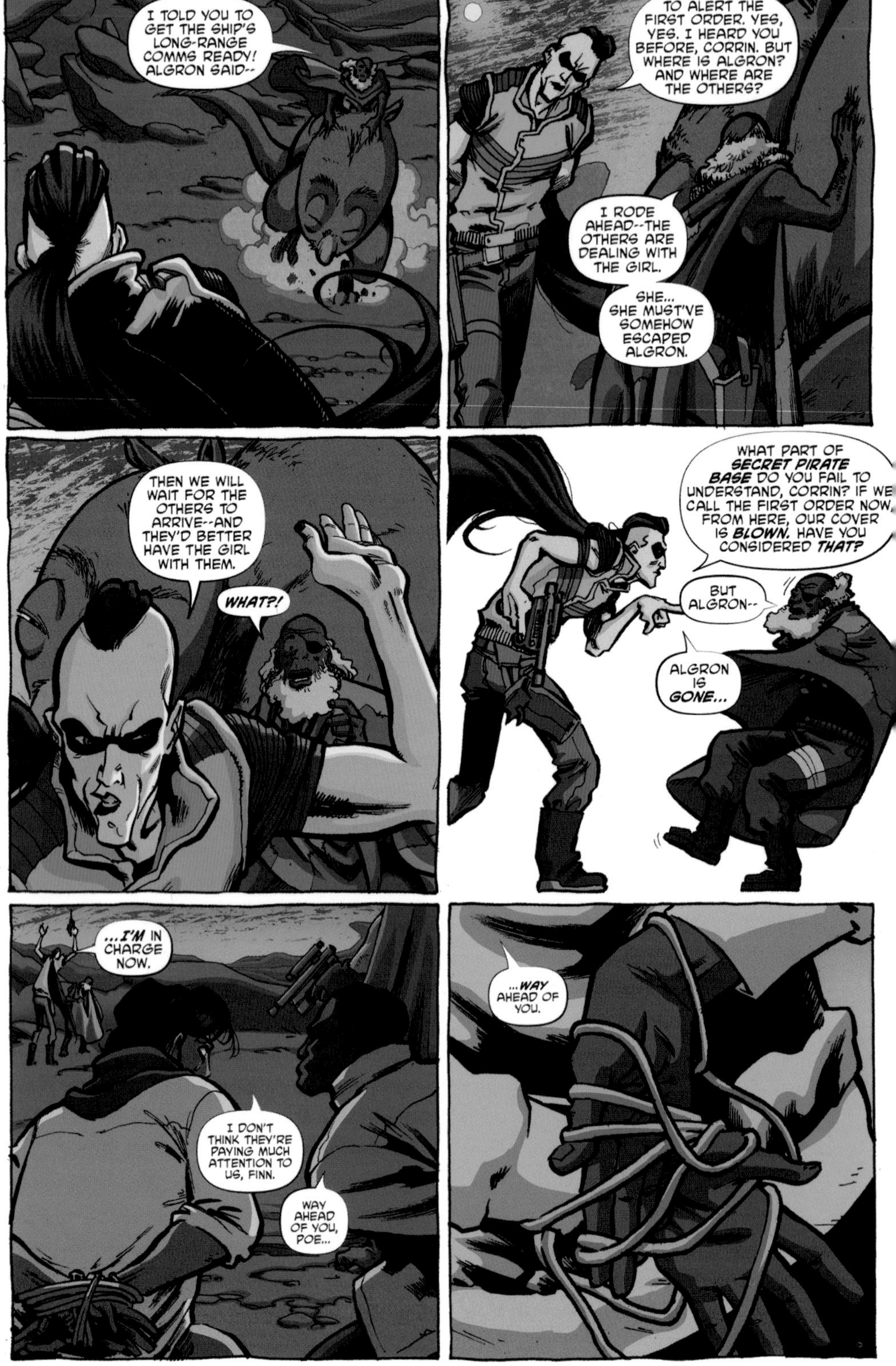
I TOLD YOU TO GET THE SHIP'S LONG-RANGE COMMS READY! ALGRON SAID--
TO ALERT THE FIRST ORDER. YES, YES. I HEARD YOU BEFORE, CORRIN. BUT WHERE IS ALGRON? AND WHERE ARE THE OTHERS?
I RODE AHEAD--THE OTHERS ARE DEALING WITH THE GIRL.
SHE... SHE MUST'VE SOMEHOW ESCAPED ALGRON.
THEN WE WILL WAIT FOR THE OTHERS TO ARRIVE--AND THEY'D BETTER HAVE THE GIRL WITH THEM.
WHAT?!
WHAT PART OF SECRET PIRATE BASE DO YOU FAIL TO UNDERSTAND, CORRIN? IF WE CALL THE FIRST ORDER NOW, FROM HERE, OUR COVER IS BLOWN. HAVE YOU CONSIDERED THAT?
BUT ALGRON--
ALGRON IS GONE...
...I'M IN CHARGE NOW.
I DON'T THINK THEY'RE PAYING MUCH ATTENTION TO US, FINN.
WAY AHEAD OF YOU, POE...
...WAY AHEAD OF YOU.

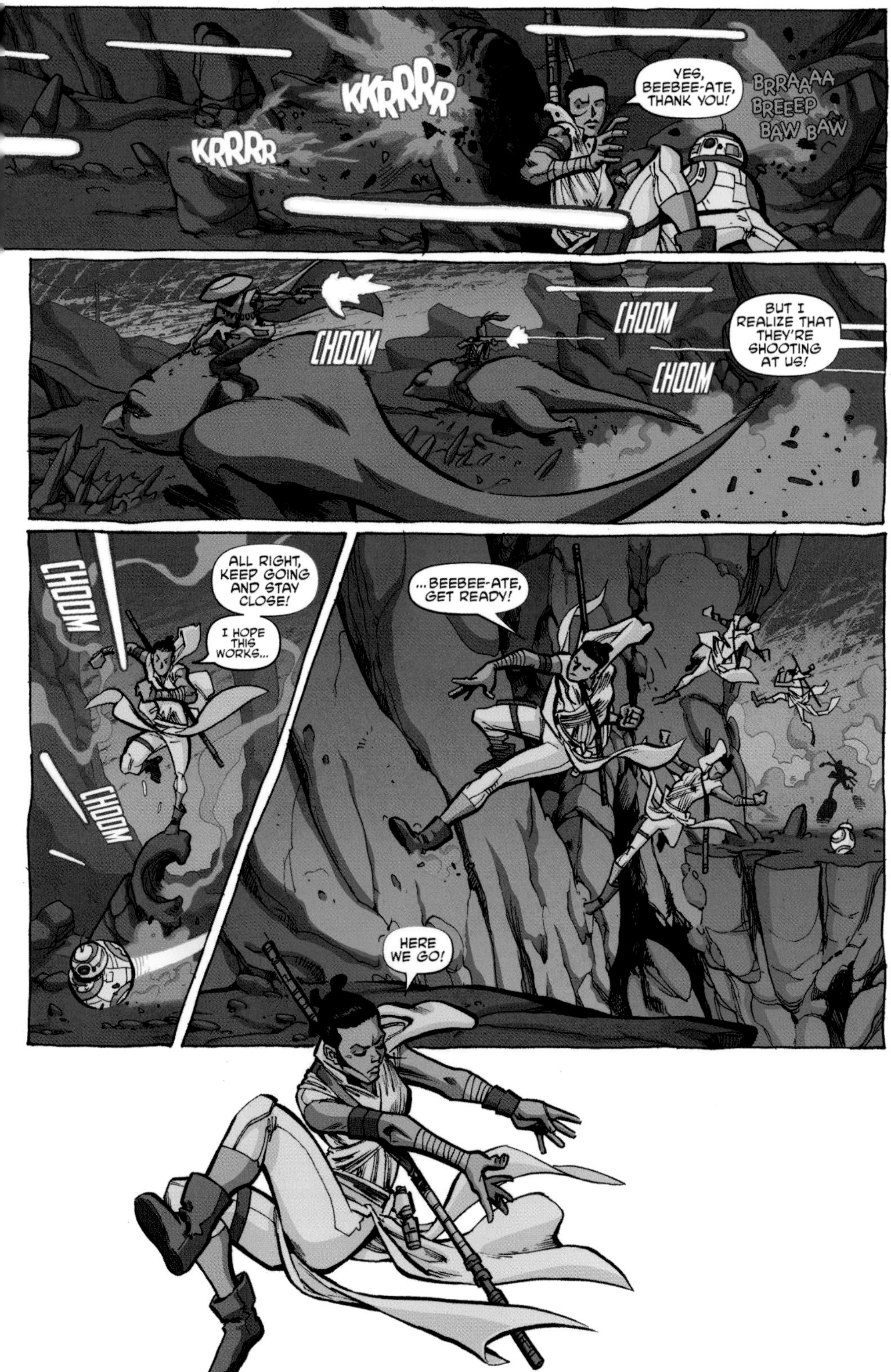
KRRRR
KKRRRRR
YES, BEEBEE-ATE, THANK YOU!
BRRAAAA BREEEP BAW BAW
CHOOM
CHOOM
CHOOM
BUT I REALIZE THAT THEY'RE SHOOTING AT US!
CHOOM
ALL RIGHT, KEEP GOING AND STAY CLOSE!
I HOPE THIS WORKS...
CHOOM
...BEEBEE-ATE, GET READY!
HERE WE GO!

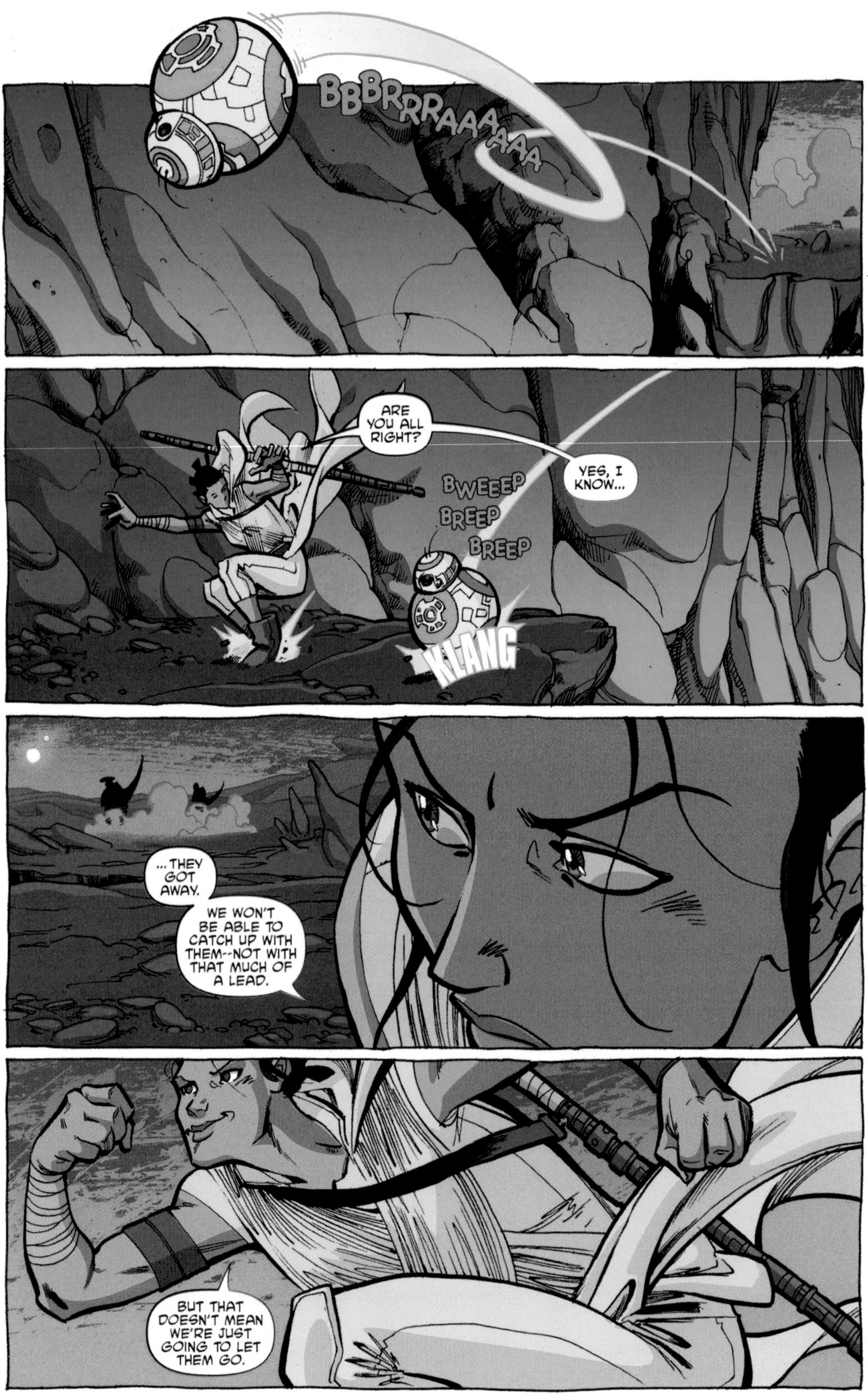
BBBRRRAAAAAAA
ARE YOU ALL RIGHT?
YES, I KNOW...
BWEEEP
BREEP
BREEP
KLANG
...THEY GOT AWAY.
WE WON'T BE ABLE TO CATCH UP WITH THEM--NOT WITH THAT MUCH OF A LEAD.
BUT THAT DOESN'T MEAN WE'RE JUST GOING TO LET THEM GO.

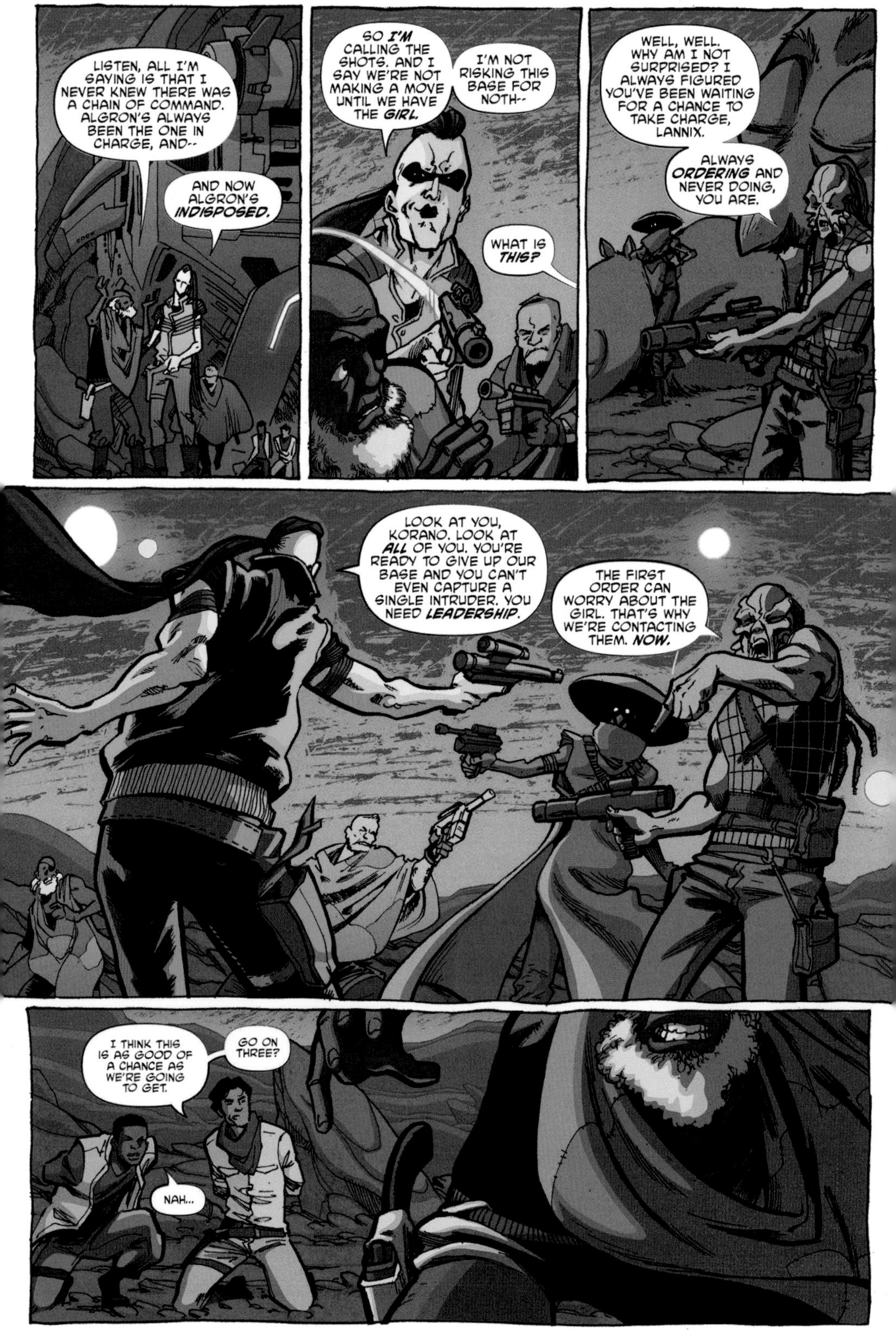
LISTEN, ALL I'M SAYING IS THAT I NEVER KNEW THERE WAS A CHAIN OF COMMAND. ALGRON'S ALWAYS BEEN THE ONE IN CHARGE, AND--
AND NOW ALGRON'S *INDISPOSED.*
SO *I'M* CALLING THE SHOTS. AND I SAY WE'RE NOT MAKING A MOVE UNTIL WE HAVE THE *GIRL.*
I'M NOT RISKING THIS BASE FOR NOTH--
WHAT IS *THIS?*
WELL, WELL. WHY AM I NOT SURPRISED? I ALWAYS FIGURED YOU'VE BEEN WAITING FOR A CHANCE TO TAKE CHARGE, LANNIX.
ALWAYS *ORDERING* AND NEVER DOING, YOU ARE.
LOOK AT YOU, KORANO. LOOK AT *ALL* OF YOU. YOU'RE READY TO GIVE UP OUR BASE AND YOU CAN'T EVEN CAPTURE A SINGLE INTRUDER. YOU NEED *LEADERSHIP*.
THE FIRST ORDER CAN WORRY ABOUT THE GIRL. THAT'S WHY WE'RE CONTACTING THEM. *NOW.*
I THINK THIS IS AS GOOD OF A CHANCE AS WE'RE GOING TO GET.
GO ON THREE?
NAH...

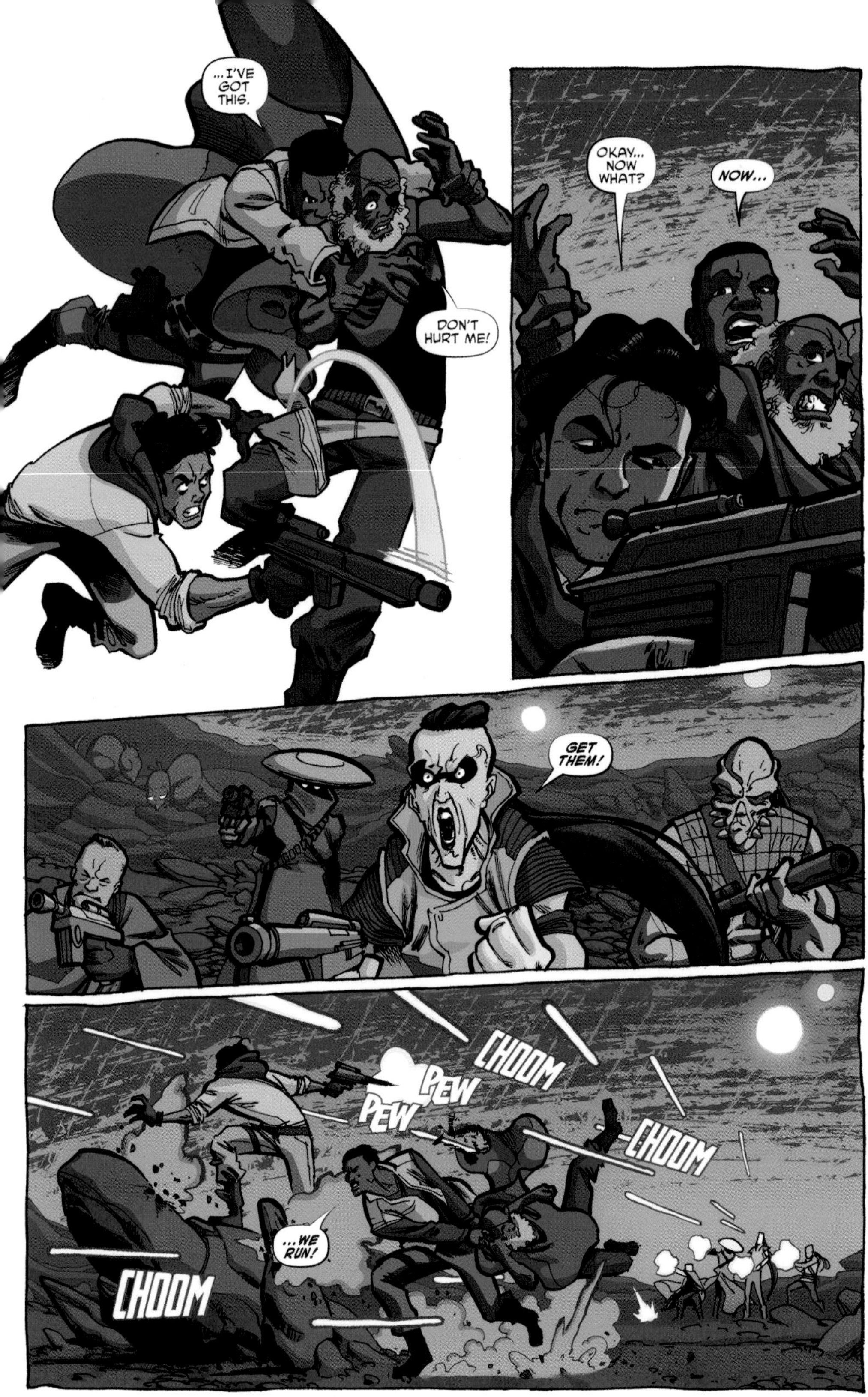
...I'VE GOT THIS.
DON'T HURT ME!
OKAY... NOW WHAT?
NOW...
GET THEM!
CHOOM
PEW
PEW
CHOOM
...WE RUN!
CHOOM

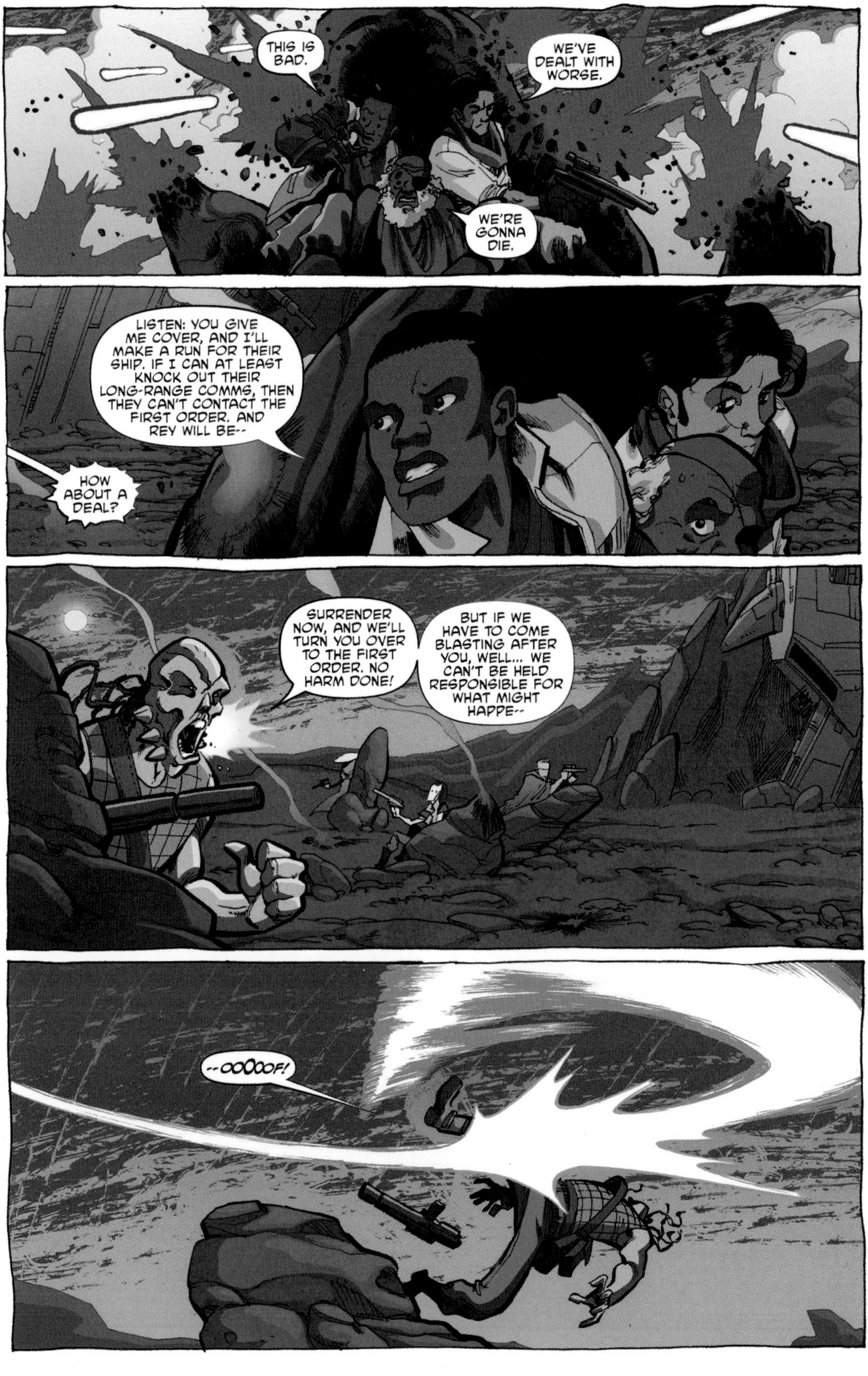
THIS IS BAD.
WE'VE DEALT WITH WORSE.
WE'RE GONNA DIE.
LISTEN: YOU GIVE ME COVER, AND I'LL MAKE A RUN FOR THEIR SHIP. IF I CAN AT LEAST KNOCK OUT THEIR LONG-RANGE COMMS, THEN THEY CAN'T CONTACT THE FIRST ORDER. AND REY WILL BE--
HOW ABOUT A DEAL?
SURRENDER NOW, AND WE'LL TURN YOU OVER TO THE FIRST ORDER. NO HARM DONE!
BUT IF WE HAVE TO COME BLASTING AFTER YOU, WELL... WE CAN'T BE HELD RESPONSIBLE FOR WHAT MIGHT HAPPE--
--OOOOOF!

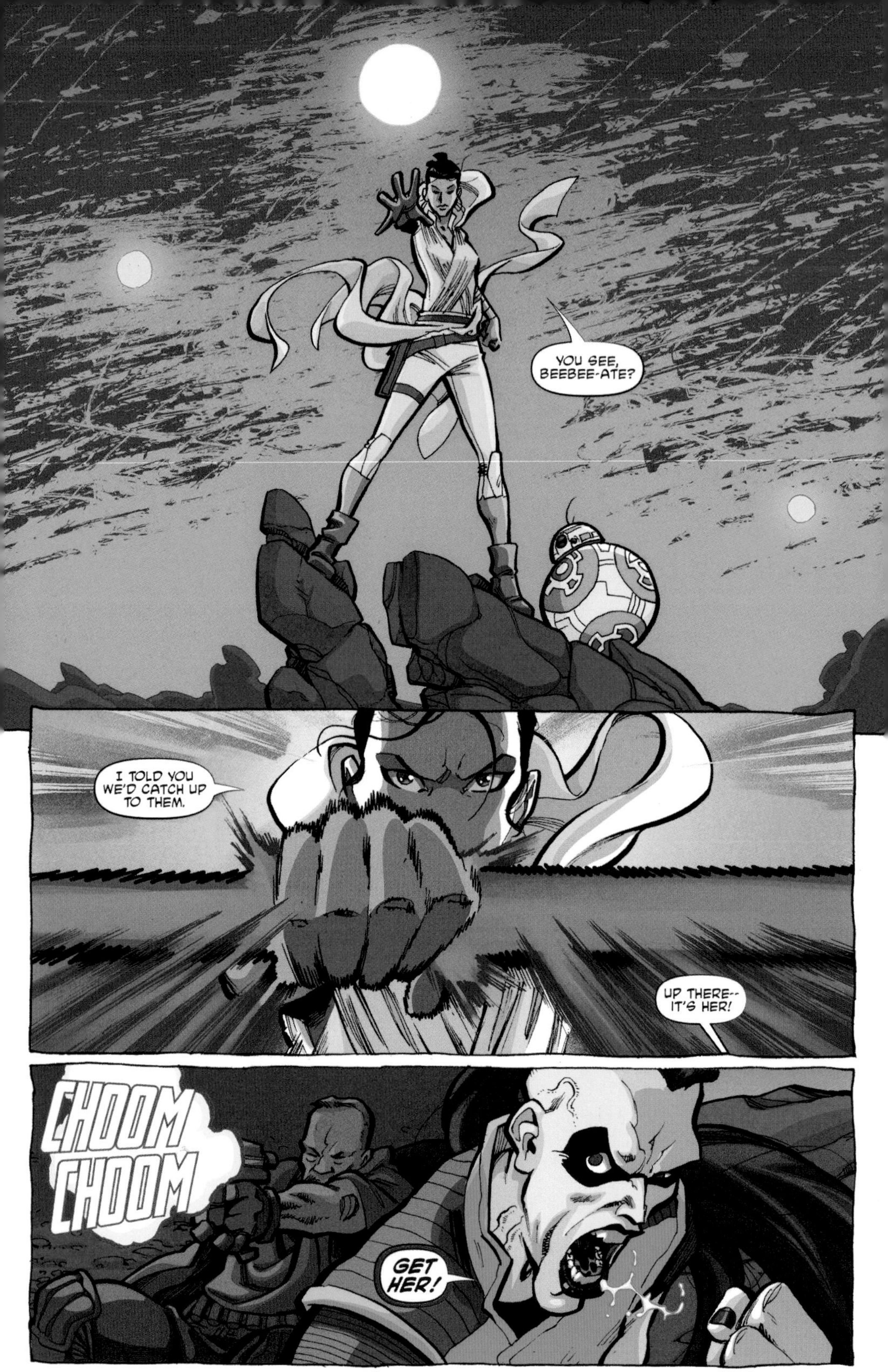
YOU SEE, BEEBEE-ATE?
I TOLD YOU WE'D CATCH UP TO THEM.
UP THERE-- IT'S HER!
CHOOM CHOOM
GET HER!

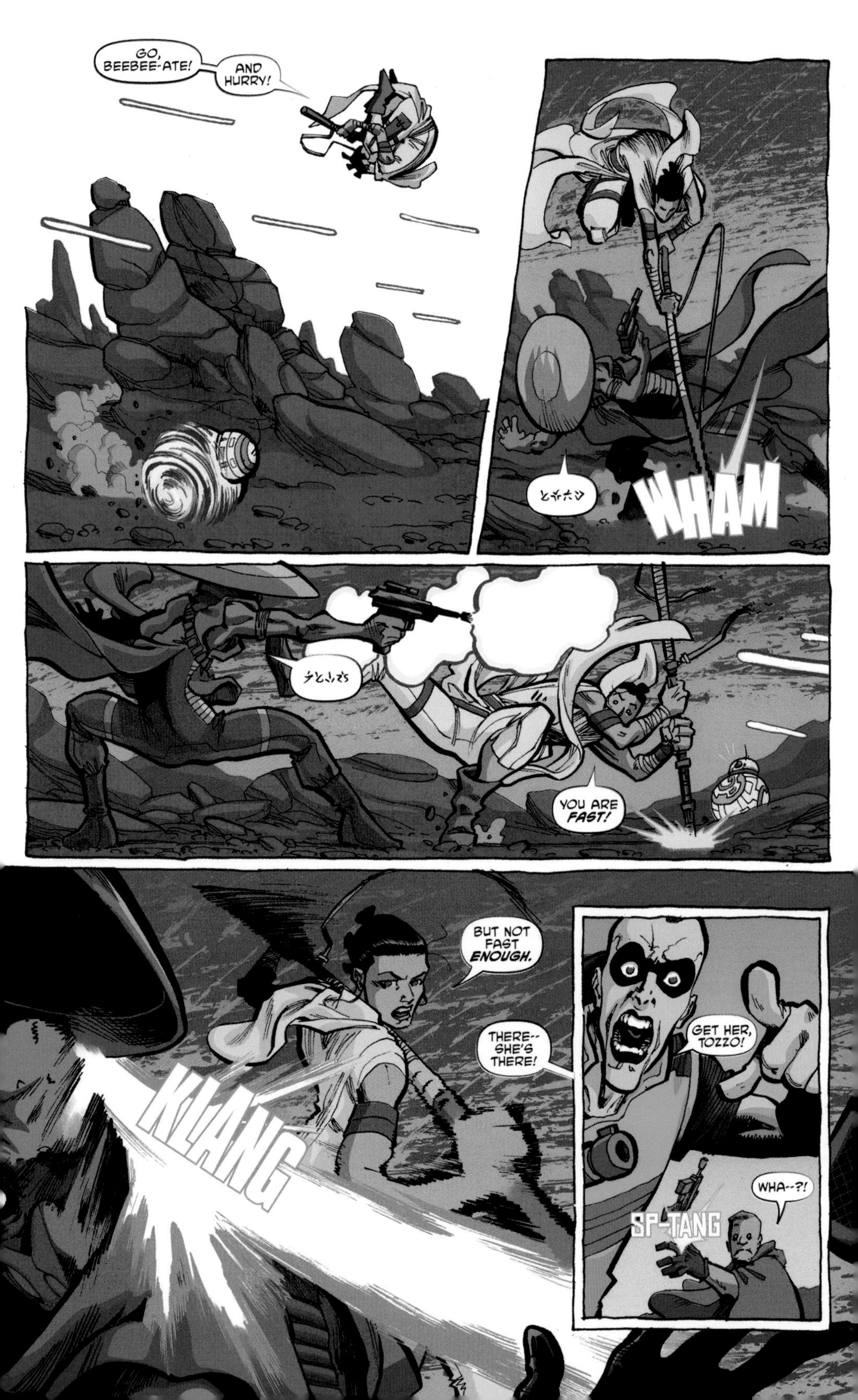
GO, BEEBEE-ATE!
AND HURRY!
WHAM
YOU ARE FAST!
BUT NOT FAST ENOUGH.
KLANG
THERE-- SHE'S THERE!
GET HER, TOZZO!
WHA--?!
SP-TANG

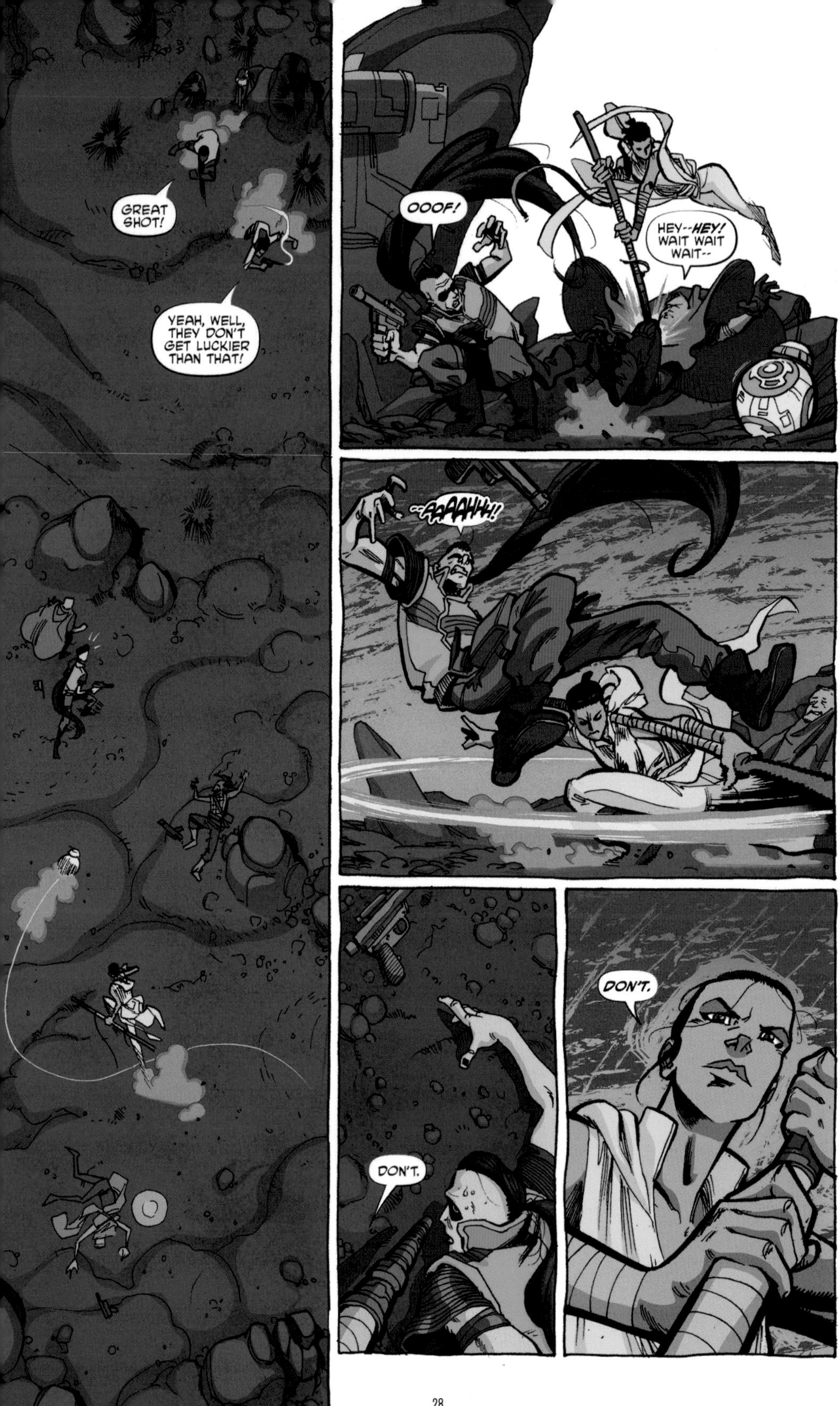
GREAT SHOT!
YEAH, WELL, THEY DON'T GET LUCKIER THAN THAT!
OOOF!
HEY--HEY! WAIT WAIT WAIT--
--AAAAHHH!
DON'T.
DON'T.

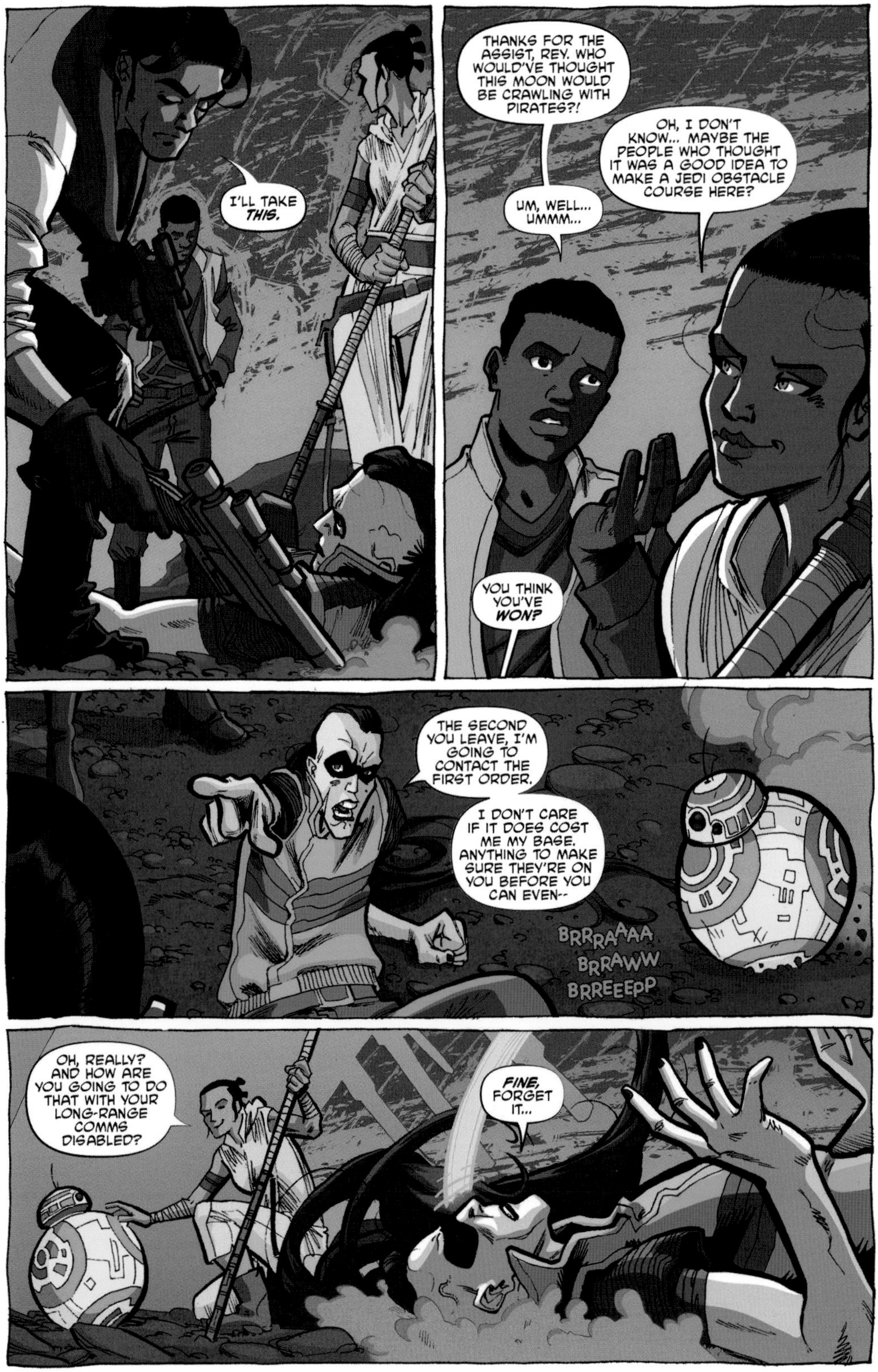
I'LL TAKE *THIS.*
THANKS FOR THE ASSIST, REY. WHO WOULD'VE THOUGHT THIS MOON WOULD BE CRAWLING WITH PIRATES?!
OH, I DON'T KNOW... MAYBE THE PEOPLE WHO THOUGHT IT WAS A GOOD IDEA TO MAKE A JEDI OBSTACLE COURSE HERE?
UM, WELL... UMMM...
YOU THINK YOU'VE *WON?*
THE SECOND YOU LEAVE, I'M GOING TO CONTACT THE FIRST ORDER.
I DON'T CARE IF IT DOES COST ME MY BASE. ANYTHING TO MAKE SURE THEY'RE ON YOU BEFORE YOU CAN EVEN--
BRRRAAAA
BRRAWW
BRREEEPP
OH, REALLY? AND HOW ARE YOU GOING TO DO THAT WITH YOUR LONG-RANGE COMMS DISABLED?
*FINE,* FORGET IT...

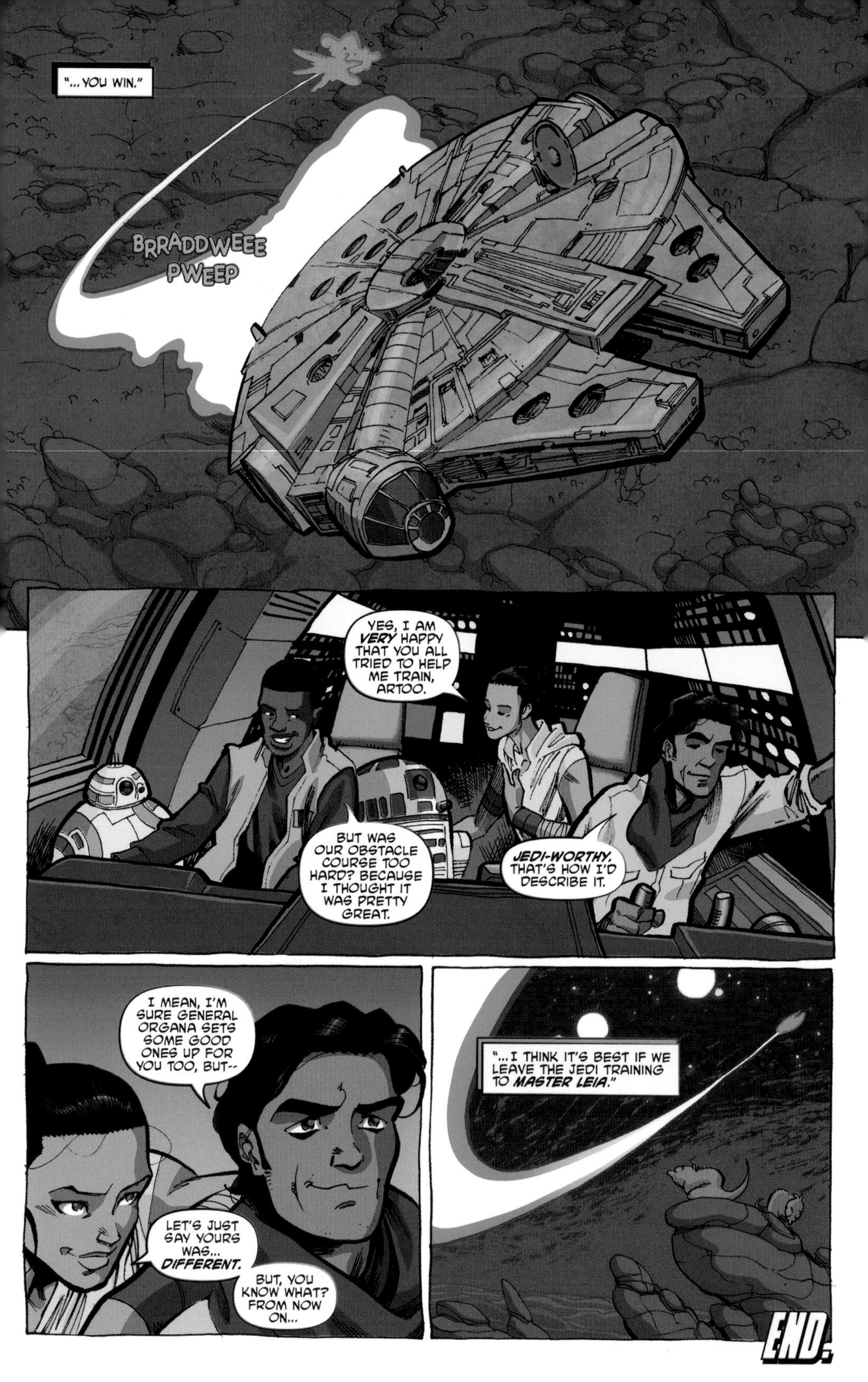
"...YOU WIN."
BRRADDWEEE PWEEP
YES, I AM VERY HAPPY THAT YOU ALL TRIED TO HELP ME TRAIN, ARTOO.
BUT WAS OUR OBSTACLE COURSE TOO HARD? BECAUSE I THOUGHT IT WAS PRETTY GREAT.
JEDI-WORTHY. THAT'S HOW I'D DESCRIBE IT.
I MEAN, I'M SURE GENERAL ORGANA SETS SOME GOOD ONES UP FOR YOU TOO, BUT--
LET'S JUST SAY YOURS WAS... DIFFERENT.
BUT, YOU KNOW WHAT? FROM NOW ON...
"...I THINK IT'S BEST IF WE LEAVE THE JEDI TRAINING TO MASTER LEIA."
END.

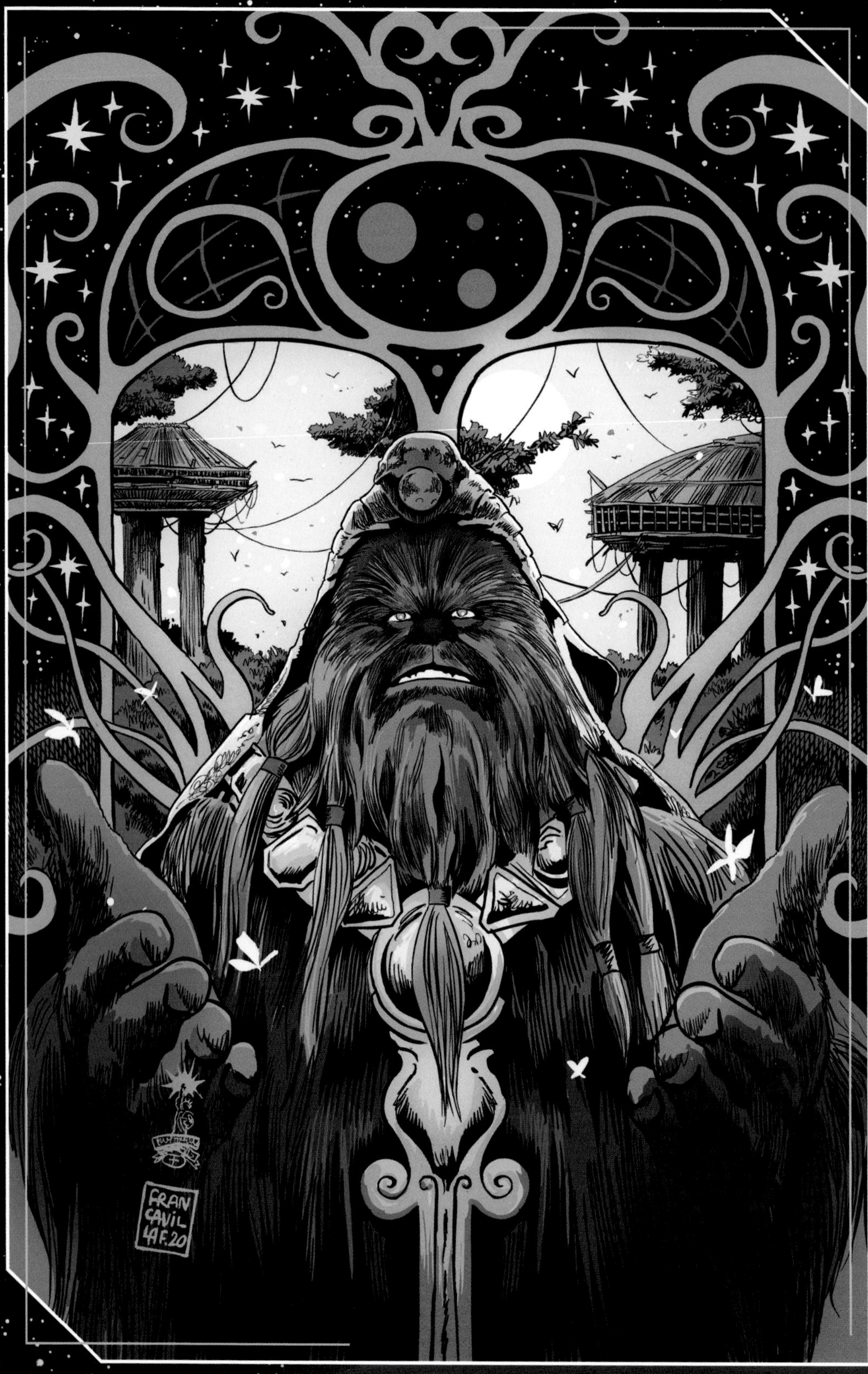
FRAN CAVIL LA F.20

ART BY **FRANCESCO FRANCAVILLA**

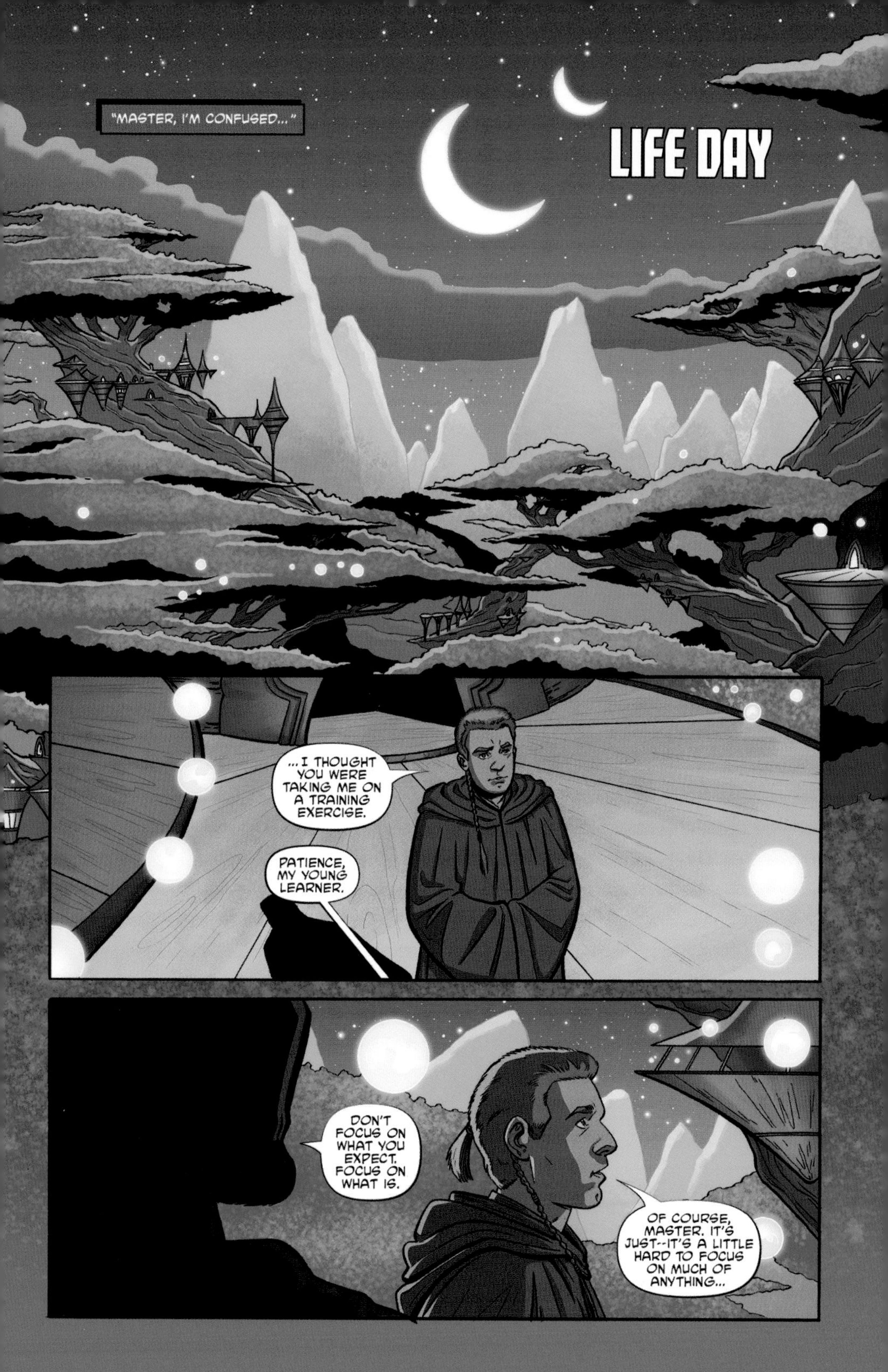
"MASTER, I'M CONFUSED..."
LIFE DAY
...I THOUGHT YOU WERE TAKING ME ON A TRAINING EXERCISE.
PATIENCE, MY YOUNG LEARNER.
DON'T FOCUS ON WHAT YOU EXPECT. FOCUS ON WHAT IS.
OF COURSE, MASTER. IT'S JUST--IT'S A LITTLE HARD TO FOCUS ON MUCH OF ANYTHING...

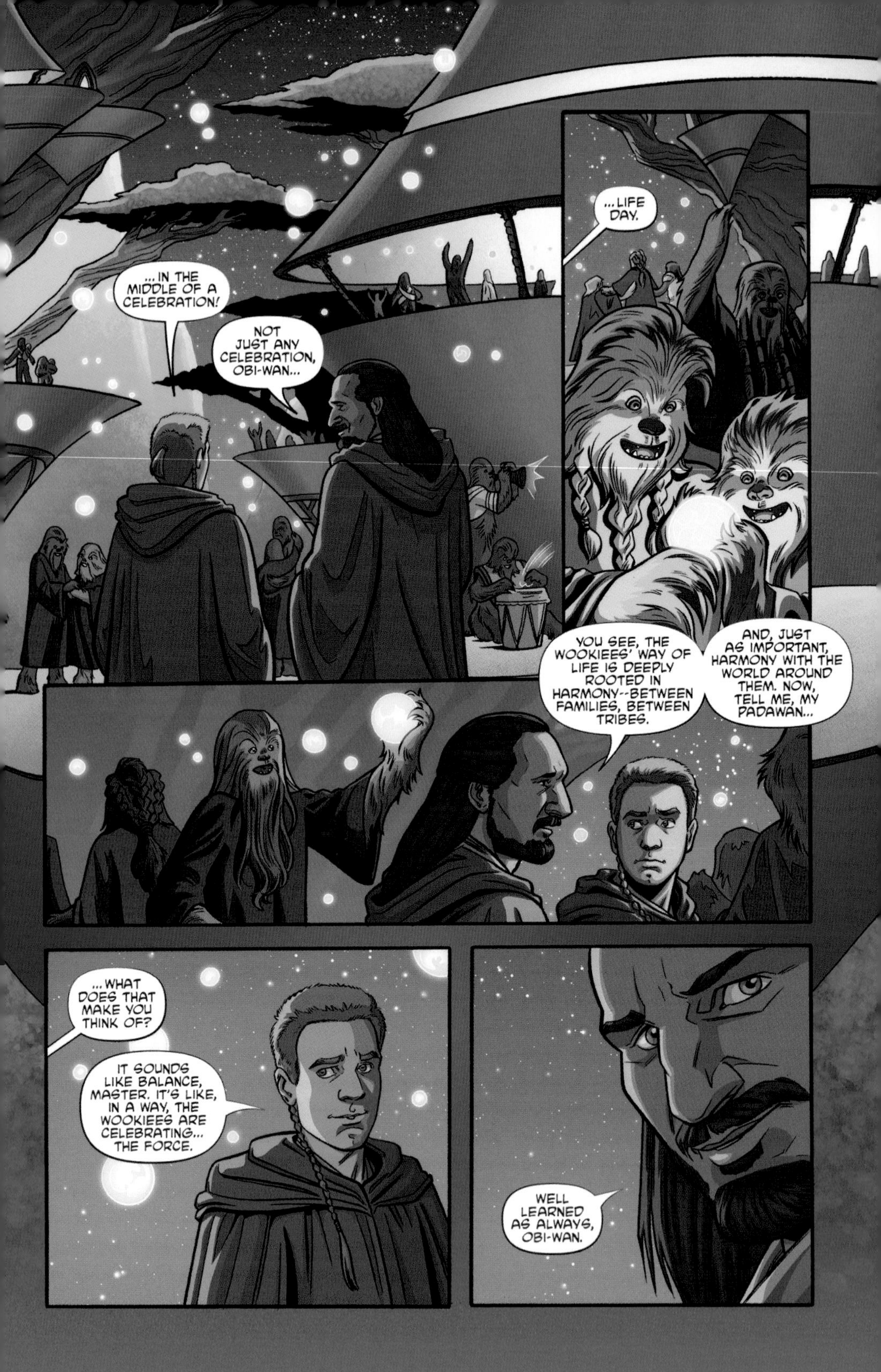
...IN THE MIDDLE OF A CELEBRATION!
NOT JUST ANY CELEBRATION, OBI-WAN...
...LIFE DAY.
YOU SEE, THE WOOKIEES' WAY OF LIFE IS DEEPLY ROOTED IN HARMONY--BETWEEN FAMILIES, BETWEEN TRIBES.
AND, JUST AS IMPORTANT, HARMONY WITH THE WORLD AROUND THEM. NOW, TELL ME, MY PADAWAN...
...WHAT DOES THAT MAKE YOU THINK OF?
IT SOUNDS LIKE BALANCE, MASTER. IT'S LIKE, IN A WAY, THE WOOKIEES ARE CELEBRATING... THE FORCE.
WELL LEARNED AS ALWAYS, OBI-WAN.

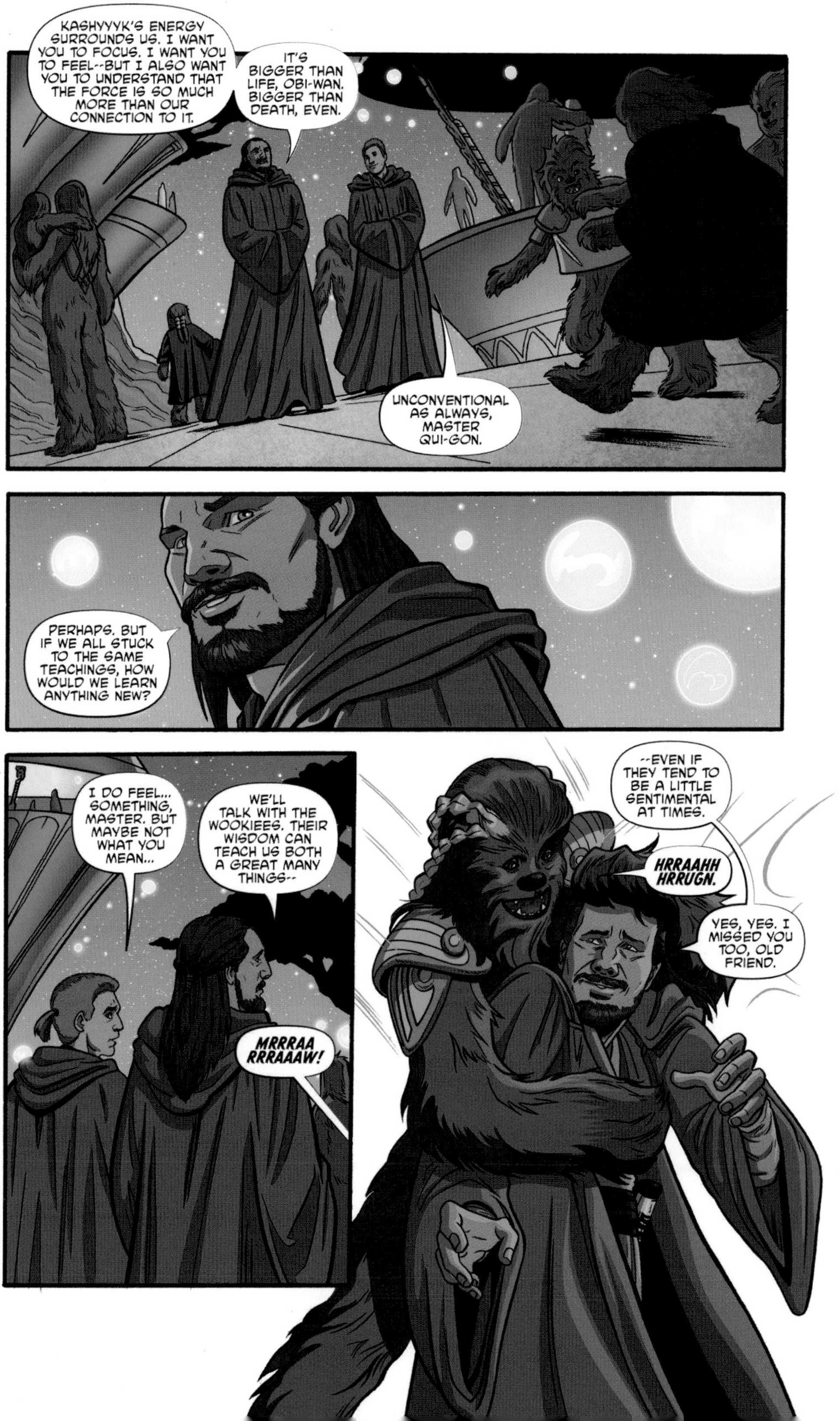
KASHYYYK'S ENERGY SURROUNDS US. I WANT YOU TO FOCUS. I WANT YOU TO FEEL--BUT I ALSO WANT YOU TO UNDERSTAND THAT THE FORCE IS SO MUCH MORE THAN OUR CONNECTION TO IT.
IT'S BIGGER THAN LIFE, OBI-WAN. BIGGER THAN DEATH, EVEN.
UNCONVENTIONAL AS ALWAYS, MASTER QUI-GON.
PERHAPS. BUT IF WE ALL STUCK TO THE SAME TEACHINGS, HOW WOULD WE LEARN ANYTHING NEW?
I DO FEEL... SOMETHING, MASTER. BUT MAYBE NOT WHAT YOU MEAN...
WE'LL TALK WITH THE WOOKIEES. THEIR WISDOM CAN TEACH US BOTH A GREAT MANY THINGS--
MRRRAA RRRAAAW!
--EVEN IF THEY TEND TO BE A LITTLE SENTIMENTAL AT TIMES.
HRRAAHH HRRUGN.
YES, YES. I MISSED YOU TOO, OLD FRIEND.

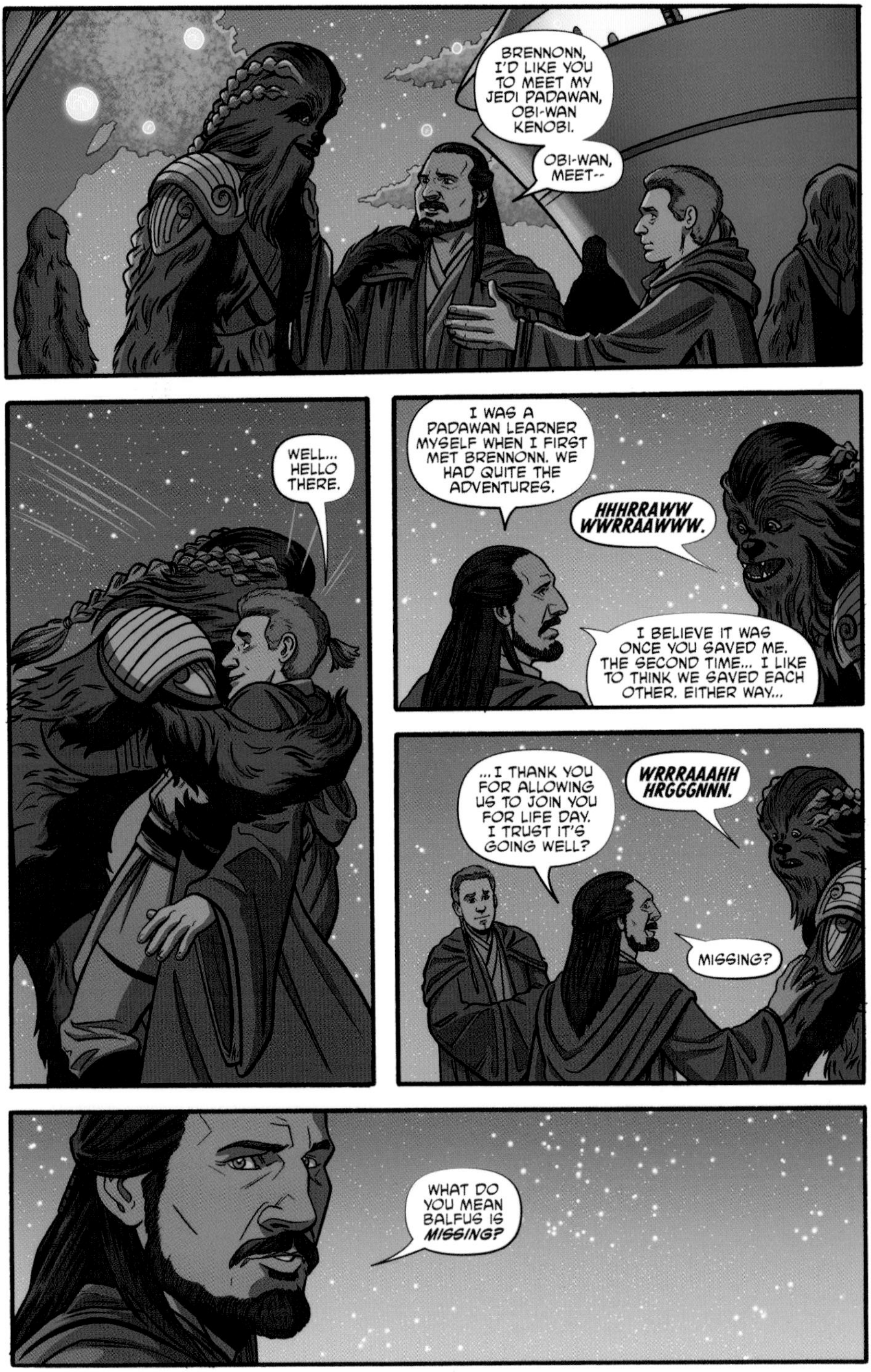
BRENNONN, I'D LIKE YOU TO MEET MY JEDI PADAWAN, OBI-WAN KENOBI.
OBI-WAN, MEET--
WELL... HELLO THERE.
I WAS A PADAWAN LEARNER MYSELF WHEN I FIRST MET BRENNONN. WE HAD QUITE THE ADVENTURES.
HHHRRAWW WWRRAAWWW.
I BELIEVE IT WAS ONCE YOU SAVED ME. THE SECOND TIME... I LIKE TO THINK WE SAVED EACH OTHER. EITHER WAY...
...I THANK YOU FOR ALLOWING US TO JOIN YOU FOR LIFE DAY. I TRUST IT'S GOING WELL?
WRRRAAAHH HRGGGNNN.
MISSING?
WHAT DO YOU MEAN BALFUS IS MISSING?

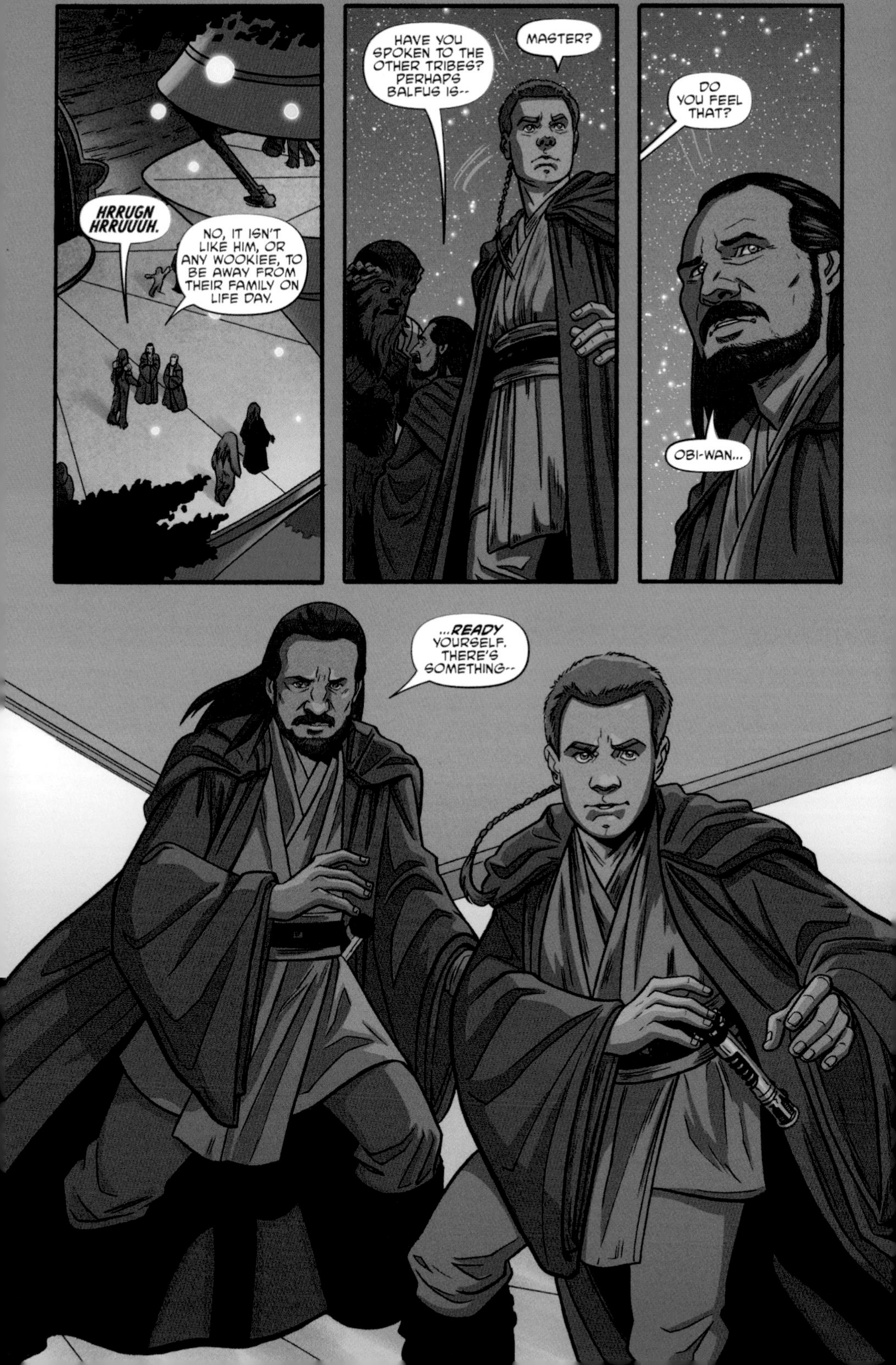
HRRUGN HRRUUUH.
NO, IT ISN'T LIKE HIM, OR ANY WOOKIEE, TO BE AWAY FROM THEIR FAMILY ON LIFE DAY.
HAVE YOU SPOKEN TO THE OTHER TRIBES? PERHAPS BALFUS IS--
MASTER?
DO YOU FEEL THAT?
OBI-WAN...
...READY YOURSELF. THERE'S SOMETHING--

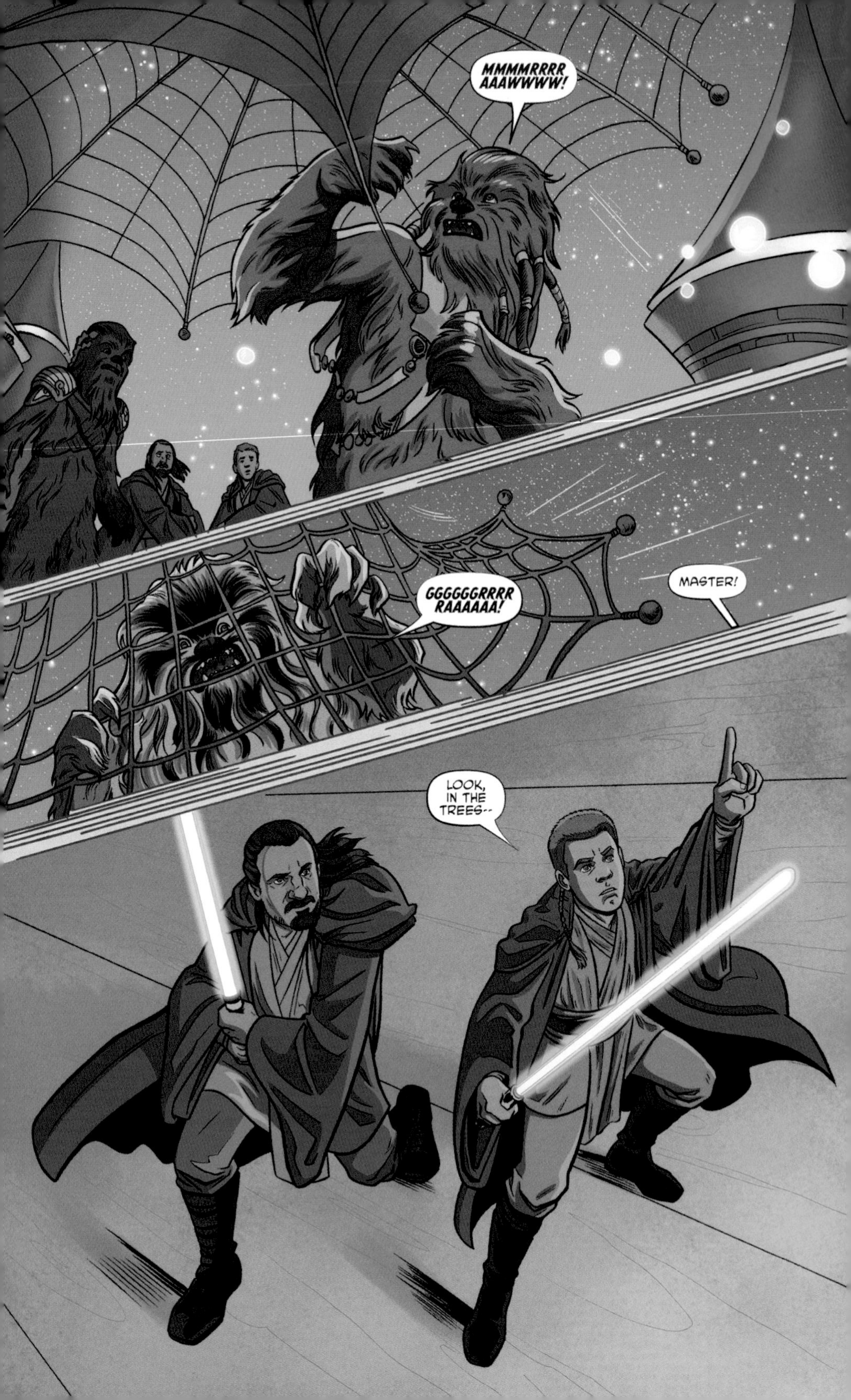
MMMMRRRR AAAWWWW!
GGGGGGRRRR RAAAAAA!
MASTER!
LOOK, IN THE TREES--

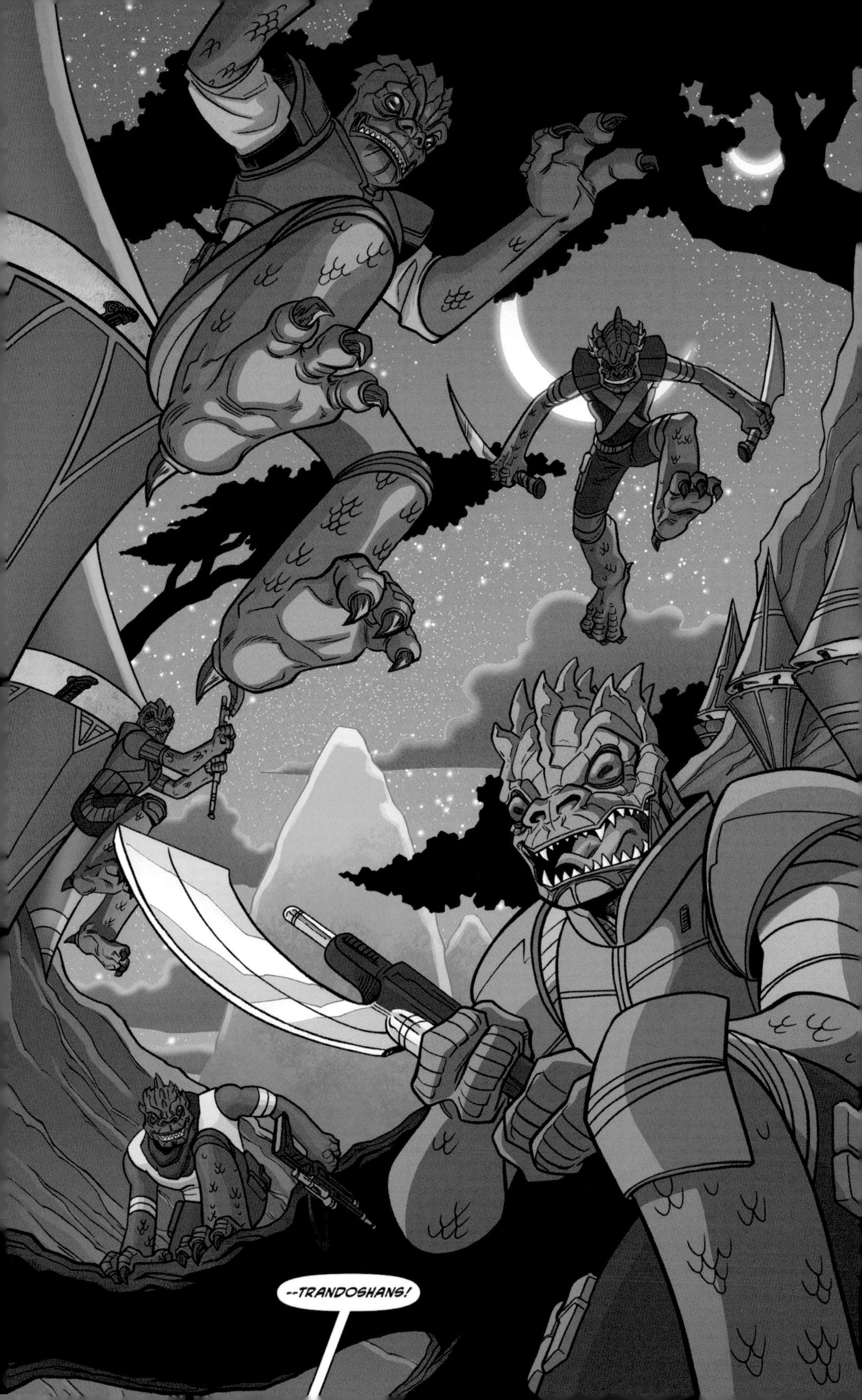
--TRANDOSHANS!

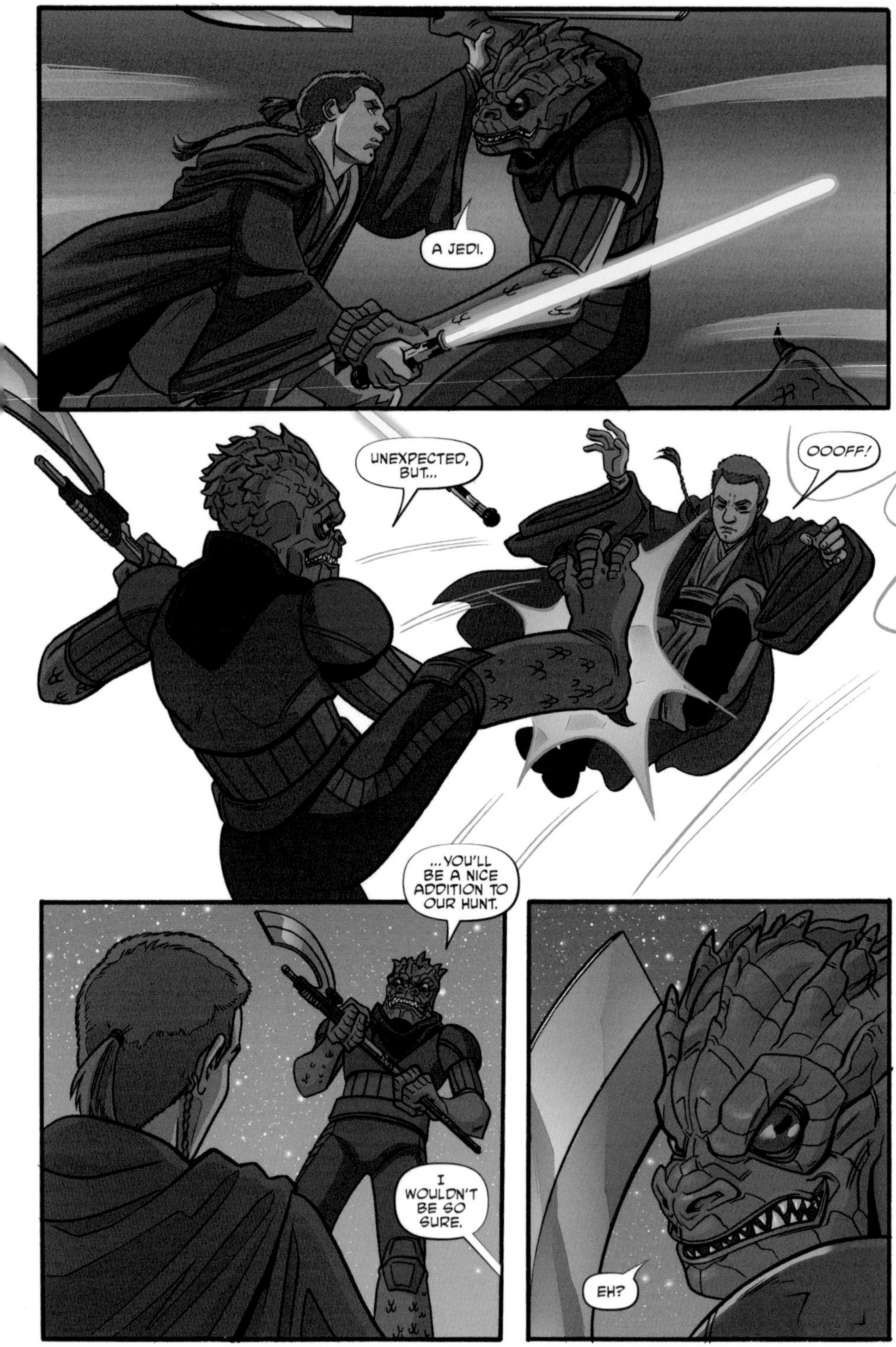
A JEDI.
UNEXPECTED, BUT...
OOOFF!
...YOU'LL BE A NICE ADDITION TO OUR HUNT.
I WOULDN'T BE SO SURE.
EH?

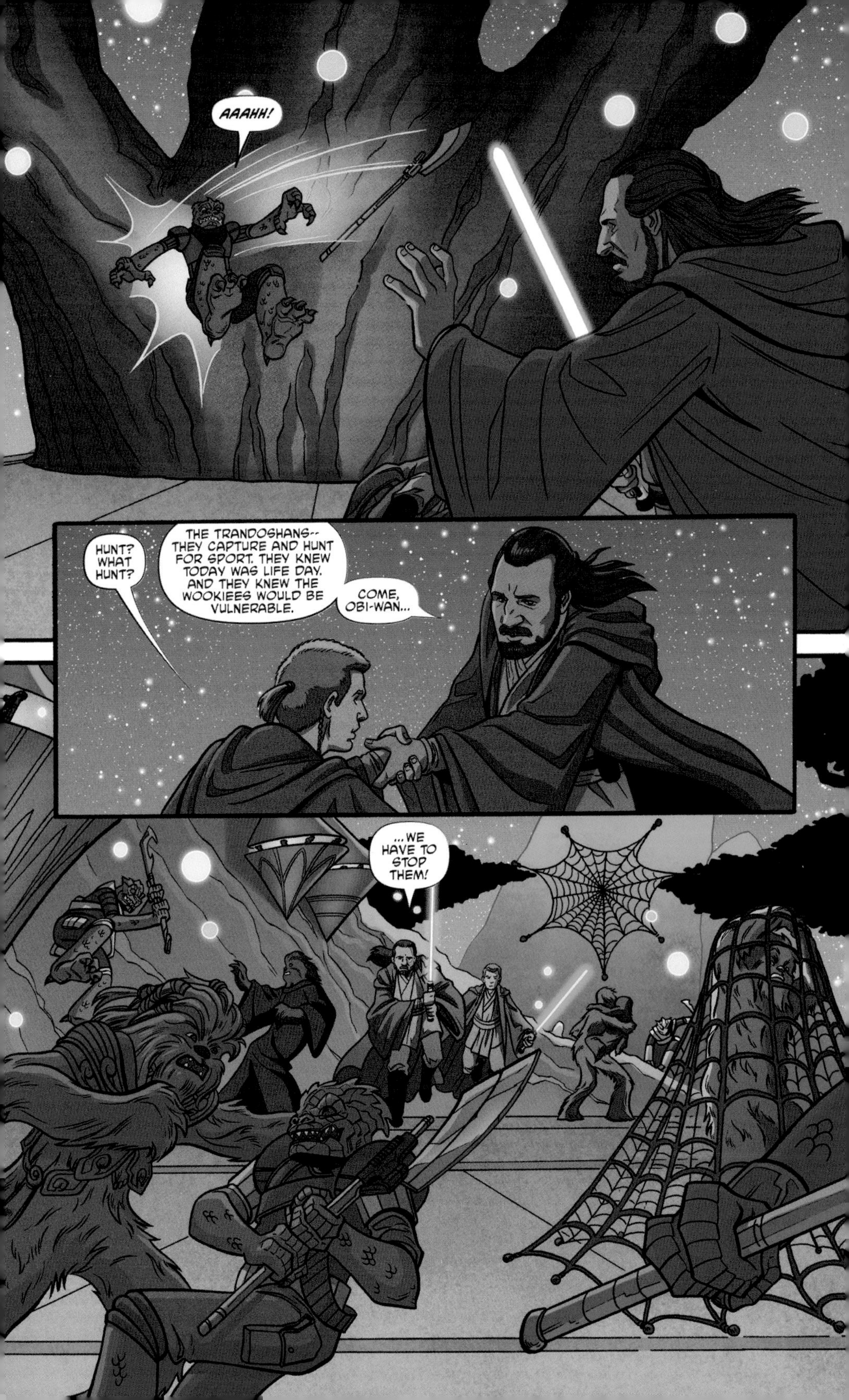
AAAHH!
HUNT? WHAT HUNT?
THE TRANDOSHANS-- THEY CAPTURE AND HUNT FOR SPORT. THEY KNEW TODAY WAS LIFE DAY. AND THEY KNEW THE WOOKIEES WOULD BE VULNERABLE.
COME, OBI-WAN...
...WE HAVE TO STOP THEM!

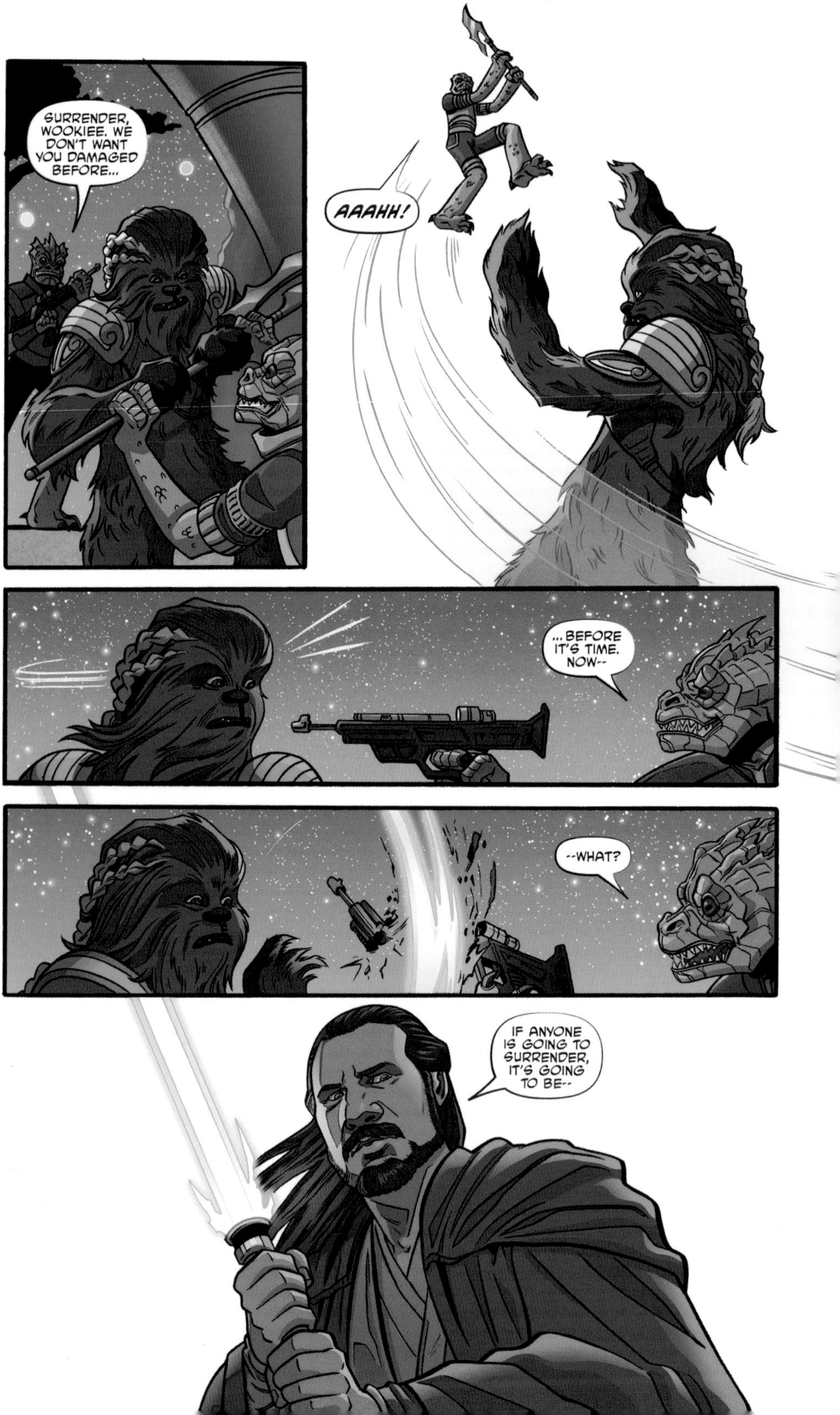
SURRENDER, WOOKIEE. WE DON'T WANT YOU DAMAGED BEFORE...
AAAHH!
...BEFORE IT'S TIME. NOW--
--WHAT?
IF ANYONE IS GOING TO SURRENDER, IT'S GOING TO BE--

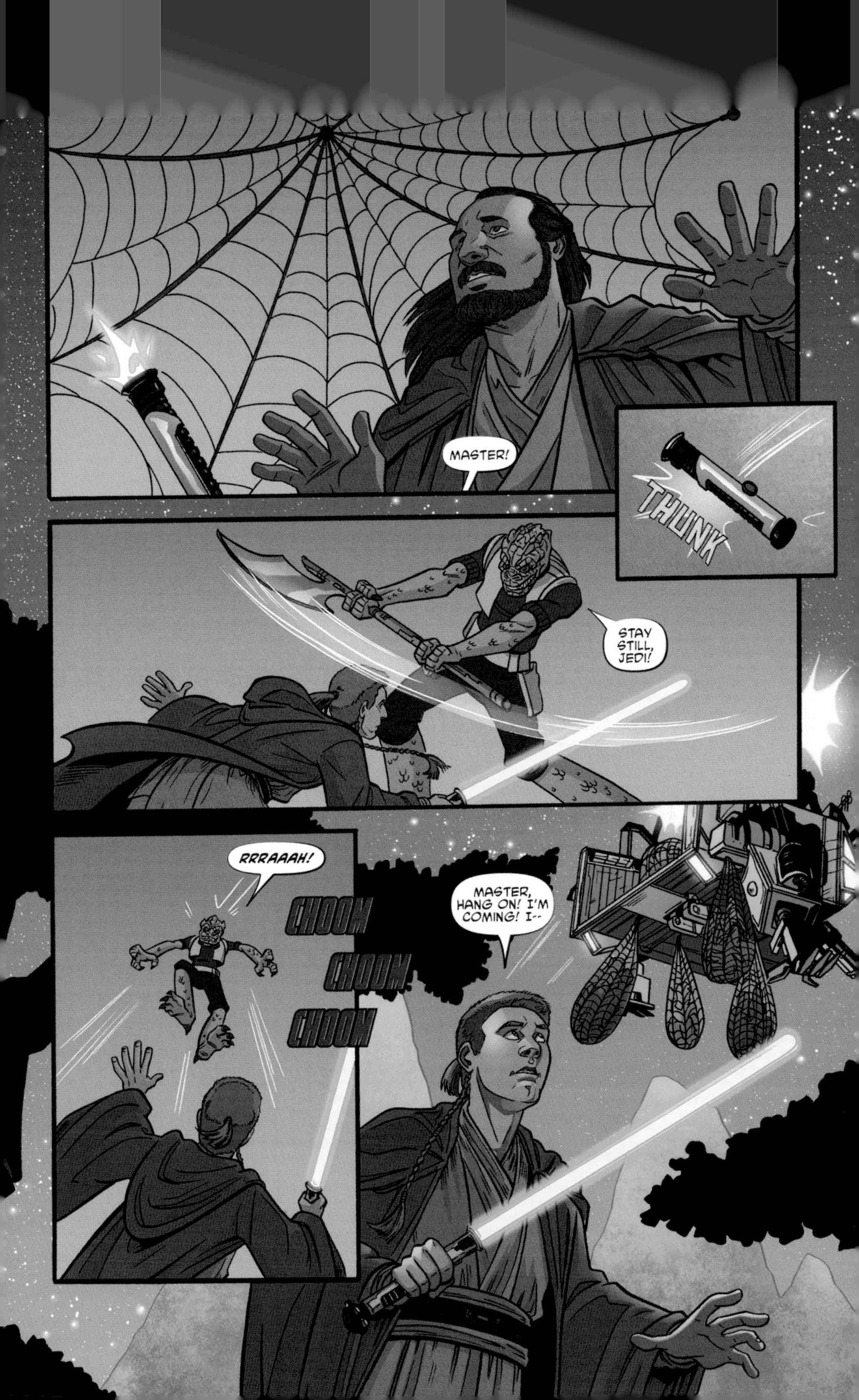
MASTER!
THUNK
STAY STILL, JEDI!
RRRAAAH!
CHOOM
CHOOM
CHOOM
MASTER, HANG ON! I'M COMING! I--

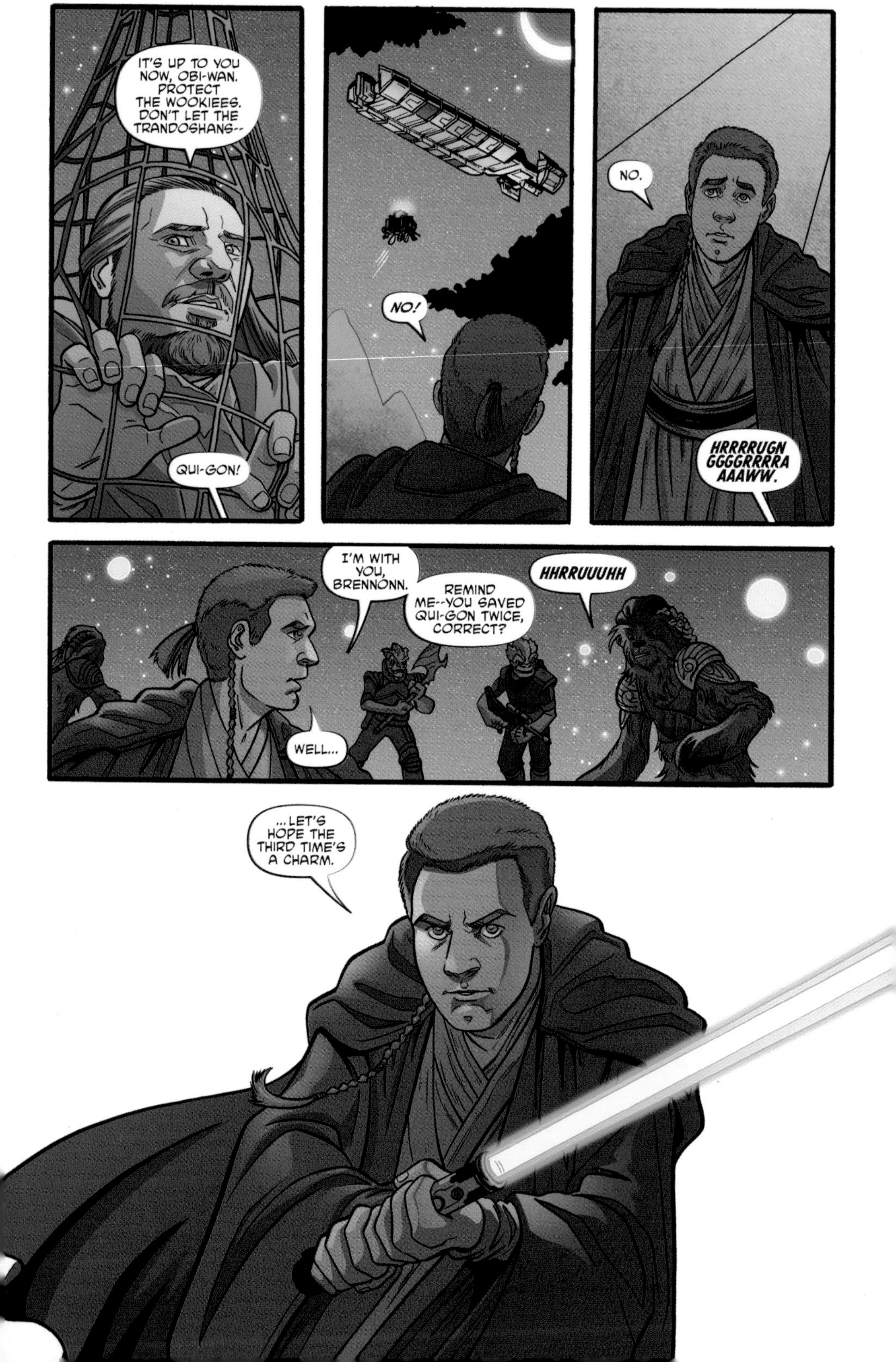
IT'S UP TO YOU NOW, OBI-WAN. PROTECT THE WOOKIEES. DON'T LET THE TRANDOSHANS--
QUI-GON!
NO!
NO.
HRRRRUGN GGGGRRRRA AAAWW.
I'M WITH YOU, BRENNONN.
REMIND ME--YOU SAVED QUI-GON TWICE, CORRECT?
HHRRUUUHH
WELL...
...LET'S HOPE THE THIRD TIME'S A CHARM.

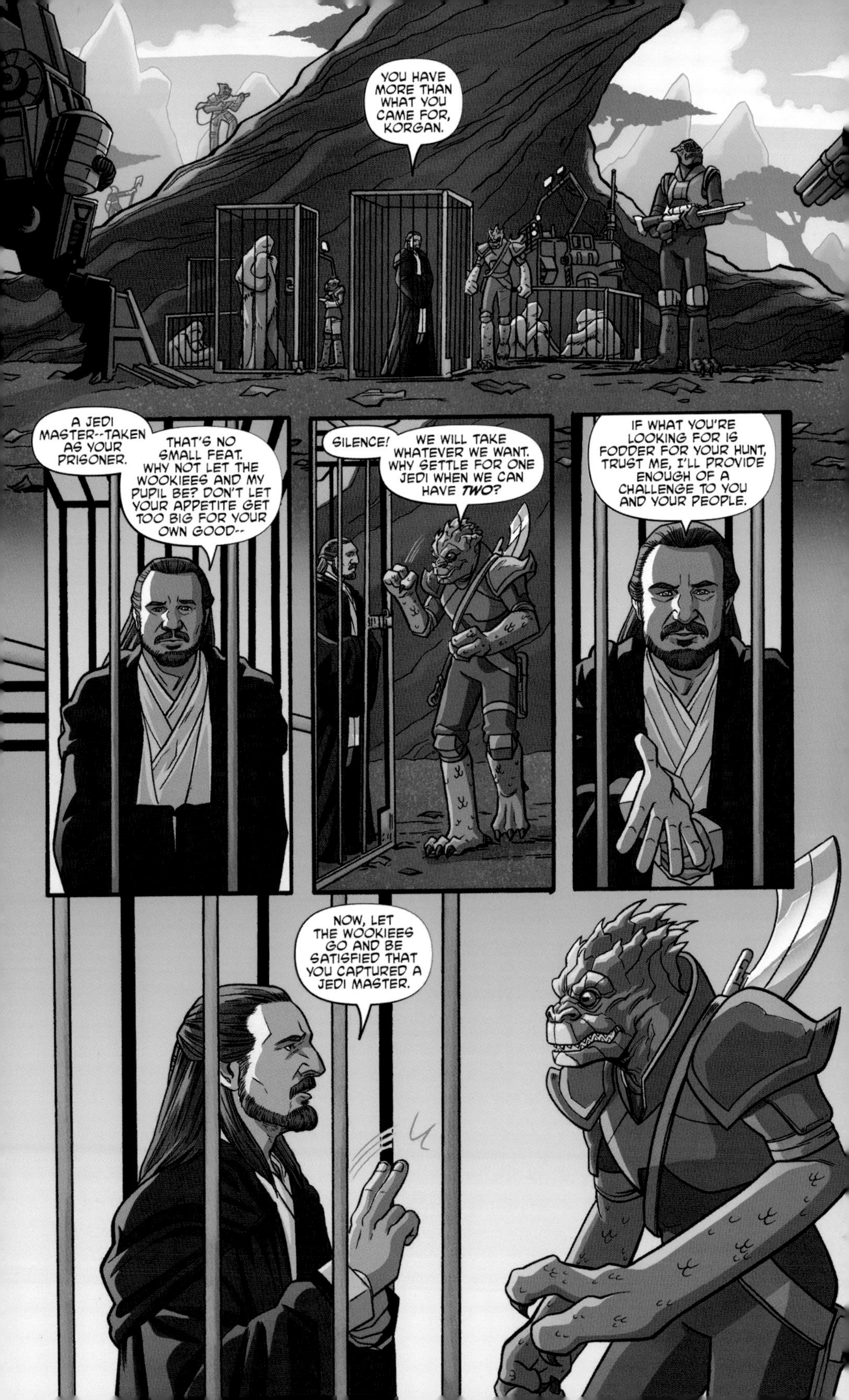
YOU HAVE MORE THAN WHAT YOU CAME FOR, KORGAN.
A JEDI MASTER--TAKEN AS YOUR PRISONER.
THAT'S NO SMALL FEAT. WHY NOT LET THE WOOKIEES AND MY PUPIL BE? DON'T LET YOUR APPETITE GET TOO BIG FOR YOUR OWN GOOD--
SILENCE!
WE WILL TAKE WHATEVER WE WANT. WHY SETTLE FOR ONE JEDI WHEN WE CAN HAVE *TWO*?
IF WHAT YOU'RE LOOKING FOR IS FODDER FOR YOUR HUNT, TRUST ME, I'LL PROVIDE ENOUGH OF A CHALLENGE TO YOU AND YOUR PEOPLE.
NOW, LET THE WOOKIEES GO AND BE SATISFIED THAT YOU CAPTURED A JEDI MASTER.

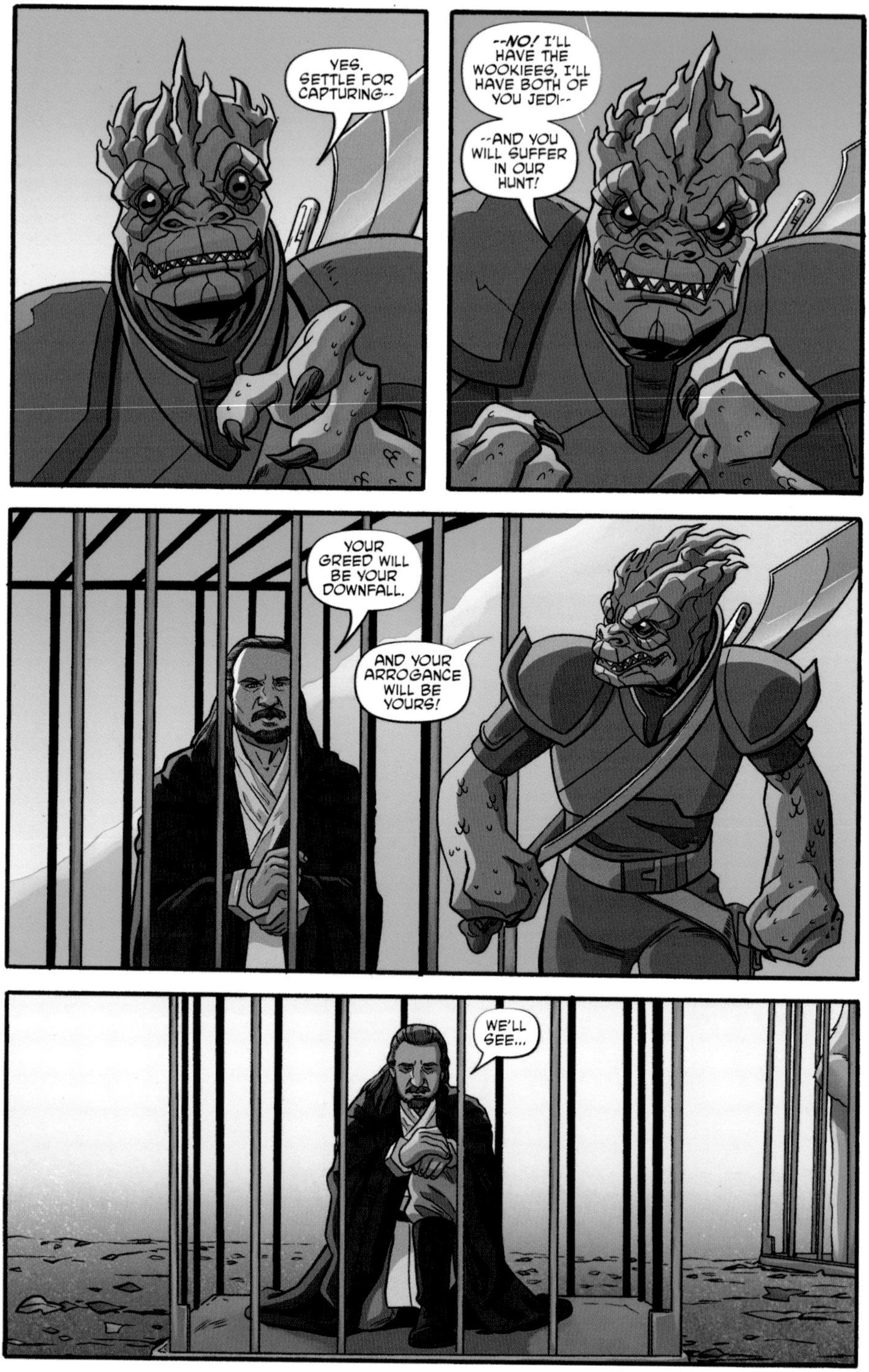
YES. SETTLE FOR CAPTURING--
--NO! I'LL HAVE THE WOOKIEES, I'LL HAVE BOTH OF YOU JEDI--
--AND YOU WILL SUFFER IN OUR HUNT!
YOUR GREED WILL BE YOUR DOWNFALL.
AND YOUR ARROGANCE WILL BE YOURS!
WE'LL SEE...

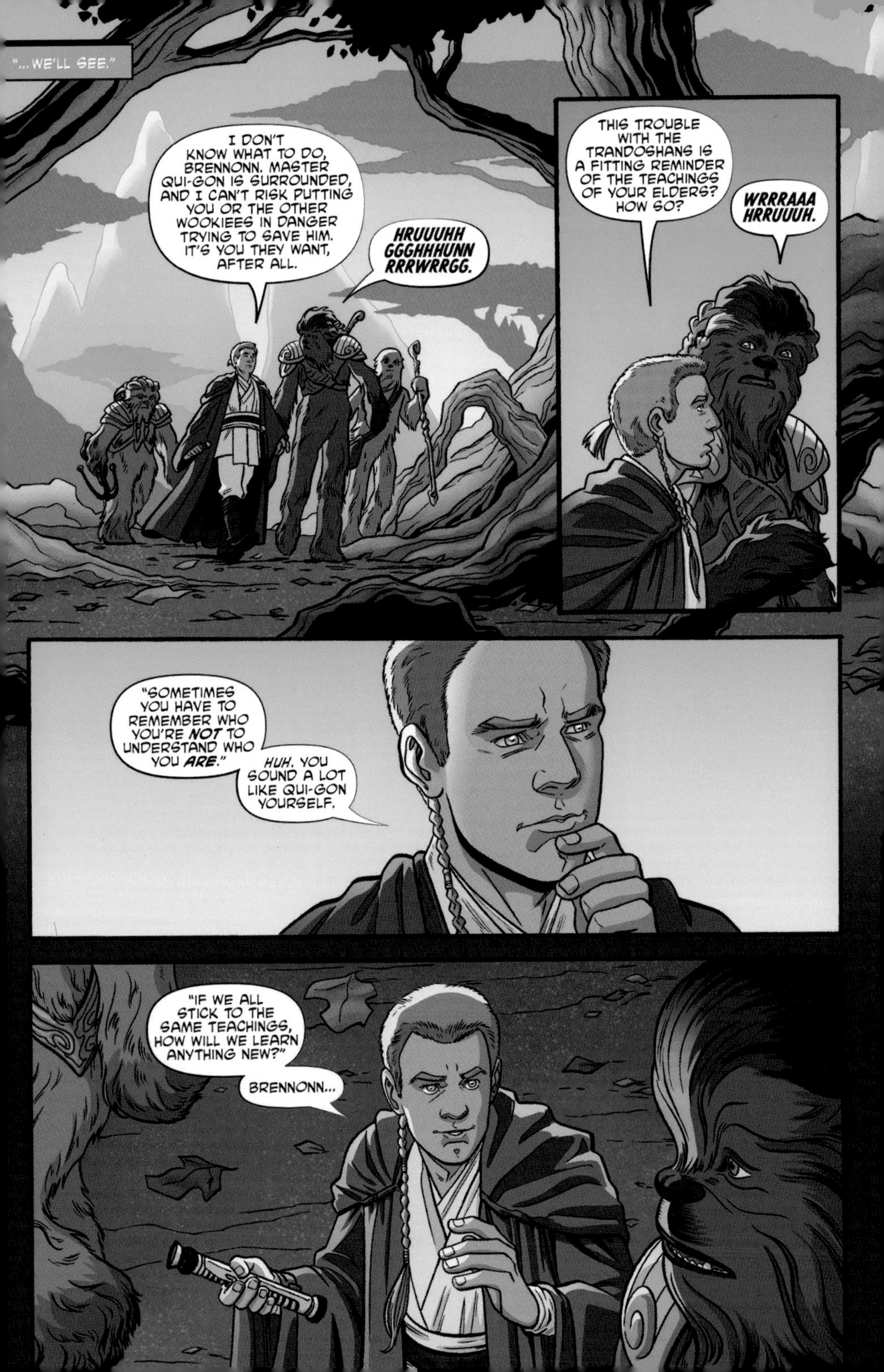
"...WE'LL SEE."
I DON'T KNOW WHAT TO DO, BRENNONN. MASTER QUI-GON IS SURROUNDED, AND I CAN'T RISK PUTTING YOU OR THE OTHER WOOKIEES IN DANGER TRYING TO SAVE HIM. IT'S YOU THEY WANT, AFTER ALL.
HRUUUHH GGGHHHUNN RRRWRRGG.
THIS TROUBLE WITH THE TRANDOSHANS IS A FITTING REMINDER OF THE TEACHINGS OF YOUR ELDERS? HOW SO?
WRRRAAA HRRUUUH.
"SOMETIMES YOU HAVE TO REMEMBER WHO YOU'RE NOT TO UNDERSTAND WHO YOU ARE."
HUH. YOU SOUND A LOT LIKE QUI-GON YOURSELF.
"IF WE ALL STICK TO THE SAME TEACHINGS, HOW WILL WE LEARN ANYTHING NEW?"
BRENNONN...

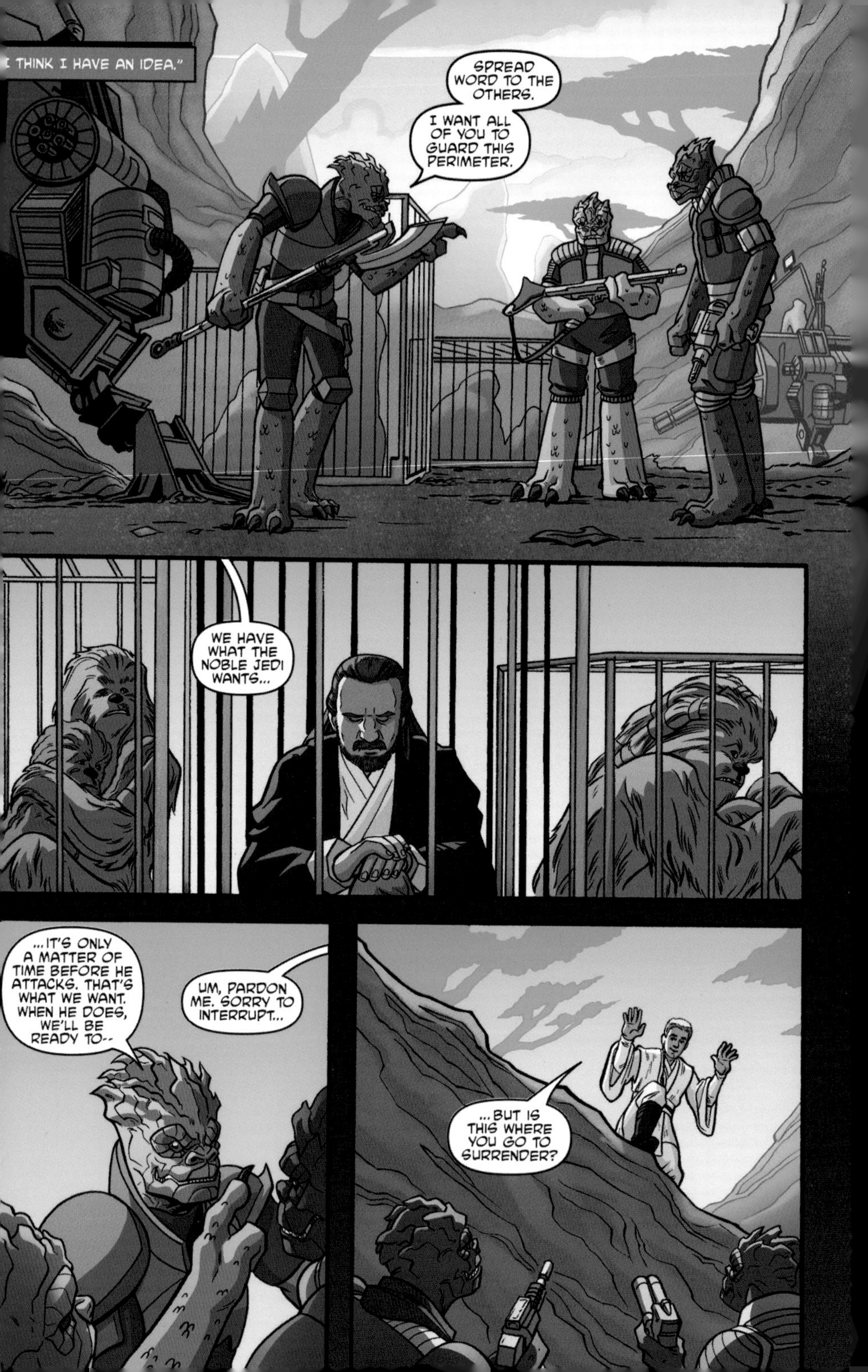
I THINK I HAVE AN IDEA."
SPREAD WORD TO THE OTHERS.
I WANT ALL OF YOU TO GUARD THIS PERIMETER.
WE HAVE WHAT THE NOBLE JEDI WANTS...
...IT'S ONLY A MATTER OF TIME BEFORE HE ATTACKS. THAT'S WHAT WE WANT. WHEN HE DOES, WE'LL BE READY TO--
UM, PARDON ME. SORRY TO INTERRUPT...
...BUT IS THIS WHERE YOU GO TO SURRENDER?

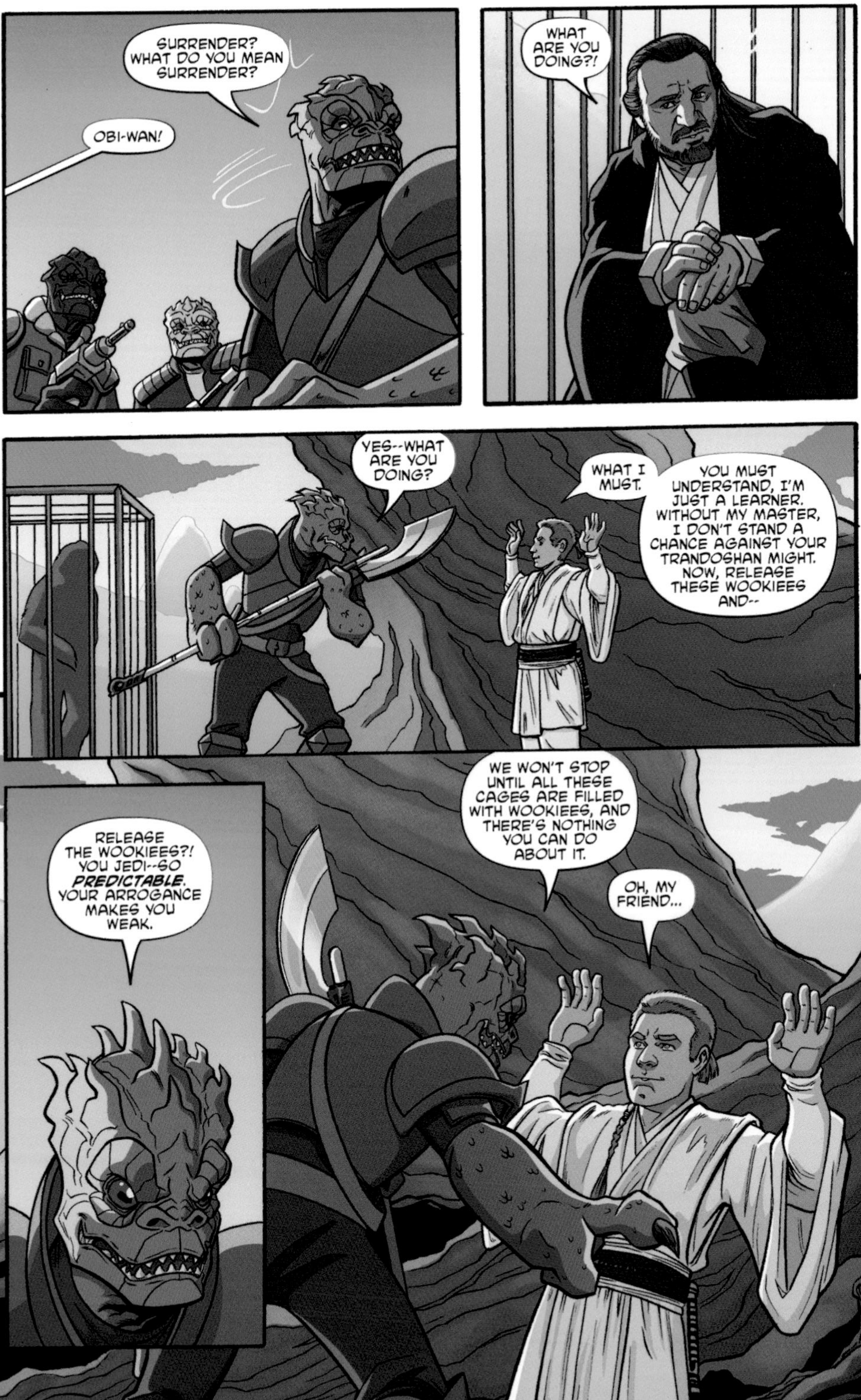
SURRENDER? WHAT DO YOU MEAN SURRENDER?
OBI-WAN!
WHAT ARE YOU DOING?!
YES--WHAT ARE YOU DOING?
WHAT I MUST.
YOU MUST UNDERSTAND, I'M JUST A LEARNER. WITHOUT MY MASTER, I DON'T STAND A CHANCE AGAINST YOUR TRANDOSHAN MIGHT. NOW, RELEASE THESE WOOKIEES AND--
RELEASE THE WOOKIEES?! YOU JEDI--SO *PREDICTABLE*. YOUR ARROGANCE MAKES YOU WEAK.
WE WON'T STOP UNTIL ALL THESE CAGES ARE FILLED WITH WOOKIEES, AND THERE'S NOTHING YOU CAN DO ABOUT IT.
OH, MY FRIEND...

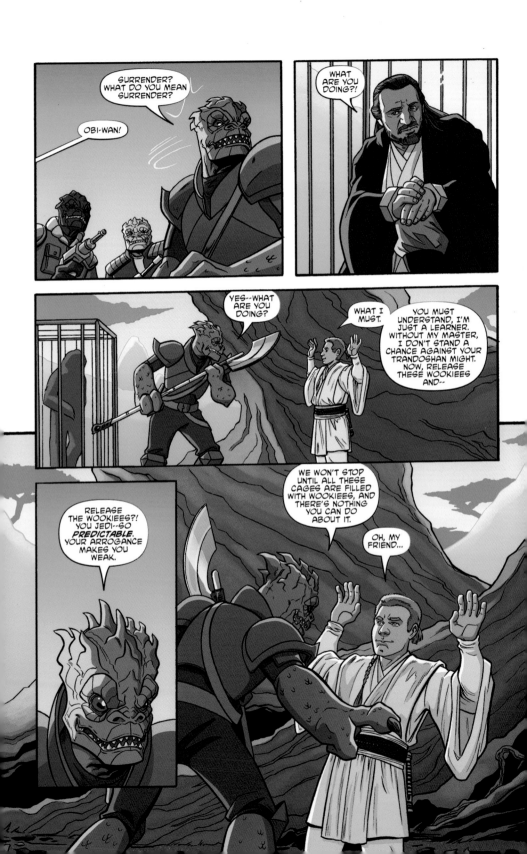

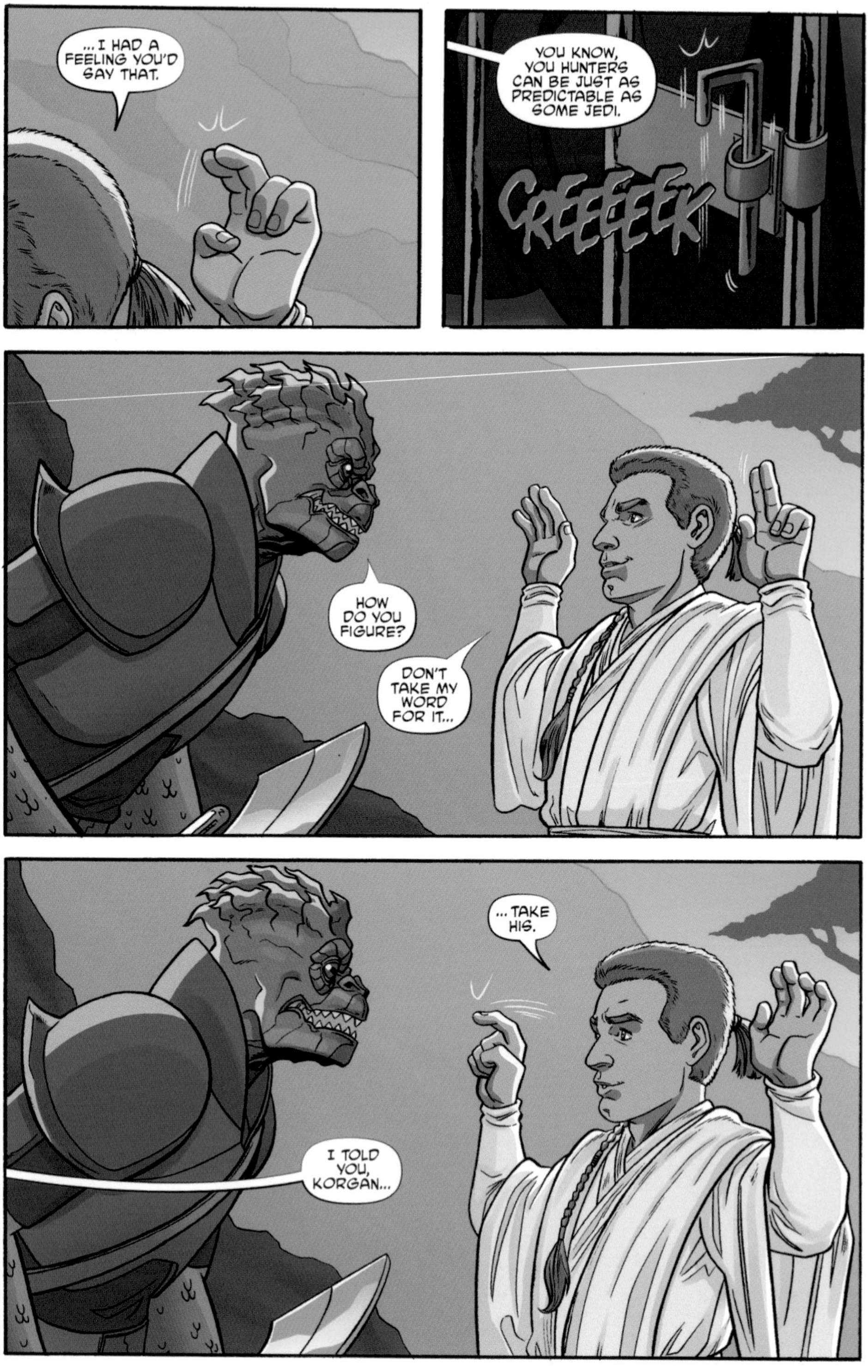
...I HAD A FEELING YOU'D SAY THAT.
YOU KNOW, YOU HUNTERS CAN BE JUST AS PREDICTABLE AS SOME JEDI.
CREEEEEK
HOW DO YOU FIGURE?
DON'T TAKE MY WORD FOR IT...
...TAKE HIS.
I TOLD YOU, KORGAN...

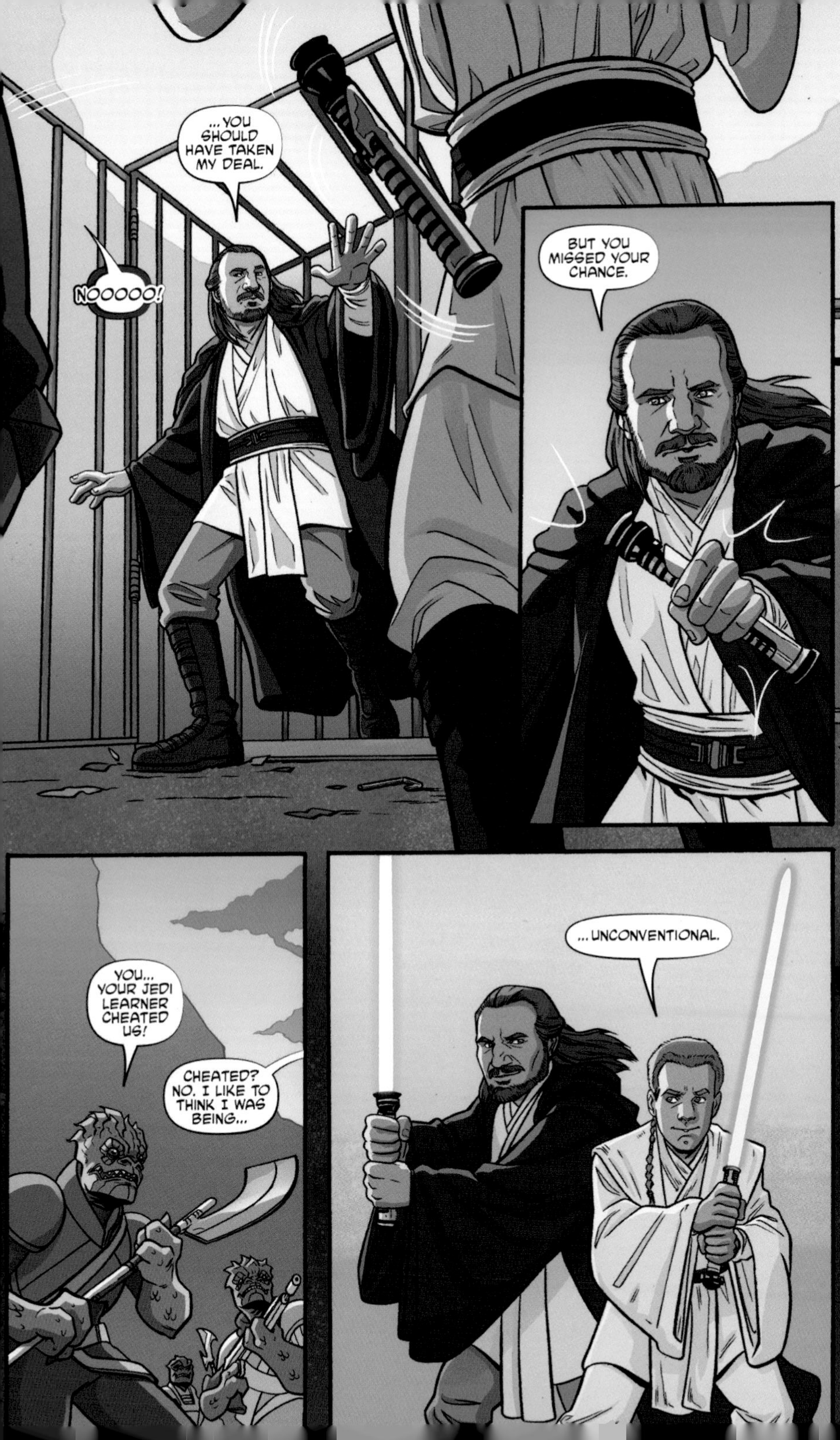
...YOU SHOULD HAVE TAKEN MY DEAL.
NOOOOO!
BUT YOU MISSED YOUR CHANCE.
YOU... YOUR JEDI LEARNER CHEATED US!
CHEATED? NO. I LIKE TO THINK I WAS BEING...
...UNCONVENTIONAL.

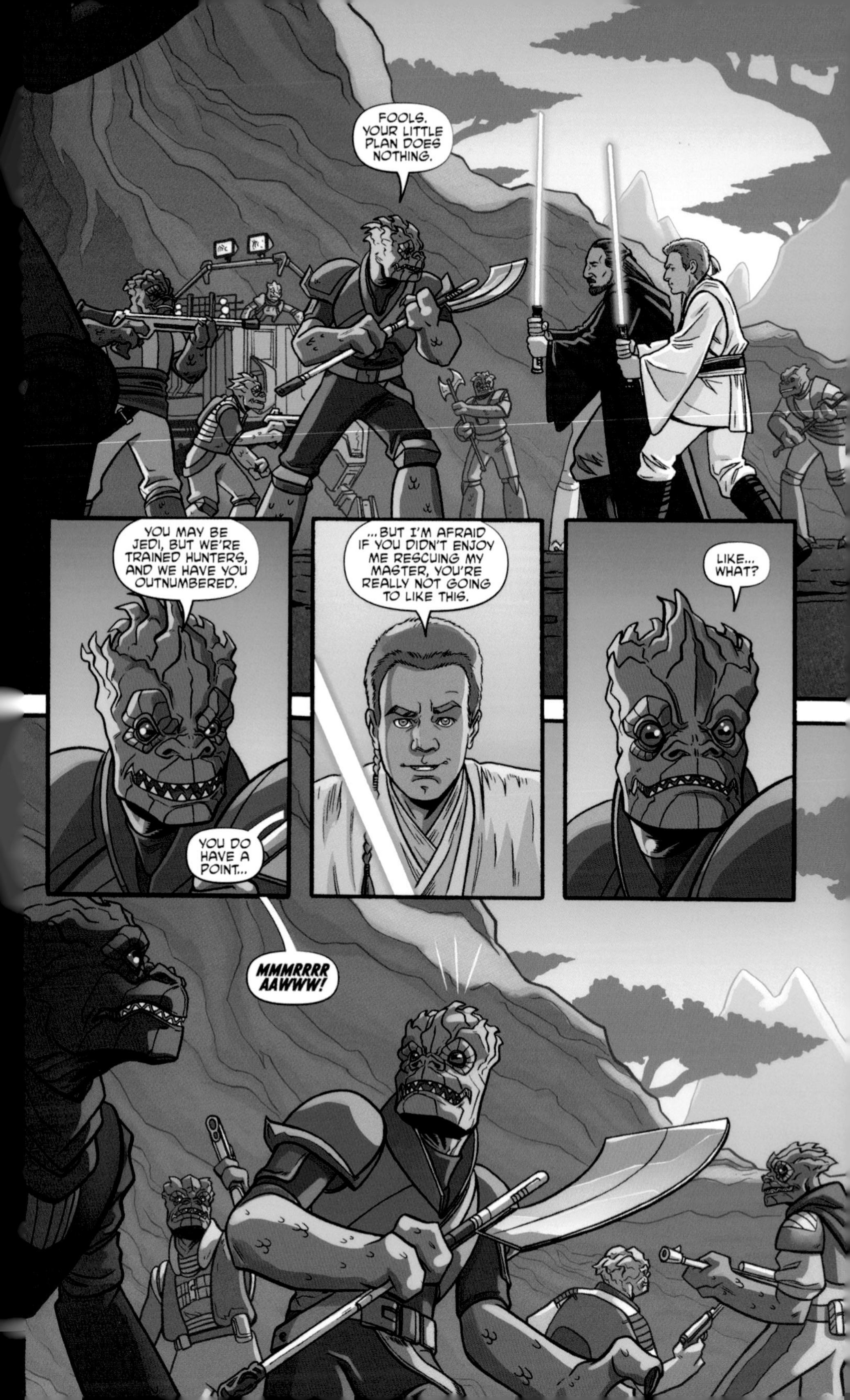
FOOLS. YOUR LITTLE PLAN DOES NOTHING.
YOU MAY BE JEDI, BUT WE'RE TRAINED HUNTERS, AND WE HAVE YOU OUTNUMBERED.
...BUT I'M AFRAID IF YOU DIDN'T ENJOY ME RESCUING MY MASTER, YOU'RE REALLY NOT GOING TO LIKE THIS.
LIKE... WHAT?
YOU DO HAVE A POINT...
MMMRRRR AAWWW!

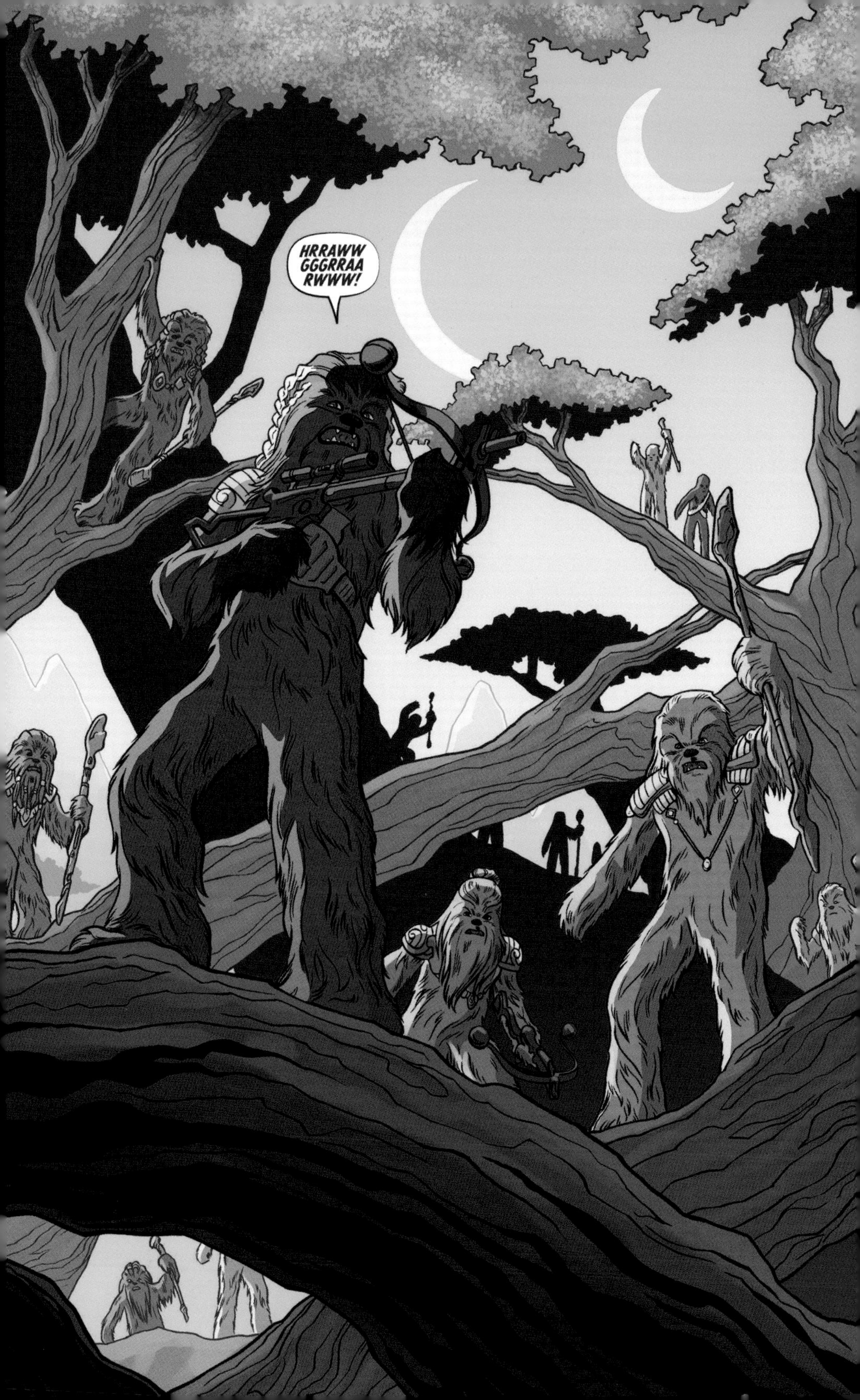
HRRAWW GGGRRAA RWWW!

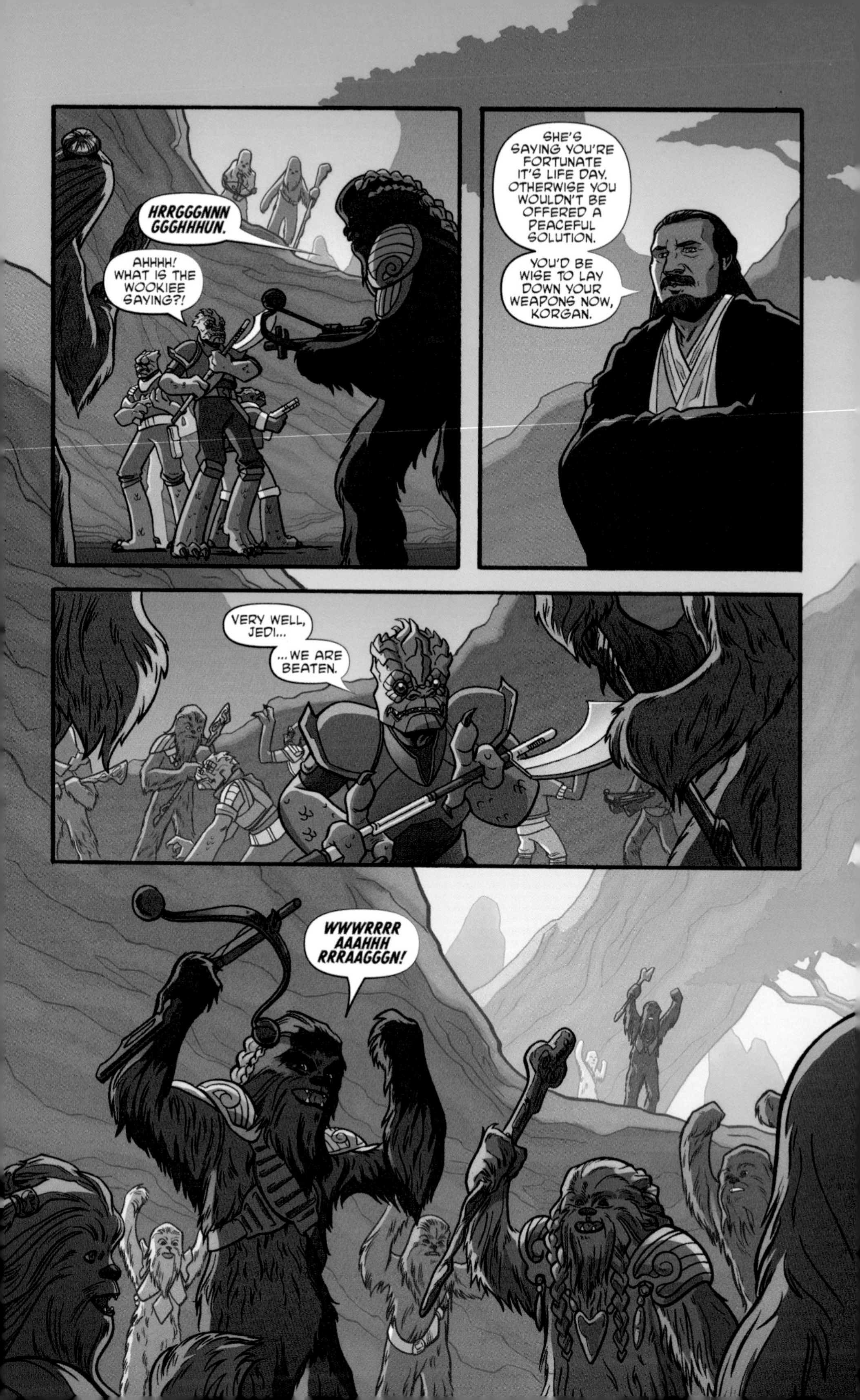
HRRGGGNNN GGGHHHUN.
AHHHH! WHAT IS THE WOOKIEE SAYING?!
SHE'S SAYING YOU'RE FORTUNATE IT'S LIFE DAY. OTHERWISE YOU WOULDN'T BE OFFERED A PEACEFUL SOLUTION.
YOU'D BE WISE TO LAY DOWN YOUR WEAPONS NOW, KORGAN.
VERY WELL, JEDI...
...WE ARE BEATEN.
WWWRRRR AAAHHHH RRRAAGGGN!

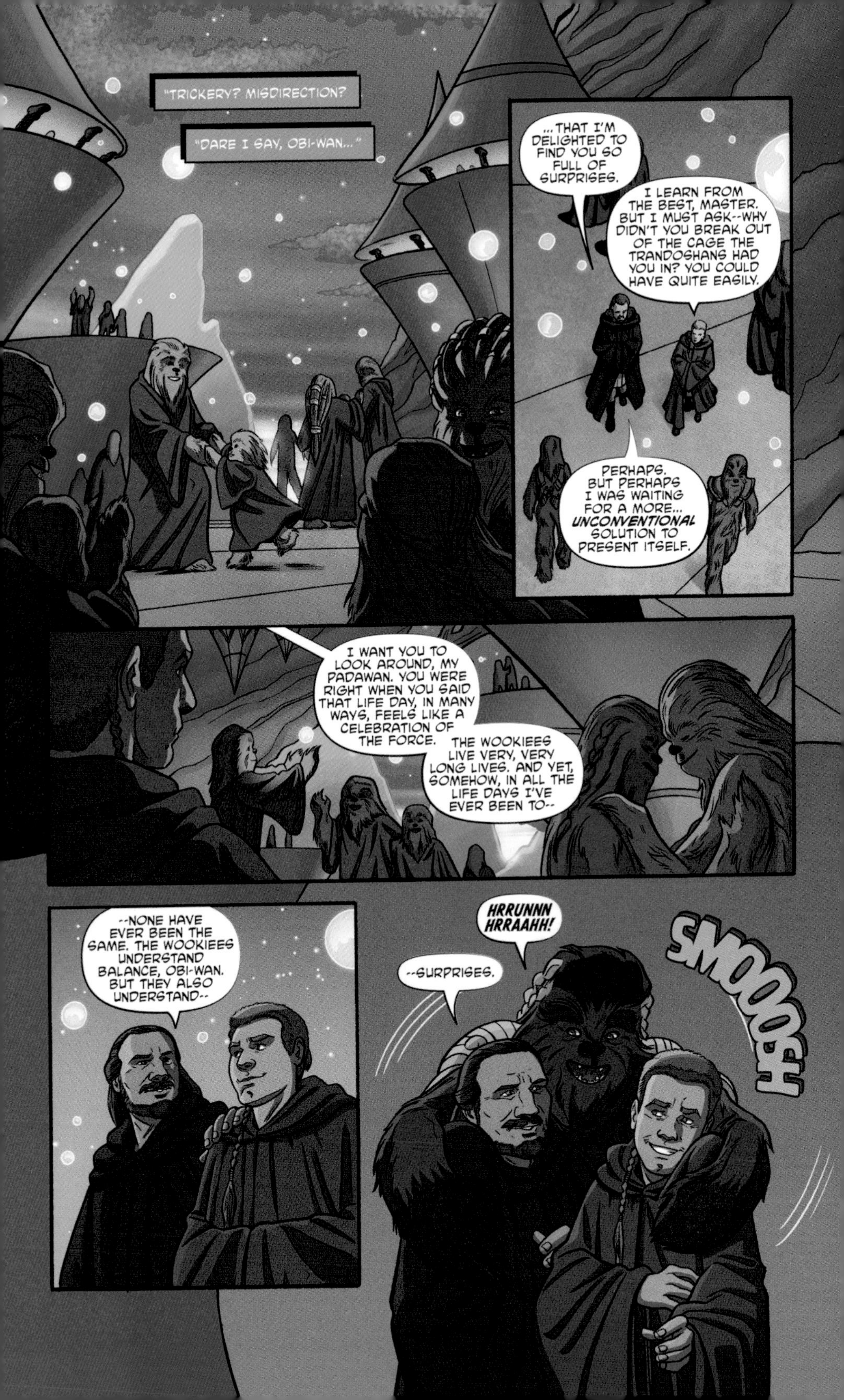
"TRICKERY? MISDIRECTION?
"DARE I SAY, OBI-WAN..."
...THAT I'M DELIGHTED TO FIND YOU SO FULL OF SURPRISES.
I LEARN FROM THE BEST, MASTER. BUT I MUST ASK--WHY DIDN'T YOU BREAK OUT OF THE CAGE THE TRANDOSHANS HAD YOU IN? YOU COULD HAVE QUITE EASILY.
PERHAPS. BUT PERHAPS I WAS WAITING FOR A MORE... UNCONVENTIONAL SOLUTION TO PRESENT ITSELF.
I WANT YOU TO LOOK AROUND, MY PADAWAN. YOU WERE RIGHT WHEN YOU SAID THAT LIFE DAY, IN MANY WAYS, FEELS LIKE A CELEBRATION OF THE FORCE.
THE WOOKIEES LIVE VERY, VERY LONG LIVES. AND YET, SOMEHOW, IN ALL THE LIFE DAYS I'VE EVER BEEN TO--
--NONE HAVE EVER BEEN THE SAME. THE WOOKIEES UNDERSTAND BALANCE, OBI-WAN. BUT THEY ALSO UNDERSTAND--
--SURPRISES.
HRRUNNN HRRAAHH!
SMOOOSH

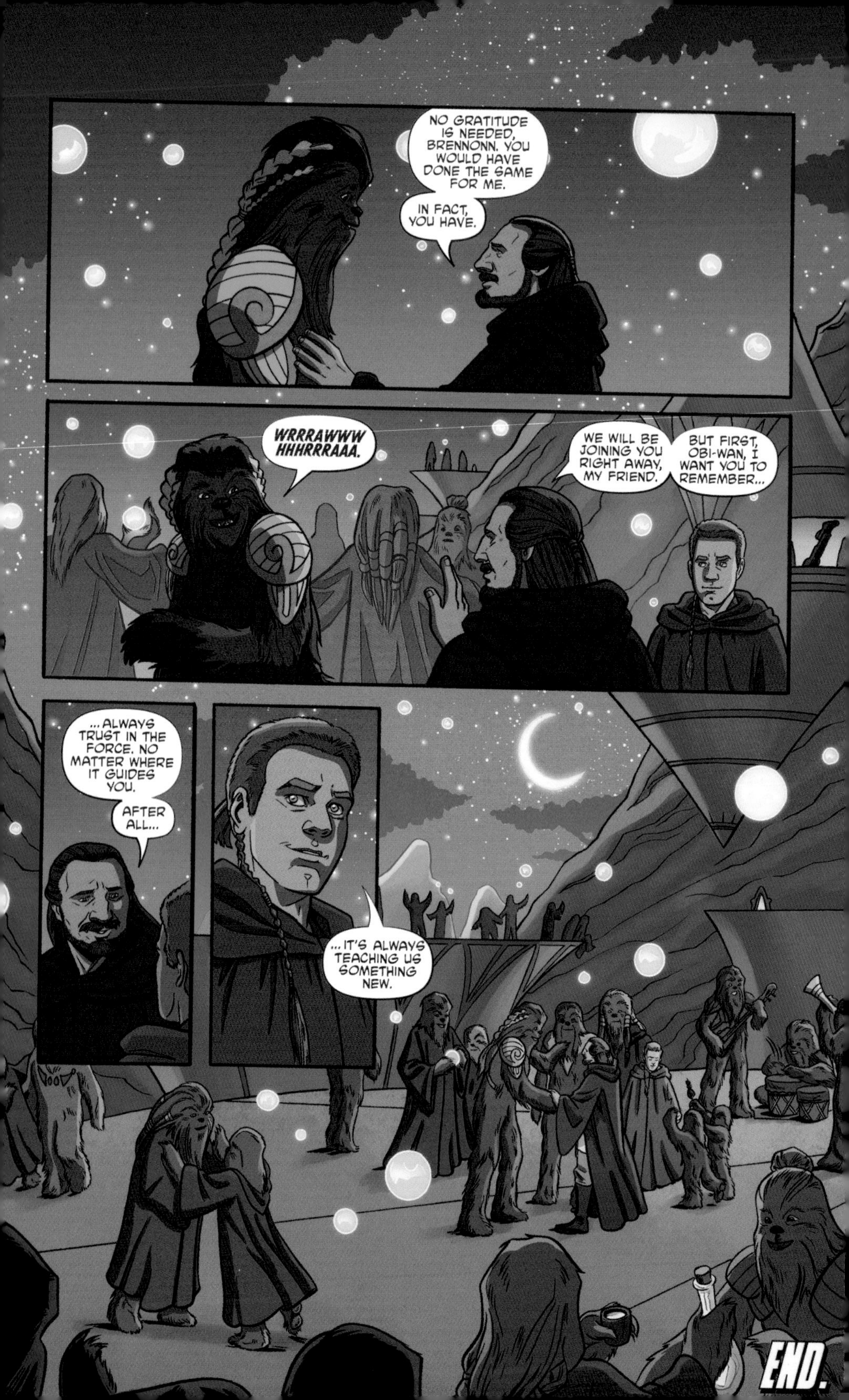
NO GRATITUDE IS NEEDED, BRENNONN. YOU WOULD HAVE DONE THE SAME FOR ME.
IN FACT, YOU HAVE.
WRRRAWWW HHHRRRAAA.
WE WILL BE JOINING YOU RIGHT AWAY, MY FRIEND.
BUT FIRST, OBI-WAN, I WANT YOU TO REMEMBER...
...ALWAYS TRUST IN THE FORCE. NO MATTER WHERE IT GUIDES YOU.
AFTER ALL...
...IT'S ALWAYS TEACHING US SOMETHING NEW.
END.

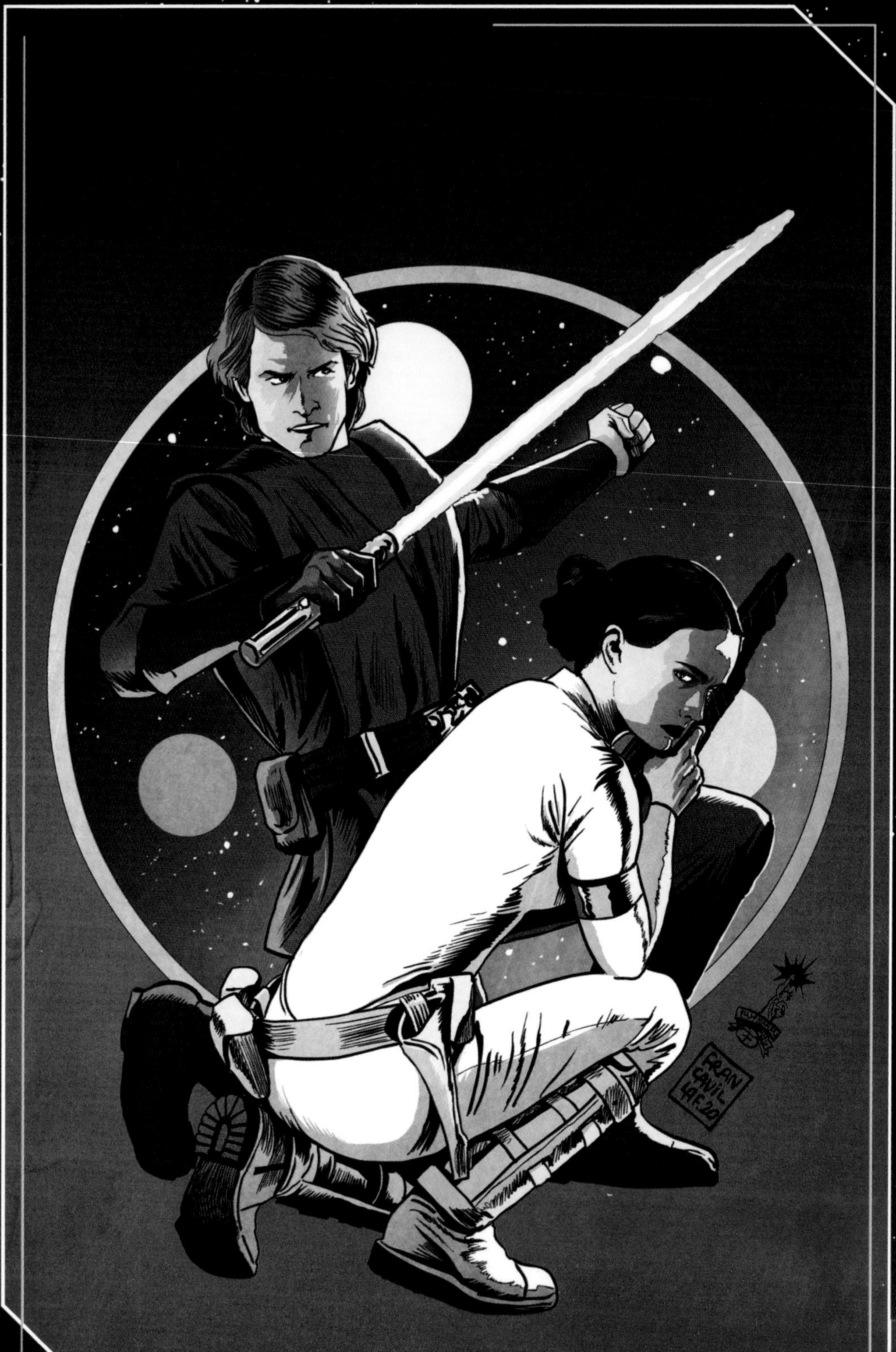

ART BY FRANCESCO FRANCAVILLA

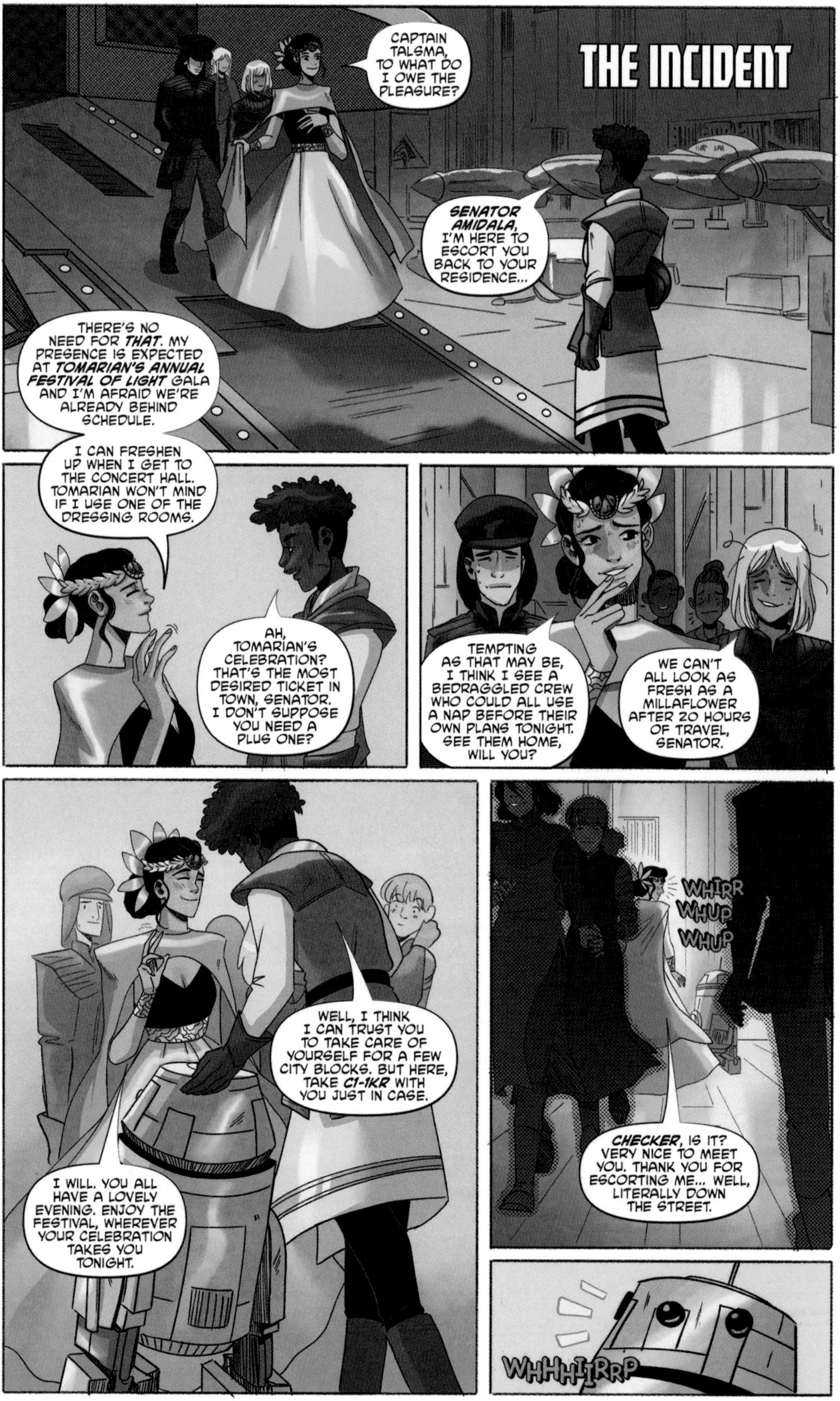
CAPTAIN TALSMA, TO WHAT DO I OWE THE PLEASURE?
THE INCIDENT
SENATOR AMIDALA, I'M HERE TO ESCORT YOU BACK TO YOUR RESIDENCE...
THERE'S NO NEED FOR THAT. MY PRESENCE IS EXPECTED AT TOMARIAN'S ANNUAL FESTIVAL OF LIGHT GALA AND I'M AFRAID WE'RE ALREADY BEHIND SCHEDULE.
I CAN FRESHEN UP WHEN I GET TO THE CONCERT HALL. TOMARIAN WON'T MIND IF I USE ONE OF THE DRESSING ROOMS.
AH, TOMARIAN'S CELEBRATION? THAT'S THE MOST DESIRED TICKET IN TOWN, SENATOR. I DON'T SUPPOSE YOU NEED A PLUS ONE?
TEMPTING AS THAT MAY BE, I THINK I SEE A BEDRAGGLED CREW WHO COULD ALL USE A NAP BEFORE THEIR OWN PLANS TONIGHT. SEE THEM HOME, WILL YOU?
WE CAN'T ALL LOOK AS FRESH AS A MILLAFLOWER AFTER 20 HOURS OF TRAVEL, SENATOR.
WELL, I THINK I CAN TRUST YOU TO TAKE CARE OF YOURSELF FOR A FEW CITY BLOCKS. BUT HERE, TAKE C1-1KR WITH YOU JUST IN CASE.
I WILL. YOU ALL HAVE A LOVELY EVENING. ENJOY THE FESTIVAL, WHEREVER YOUR CELEBRATION TAKES YOU TONIGHT.
WHIRR
WHUP
WHUP
CHECKER, IS IT? VERY NICE TO MEET YOU. THANK YOU FOR ESCORTING ME... WELL, LITERALLY DOWN THE STREET.
WHHHIRRP

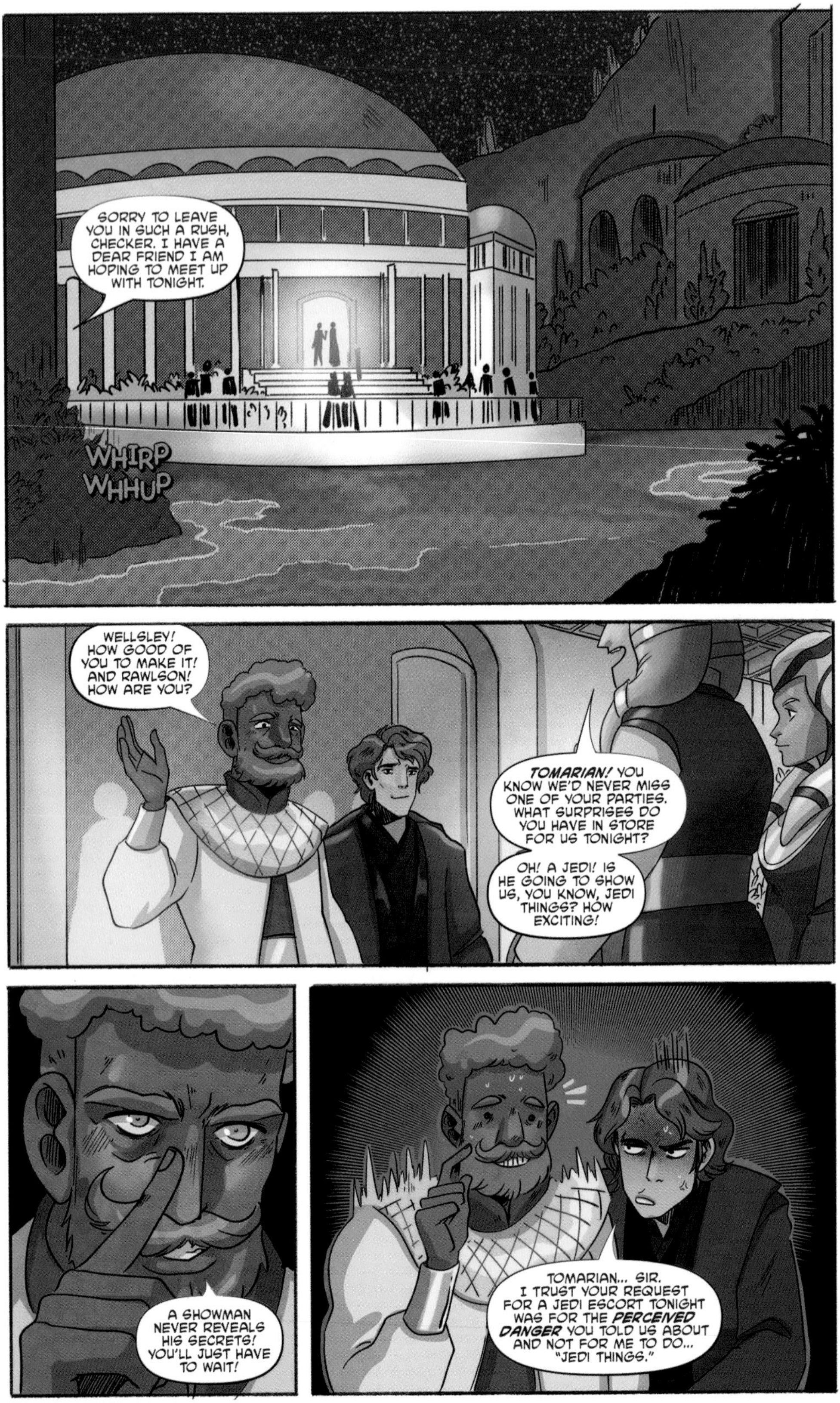
SORRY TO LEAVE YOU IN SUCH A RUSH, CHECKER. I HAVE A DEAR FRIEND I AM HOPING TO MEET UP WITH TONIGHT.
WHIRP WHHUP
WELLSLEY! HOW GOOD OF YOU TO MAKE IT! AND RAWLSON! HOW ARE YOU?
TOMARIAN! YOU KNOW WE'D NEVER MISS ONE OF YOUR PARTIES. WHAT SURPRISES DO YOU HAVE IN STORE FOR US TONIGHT?
OH! A JEDI! IS HE GOING TO SHOW US, YOU KNOW, JEDI THINGS? HOW EXCITING!
A SHOWMAN NEVER REVEALS HIS SECRETS! YOU'LL JUST HAVE TO WAIT!
TOMARIAN... SIR. I TRUST YOUR REQUEST FOR A JEDI ESCORT TONIGHT WAS FOR THE PERCEIVED DANGER YOU TOLD US ABOUT AND NOT FOR ME TO DO... "JEDI THINGS."

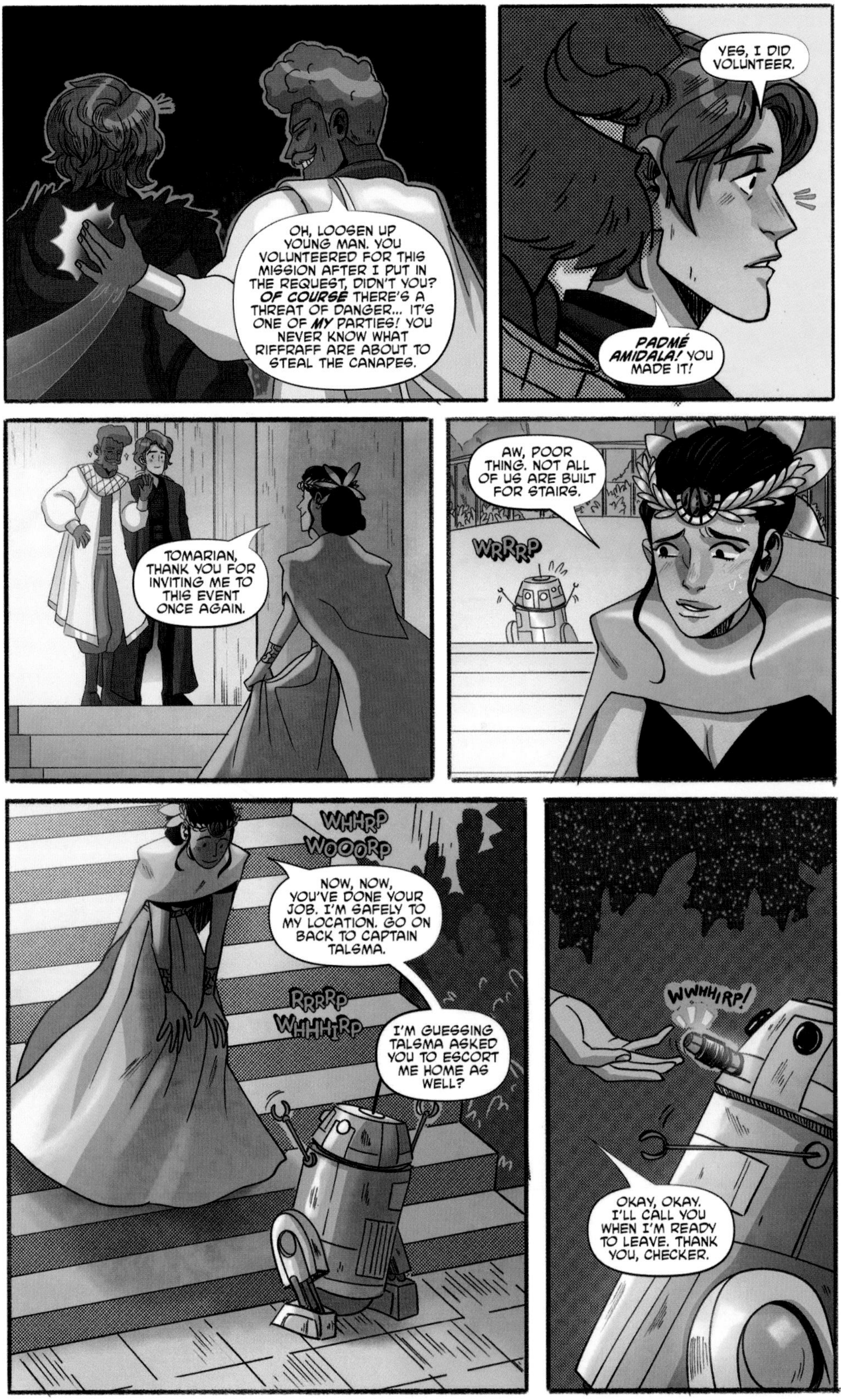

OH, LOOSEN UP YOUNG MAN. YOU VOLUNTEERED FOR THIS MISSION AFTER I PUT IN THE REQUEST, DIDN'T YOU? OF COURSE THERE'S A THREAT OF DANGER... IT'S ONE OF MY PARTIES! YOU NEVER KNOW WHAT RIFFRAFF ARE ABOUT TO STEAL THE CANAPES.
YES, I DID VOLUNTEER.
PADMÉ AMIDALA! YOU MADE IT!
TOMARIAN, THANK YOU FOR INVITING ME TO THIS EVENT ONCE AGAIN.
AW, POOR THING. NOT ALL OF US ARE BUILT FOR STAIRS.
WRRRP
WHHRP
WOOORP
NOW, NOW, YOU'VE DONE YOUR JOB. I'M SAFELY TO MY LOCATION. GO ON BACK TO CAPTAIN TALSMA.
RRRRP
WHHHIRP
I'M GUESSING TALSMA ASKED YOU TO ESCORT ME HOME AS WELL?
WWHHIRP!
OKAY, OKAY. I'LL CALL YOU WHEN I'M READY TO LEAVE. THANK YOU, CHECKER.

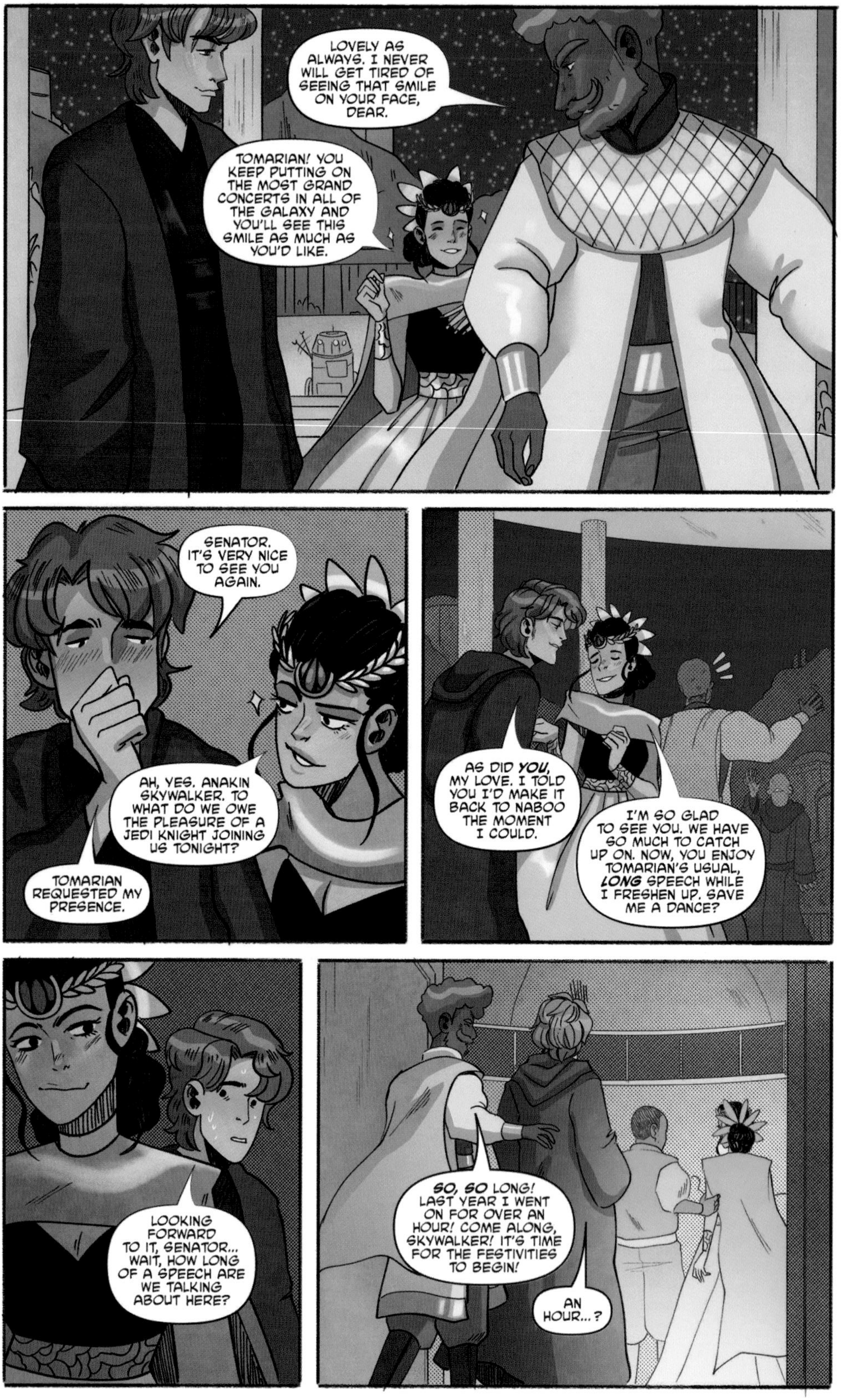

TOMARIAN! YOU KEEP PUTTING ON THE MOST GRAND CONCERTS IN ALL OF THE GALAXY AND YOU'LL SEE THIS SMILE AS MUCH AS YOU'D LIKE.
LOVELY AS ALWAYS. I NEVER WILL GET TIRED OF SEEING THAT SMILE ON YOUR FACE, DEAR.
SENATOR. IT'S VERY NICE TO SEE YOU AGAIN.
AH, YES. ANAKIN SKYWALKER. TO WHAT DO WE OWE THE PLEASURE OF A JEDI KNIGHT JOINING US TONIGHT?
TOMARIAN REQUESTED MY PRESENCE.
AS DID *YOU*, MY LOVE. I TOLD YOU I'D MAKE IT BACK TO NABOO THE MOMENT I COULD.
I'M SO GLAD TO SEE YOU. WE HAVE SO MUCH TO CATCH UP ON. NOW, YOU ENJOY TOMARIAN'S USUAL, ***LONG*** SPEECH WHILE I FRESHEN UP. SAVE ME A DANCE?
LOOKING FORWARD TO IT, SENATOR... WAIT, HOW LONG OF A SPEECH ARE WE TALKING ABOUT HERE?
***SO, SO*** LONG! LAST YEAR I WENT ON FOR OVER AN HOUR! COME ALONG, SKYWALKER! IT'S TIME FOR THE FESTIVITIES TO BEGIN!
AN HOUR...?

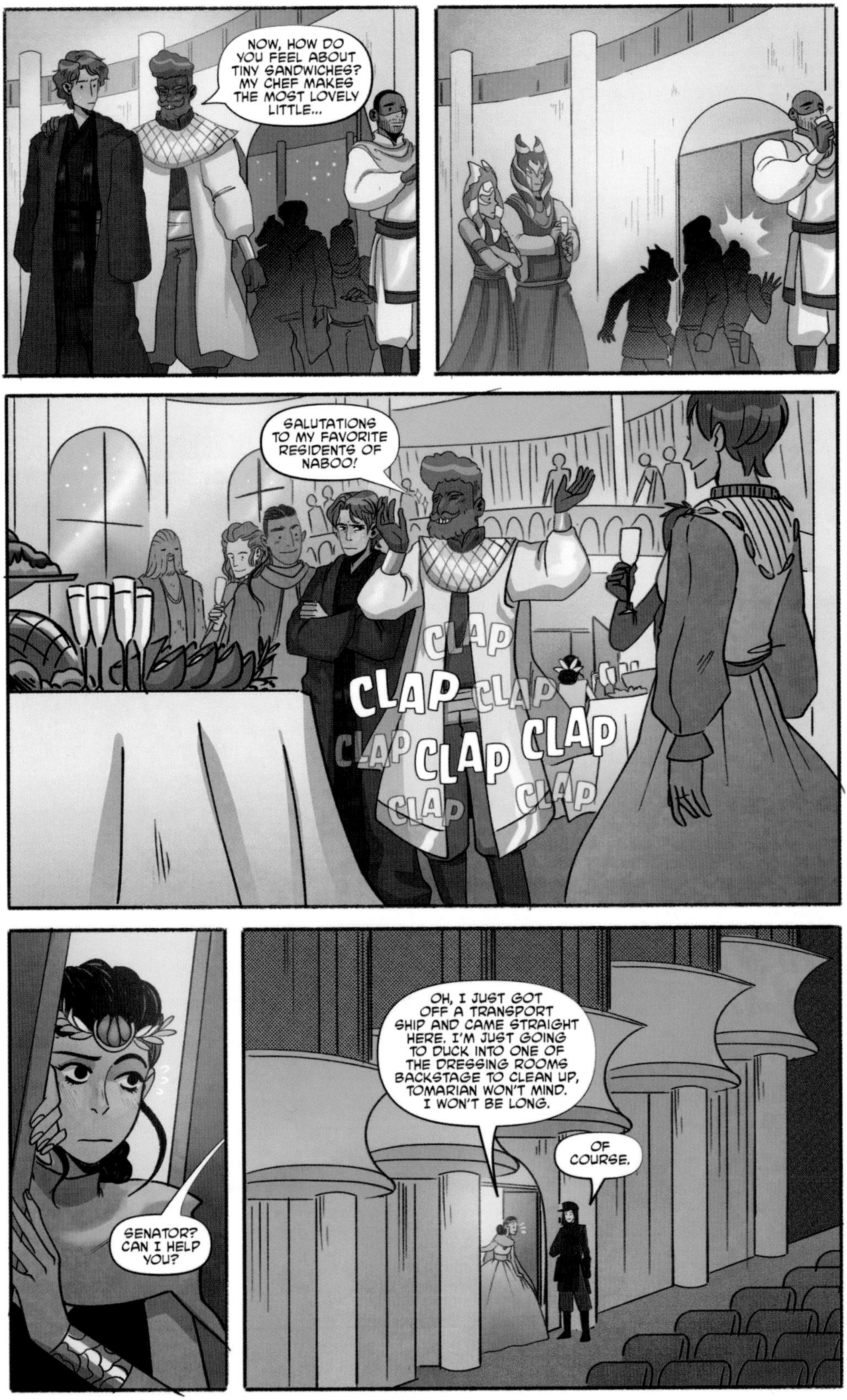
NOW, HOW DO YOU FEEL ABOUT TINY SANDWICHES? MY CHEF MAKES THE MOST LOVELY LITTLE...
SALUTATIONS TO MY FAVORITE RESIDENTS OF NABOO!
CLAP CLAP CLAP CLAP CLAP CLAP CLAP CLAP
SENATOR? CAN I HELP YOU?
OH, I JUST GOT OFF A TRANSPORT SHIP AND CAME STRAIGHT HERE. I'M JUST GOING TO DUCK INTO ONE OF THE DRESSING ROOMS BACKSTAGE TO CLEAN UP, TOMARIAN WON'T MIND. I WON'T BE LONG.
OF COURSE.

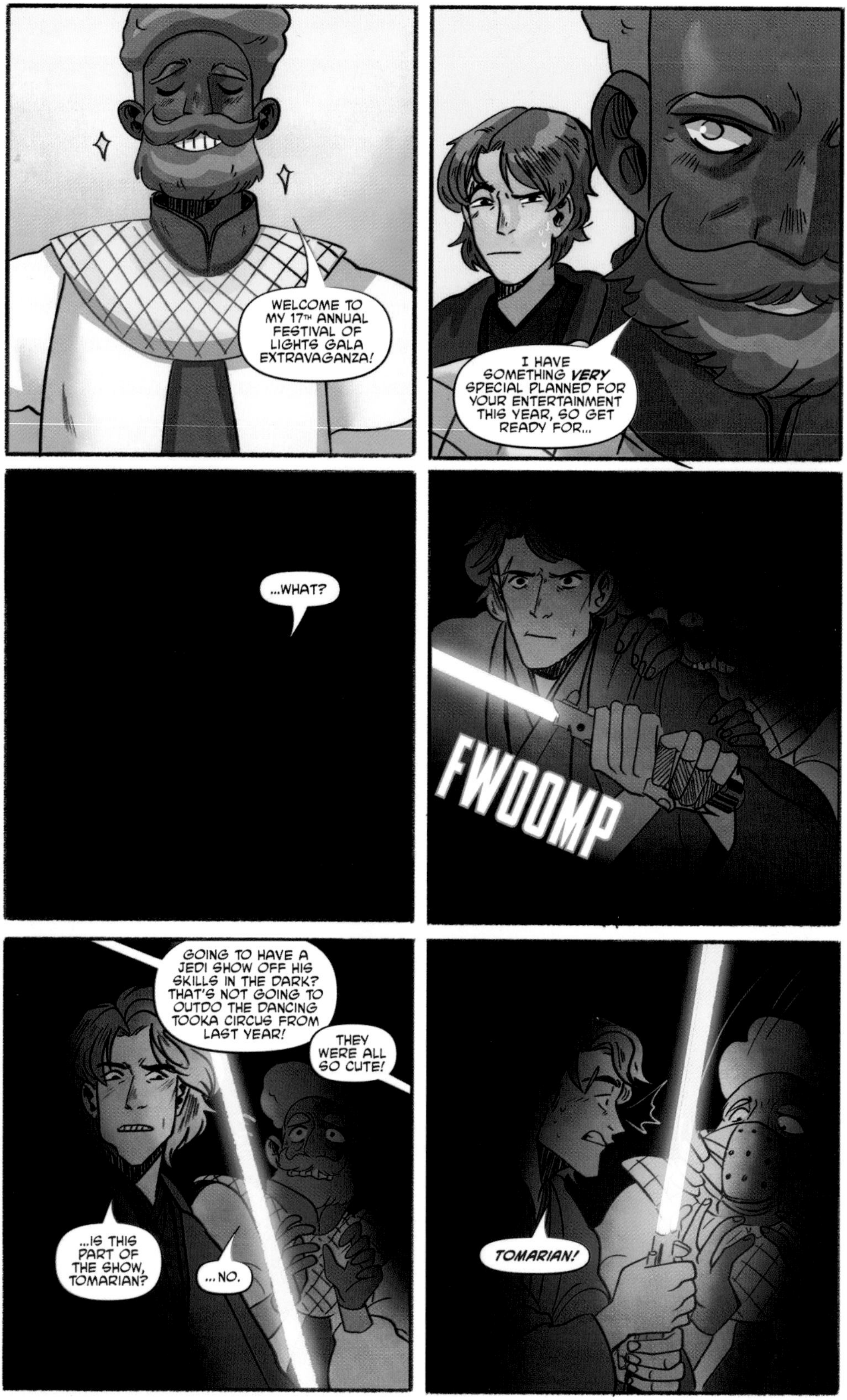
WELCOME TO MY 17TH ANNUAL FESTIVAL OF LIGHTS GALA EXTRAVAGANZA!
I HAVE SOMETHING VERY SPECIAL PLANNED FOR YOUR ENTERTAINMENT THIS YEAR, SO GET READY FOR...
...WHAT?
FWOOMP
GOING TO HAVE A JEDI SHOW OFF HIS SKILLS IN THE DARK? THAT'S NOT GOING TO OUTDO THE DANCING TOOKA CIRCUS FROM LAST YEAR!
THEY WERE ALL SO CUTE!
...IS THIS PART OF THE SHOW, TOMARIAN?
...NO.
TOMARIAN!

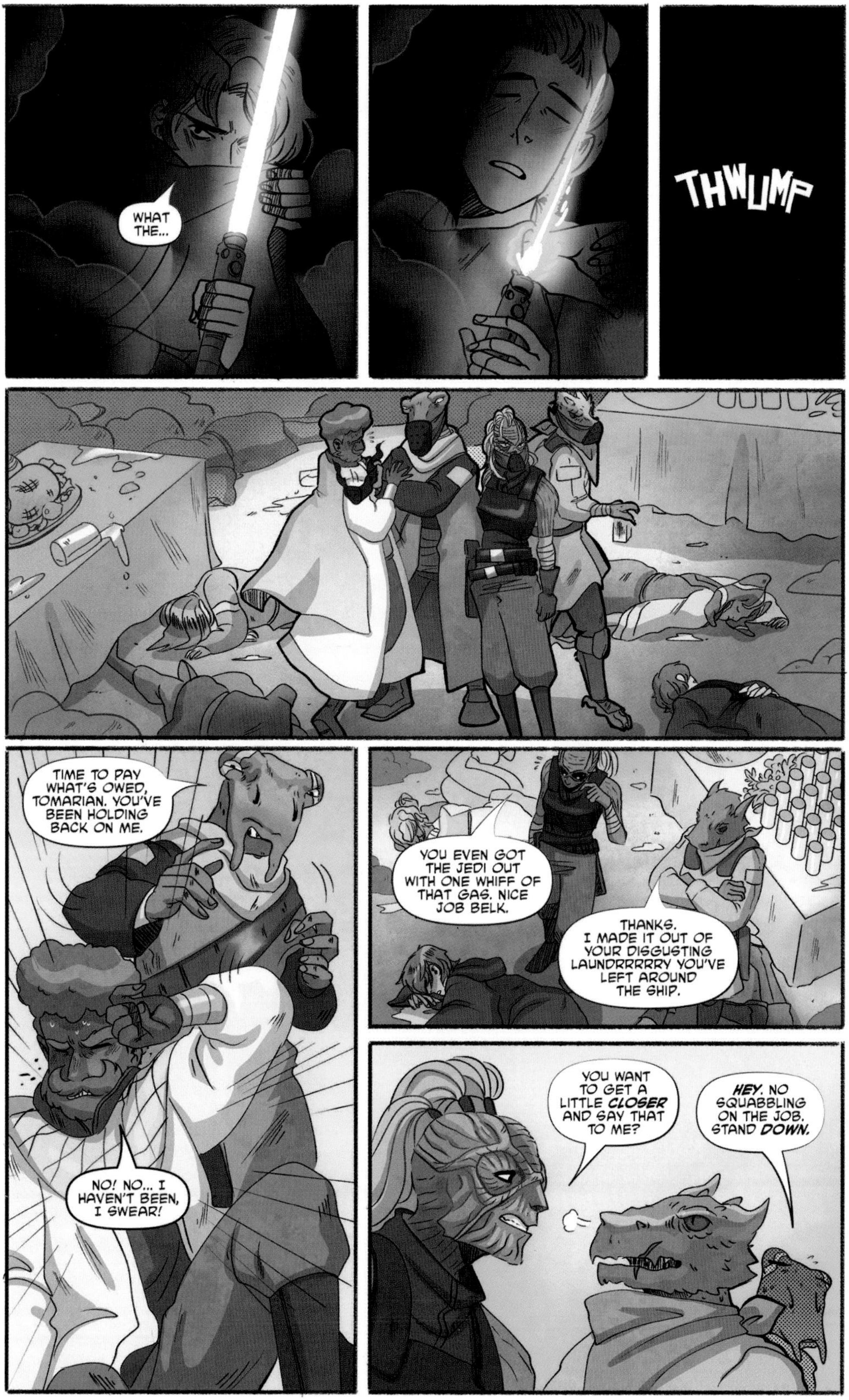
WHAT THE...
THWUMP
TIME TO PAY WHAT'S OWED, TOMARIAN. YOU'VE BEEN HOLDING BACK ON ME.
NO! NO... I HAVEN'T BEEN, I SWEAR!
YOU EVEN GOT THE JEDI OUT WITH ONE WHIFF OF THAT GAS. NICE JOB BELK.
THANKS. I MADE IT OUT OF YOUR DISGUSTING LAUNDRRRRRY YOU'VE LEFT AROUND THE SHIP.
YOU WANT TO GET A LITTLE CLOSER AND SAY THAT TO ME?
HEY. NO SQUABBLING ON THE JOB. STAND DOWN.

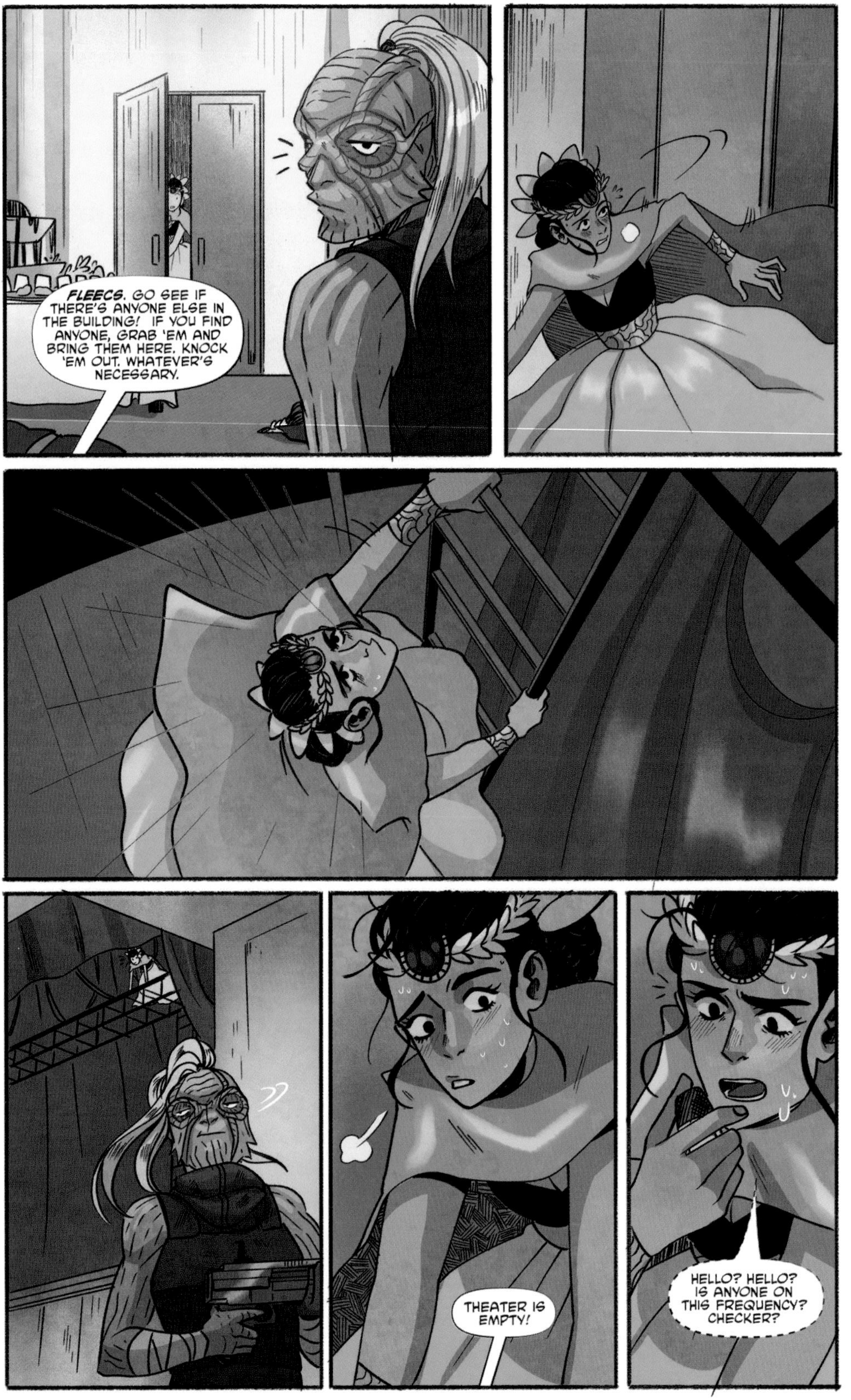
FLEECS. GO SEE IF THERE'S ANYONE ELSE IN THE BUILDING! IF YOU FIND ANYONE, GRAB 'EM AND BRING THEM HERE. KNOCK 'EM OUT. WHATEVER'S NECESSARY.
THEATER IS EMPTY!
HELLO? HELLO? IS ANYONE ON THIS FREQUENCY? CHECKER?

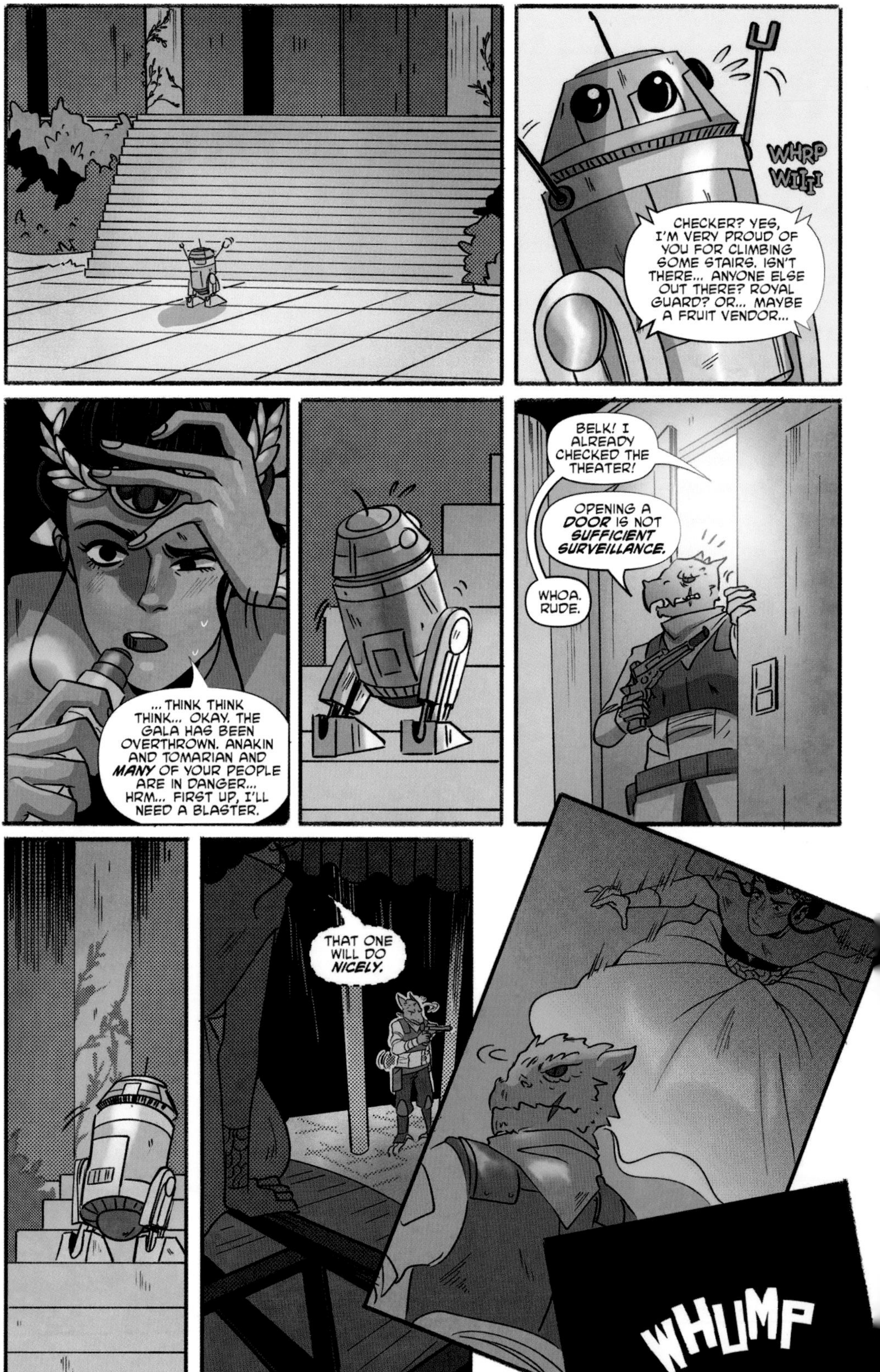
WHRP WIIII
CHECKER? YES, I'M VERY PROUD OF YOU FOR CLIMBING SOME STAIRS. ISN'T THERE... ANYONE ELSE OUT THERE? ROYAL GUARD? OR... MAYBE A FRUIT VENDOR...
...THINK THINK THINK... OKAY. THE GALA HAS BEEN OVERTHROWN. ANAKIN AND TOMARIAN AND MANY OF YOUR PEOPLE ARE IN DANGER... HRM... FIRST UP, I'LL NEED A BLASTER.
BELK! I ALREADY CHECKED THE THEATER!
OPENING A DOOR IS NOT SUFFICIENT SURVEILLANCE.
WHOA. RUDE.
THAT ONE WILL DO NICELY.
WHUMP

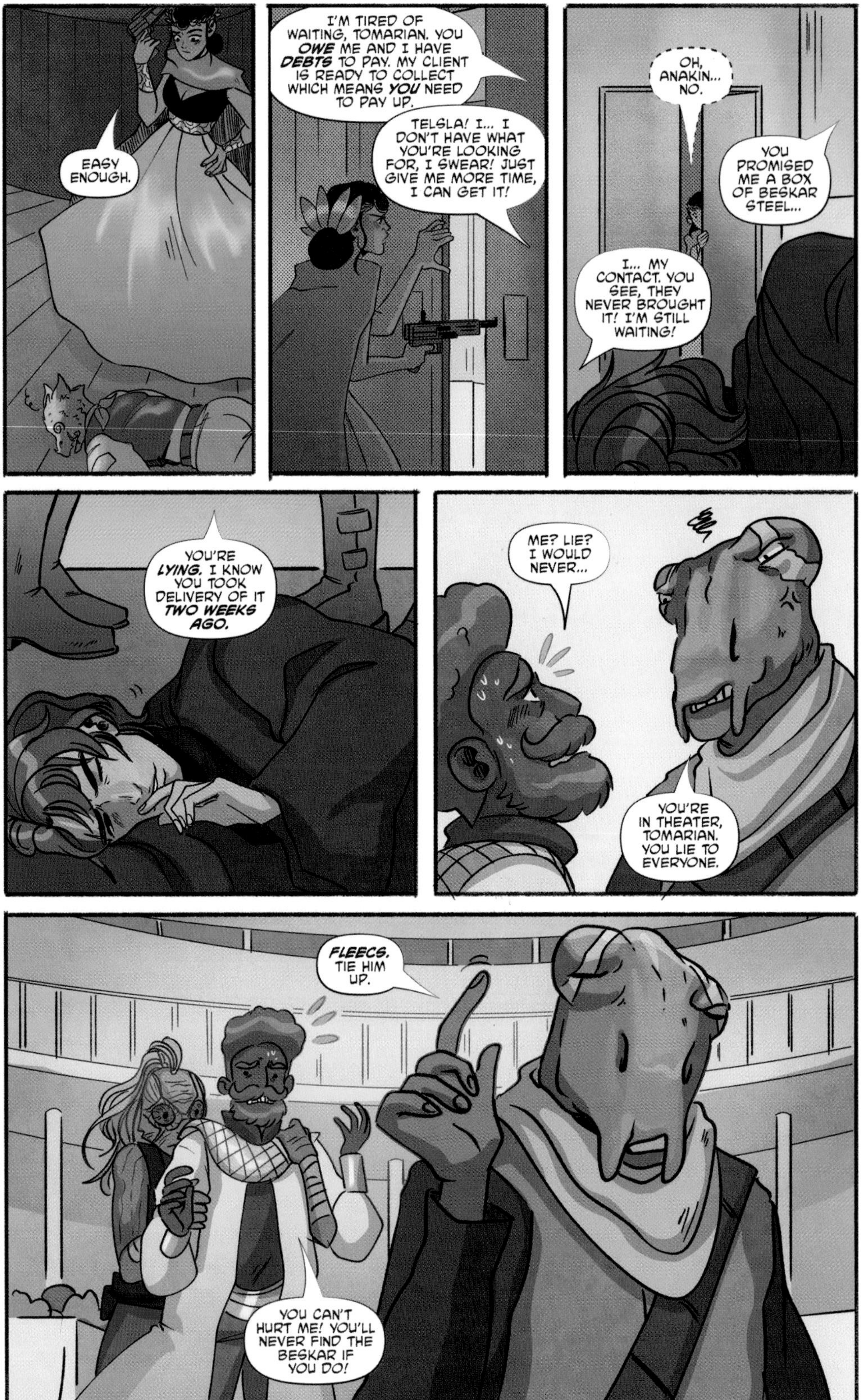
EASY ENOUGH.
I'M TIRED OF WAITING, TOMARIAN. YOU OWE ME AND I HAVE DEBTS TO PAY. MY CLIENT IS READY TO COLLECT WHICH MEANS YOU NEED TO PAY UP.
TELSLA! I... I DON'T HAVE WHAT YOU'RE LOOKING FOR, I SWEAR! JUST GIVE ME MORE TIME, I CAN GET IT!
OH, ANAKIN... NO.
YOU PROMISED ME A BOX OF BESKAR STEEL...
I... MY CONTACT. YOU SEE, THEY NEVER BROUGHT IT! I'M STILL WAITING!
YOU'RE LYING. I KNOW YOU TOOK DELIVERY OF IT TWO WEEKS AGO.
ME? LIE? I WOULD NEVER...
YOU'RE IN THEATER, TOMARIAN. YOU LIE TO EVERYONE.
FLEECS. TIE HIM UP.
YOU CAN'T HURT ME! YOU'LL NEVER FIND THE BESKAR IF YOU DO!

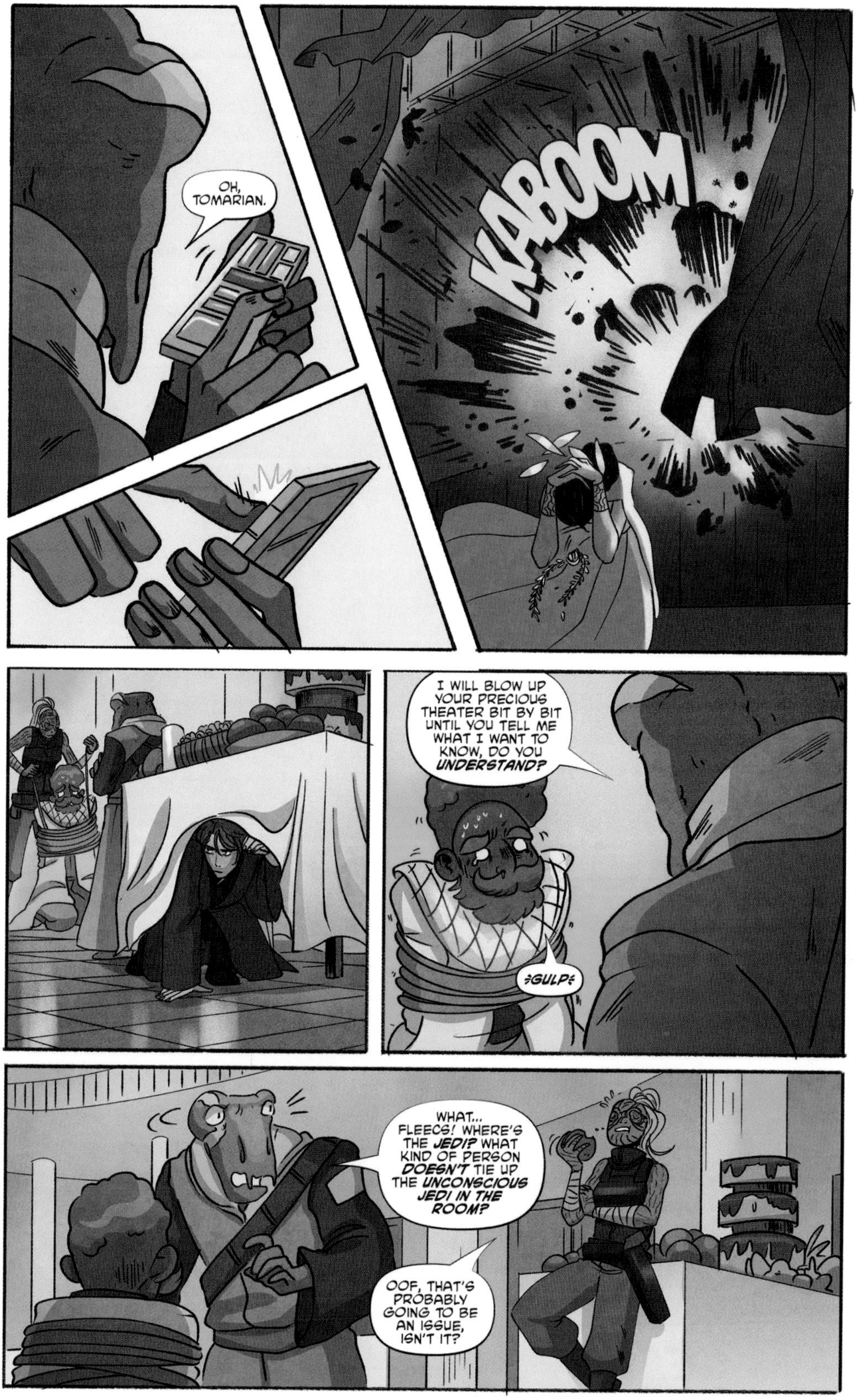
OH, TOMARIAN.
KABOOM
I WILL BLOW UP YOUR PRECIOUS THEATER BIT BY BIT UNTIL YOU TELL ME WHAT I WANT TO KNOW, DO YOU *UNDERSTAND?*
*GULP*
WHAT... FLEECS! WHERE'S THE *JEDI?* WHAT KIND OF PERSON *DOESN'T* TIE UP THE *UNCONSCIOUS JEDI IN THE ROOM?*
OOF, THAT'S PROBABLY GOING TO BE AN ISSUE, ISN'T IT?

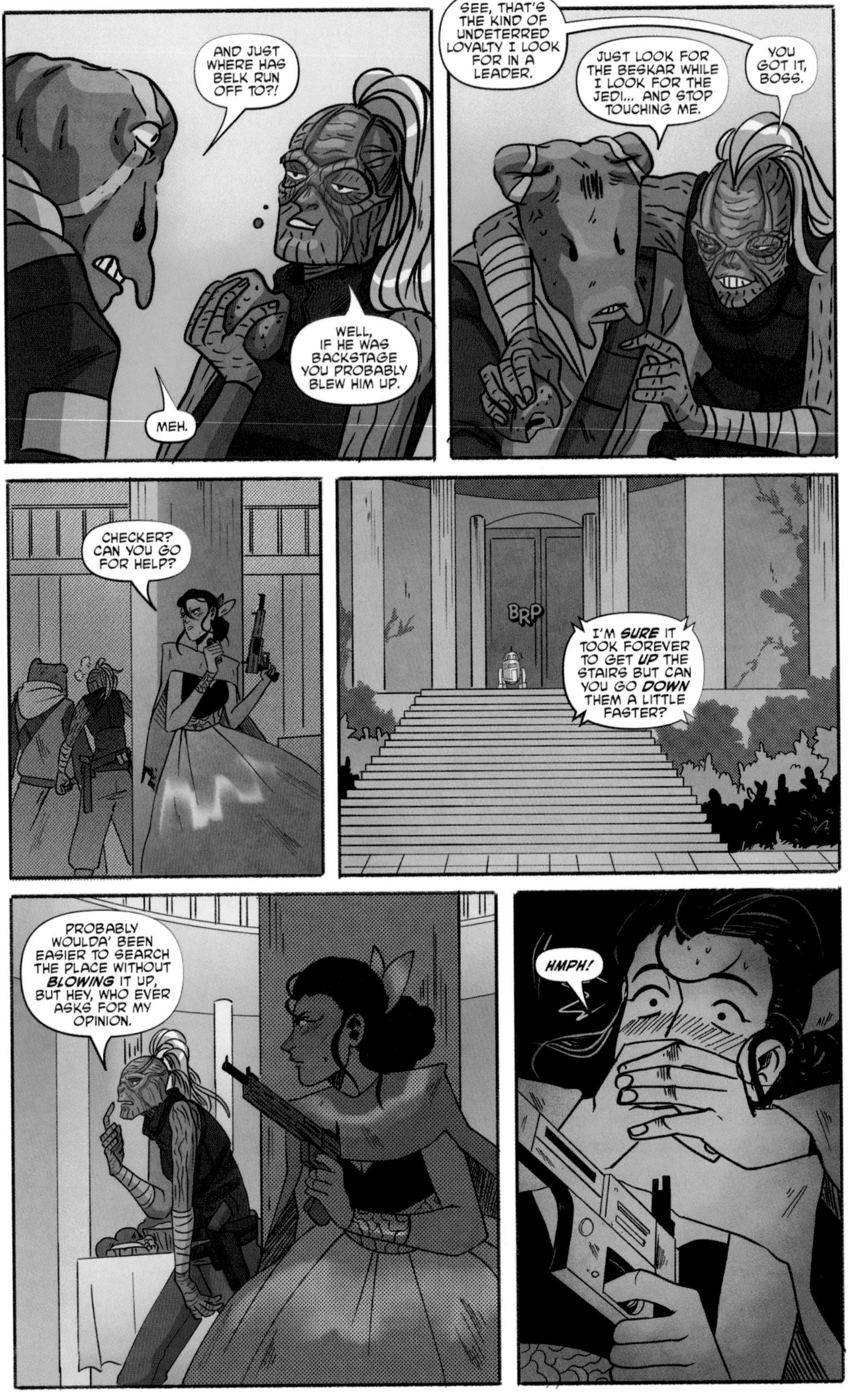
AND JUST WHERE HAS BELK RUN OFF TO?!
WELL, IF HE WAS BACKSTAGE YOU PROBABLY BLEW HIM UP.
MEH.
SEE, THAT'S THE KIND OF UNDETERRED LOYALTY I LOOK FOR IN A LEADER.
JUST LOOK FOR THE BESKAR WHILE I LOOK FOR THE JEDI... AND STOP TOUCHING ME.
YOU GOT IT, BOSS.
CHECKER? CAN YOU GO FOR HELP?
BRP
I'M SURE IT TOOK FOREVER TO GET UP THE STAIRS BUT CAN YOU GO DOWN THEM A LITTLE FASTER?
PROBABLY WOULDA' BEEN EASIER TO SEARCH THE PLACE WITHOUT BLOWING IT UP, BUT HEY, WHO EVER ASKS FOR MY OPINION.
HMPH!

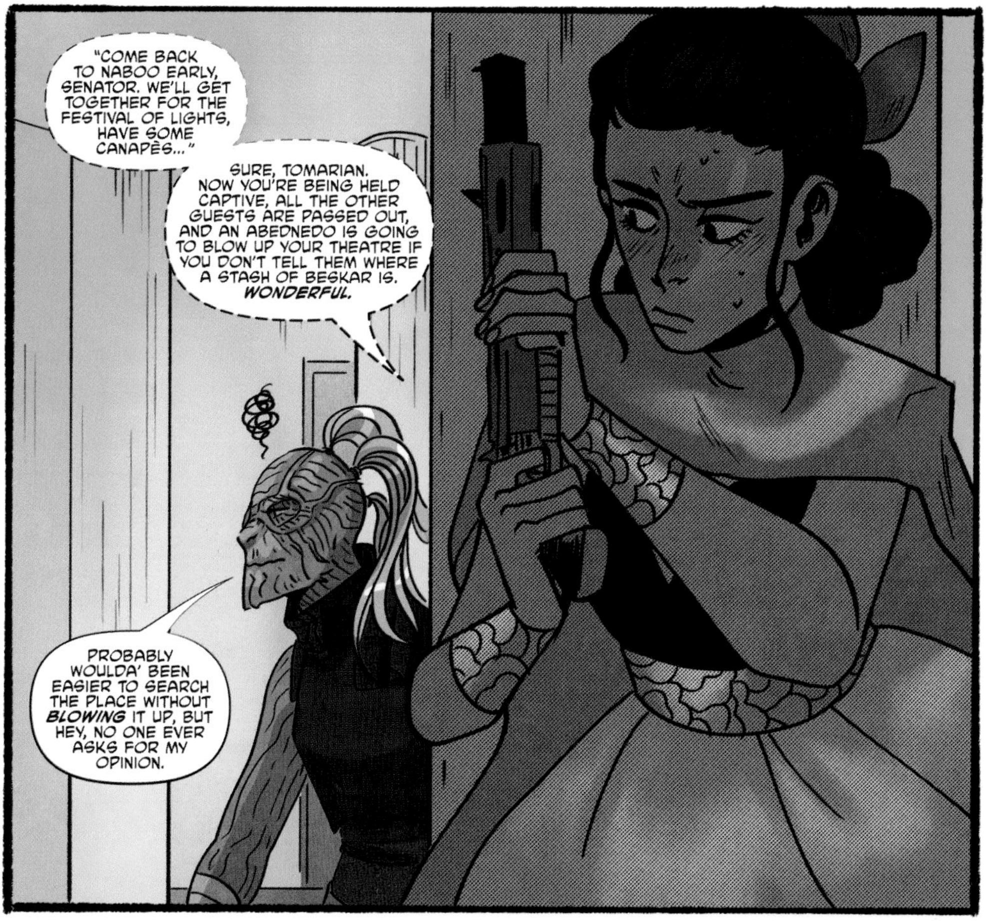
"COME BACK TO NABOO EARLY, SENATOR. WE'LL GET TOGETHER FOR THE FESTIVAL OF LIGHTS, HAVE SOME CANAPÉS..."
SURE, TOMARIAN. NOW YOU'RE BEING HELD CAPTIVE, ALL THE OTHER GUESTS ARE PASSED OUT, AND AN ABEDNEDO IS GOING TO BLOW UP YOUR THEATRE IF YOU DON'T TELL THEM WHERE A STASH OF BESKAR IS. *WONDERFUL.*
PROBABLY WOULDA' BEEN EASIER TO SEARCH THE PLACE WITHOUT *BLOWING* IT UP, BUT HEY, NO ONE EVER ASKS FOR MY OPINION.

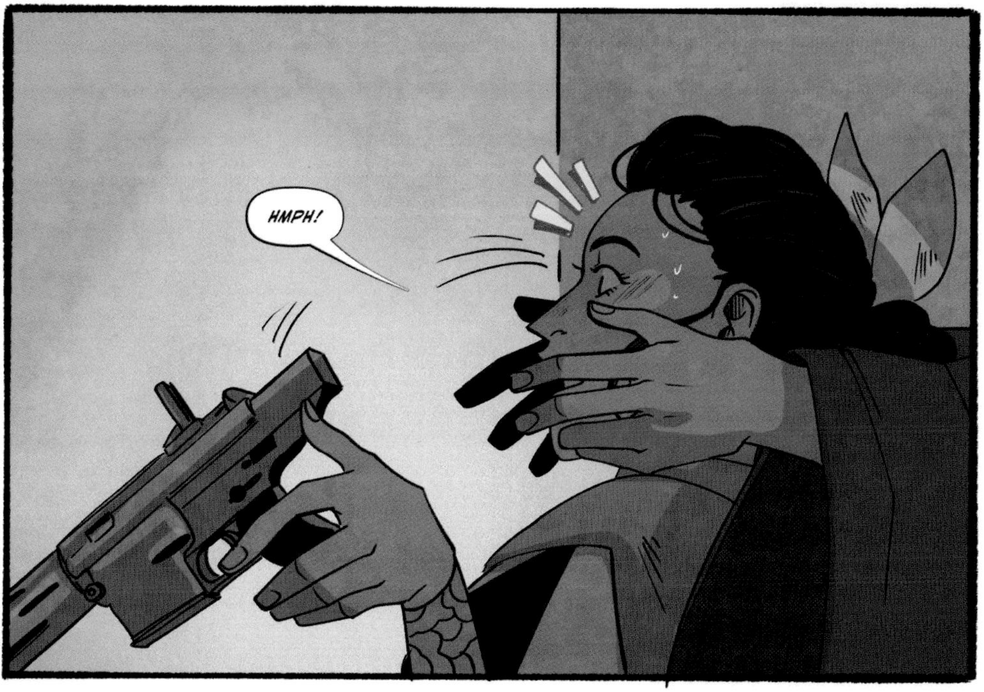
*HMPH!*

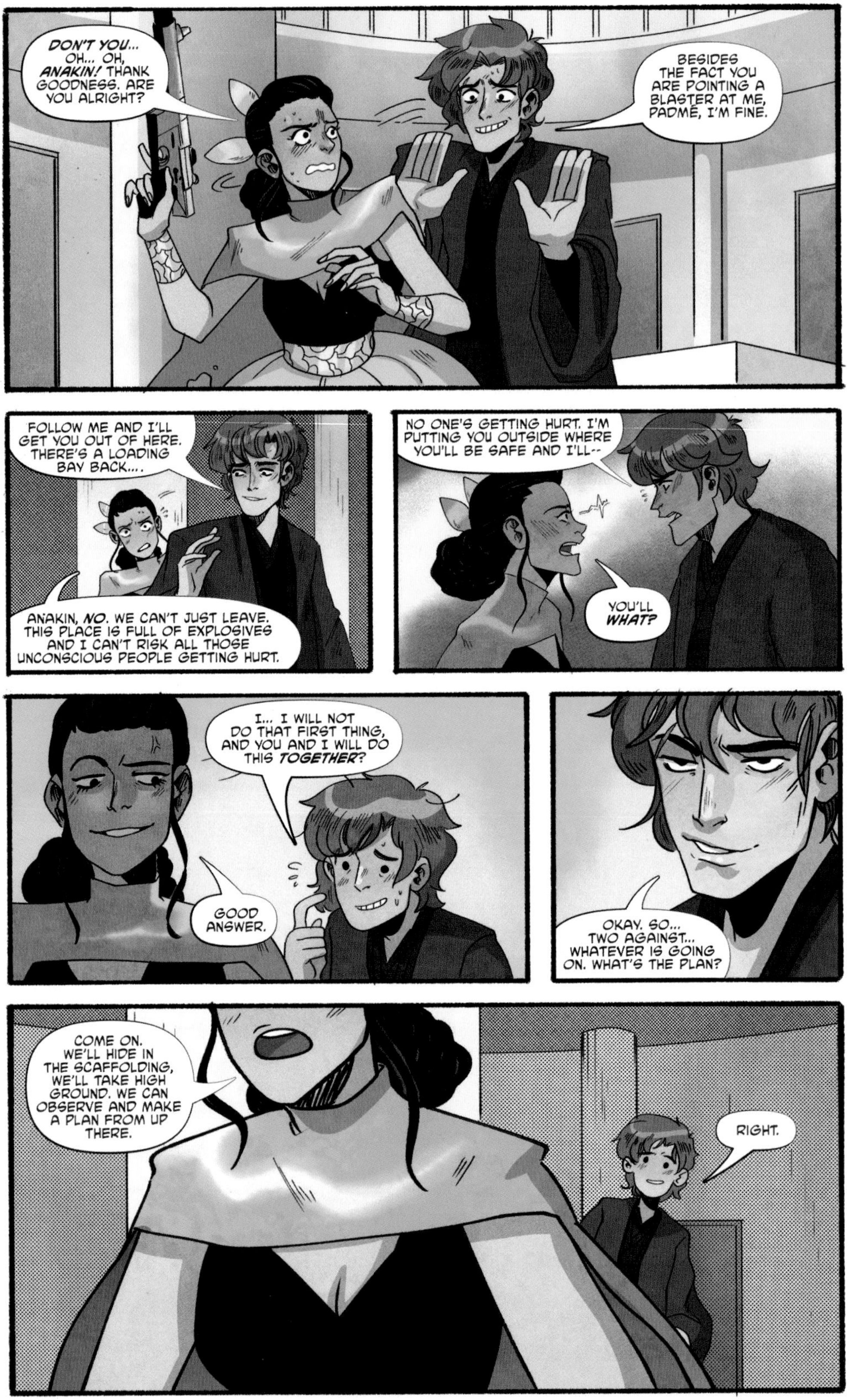
DON'T YOU... OH... OH, ANAKIN! THANK GOODNESS. ARE YOU ALRIGHT?
BESIDES THE FACT YOU ARE POINTING A BLASTER AT ME, PADMÉ, I'M FINE.
FOLLOW ME AND I'LL GET YOU OUT OF HERE. THERE'S A LOADING BAY BACK....
ANAKIN, NO. WE CAN'T JUST LEAVE. THIS PLACE IS FULL OF EXPLOSIVES AND I CAN'T RISK ALL THOSE UNCONSCIOUS PEOPLE GETTING HURT.
NO ONE'S GETTING HURT. I'M PUTTING YOU OUTSIDE WHERE YOU'LL BE SAFE AND I'LL--
YOU'LL WHAT?
I... I WILL NOT DO THAT FIRST THING, AND YOU AND I WILL DO THIS TOGETHER?
GOOD ANSWER.
OKAY. SO... TWO AGAINST... WHATEVER IS GOING ON. WHAT'S THE PLAN?
COME ON. WE'LL HIDE IN THE SCAFFOLDING, WE'LL TAKE HIGH GROUND. WE CAN OBSERVE AND MAKE A PLAN FROM UP THERE.
RIGHT.

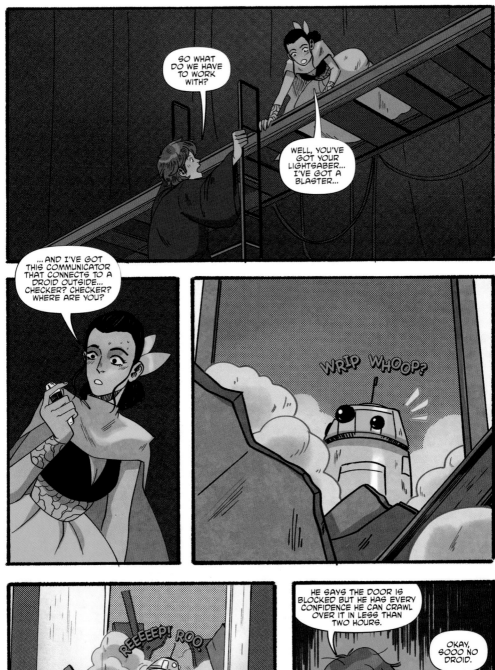

SO WHAT DO WE HAVE TO WORK WITH?

WELL, YOU'VE GOT YOUR LIGHTSABER... I'VE GOT A BLASTER...

...AND I'VE GOT THIS COMMUNICATOR THAT CONNECTS TO A DROID OUTSIDE... CHECKER? CHECKER? WHERE ARE YOU?

WRIP WHOOP?

REEEEEP! ROO.

HE SAYS THE DOOR IS BLOCKED BUT HE HAS EVERY CONFIDENCE HE CAN CRAWL OVER IT IN LESS THAN TWO HOURS.

OKAY, SOOO NO DROID.

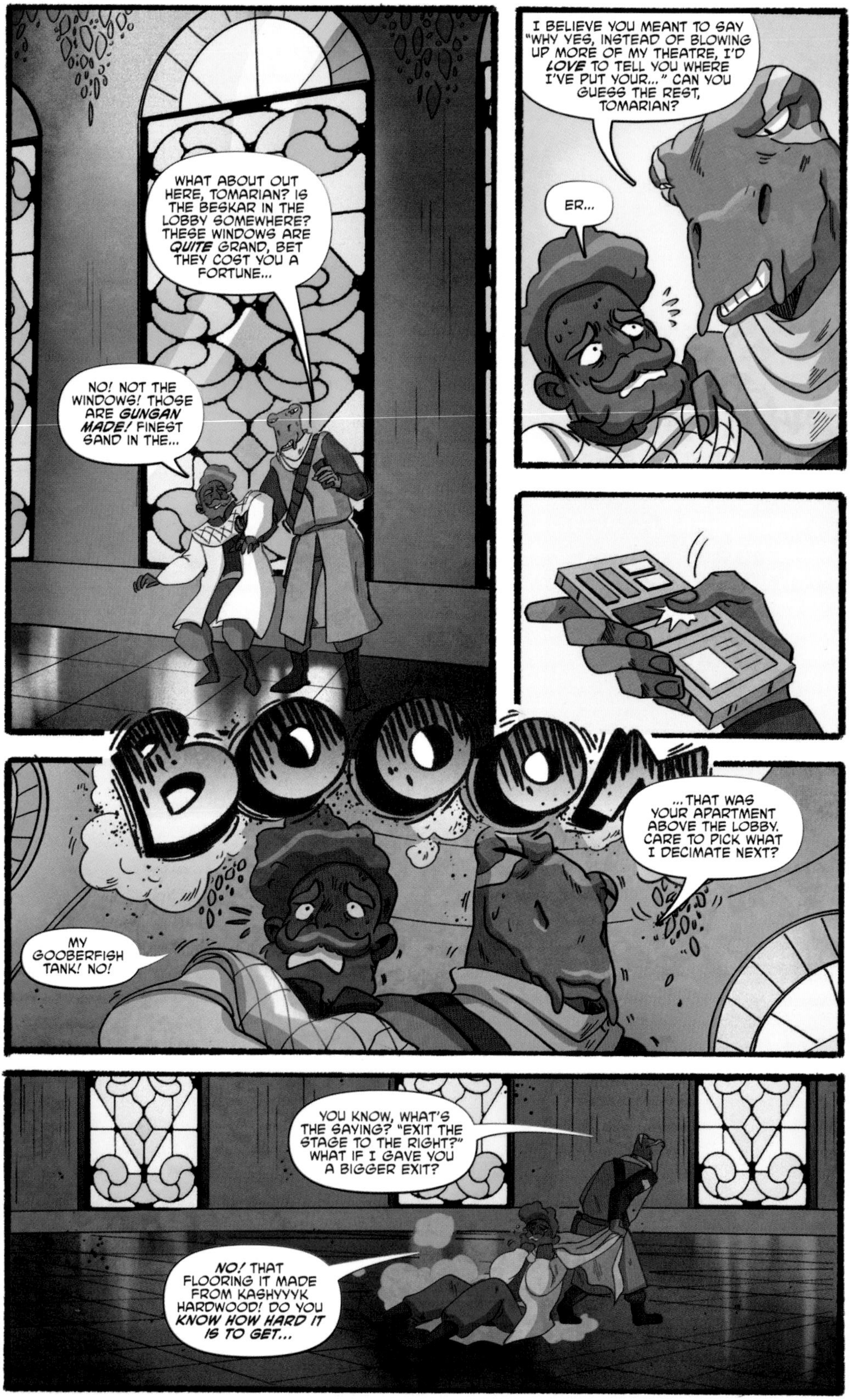
WHAT ABOUT OUT HERE, TOMARIAN? IS THE BESKAR IN THE LOBBY SOMEWHERE? THESE WINDOWS ARE *QUITE* GRAND, BET THEY COST YOU A FORTUNE...
NO! NOT THE WINDOWS! THOSE ARE *GUNGAN MADE!* FINEST SAND IN THE...
I BELIEVE YOU MEANT TO SAY "WHY YES, INSTEAD OF BLOWING UP MORE OF MY THEATRE, I'D *LOVE* TO TELL YOU WHERE I'VE PUT YOUR..." CAN YOU GUESS THE REST, TOMARIAN?
ER...
BOOOOM
...THAT WAS YOUR APARTMENT ABOVE THE LOBBY. CARE TO PICK WHAT I DECIMATE NEXT?
MY GOOBERFISH TANK! NO!
YOU KNOW, WHAT'S THE SAYING? "EXIT THE STAGE TO THE RIGHT?" WHAT IF I GAVE YOU A BIGGER EXIT?
*NO!* THAT FLOORING IT MADE FROM KASHYYYK HARDWOOD! DO YOU *KNOW HOW HARD IT IS TO GET...*

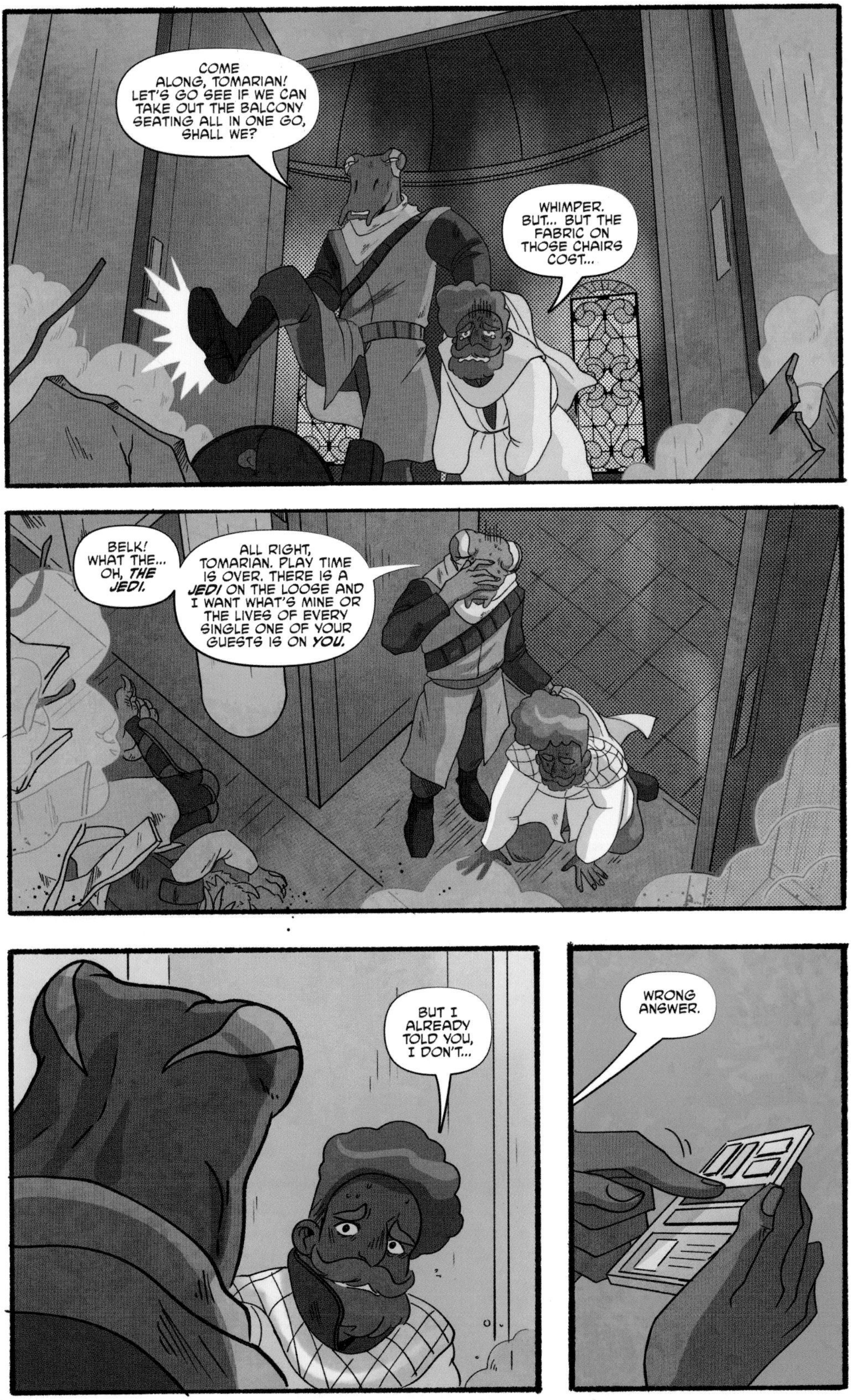
COME ALONG, TOMARIAN! LET'S GO SEE IF WE CAN TAKE OUT THE BALCONY SEATING ALL IN ONE GO, SHALL WE?
WHIMPER. BUT... BUT THE FABRIC ON THOSE CHAIRS COST...
BELK! WHAT THE... OH, *THE JEDI.*
ALL RIGHT, TOMARIAN. PLAY TIME IS OVER. THERE IS A *JEDI* ON THE LOOSE AND I WANT WHAT'S MINE OR THE LIVES OF EVERY SINGLE ONE OF YOUR GUESTS IS ON *YOU.*
BUT I ALREADY TOLD YOU, I DON'T...
WRONG ANSWER.

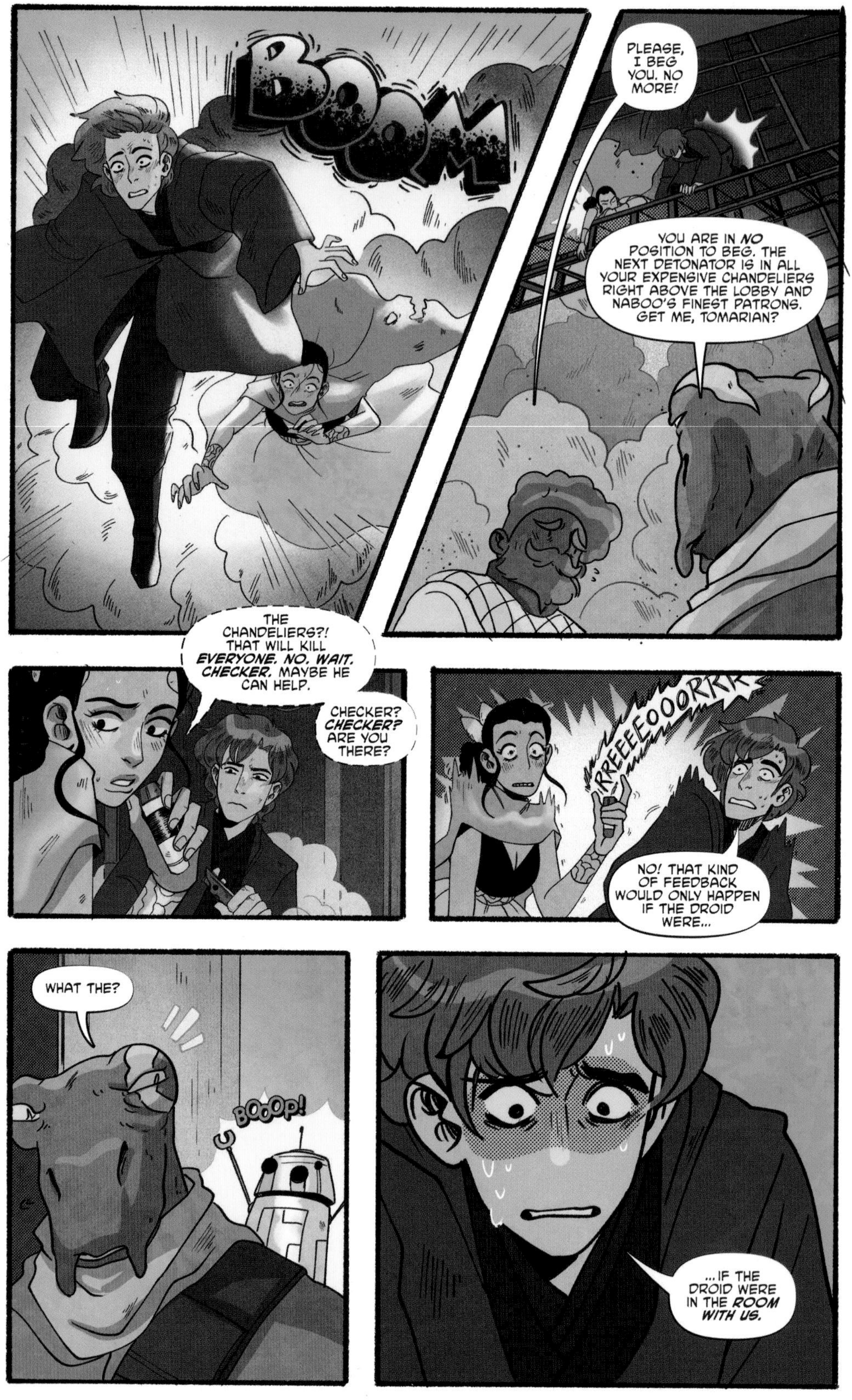
BOOM
PLEASE, I BEG YOU. NO MORE!
YOU ARE IN *NO* POSITION TO BEG. THE NEXT DETONATOR IS IN ALL YOUR EXPENSIVE CHANDELIERS RIGHT ABOVE THE LOBBY AND NABOO'S FINEST PATRONS. GET ME, TOMARIAN?
THE CHANDELIERS?! THAT WILL KILL ***EVERYONE. NO. WAIT. CHECKER.*** MAYBE HE CAN HELP.
CHECKER? ***CHECKER?*** ARE YOU THERE?
RREEEEOOORRR
NO! THAT KIND OF FEEDBACK WOULD ONLY HAPPEN IF THE DROID WERE...
WHAT THE?
BOOOP!
...IF THE DROID WERE IN THE ***ROOM WITH US.***

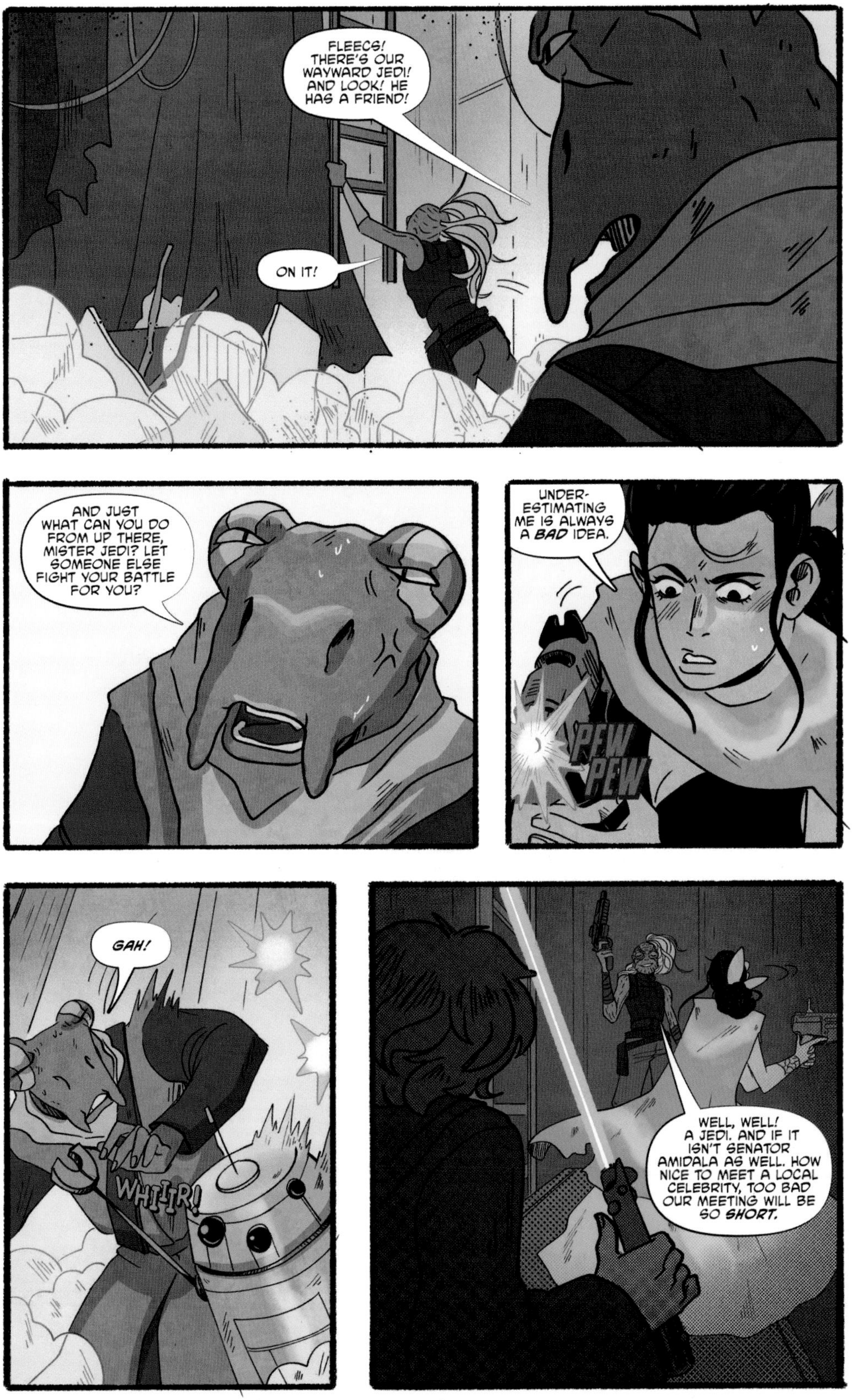

FLEECS! THERE'S OUR WAYWARD JEDI! AND LOOK! HE HAS A FRIEND!
ON IT!
AND JUST WHAT CAN YOU DO FROM UP THERE, MISTER JEDI? LET SOMEONE ELSE FIGHT YOUR BATTLE FOR YOU?
UNDER-ESTIMATING ME IS ALWAYS A *BAD* IDEA.
PEW PEW
GAH!
WHIIIR!
WELL, WELL! A JEDI. AND IF IT ISN'T SENATOR AMIDALA AS WELL. HOW NICE TO MEET A LOCAL CELEBRITY, TOO BAD OUR MEETING WILL BE SO *SHORT.*

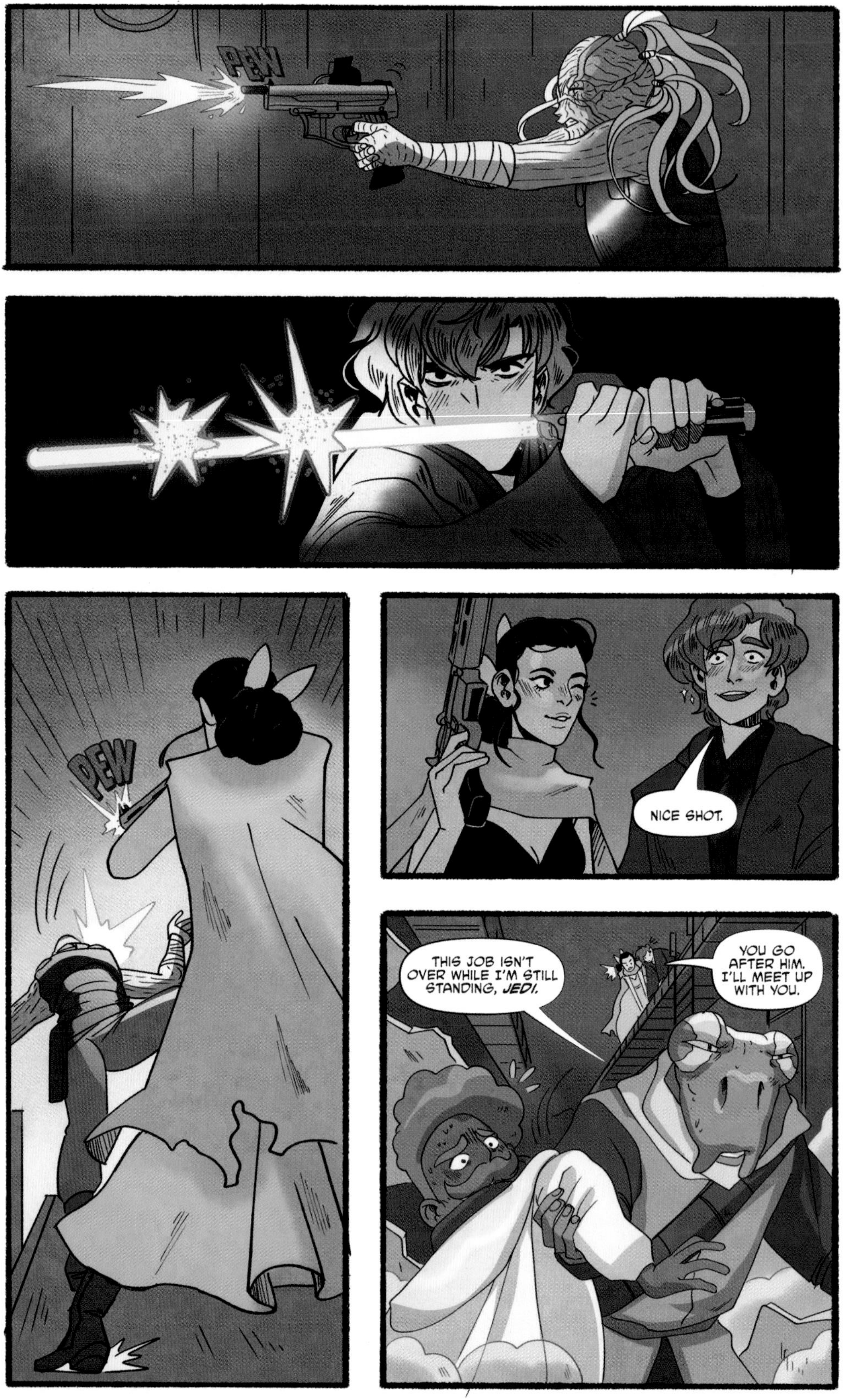
PEW
PEW
NICE SHOT.
THIS JOB ISN'T OVER WHILE I'M STILL STANDING, *JEDI.*
YOU GO AFTER HIM. I'LL MEET UP WITH YOU.

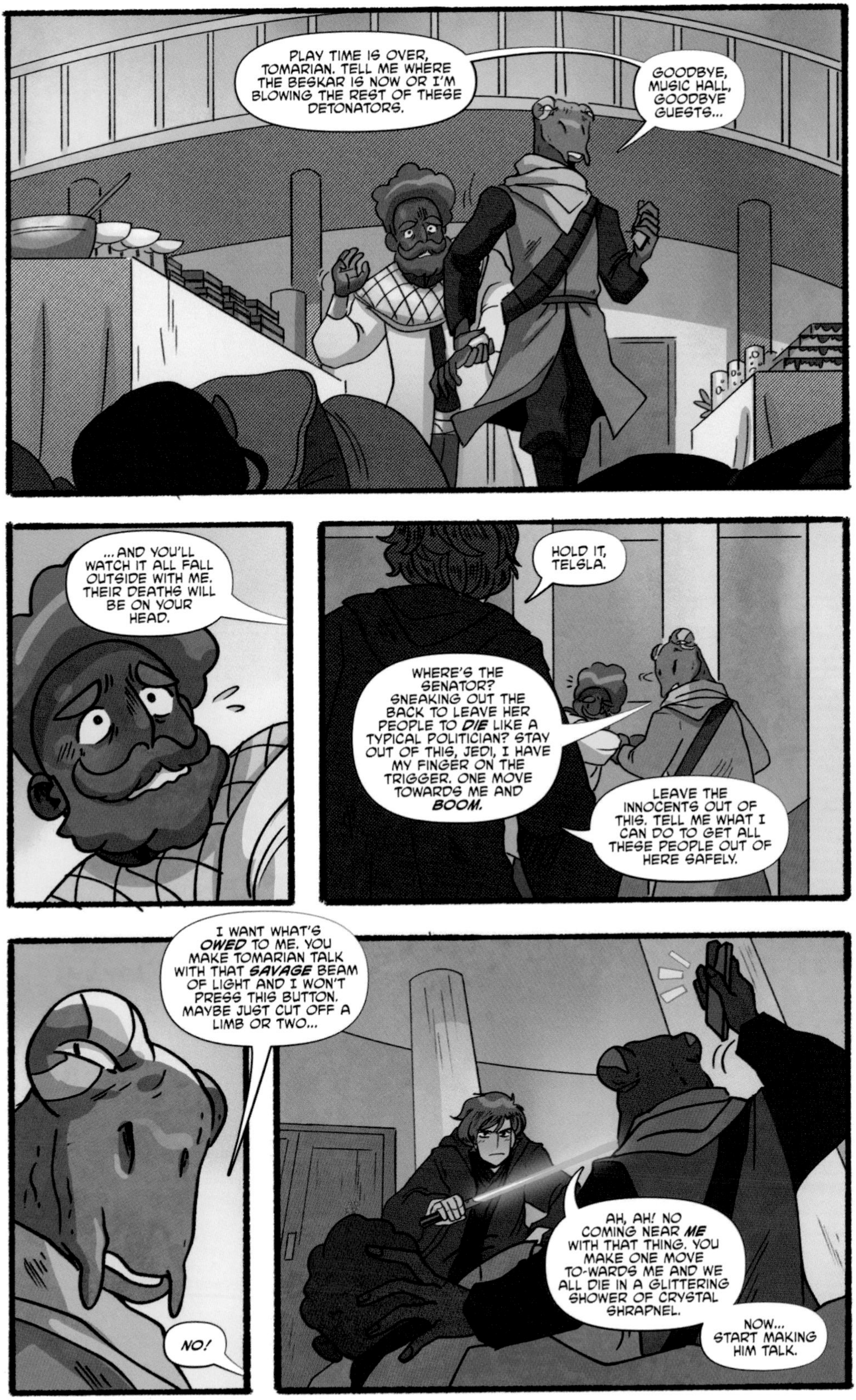
PLAY TIME IS OVER, TOMARIAN. TELL ME WHERE THE BESKAR IS NOW OR I'M BLOWING THE REST OF THESE DETONATORS.
GOODBYE, MUSIC HALL, GOODBYE GUESTS...
...AND YOU'LL WATCH IT ALL FALL OUTSIDE WITH ME. THEIR DEATHS WILL BE ON YOUR HEAD.
HOLD IT, TELSLA.
WHERE'S THE SENATOR? SNEAKING OUT THE BACK TO LEAVE HER PEOPLE TO DIE LIKE A TYPICAL POLITICIAN? STAY OUT OF THIS, JEDI, I HAVE MY FINGER ON THE TRIGGER. ONE MOVE TOWARDS ME AND BOOM.
LEAVE THE INNOCENTS OUT OF THIS. TELL ME WHAT I CAN DO TO GET ALL THESE PEOPLE OUT OF HERE SAFELY.
I WANT WHAT'S OWED TO ME. YOU MAKE TOMARIAN TALK WITH THAT SAVAGE BEAM OF LIGHT AND I WON'T PRESS THIS BUTTON. MAYBE JUST CUT OFF A LIMB OR TWO...
NO!
AH, AH! NO COMING NEAR ME WITH THAT THING. YOU MAKE ONE MOVE TO-WARDS ME AND WE ALL DIE IN A GLITTERING SHOWER OF CRYSTAL SHRAPNEL.
NOW... START MAKING HIM TALK.

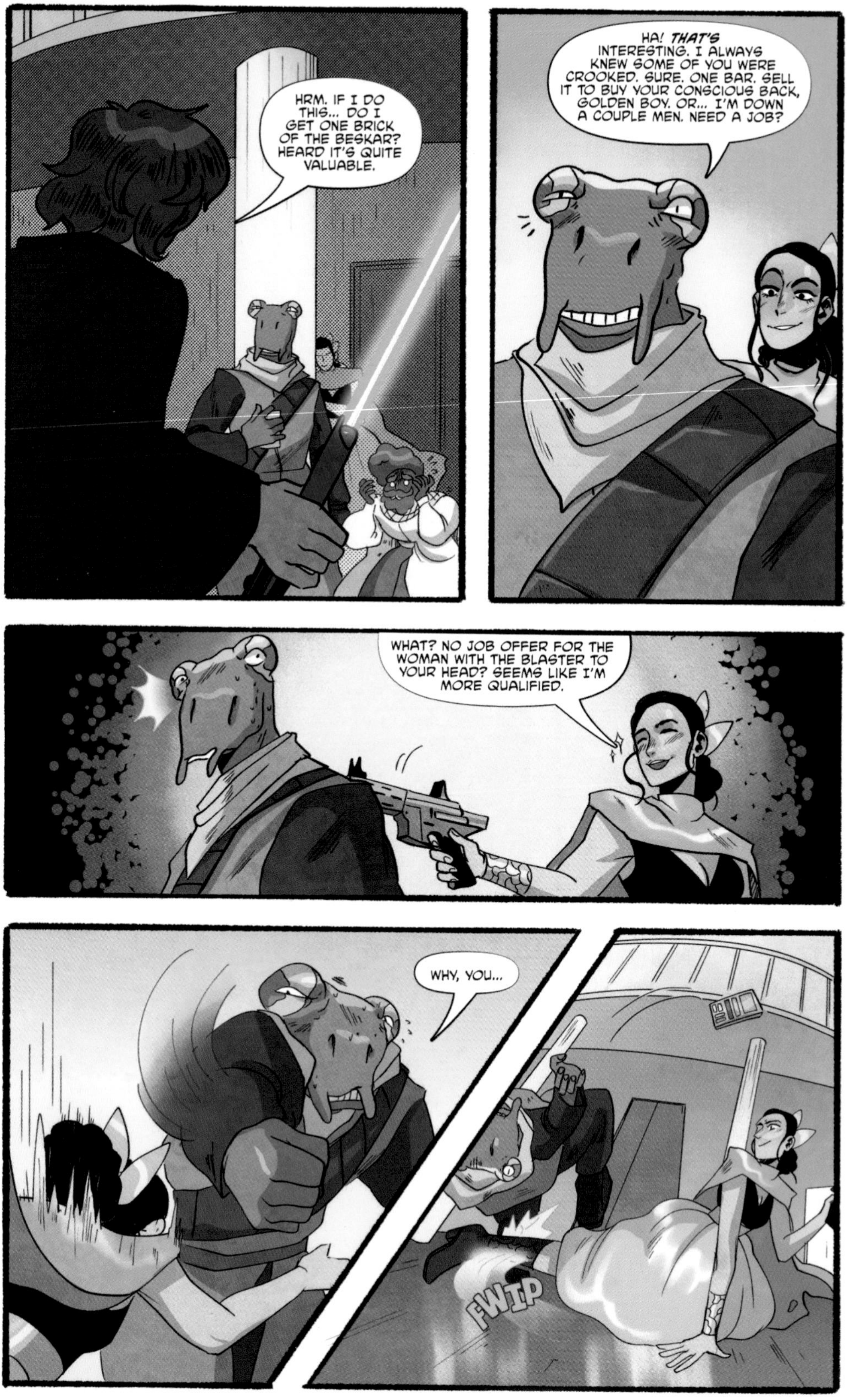
HRM. IF I DO THIS... DO I GET ONE BRICK OF THE BESKAR? HEARD IT'S QUITE VALUABLE.
HA! *THAT'S* INTERESTING. I ALWAYS KNEW SOME OF YOU WERE CROOKED. SURE. ONE BAR. SELL IT TO BUY YOUR CONSCIOUS BACK, GOLDEN BOY. OR... I'M DOWN A COUPLE MEN. NEED A JOB?
WHAT? NO JOB OFFER FOR THE WOMAN WITH THE BLASTER TO YOUR HEAD? SEEMS LIKE I'M MORE QUALIFIED.
WHY, YOU...
FWIP

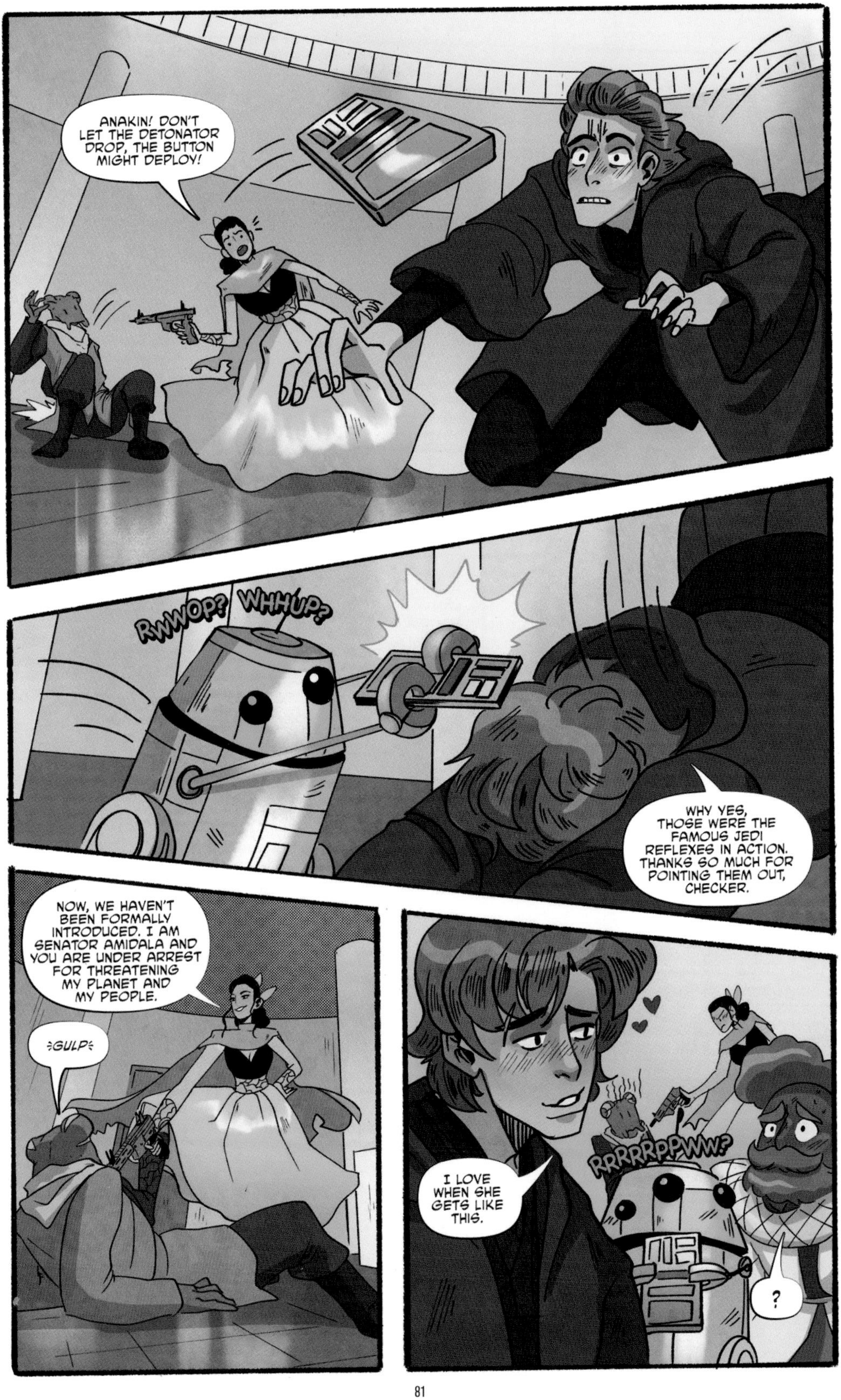

ANAKIN! DON'T LET THE DETONATOR DROP, THE BUTTON MIGHT DEPLOY!
RWWOP? WHHUP?
WHY YES, THOSE WERE THE FAMOUS JEDI REFLEXES IN ACTION. THANKS SO MUCH FOR POINTING THEM OUT, CHECKER.
NOW, WE HAVEN'T BEEN FORMALLY INTRODUCED. I AM SENATOR AMIDALA AND YOU ARE UNDER ARREST FOR THREATENING MY PLANET AND MY PEOPLE.
GULP
I LOVE WHEN SHE GETS LIKE THIS.
RRRRRPPWW?
?

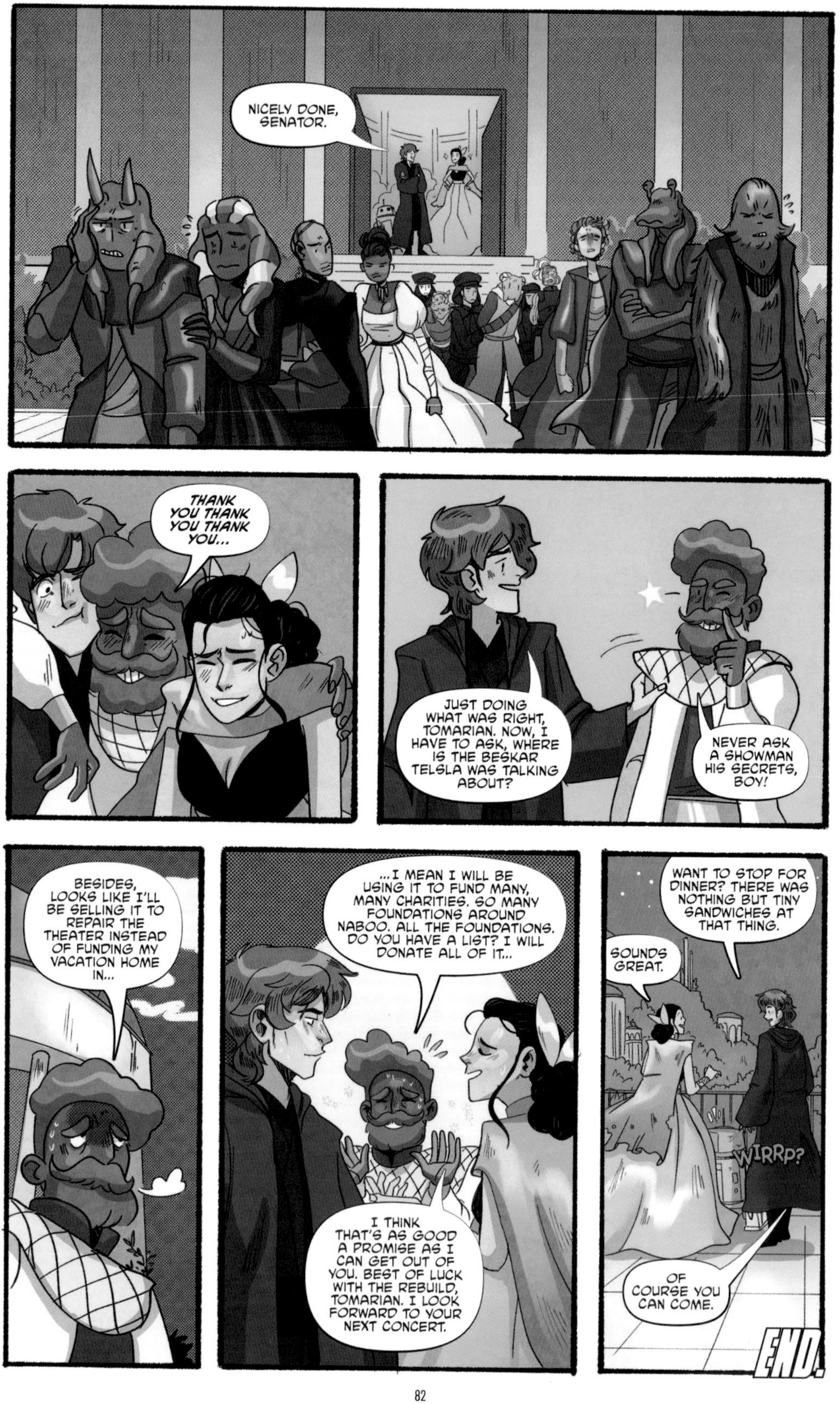
NICELY DONE, SENATOR.
THANK YOU THANK YOU THANK YOU...
JUST DOING WHAT WAS RIGHT, TOMARIAN. NOW, I HAVE TO ASK, WHERE IS THE BESKAR TELSLA WAS TALKING ABOUT?
NEVER ASK A SHOWMAN HIS SECRETS, BOY!
BESIDES, LOOKS LIKE I'LL BE SELLING IT TO REPAIR THE THEATER INSTEAD OF FUNDING MY VACATION HOME IN...
...I MEAN I WILL BE USING IT TO FUND MANY, MANY CHARITIES. SO MANY FOUNDATIONS AROUND NABOO. ALL THE FOUNDATIONS. DO YOU HAVE A LIST? I WILL DONATE ALL OF IT...
I THINK THAT'S AS GOOD A PROMISE AS I CAN GET OUT OF YOU. BEST OF LUCK WITH THE REBUILD, TOMARIAN. I LOOK FORWARD TO YOUR NEXT CONCERT.
WANT TO STOP FOR DINNER? THERE WAS NOTHING BUT TINY SANDWICHES AT THAT THING.
SOUNDS GREAT.
WIRRP?
OF COURSE YOU CAN COME.
END.

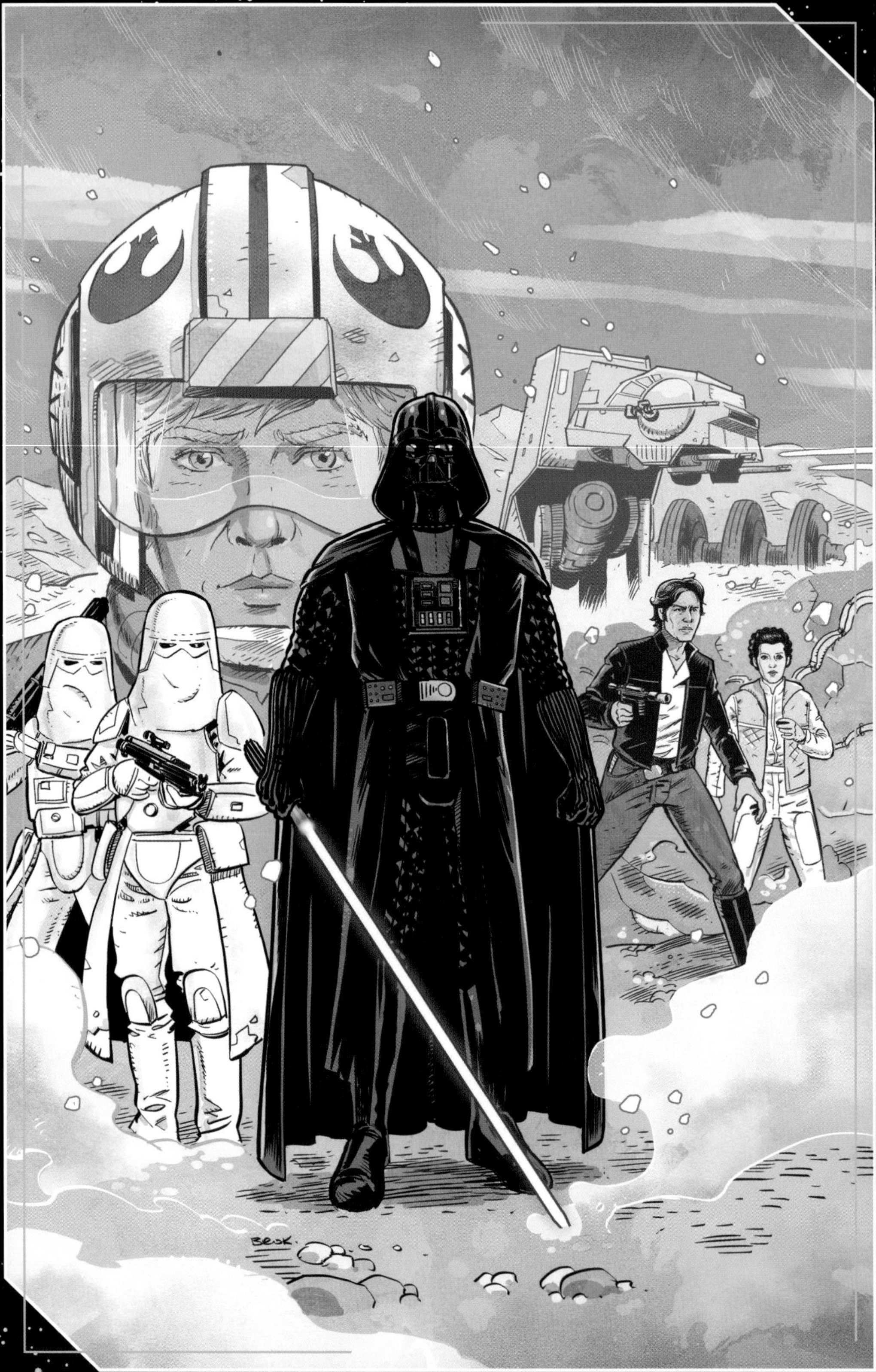

ART BY NICK BROKENSHIRE

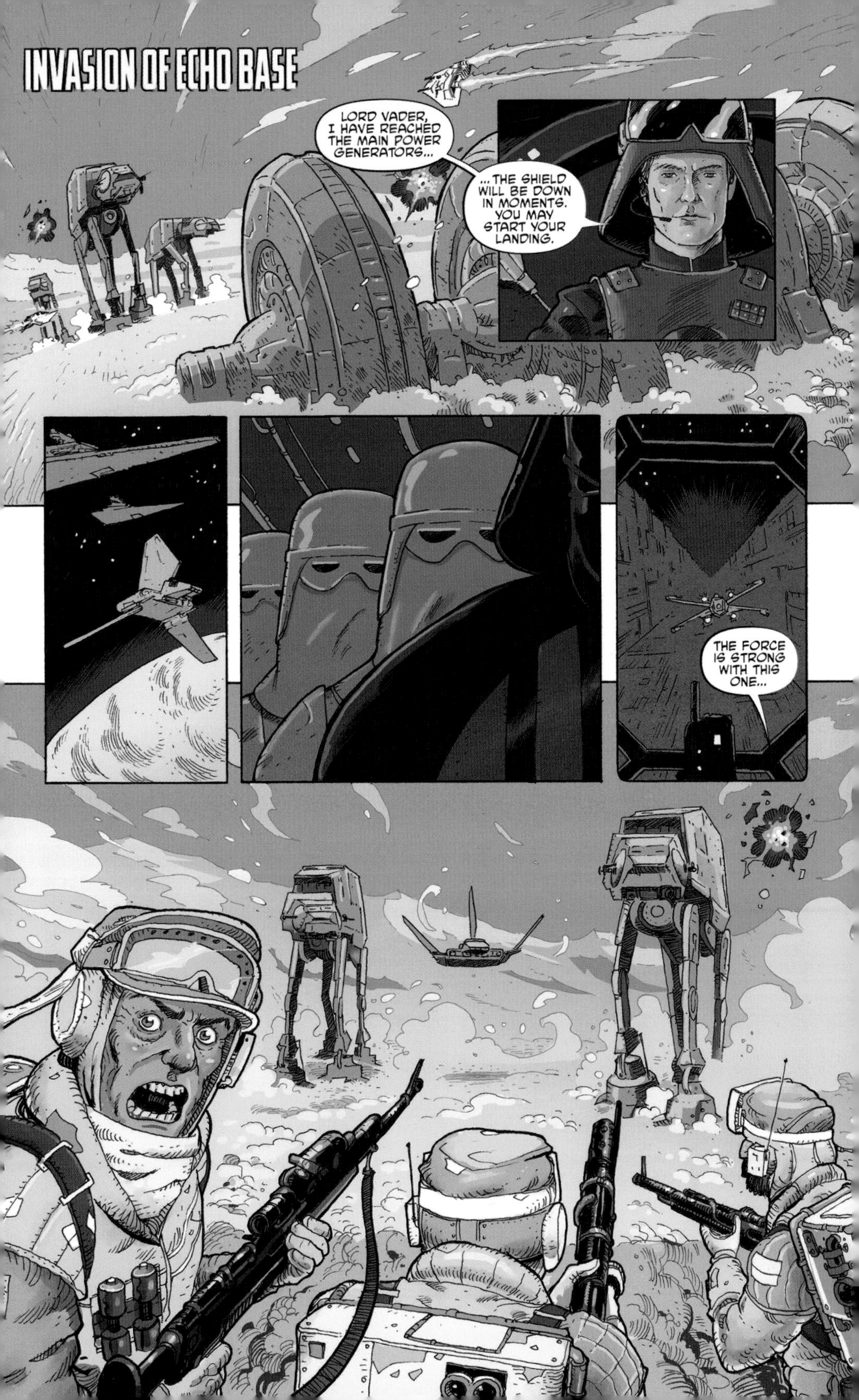
INVASION OF ECHO BASE
LORD VADER, I HAVE REACHED THE MAIN POWER GENERATORS...
...THE SHIELD WILL BE DOWN IN MOMENTS. YOU MAY START YOUR LANDING.
THE FORCE IS STRONG WITH THIS ONE...

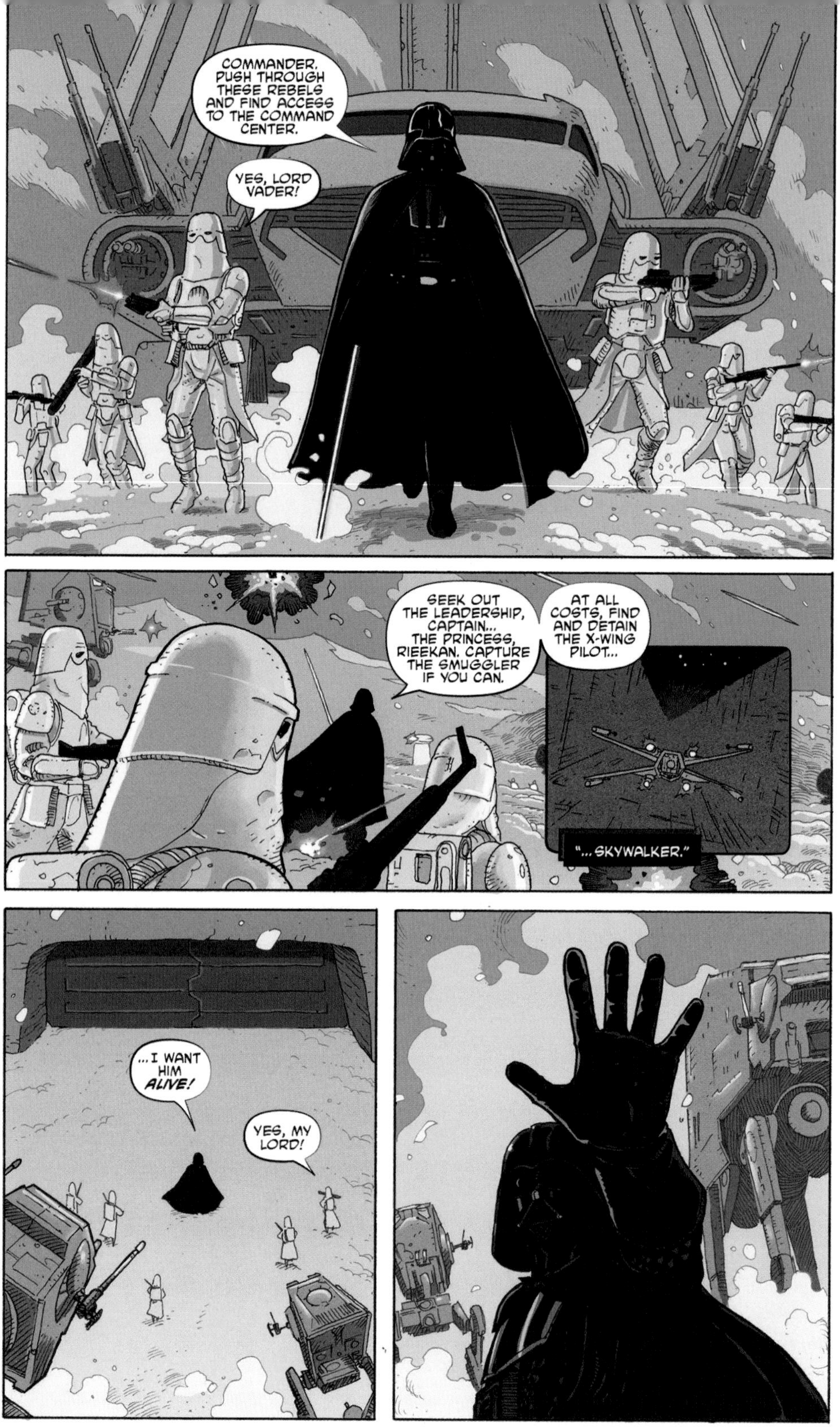
COMMANDER. PUSH THROUGH THESE REBELS AND FIND ACCESS TO THE COMMAND CENTER.
YES, LORD VADER!
SEEK OUT THE LEADERSHIP, CAPTAIN... THE PRINCESS, RIEEKAN. CAPTURE THE SMUGGLER IF YOU CAN.
AT ALL COSTS, FIND AND DETAIN THE X-WING PILOT...
"...SKYWALKER."
...I WANT HIM ALIVE!
YES, MY LORD!

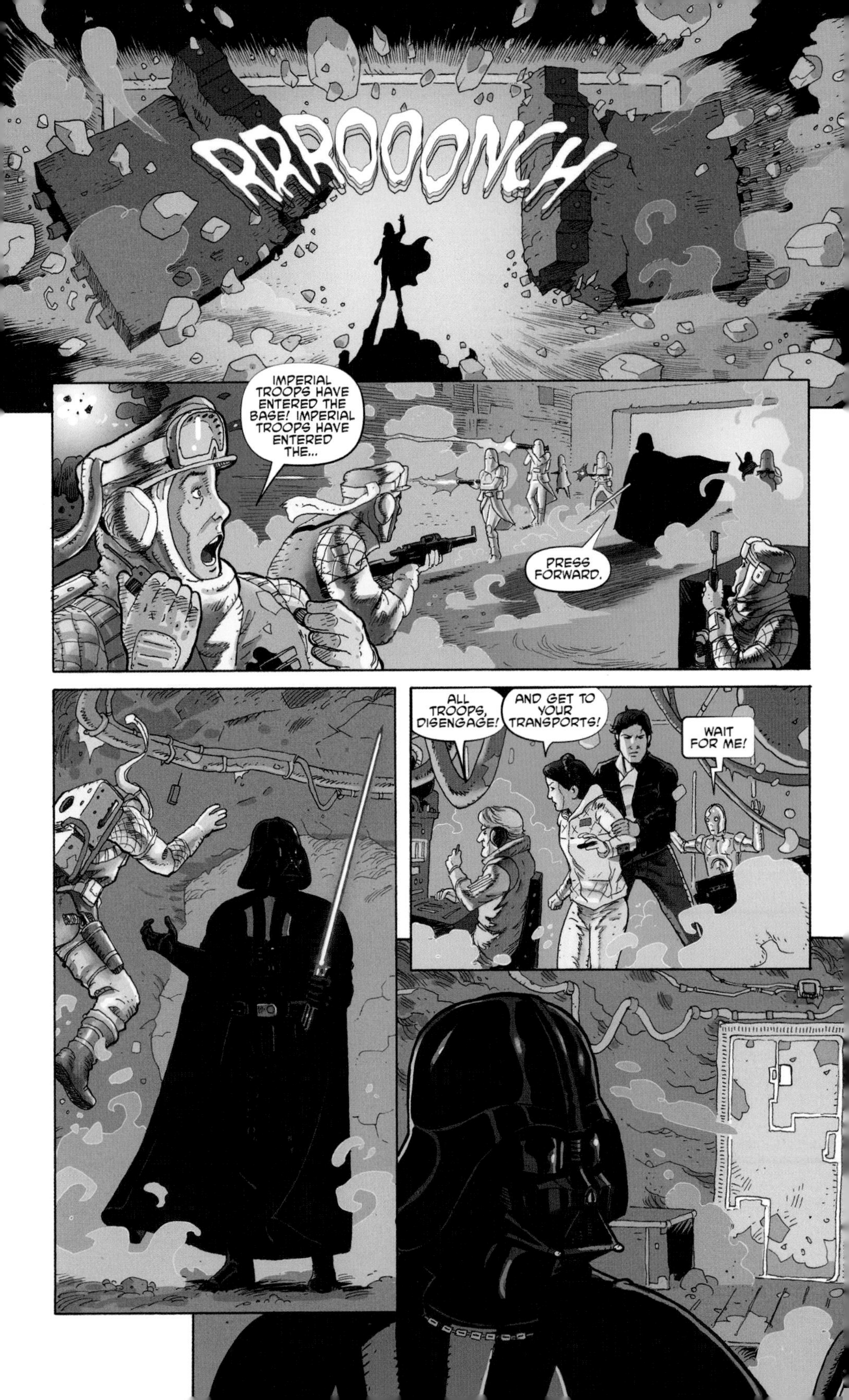
ARRROOONCH
IMPERIAL TROOPS HAVE ENTERED THE BASE! IMPERIAL TROOPS HAVE ENTERED THE...
PRESS FORWARD.
ALL TROOPS, DISENGAGE!
AND GET TO YOUR TRANSPORTS!
WAIT FOR ME!

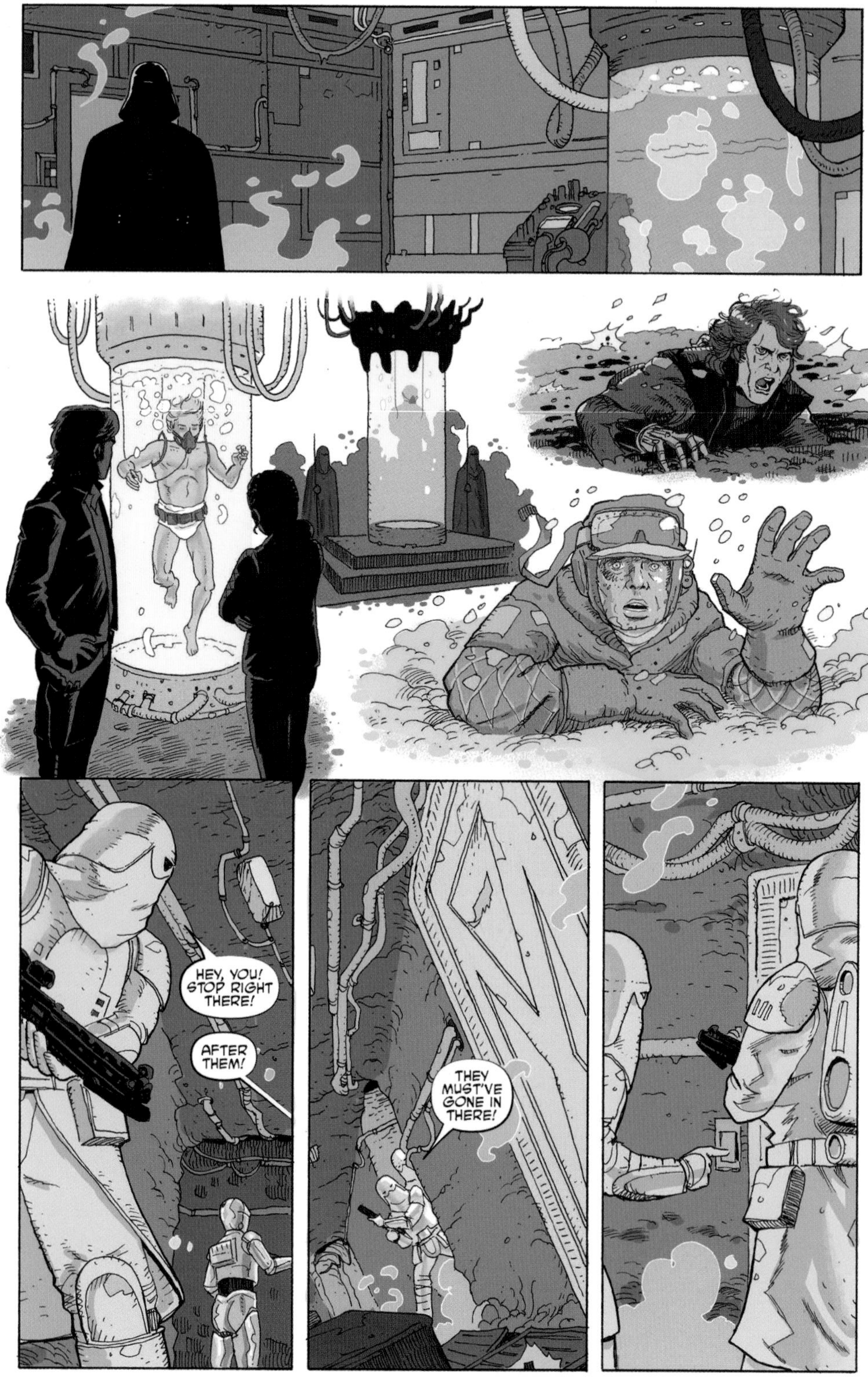
HEY, YOU! STOP RIGHT THERE!
AFTER THEM!
THEY MUST'VE GONE IN THERE!

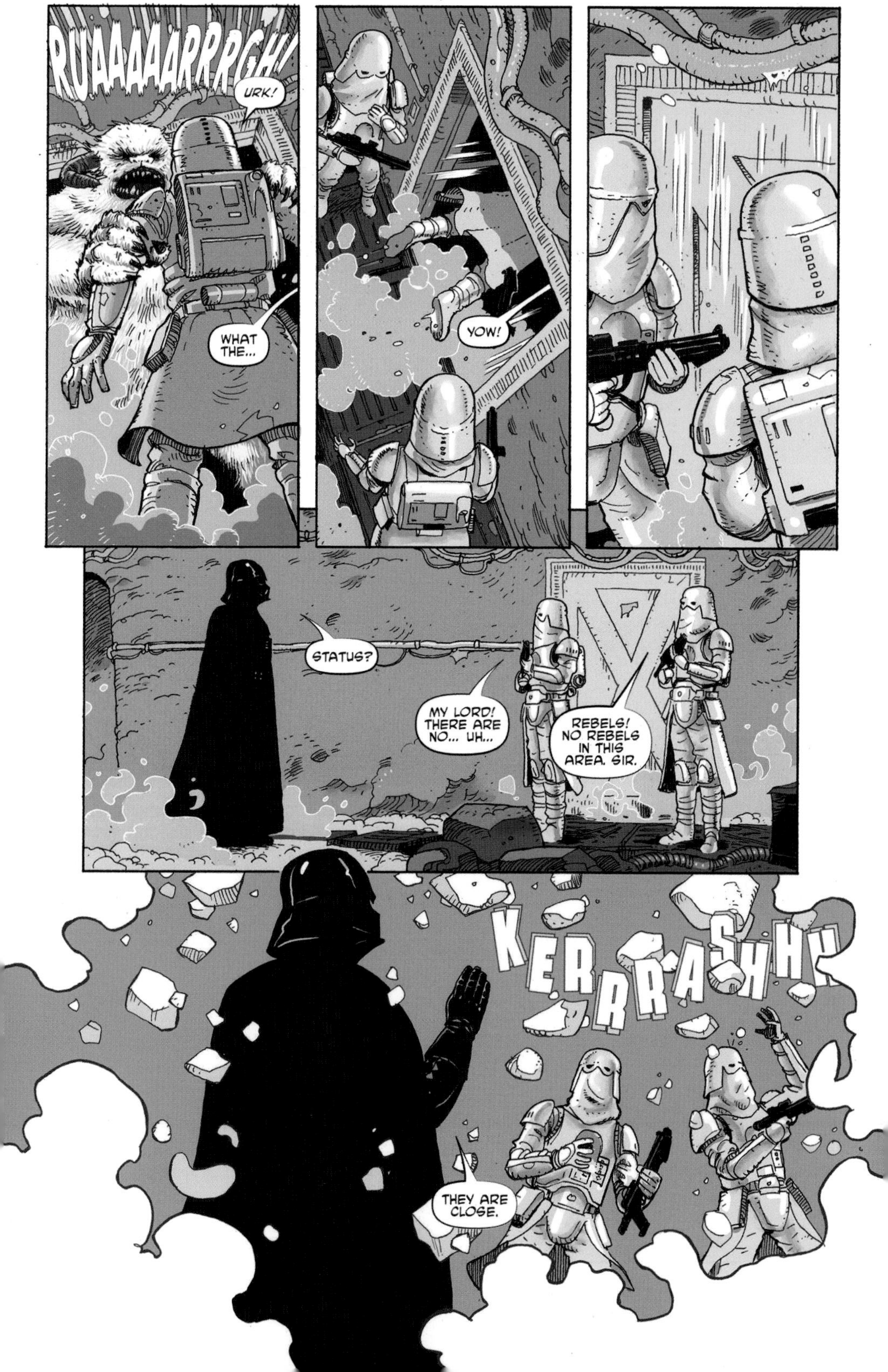
RUAAAAARRRGH!
URK!
WHAT THE...
YOW!
STATUS?
MY LORD! THERE ARE NO... UH...
REBELS! NO REBELS IN THIS AREA. SIR.
KERRRASHHH
THEY ARE CLOSE.

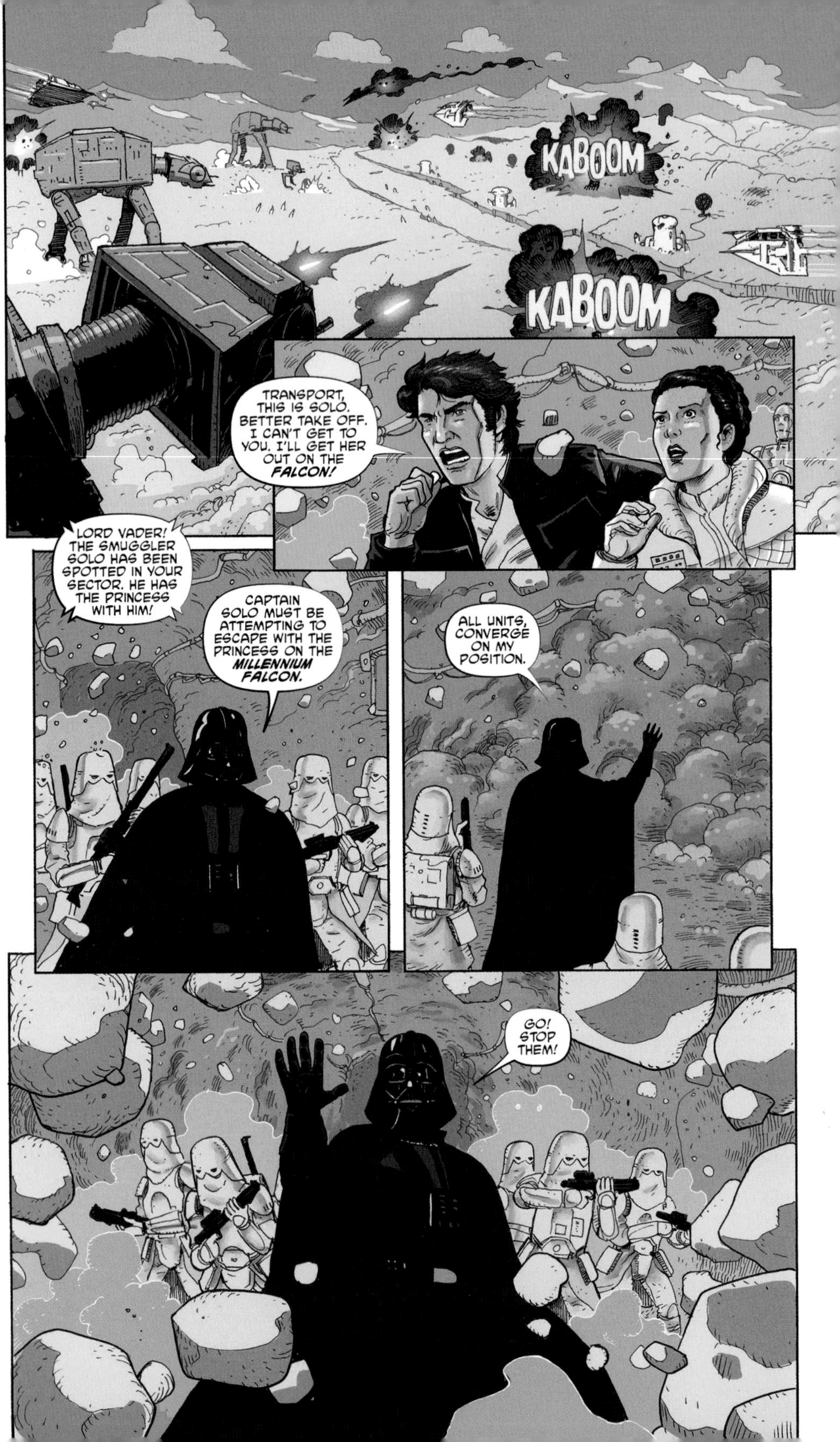
KABOOM
KABOOM
TRANSPORT, THIS IS SOLO. BETTER TAKE OFF. I CAN'T GET TO YOU. I'LL GET HER OUT ON THE FALCON!
LORD VADER! THE SMUGGLER SOLO HAS BEEN SPOTTED IN YOUR SECTOR. HE HAS THE PRINCESS WITH HIM!
CAPTAIN SOLO MUST BE ATTEMPTING TO ESCAPE WITH THE PRINCESS ON THE MILLENNIUM FALCON.
ALL UNITS, CONVERGE ON MY POSITION.
GO! STOP THEM!

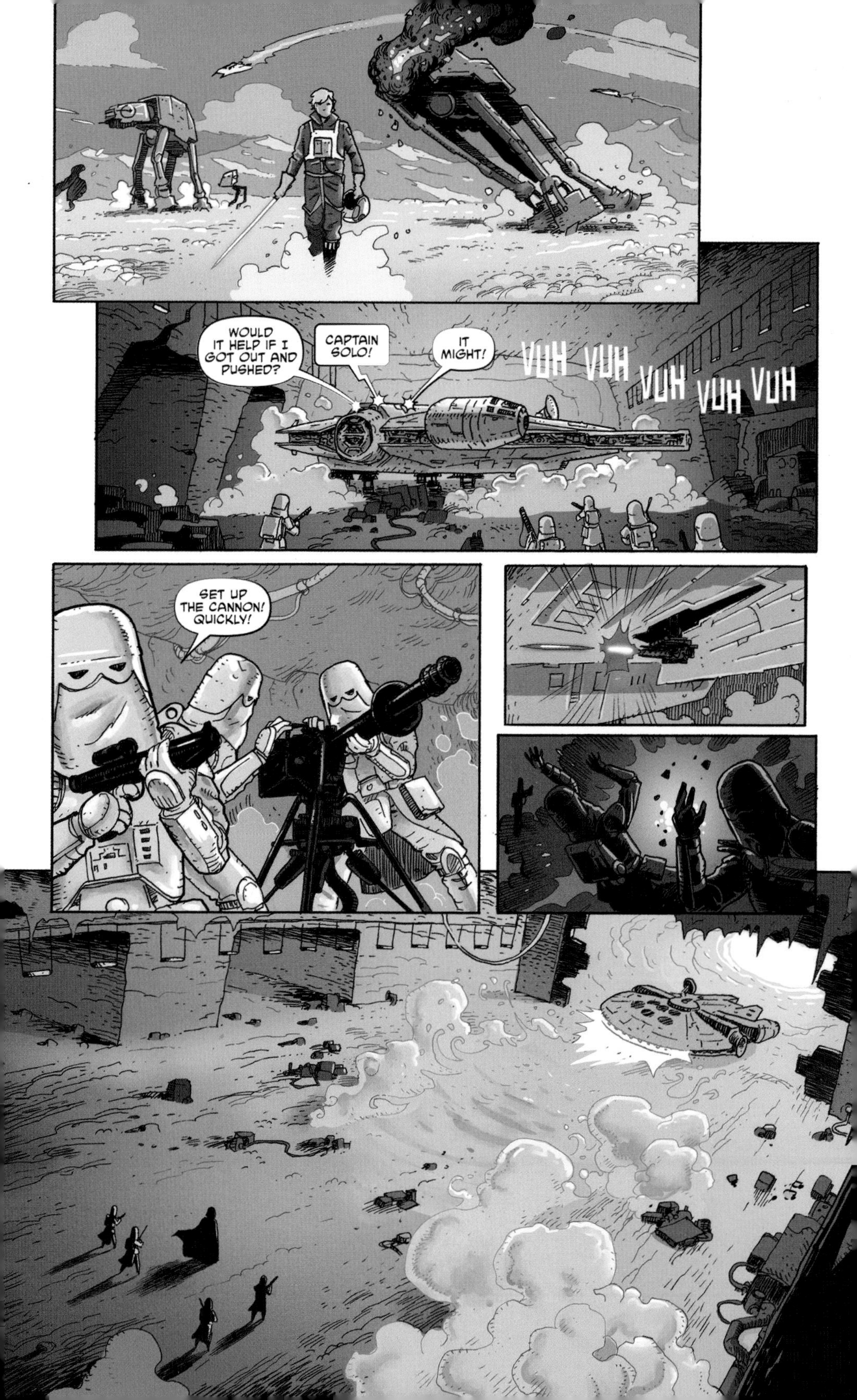
WOULD IT HELP IF I GOT OUT AND PUSHED?
CAPTAIN SOLO!
IT MIGHT!
VUH VUH VUH VUH VUH
SET UP THE CANNON! QUICKLY!

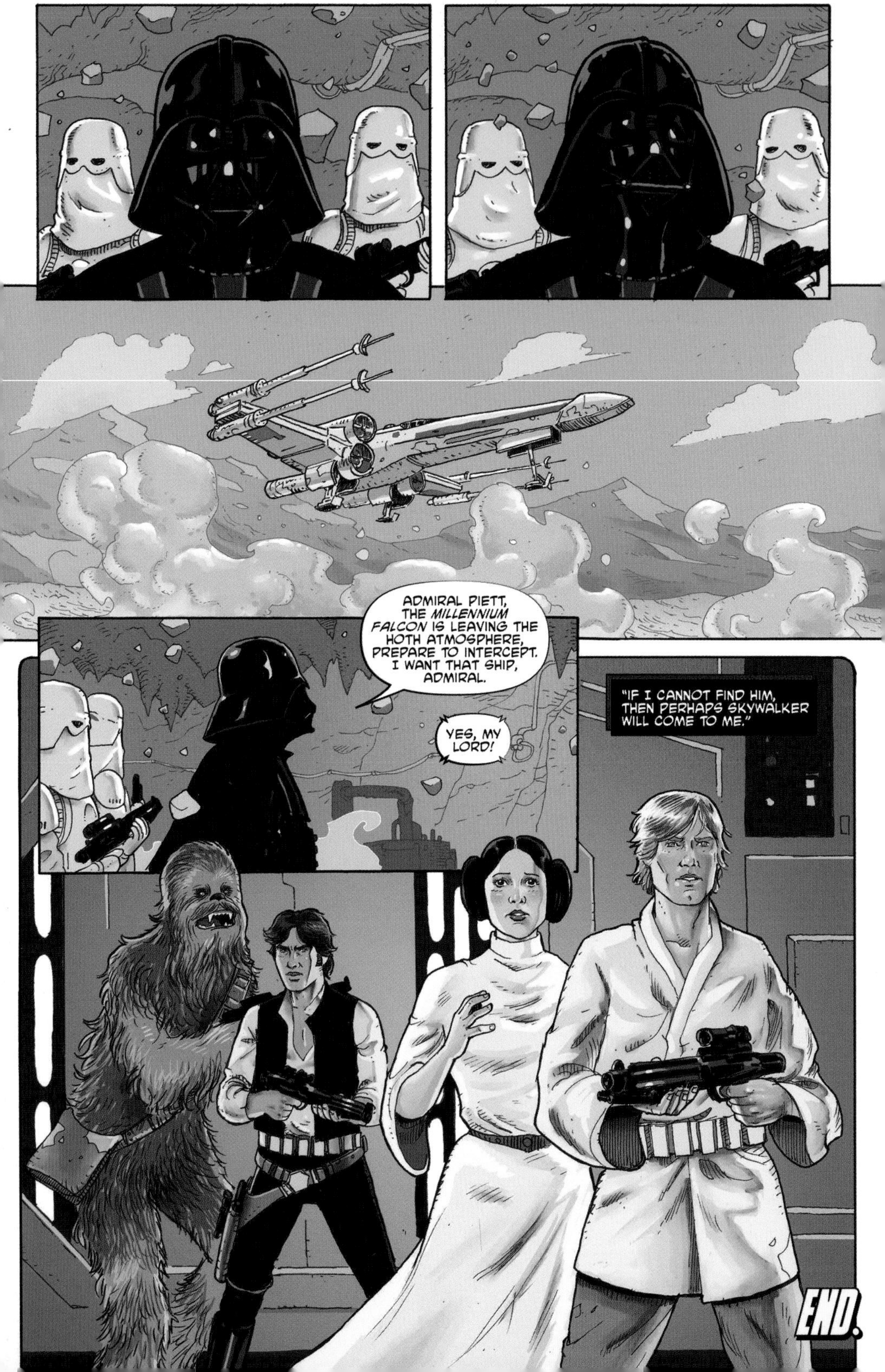
ADMIRAL PIETT, THE *MILLENNIUM FALCON* IS LEAVING THE HOTH ATMOSPHERE, PREPARE TO INTERCEPT. I WANT THAT SHIP, ADMIRAL.
YES, MY LORD!
"IF I CANNOT FIND HIM, THEN PERHAPS SKYWALKER WILL COME TO ME."
END.

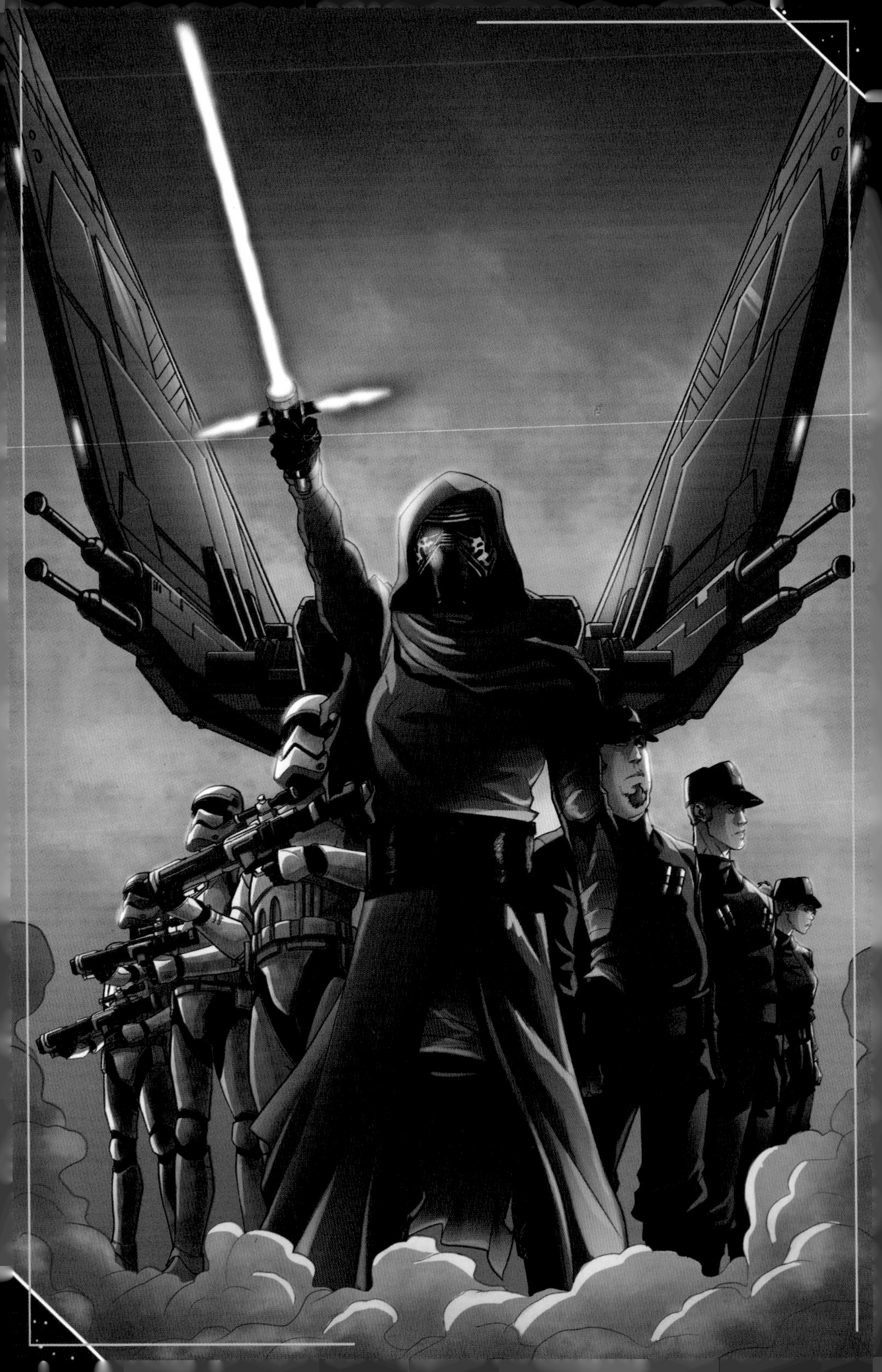

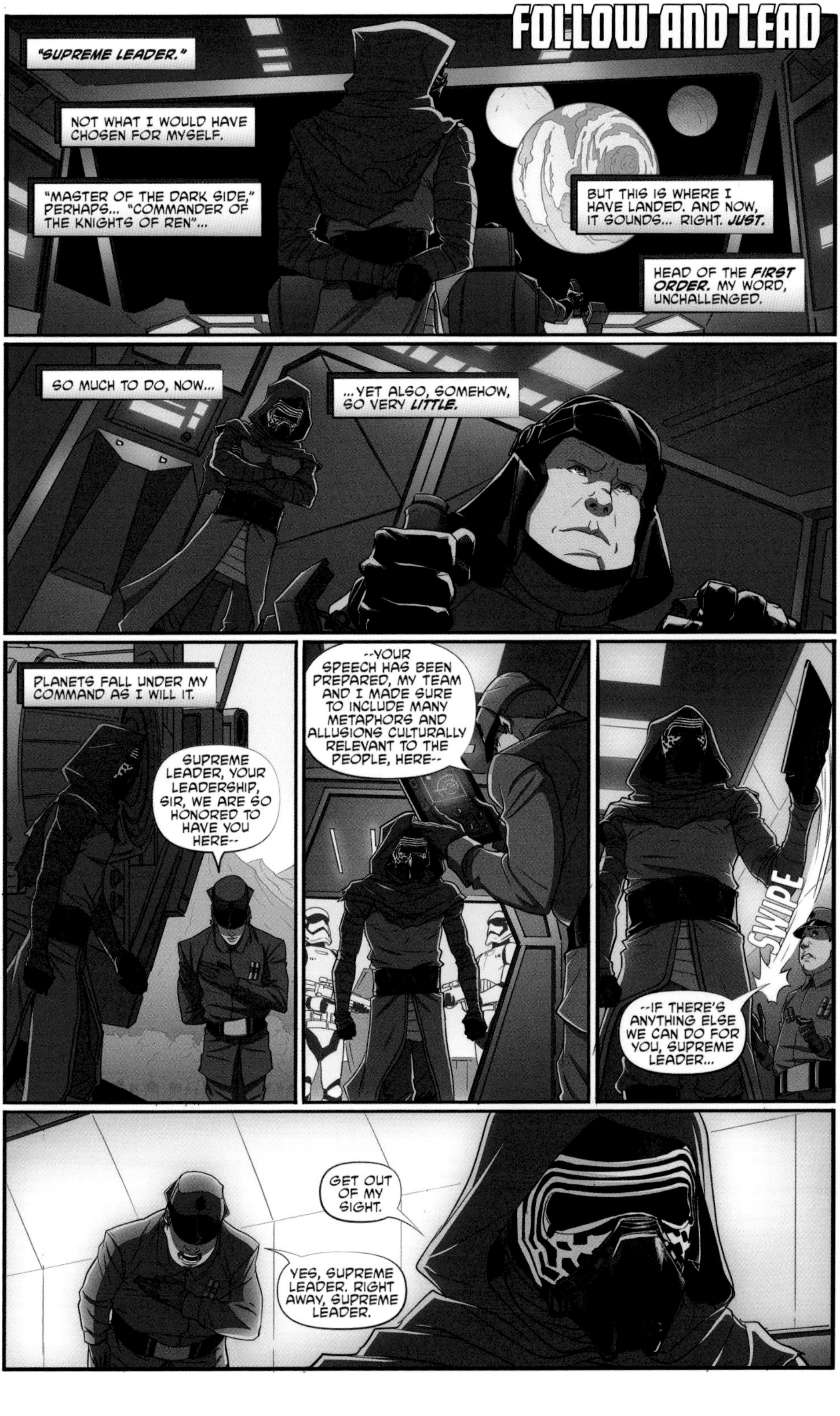
FOLLOW AND LEAD
"SUPREME LEADER."
NOT WHAT I WOULD HAVE CHOSEN FOR MYSELF.
"MASTER OF THE DARK SIDE," PERHAPS... "COMMANDER OF THE KNIGHTS OF REN"...
BUT THIS IS WHERE I HAVE LANDED. AND NOW, IT SOUNDS... RIGHT. JUST.
HEAD OF THE FIRST ORDER. MY WORD, UNCHALLENGED.
SO MUCH TO DO, NOW...
...YET ALSO, SOMEHOW, SO VERY LITTLE.
PLANETS FALL UNDER MY COMMAND AS I WILL IT.
SUPREME LEADER, YOUR LEADERSHIP, SIR, WE ARE SO HONORED TO HAVE YOU HERE--
--YOUR SPEECH HAS BEEN PREPARED, MY TEAM AND I MADE SURE TO INCLUDE MANY METAPHORS AND ALLUSIONS CULTURALLY RELEVANT TO THE PEOPLE, HERE--
SWIPE
--IF THERE'S ANYTHING ELSE WE CAN DO FOR YOU, SUPREME LEADER...
GET OUT OF MY SIGHT.
YES, SUPREME LEADER. RIGHT AWAY, SUPREME LEADER.

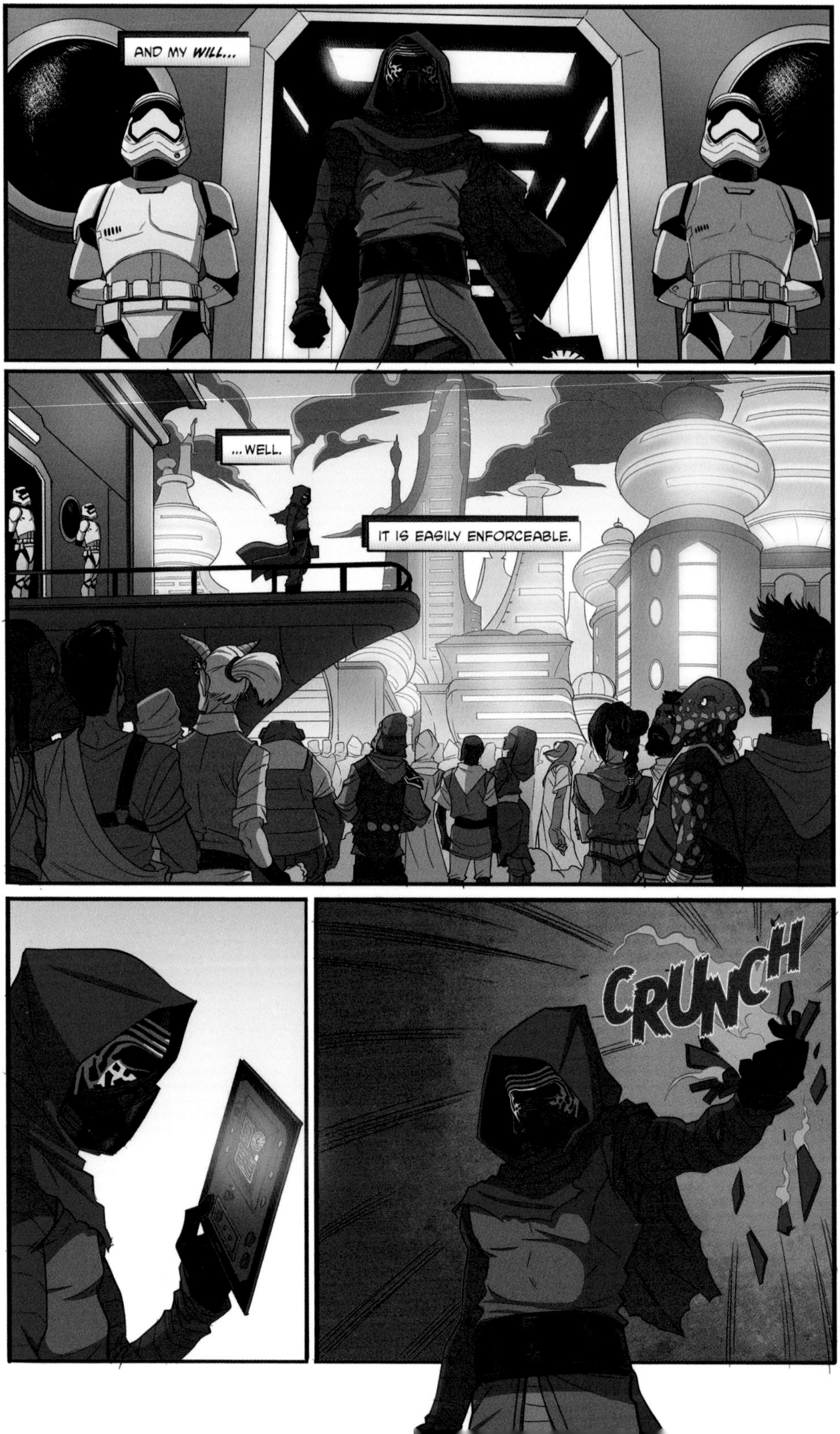
AND MY WILL...
...WELL.
IT IS EASILY ENFORCEABLE.
CRUNCH

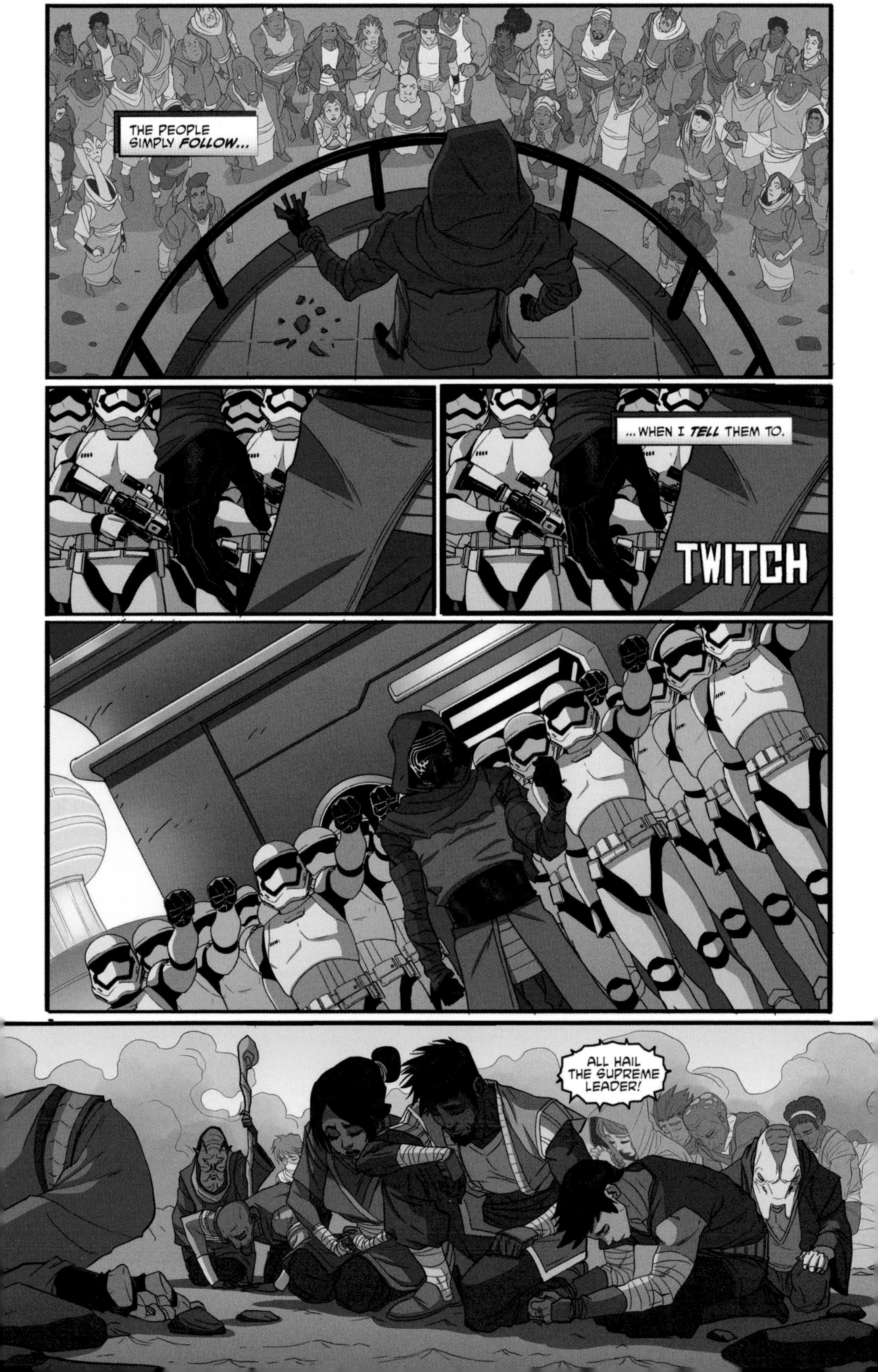
THE PEOPLE SIMPLY *FOLLOW*...
...WHEN I *TELL* THEM TO.
TWITCH
ALL HAIL THE SUPREME LEADER!

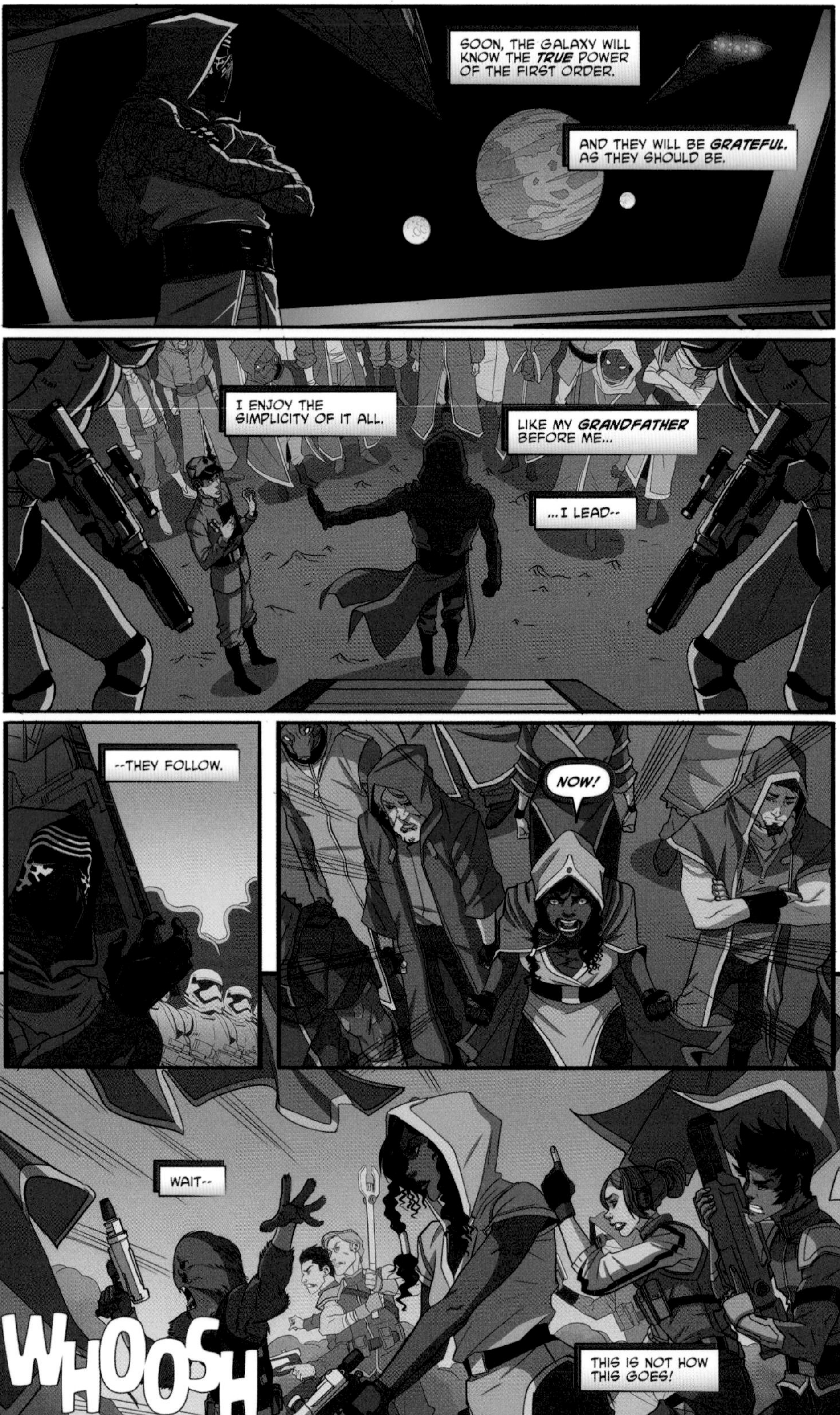
SOON, THE GALAXY WILL KNOW THE TRUE POWER OF THE FIRST ORDER.
AND THEY WILL BE GRATEFUL. AS THEY SHOULD BE.
I ENJOY THE SIMPLICITY OF IT ALL.
LIKE MY GRANDFATHER BEFORE ME...
...I LEAD--
--THEY FOLLOW.
NOW!
WAIT--
WHOOSH
THIS IS NOT HOW THIS GOES!

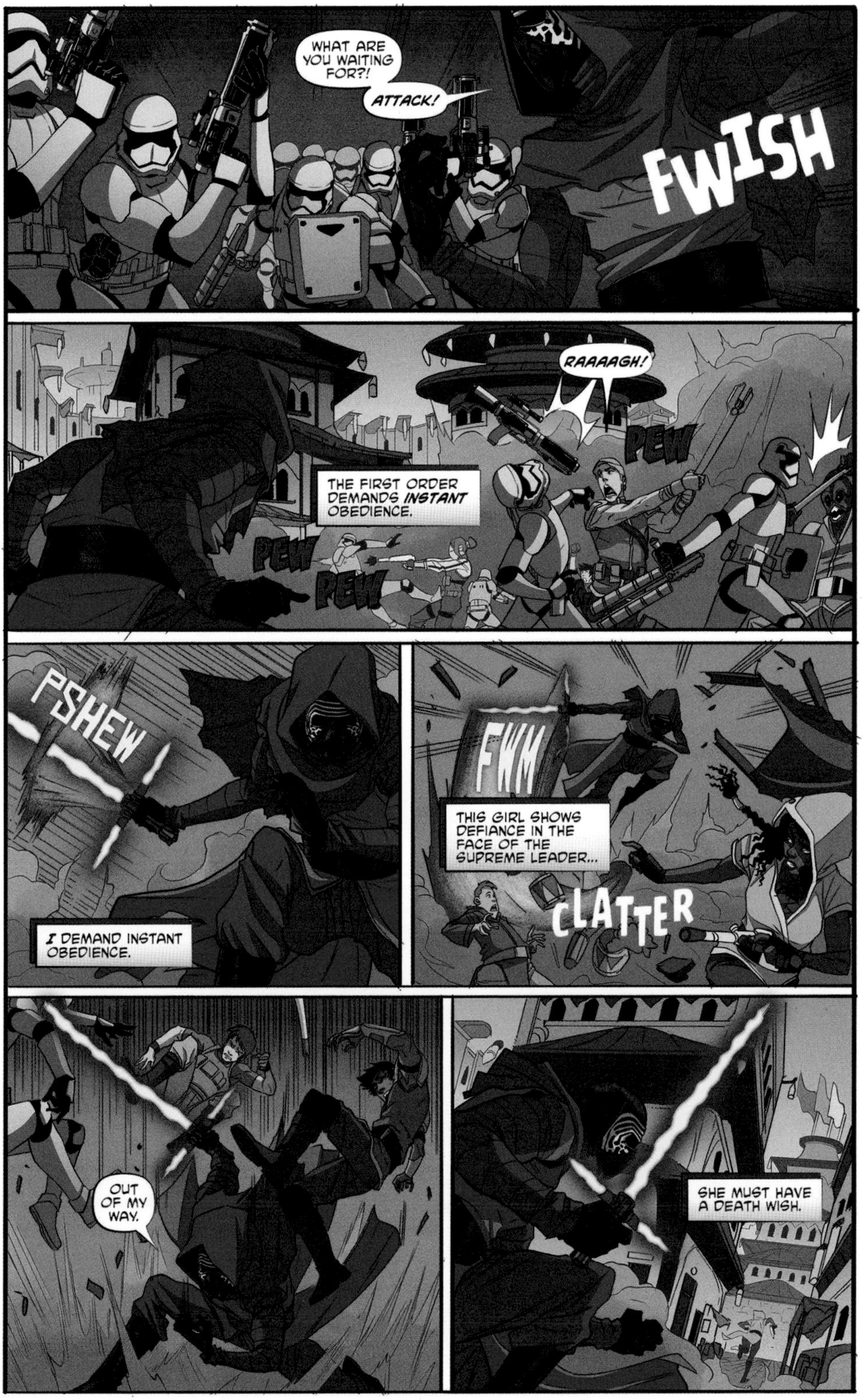
WHAT ARE YOU WAITING FOR?!
ATTACK!
FWISH
RAAAAGH!
PEW
THE FIRST ORDER DEMANDS INSTANT OBEDIENCE.
PEW
PEW
PSHEW
I DEMAND INSTANT OBEDIENCE.
FWM
THIS GIRL SHOWS DEFIANCE IN THE FACE OF THE SUPREME LEADER...
CLATTER
OUT OF MY WAY.
SHE MUST HAVE A DEATH WISH.

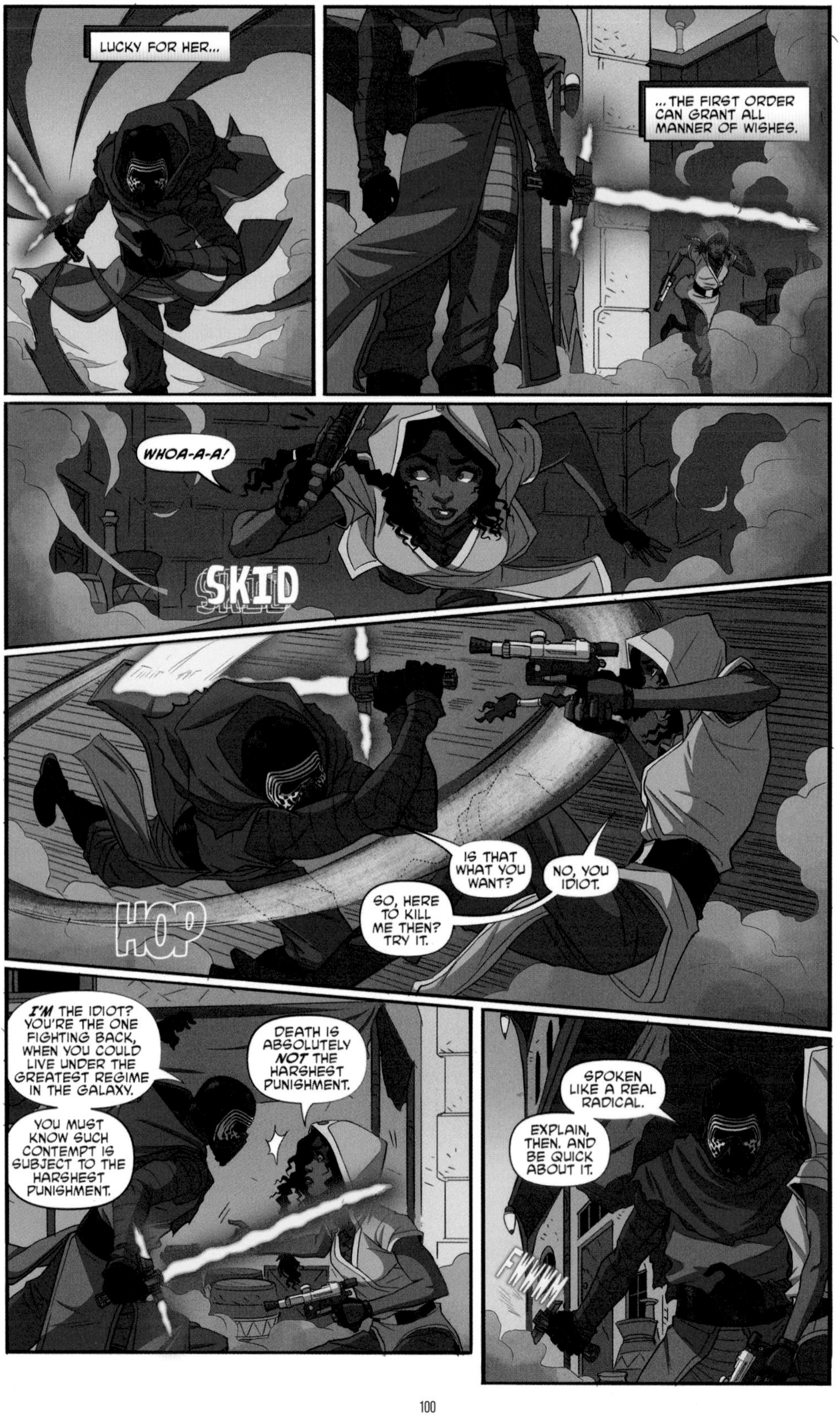

LUCKY FOR HER...
...THE FIRST ORDER CAN GRANT ALL MANNER OF WISHES.
WHOA-A-A!
SKID
HOP
SO, HERE TO KILL ME THEN? TRY IT.
IS THAT WHAT YOU WANT?
NO, YOU IDIOT.
I'M THE IDIOT? YOU'RE THE ONE FIGHTING BACK, WHEN YOU COULD LIVE UNDER THE GREATEST REGIME IN THE GALAXY.
YOU MUST KNOW SUCH CONTEMPT IS SUBJECT TO THE HARSHEST PUNISHMENT.
DEATH IS ABSOLUTELY NOT THE HARSHEST PUNISHMENT.
SPOKEN LIKE A REAL RADICAL.
EXPLAIN, THEN. AND BE QUICK ABOUT IT.
FWWWM

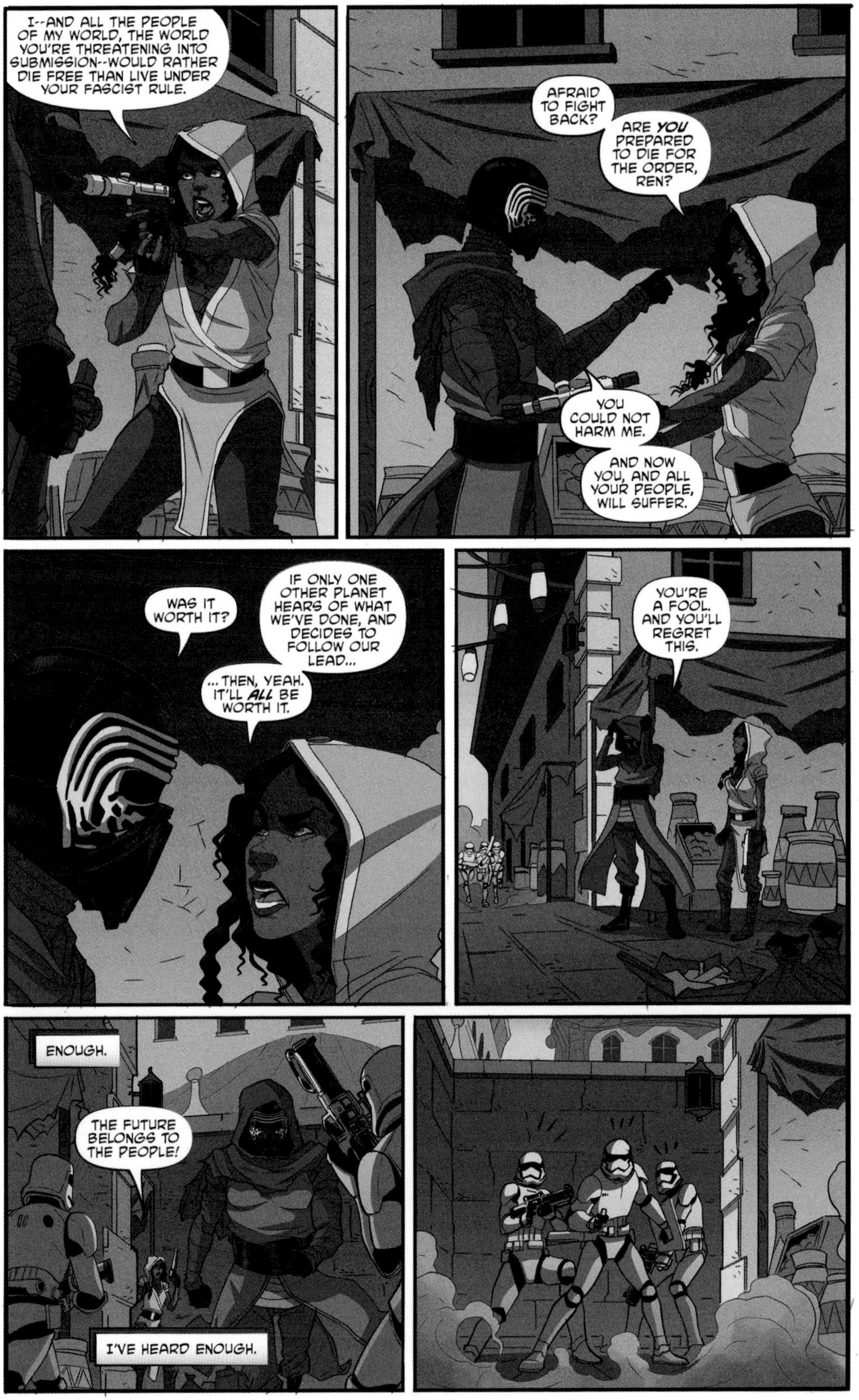
I--AND ALL THE PEOPLE OF MY WORLD, THE WORLD YOU'RE THREATENING INTO SUBMISSION--WOULD RATHER DIE FREE THAN LIVE UNDER YOUR FASCIST RULE.
AFRAID TO FIGHT BACK?
ARE YOU PREPARED TO DIE FOR THE ORDER, REN?
YOU COULD NOT HARM ME.
AND NOW YOU, AND ALL YOUR PEOPLE, WILL SUFFER.
WAS IT WORTH IT?
IF ONLY ONE OTHER PLANET HEARS OF WHAT WE'VE DONE, AND DECIDES TO FOLLOW OUR LEAD...
...THEN, YEAH. IT'LL ALL BE WORTH IT.
YOU'RE A FOOL. AND YOU'LL REGRET THIS.
ENOUGH.
THE FUTURE BELONGS TO THE PEOPLE!
I'VE HEARD ENOUGH.

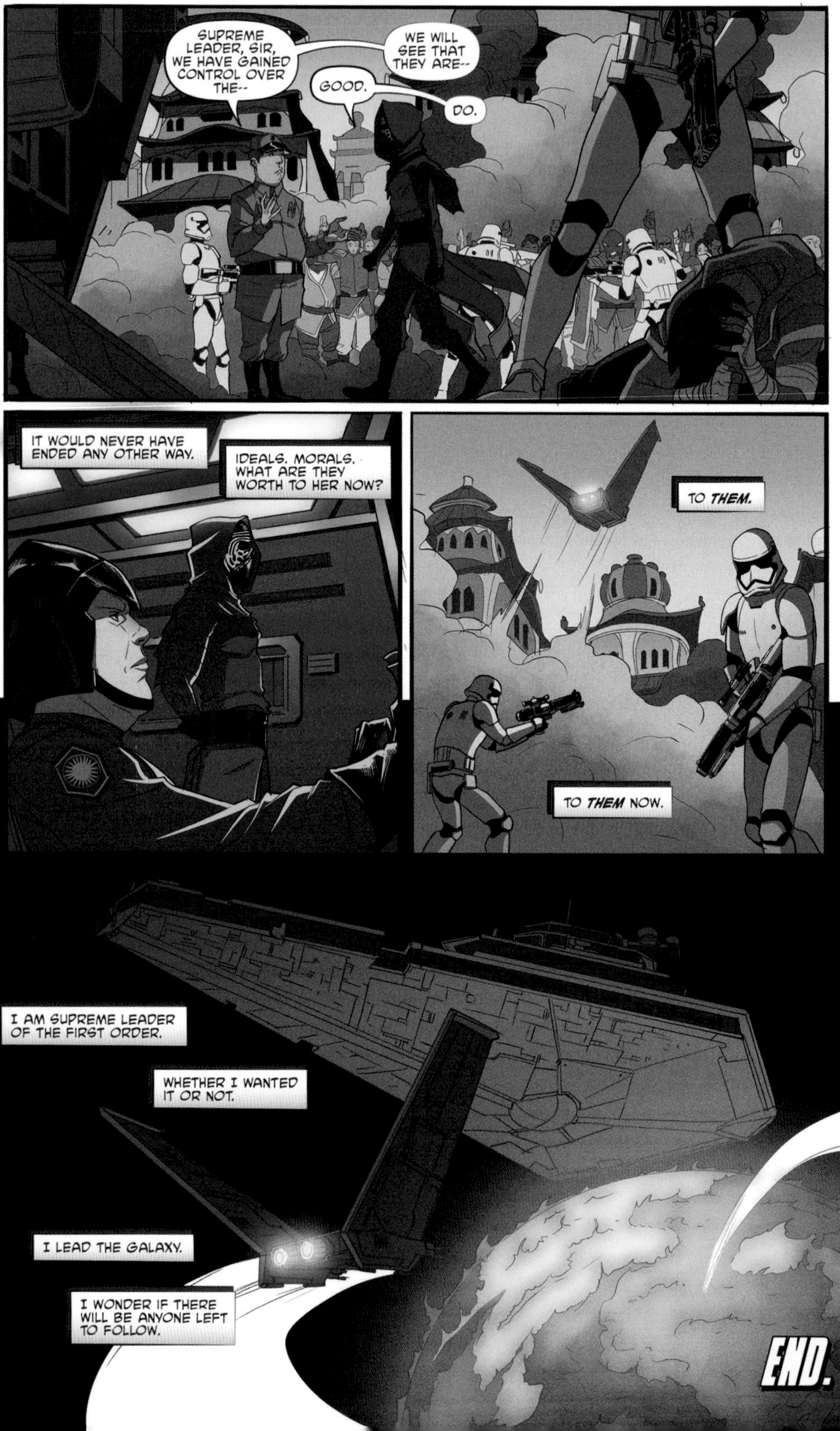
SUPREME LEADER, SIR, WE HAVE GAINED CONTROL OVER THE--
WE WILL SEE THAT THEY ARE--
GOOD.
DO.
IT WOULD NEVER HAVE ENDED ANY OTHER WAY.
IDEALS. MORALS. WHAT ARE THEY WORTH TO HER NOW?
TO *THEM.*
TO *THEM* NOW.
I AM SUPREME LEADER OF THE FIRST ORDER.
WHETHER I WANTED IT OR NOT.
I LEAD THE GALAXY.
I WONDER IF THERE WILL BE ANYONE LEFT TO FOLLOW.
END.

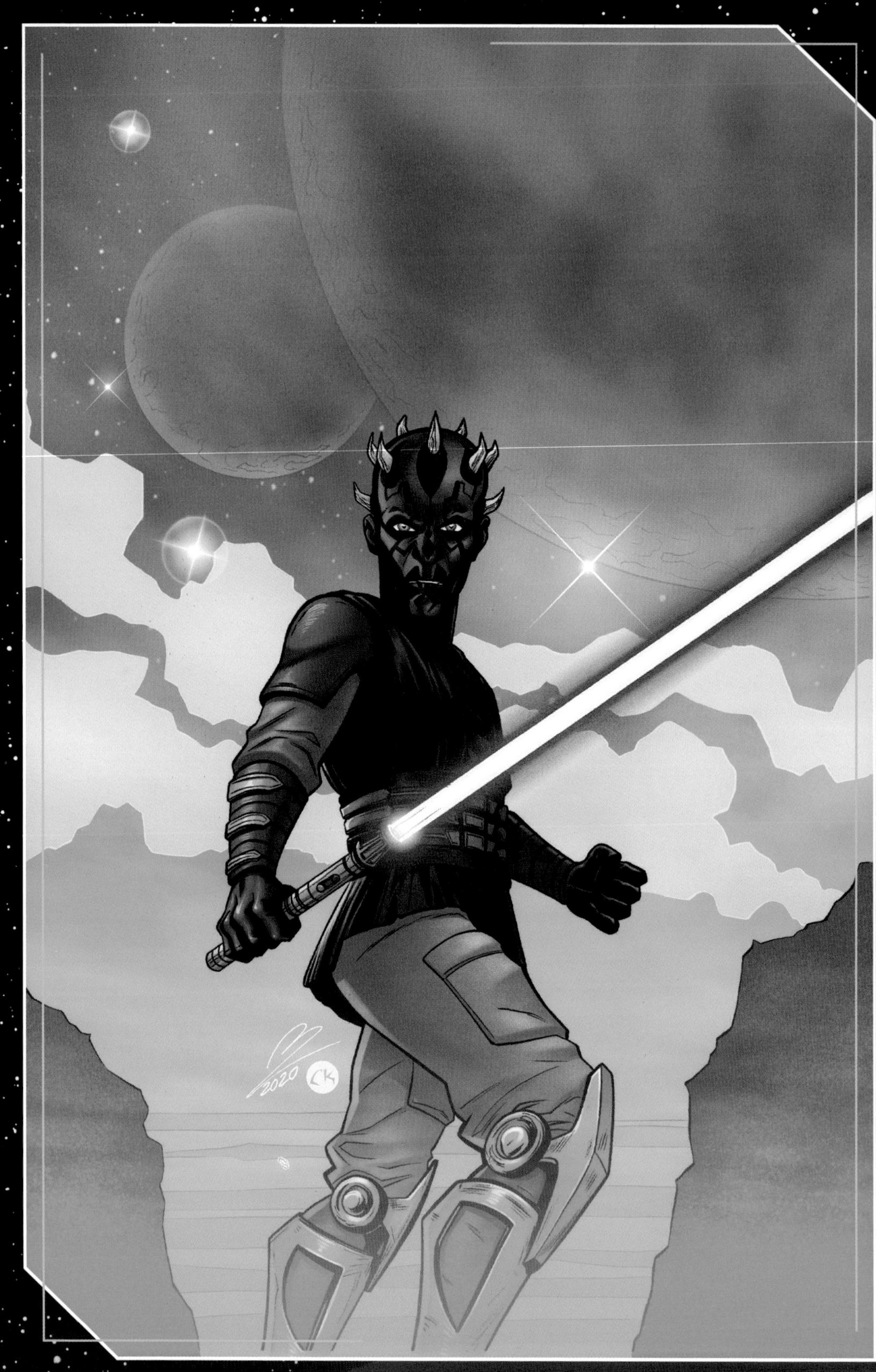

ART BY MEGAN LEVENS COLORS BY CHARLIE KIRCHOFF

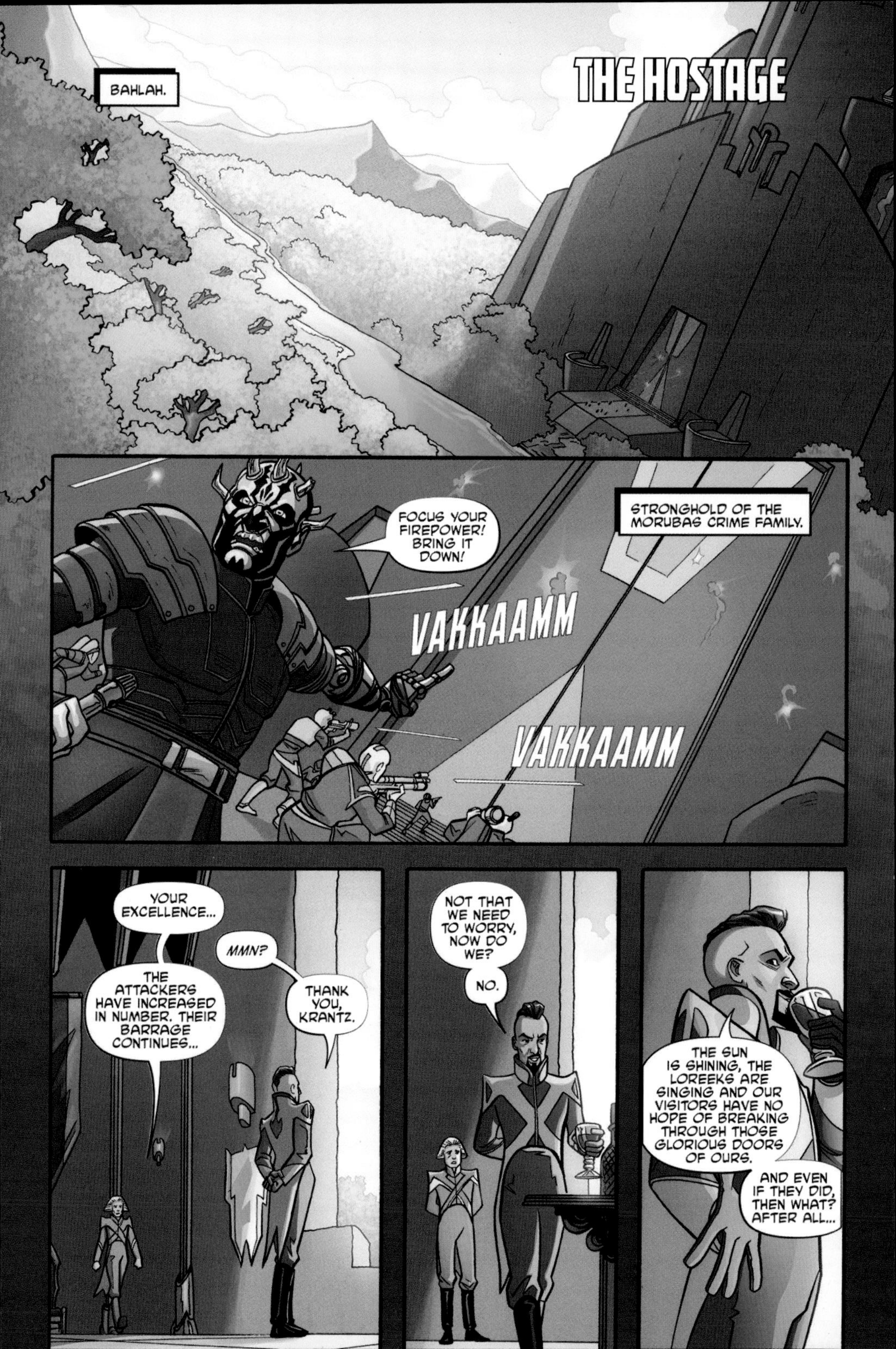
THE HOSTAGE
BAHLAH.
STRONGHOLD OF THE MORUBAS CRIME FAMILY.
FOCUS YOUR FIREPOWER! BRING IT DOWN!
VAKKAAMM
VAKKAAMM
YOUR EXCELLENCE...
MMN?
THE ATTACKERS HAVE INCREASED IN NUMBER. THEIR BARRAGE CONTINUES...
THANK YOU, KRANTZ.
NOT THAT WE NEED TO WORRY, NOW DO WE?
NO.
THE SUN IS SHINING, THE LOREEKS ARE SINGING AND OUR VISITORS HAVE NO HOPE OF BREAKING THROUGH THOSE GLORIOUS DOORS OF OURS.
AND EVEN IF THEY DID, THEN WHAT? AFTER ALL...

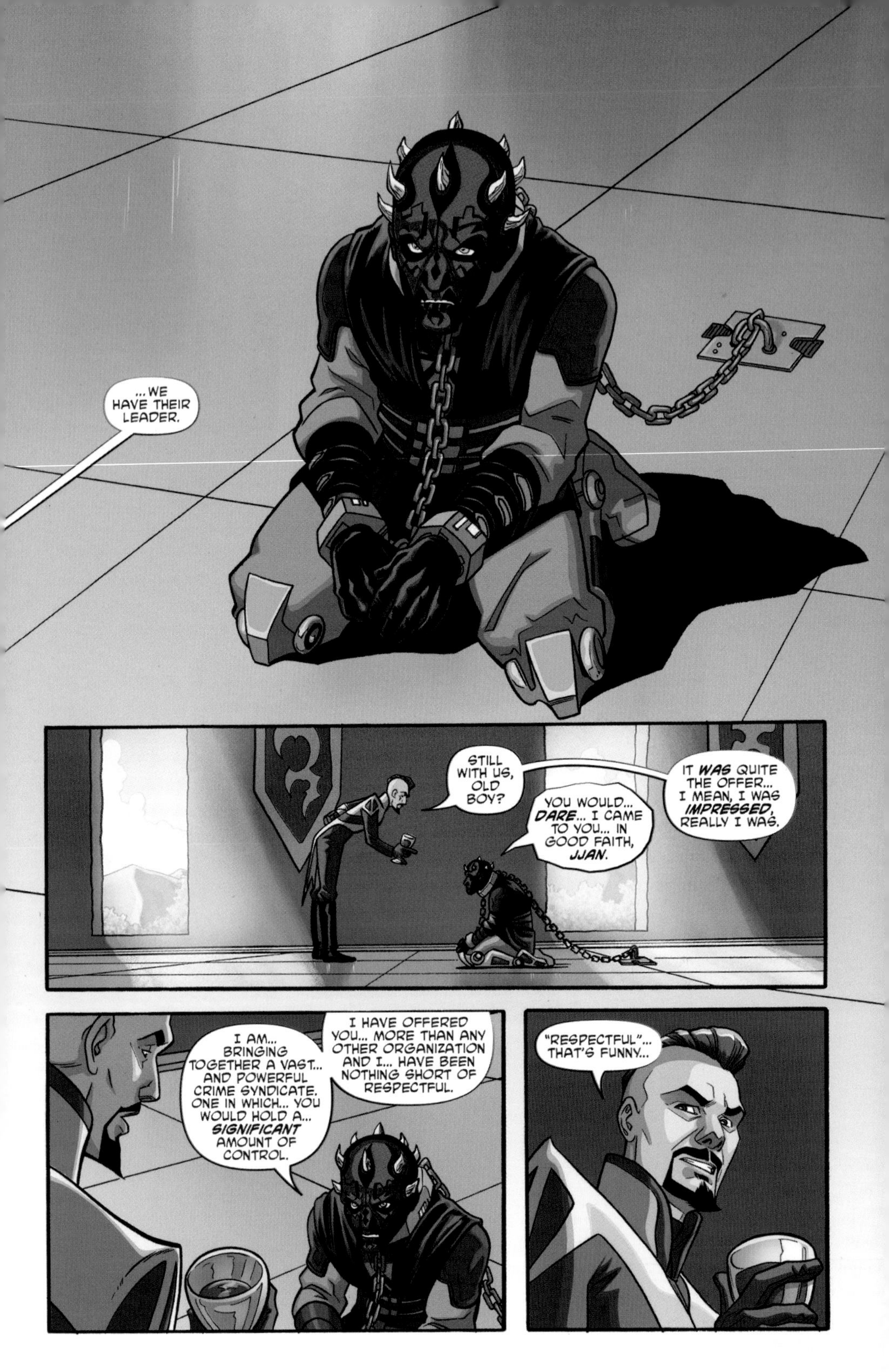
...WE HAVE THEIR LEADER.
STILL WITH US, OLD BOY?
YOU WOULD... DARE... I CAME TO YOU... IN GOOD FAITH, JJAN.
IT WAS QUITE THE OFFER... I MEAN, I WAS IMPRESSED, REALLY I WAS.
I AM... BRINGING TOGETHER A VAST... AND POWERFUL CRIME SYNDICATE. ONE IN WHICH... YOU WOULD HOLD A... SIGNIFICANT AMOUNT OF CONTROL.
I HAVE OFFERED YOU... MORE THAN ANY OTHER ORGANIZATION AND I... HAVE BEEN NOTHING SHORT OF RESPECTFUL.
"RESPECTFUL"... THAT'S FUNNY...

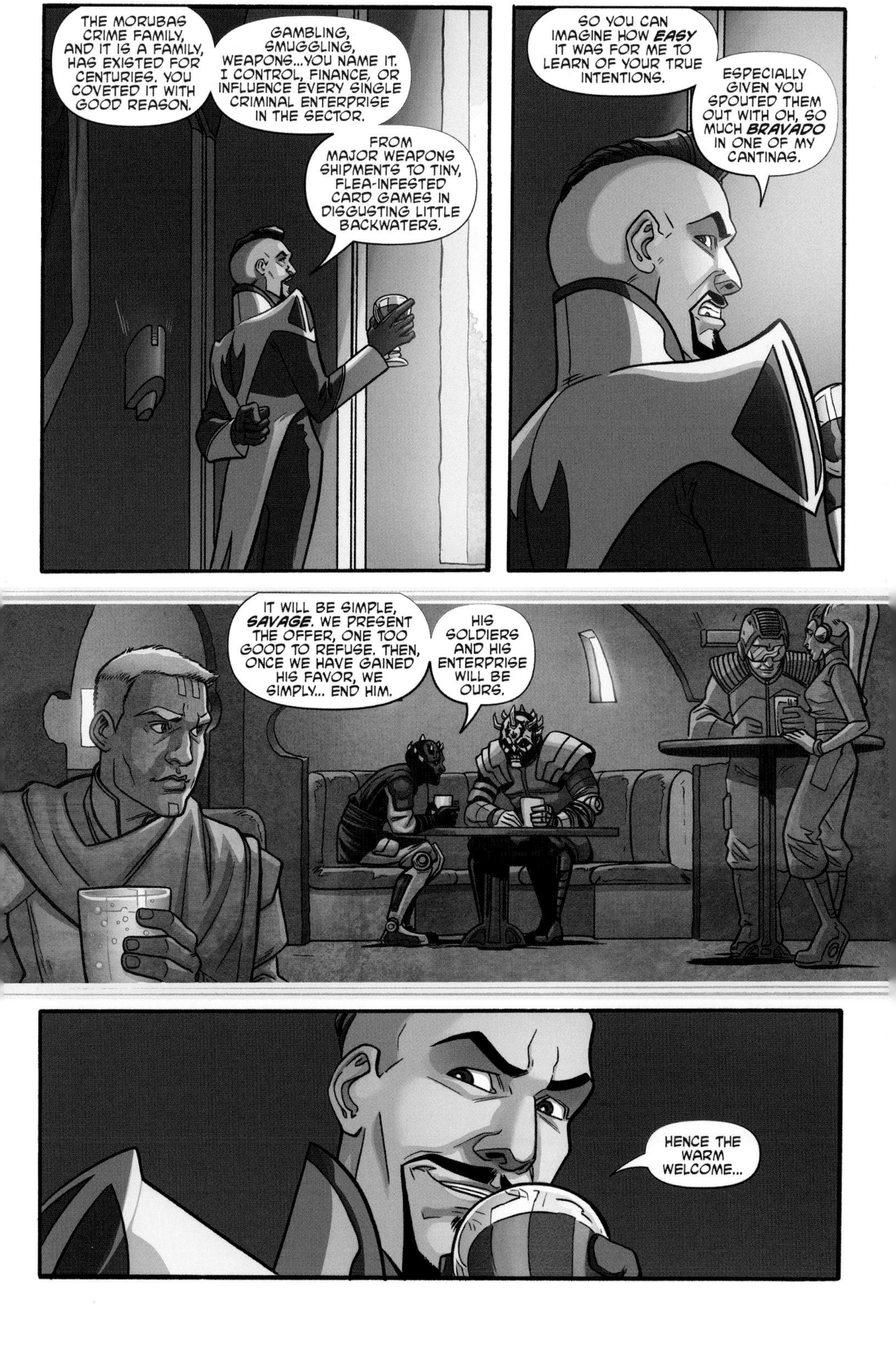
THE MORUBAS CRIME FAMILY, AND IT IS A FAMILY, HAS EXISTED FOR CENTURIES. YOU COVETED IT WITH GOOD REASON.
GAMBLING, SMUGGLING, WEAPONS...YOU NAME IT. I CONTROL, FINANCE, OR INFLUENCE EVERY SINGLE CRIMINAL ENTERPRISE IN THE SECTOR.
FROM MAJOR WEAPONS SHIPMENTS TO TINY, FLEA-INFESTED CARD GAMES IN DISGUSTING LITTLE BACKWATERS.
SO YOU CAN IMAGINE HOW EASY IT WAS FOR ME TO LEARN OF YOUR TRUE INTENTIONS.
ESPECIALLY GIVEN YOU SPOUTED THEM OUT WITH OH, SO MUCH BRAVADO IN ONE OF MY CANTINAS.
IT WILL BE SIMPLE, SAVAGE. WE PRESENT THE OFFER, ONE TOO GOOD TO REFUSE. THEN, ONCE WE HAVE GAINED HIS FAVOR, WE SIMPLY... END HIM.
HIS SOLDIERS AND HIS ENTERPRISE WILL BE OURS.
HENCE THE WARM WELCOME...

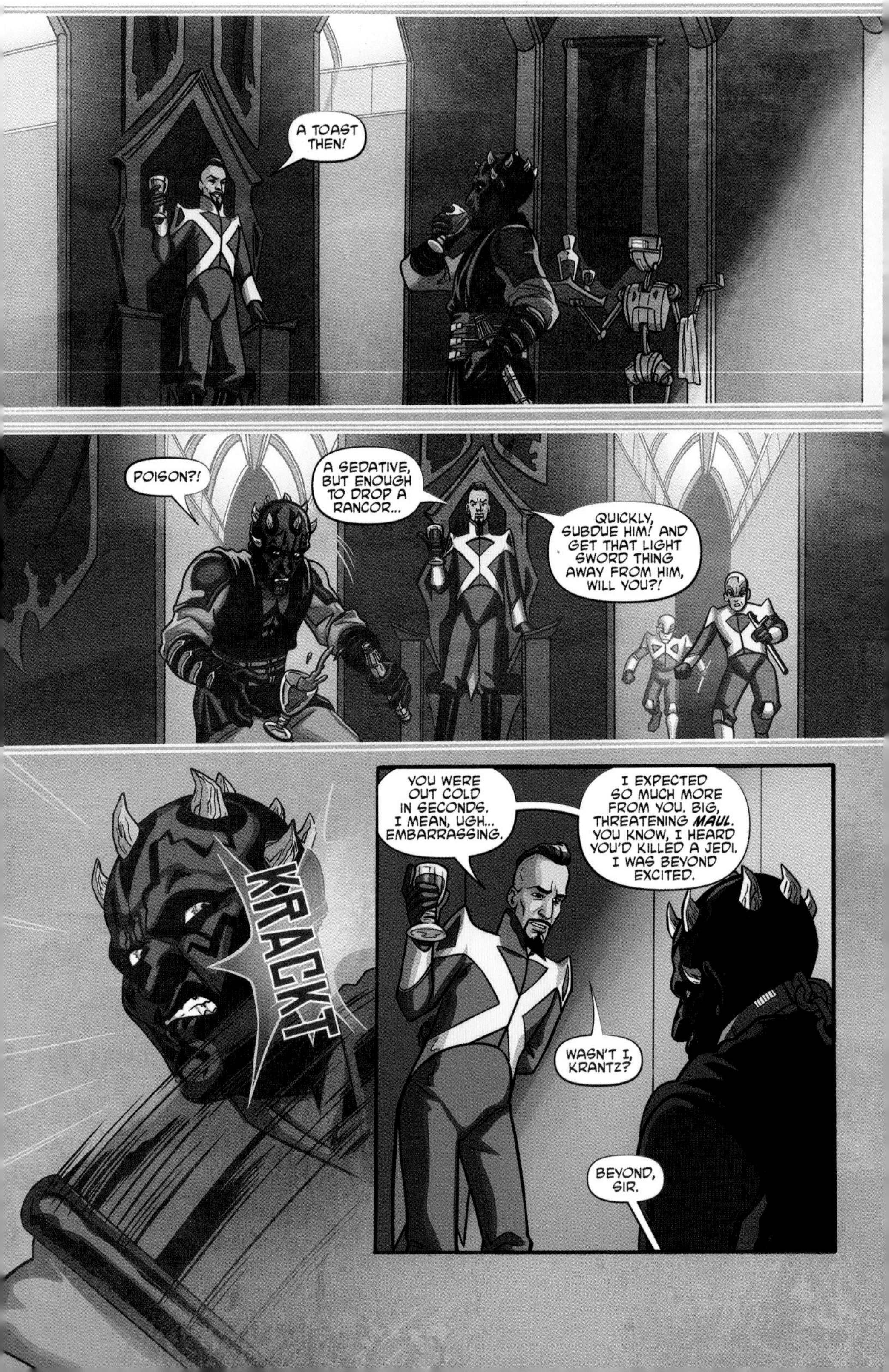
A TOAST THEN!
POISON?!
A SEDATIVE, BUT ENOUGH TO DROP A RANCOR...
QUICKLY, SUBDUE HIM! AND GET THAT LIGHT SWORD THING AWAY FROM HIM, WILL YOU?!
KRACKT
YOU WERE OUT COLD IN SECONDS. I MEAN, UGH... EMBARRASSING.
I EXPECTED SO MUCH MORE FROM YOU. BIG, THREATENING MAUL. YOU KNOW, I HEARD YOU'D KILLED A JEDI. I WAS BEYOND EXCITED.
WASN'T I, KRANTZ?
BEYOND, SIR.

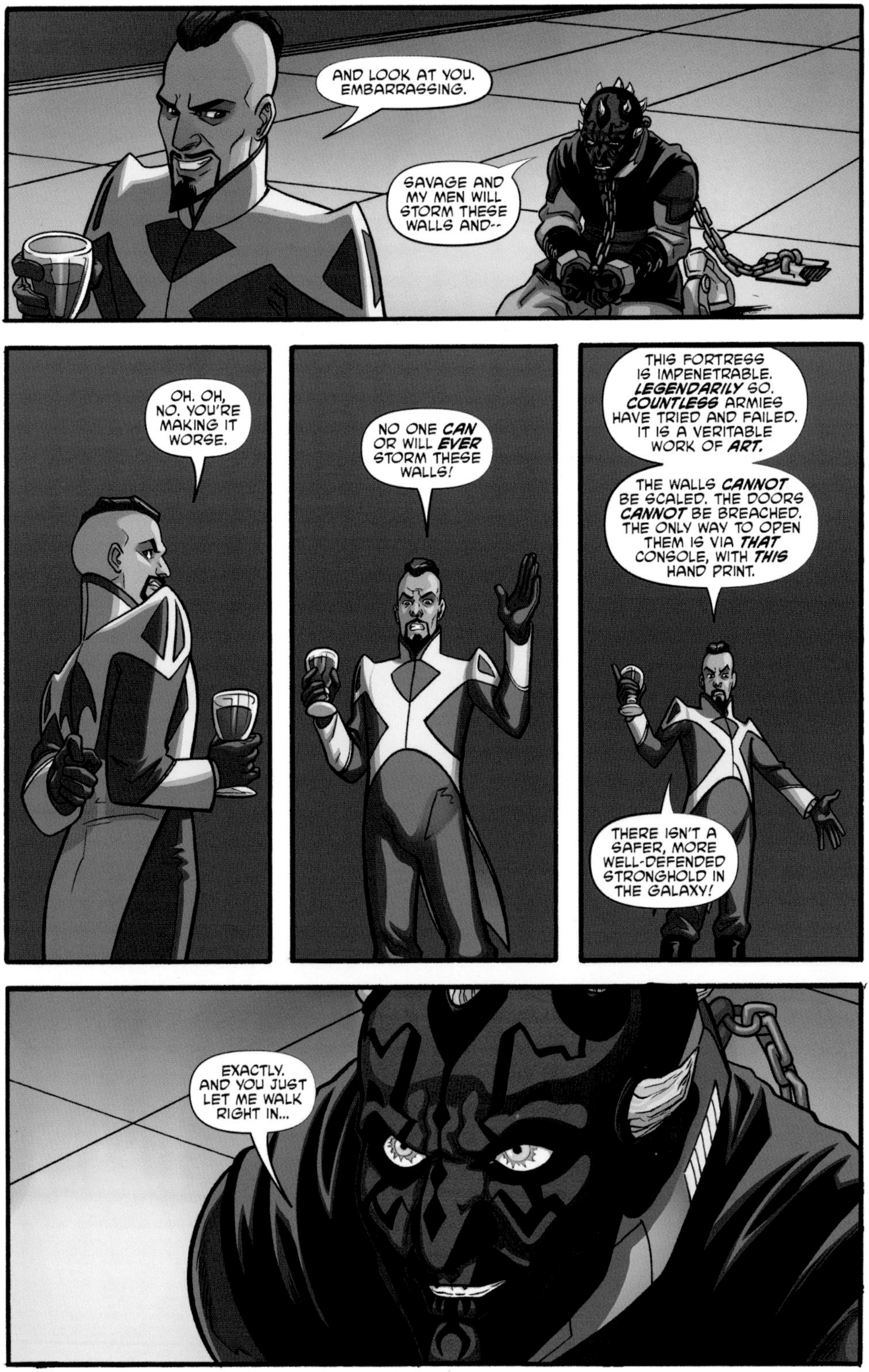
AND LOOK AT YOU. EMBARRASSING.
SAVAGE AND MY MEN WILL STORM THESE WALLS AND--
OH. OH, NO. YOU'RE MAKING IT WORSE.
NO ONE CAN OR WILL EVER STORM THESE WALLS!
THIS FORTRESS IS IMPENETRABLE. LEGENDARILY SO. COUNTLESS ARMIES HAVE TRIED AND FAILED. IT IS A VERITABLE WORK OF ART.
THE WALLS CANNOT BE SCALED. THE DOORS CANNOT BE BREACHED. THE ONLY WAY TO OPEN THEM IS VIA THAT CONSOLE, WITH THIS HAND PRINT.
THERE ISN'T A SAFER, MORE WELL-DEFENDED STRONGHOLD IN THE GALAXY!
EXACTLY. AND YOU JUST LET ME WALK RIGHT IN...

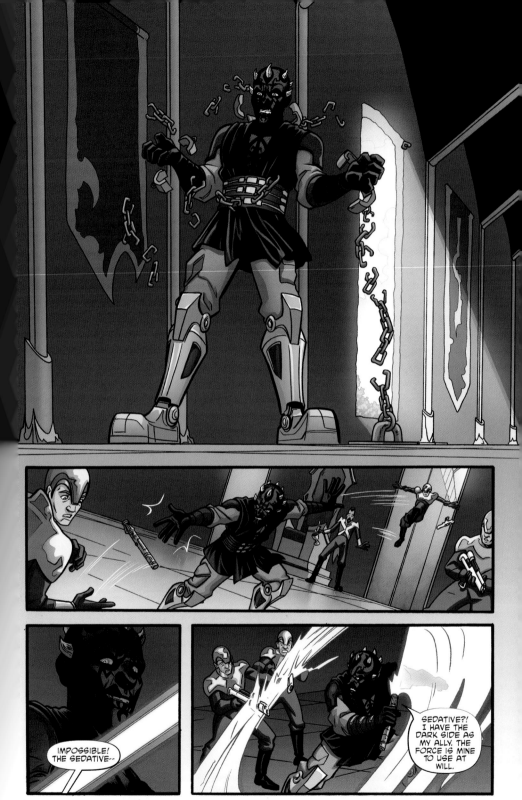

IMPOSSIBLE!
THE SEDATIVE--

SEDATIVE?!
I HAVE THE
DARK SIDE AS
MY ALLY. THE
FORCE IS MINE
TO USE AT
WILL.

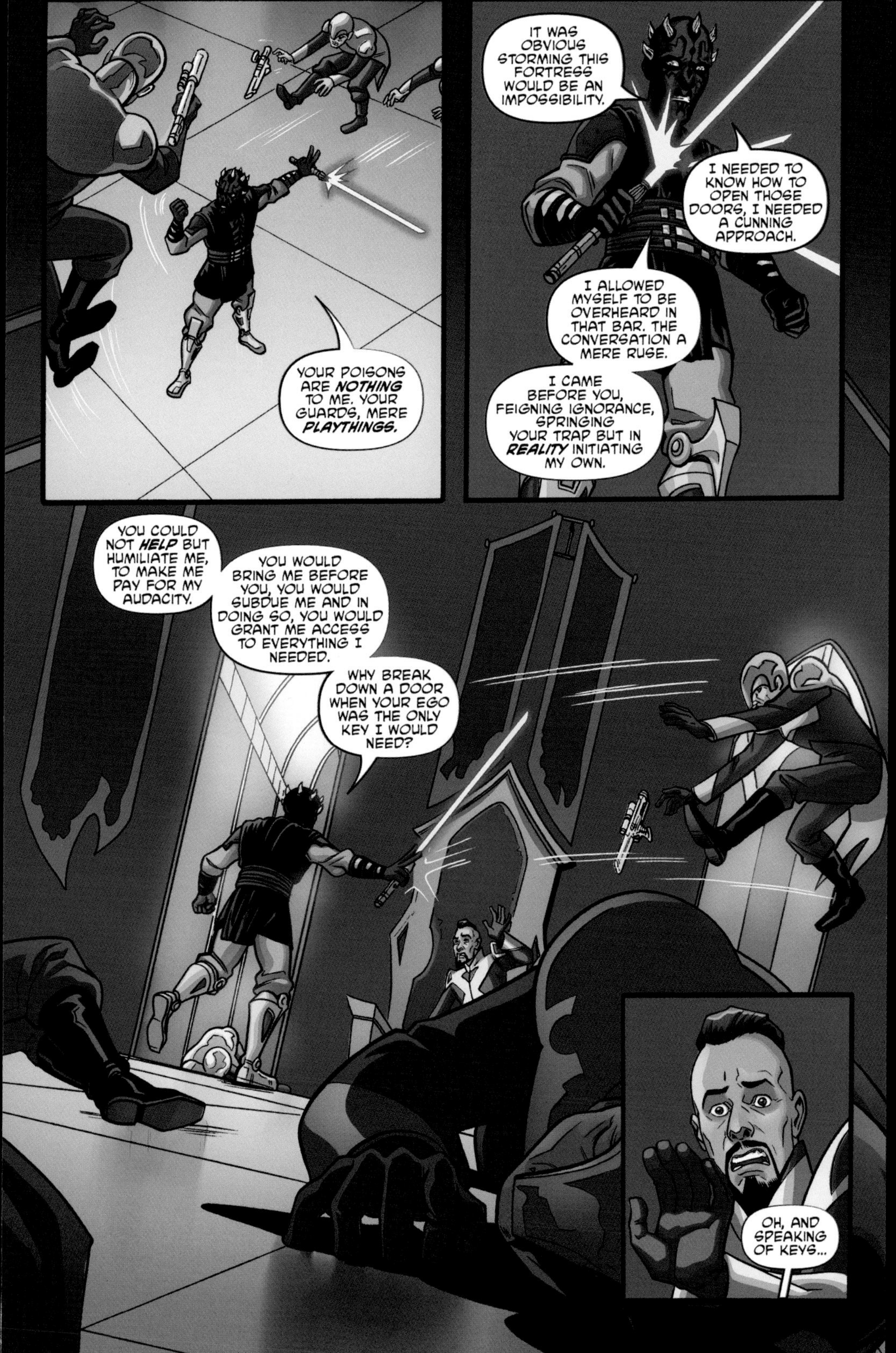

YOUR POISONS ARE *NOTHING* TO ME. YOUR GUARDS, MERE *PLAYTHINGS.*
IT WAS OBVIOUS STORMING THIS FORTRESS WOULD BE AN IMPOSSIBILITY.
I NEEDED TO KNOW HOW TO OPEN THOSE DOORS, I NEEDED A CUNNING APPROACH.
I ALLOWED MYSELF TO BE OVERHEARD IN THAT BAR. THE CONVERSATION A MERE RUSE.
I CAME BEFORE YOU, FEIGNING IGNORANCE, SPRINGING YOUR TRAP BUT IN *REALITY* INITIATING MY OWN.
YOU COULD NOT *HELP* BUT HUMILIATE ME, TO MAKE ME PAY FOR MY AUDACITY.
YOU WOULD BRING ME BEFORE YOU, YOU WOULD SUBDUE ME AND IN DOING SO, YOU WOULD GRANT ME ACCESS TO EVERYTHING I NEEDED.
WHY BREAK DOWN A DOOR WHEN YOUR EGO WAS THE ONLY KEY I WOULD NEED?
OH, AND SPEAKING OF KEYS...

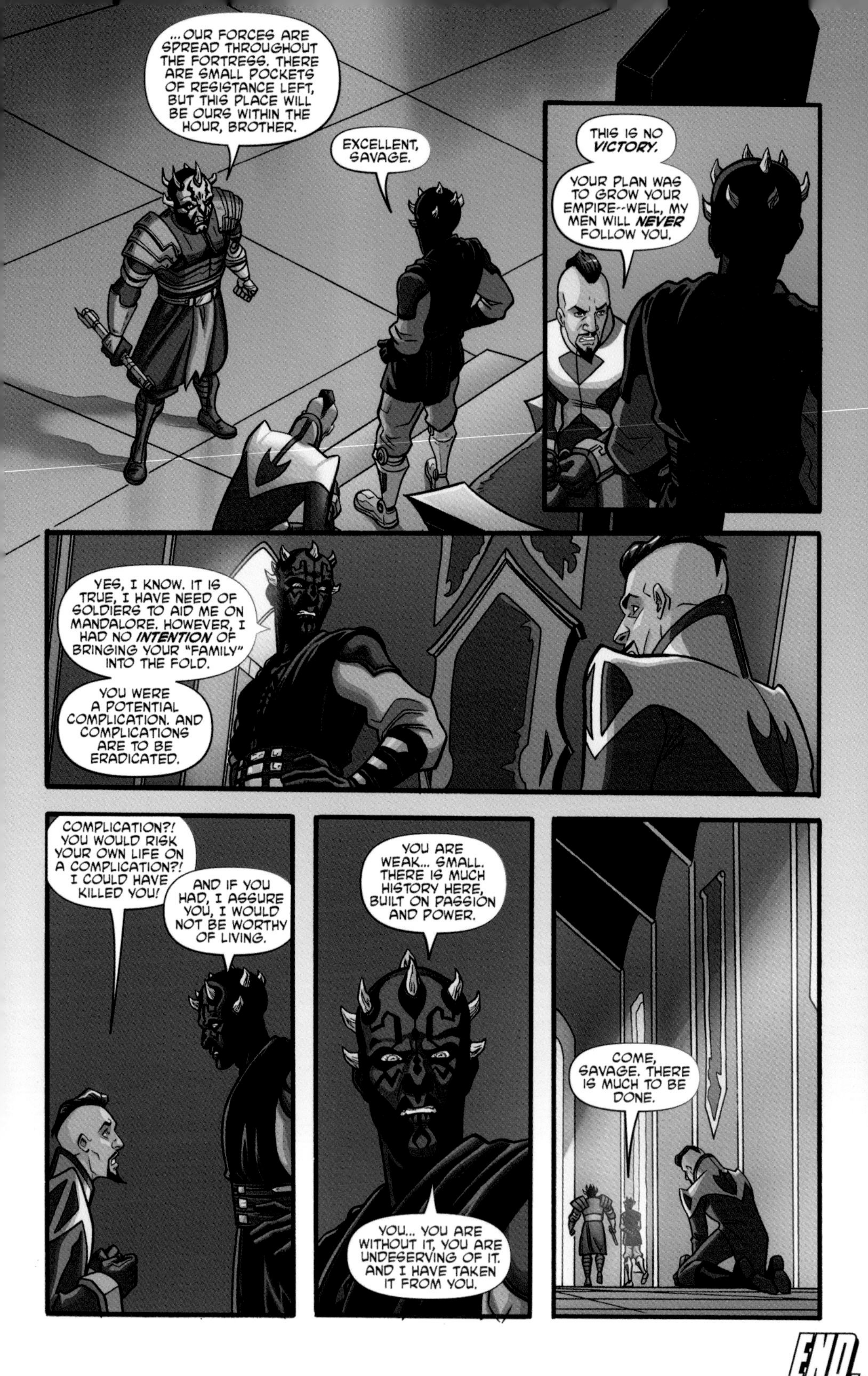
...OUR FORCES ARE SPREAD THROUGHOUT THE FORTRESS. THERE ARE SMALL POCKETS OF RESISTANCE LEFT, BUT THIS PLACE WILL BE OURS WITHIN THE HOUR, BROTHER.
EXCELLENT, SAVAGE.
THIS IS NO *VICTORY.*
YOUR PLAN WAS TO GROW YOUR EMPIRE--WELL, MY MEN WILL *NEVER* FOLLOW YOU.
YES, I KNOW. IT IS TRUE, I HAVE NEED OF SOLDIERS TO AID ME ON MANDALORE. HOWEVER, I HAD NO *INTENTION* OF BRINGING YOUR "FAMILY" INTO THE FOLD.
YOU WERE A POTENTIAL COMPLICATION. AND COMPLICATIONS ARE TO BE ERADICATED.
COMPLICATION?! YOU WOULD RISK YOUR OWN LIFE ON A COMPLICATION?! I COULD HAVE KILLED YOU!
AND IF YOU HAD, I ASSURE YOU, I WOULD NOT BE WORTHY OF LIVING.
YOU ARE WEAK... SMALL. THERE IS MUCH HISTORY HERE, BUILT ON PASSION AND POWER.
YOU... YOU ARE WITHOUT IT, YOU ARE UNDESERVING OF IT. AND I HAVE TAKEN IT FROM YOU.
COME, SAVAGE. THERE IS MUCH TO BE DONE.
END.

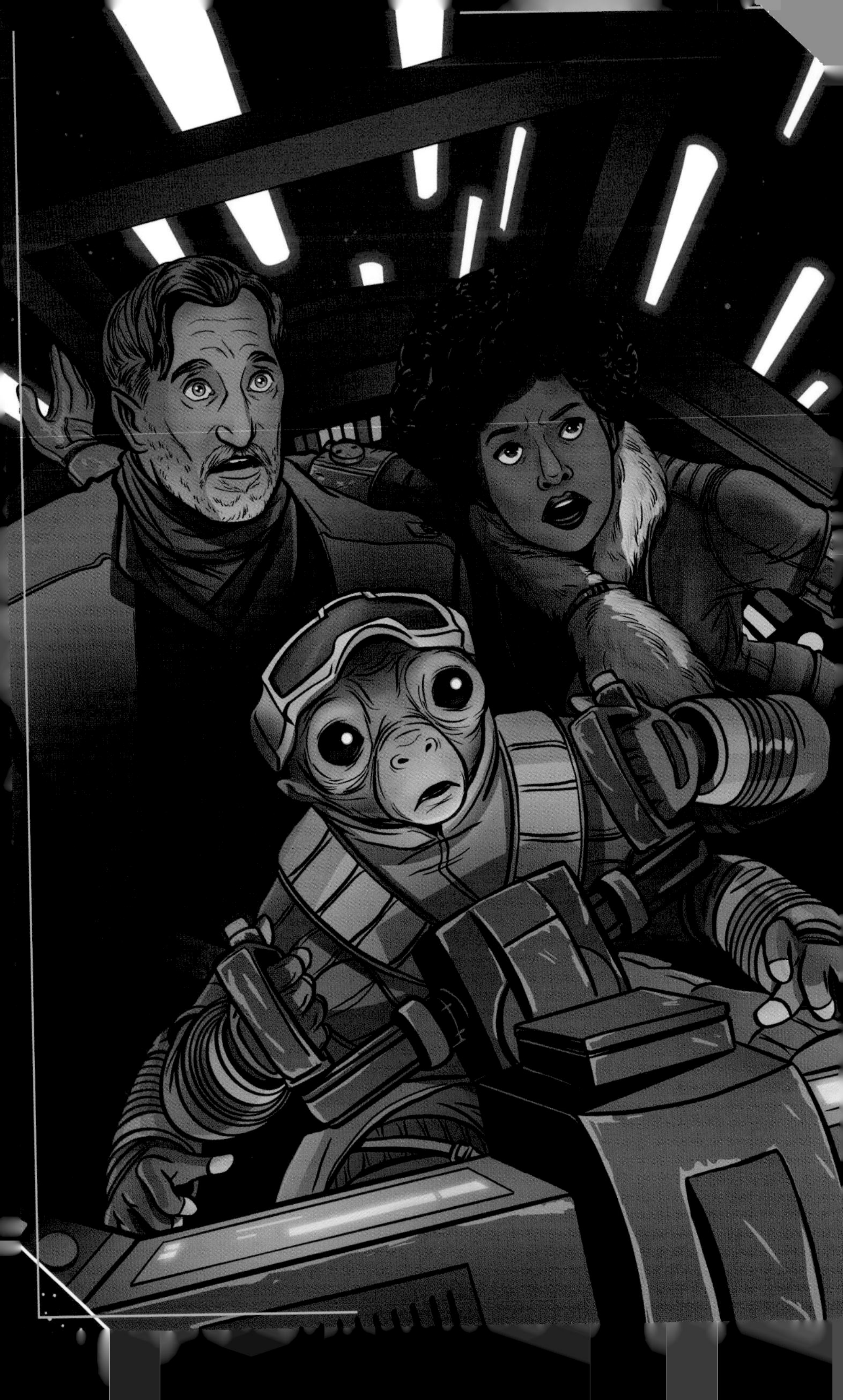

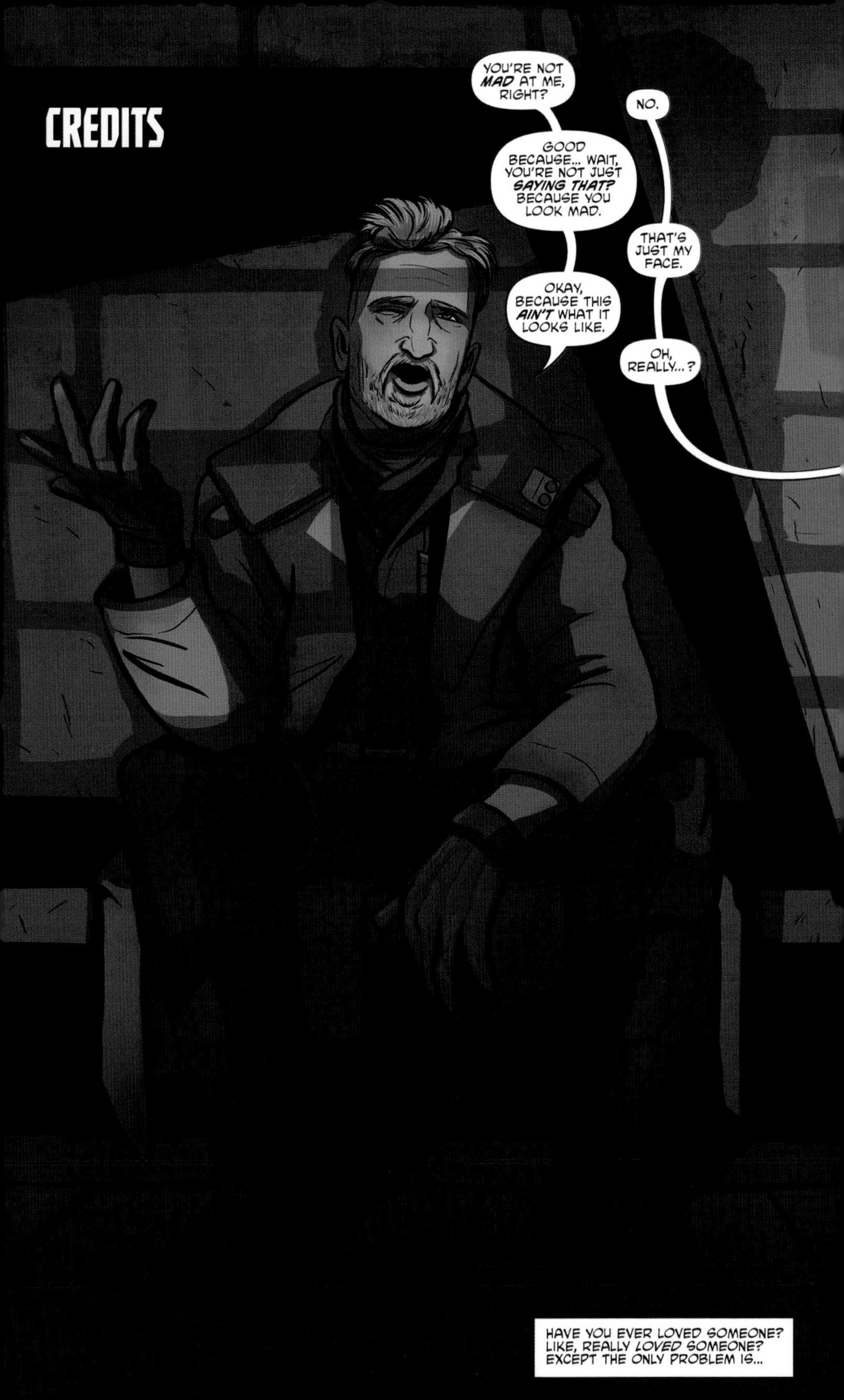
CREDITS
YOU'RE NOT *MAD* AT ME, RIGHT?
NO.
GOOD BECAUSE... WAIT, YOU'RE NOT JUST *SAYING THAT?* BECAUSE YOU LOOK MAD.
THAT'S JUST MY FACE.
OKAY, BECAUSE THIS *AIN'T* WHAT IT LOOKS LIKE.
OH, REALLY...?
HAVE YOU EVER LOVED SOMEONE? LIKE, REALLY *LOVED* SOMEONE? EXCEPT THE ONLY PROBLEM IS...

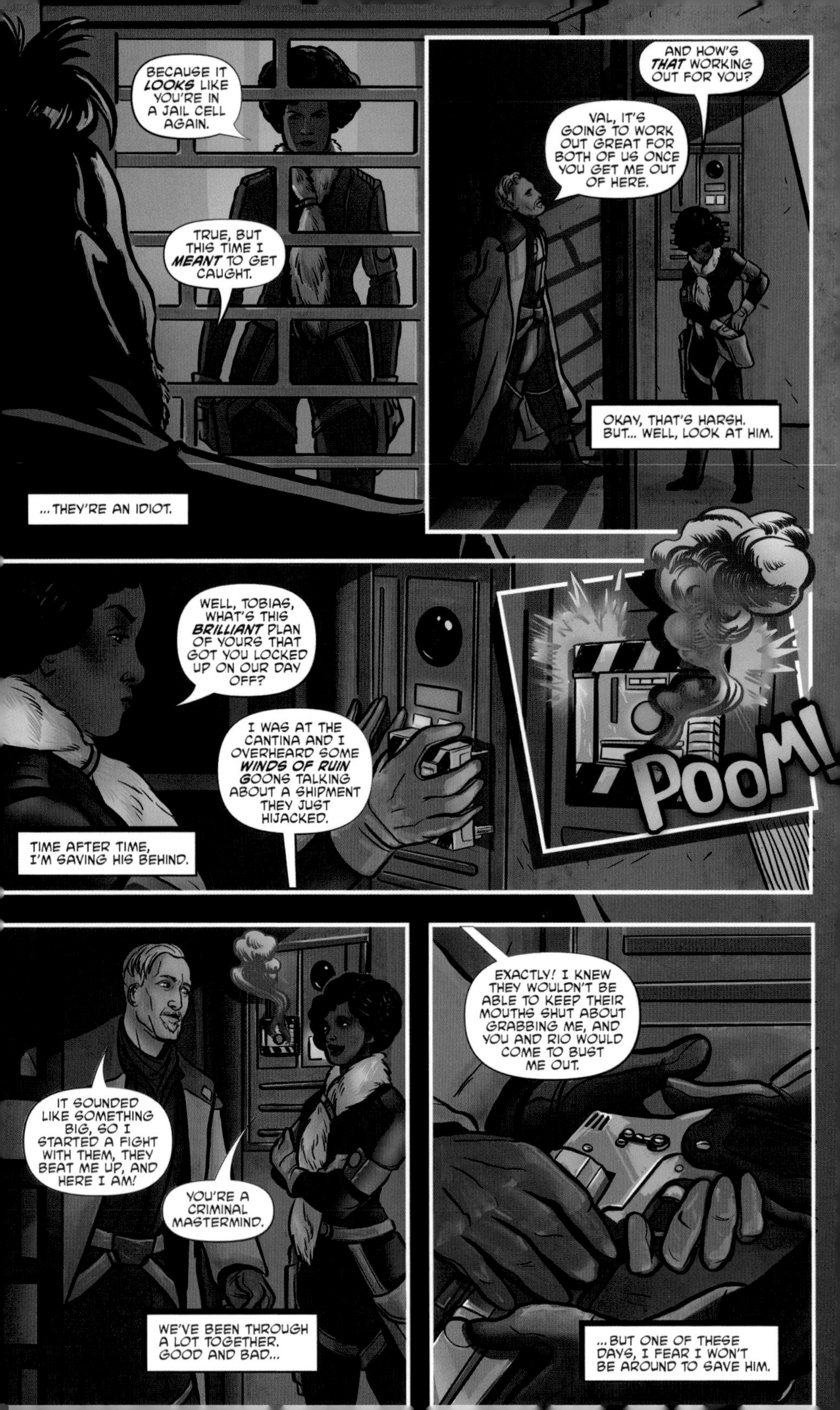
BECAUSE IT LOOKS LIKE YOU'RE IN A JAIL CELL AGAIN.
TRUE, BUT THIS TIME I MEANT TO GET CAUGHT.
...THEY'RE AN IDIOT.
AND HOW'S THAT WORKING OUT FOR YOU?
VAL, IT'S GOING TO WORK OUT GREAT FOR BOTH OF US ONCE YOU GET ME OUT OF HERE.
OKAY, THAT'S HARSH. BUT... WELL, LOOK AT HIM.
WELL, TOBIAS, WHAT'S THIS BRILLIANT PLAN OF YOURS THAT GOT YOU LOCKED UP ON OUR DAY OFF?
I WAS AT THE CANTINA AND I OVERHEARD SOME WINDS OF RUIN GOONS TALKING ABOUT A SHIPMENT THEY JUST HIJACKED.
TIME AFTER TIME, I'M SAVING HIS BEHIND.
POOM!
IT SOUNDED LIKE SOMETHING BIG, SO I STARTED A FIGHT WITH THEM, THEY BEAT ME UP, AND HERE I AM!
YOU'RE A CRIMINAL MASTERMIND.
WE'VE BEEN THROUGH A LOT TOGETHER. GOOD AND BAD...
EXACTLY! I KNEW THEY WOULDN'T BE ABLE TO KEEP THEIR MOUTHS SHUT ABOUT GRABBING ME, AND YOU AND RIO WOULD COME TO BUST ME OUT.
...BUT ONE OF THESE DAYS, I FEAR I WON'T BE AROUND TO SAVE HIM.

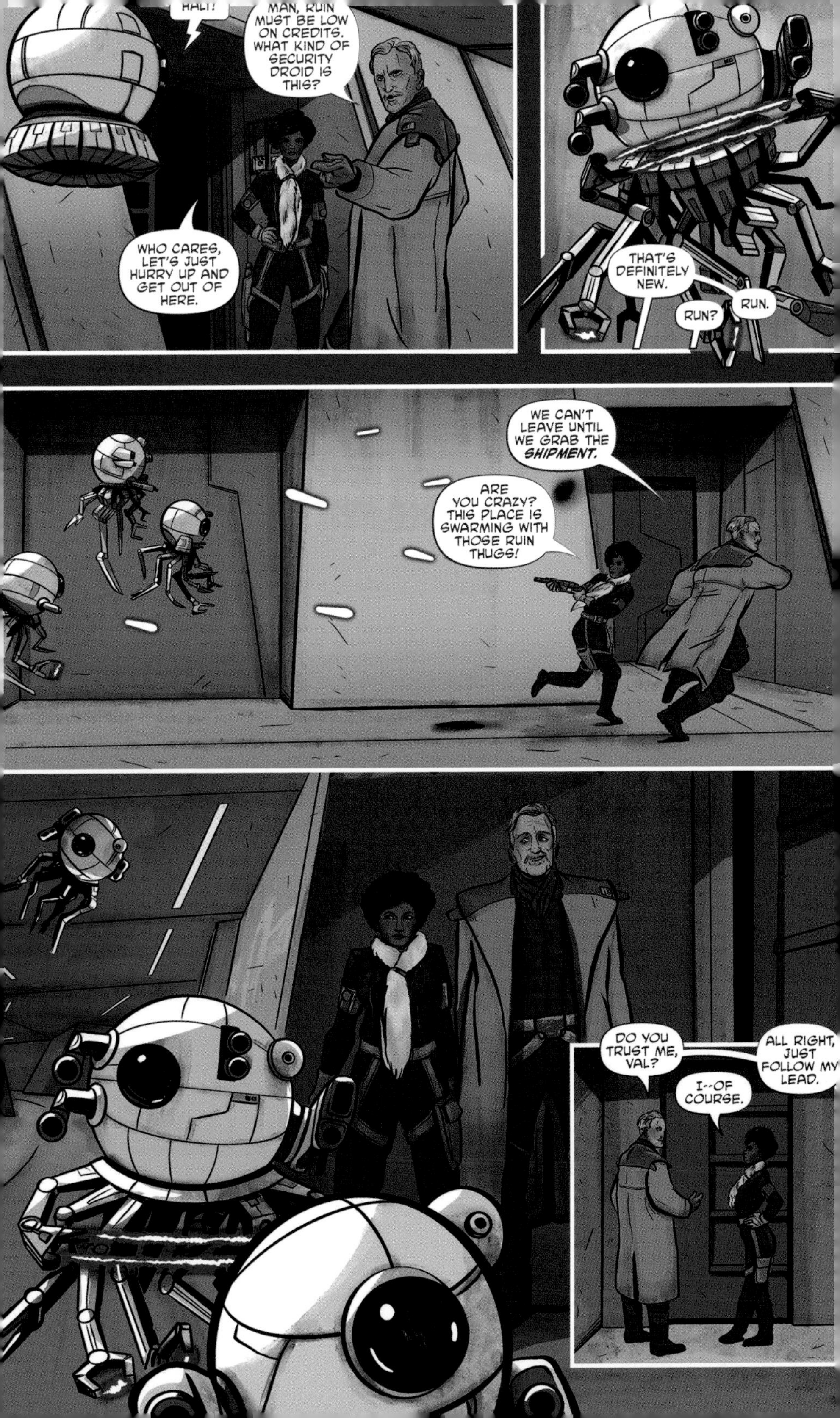
HALT!
MAN, RUIN MUST BE LOW ON CREDITS. WHAT KIND OF SECURITY DROID IS THIS?
WHO CARES, LET'S JUST HURRY UP AND GET OUT OF HERE.
THAT'S DEFINITELY NEW.
RUN?
RUN.
WE CAN'T LEAVE UNTIL WE GRAB THE SHIPMENT.
ARE YOU CRAZY? THIS PLACE IS SWARMING WITH THOSE RUIN THUGS!
DO YOU TRUST ME, VAL?
I--OF COURSE.
ALL RIGHT, JUST FOLLOW MY LEAD.

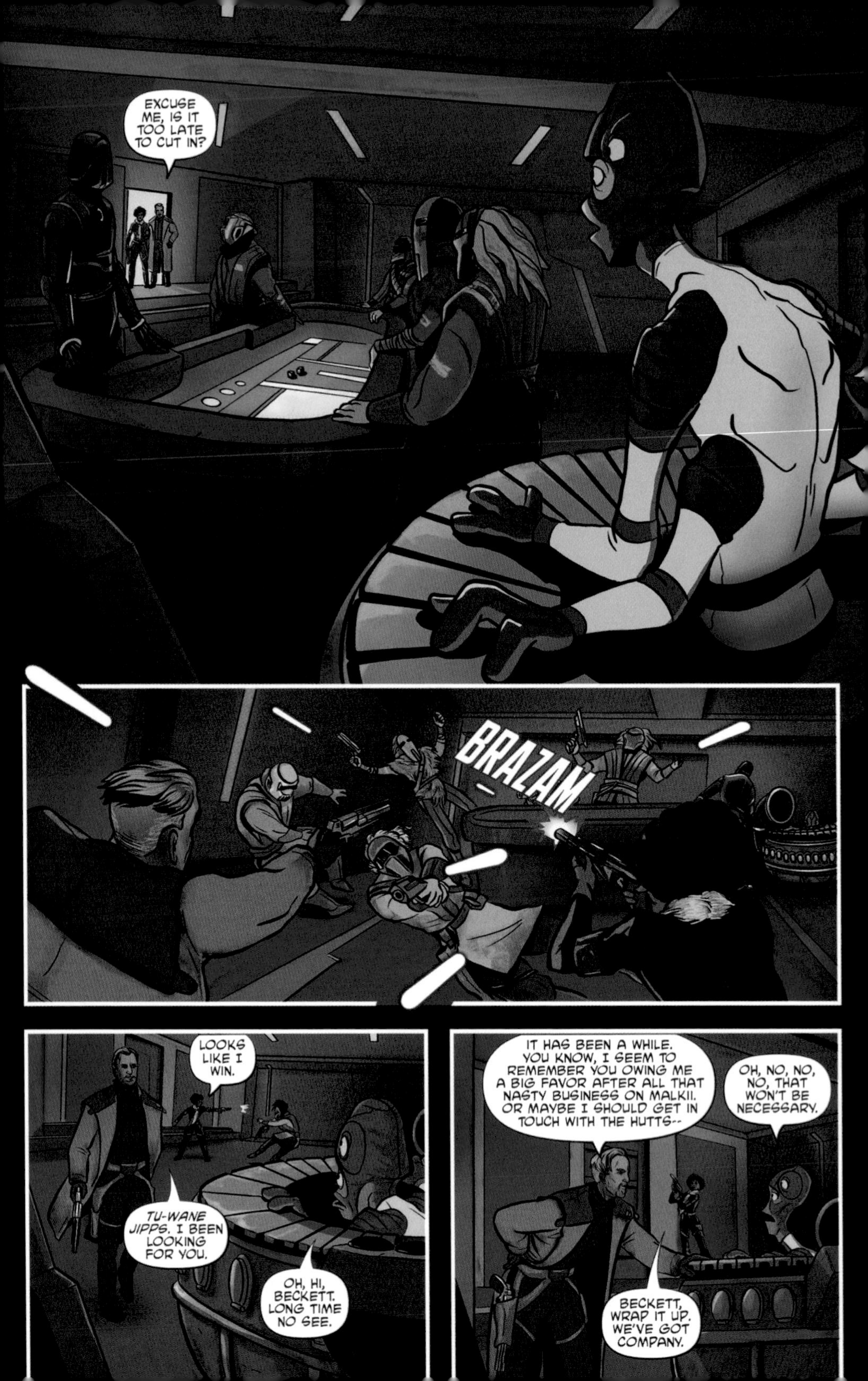
EXCUSE ME, IS IT TOO LATE TO CUT IN?
BRAZAM
LOOKS LIKE I WIN.
TU-WANE JIPPS. I BEEN LOOKING FOR YOU.
OH, HI, BECKETT. LONG TIME NO SEE.
IT HAS BEEN A WHILE. YOU KNOW, I SEEM TO REMEMBER YOU OWING ME A BIG FAVOR AFTER ALL THAT NASTY BUSINESS ON MALKII. OR MAYBE I SHOULD GET IN TOUCH WITH THE HUTTS--
OH, NO, NO, NO, THAT WON'T BE NECESSARY.
BECKETT, WRAP IT UP. WE'VE GOT COMPANY.

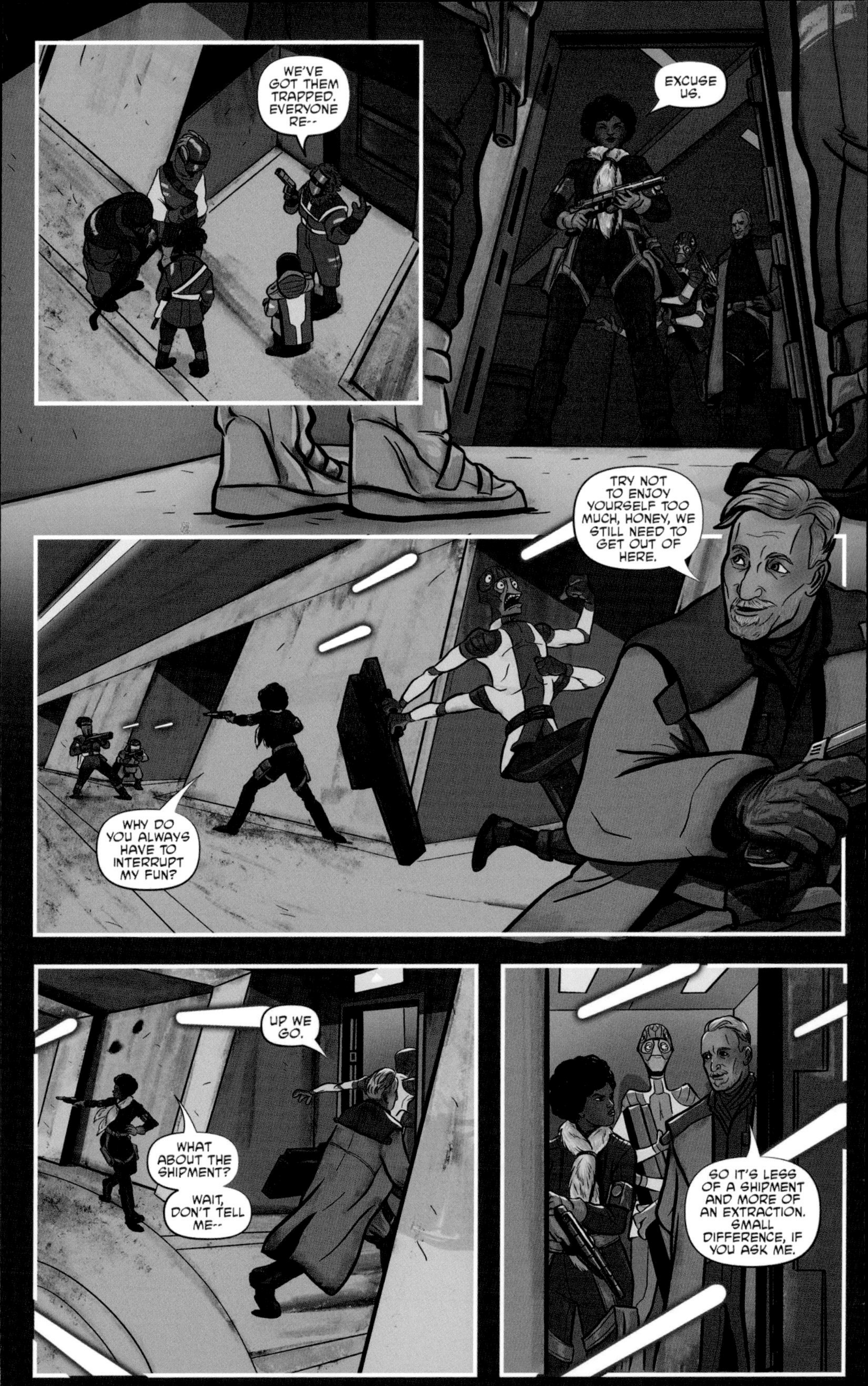
WE'VE GOT THEM TRAPPED. EVERYONE RE--
EXCUSE US.
TRY NOT TO ENJOY YOURSELF TOO MUCH, HONEY, WE STILL NEED TO GET OUT OF HERE.
WHY DO YOU ALWAYS HAVE TO INTERRUPT MY FUN?
UP WE GO.
WHAT ABOUT THE SHIPMENT?
WAIT, DON'T TELL ME--
SO IT'S LESS OF A SHIPMENT AND MORE OF AN EXTRACTION. SMALL DIFFERENCE, IF YOU ASK ME.

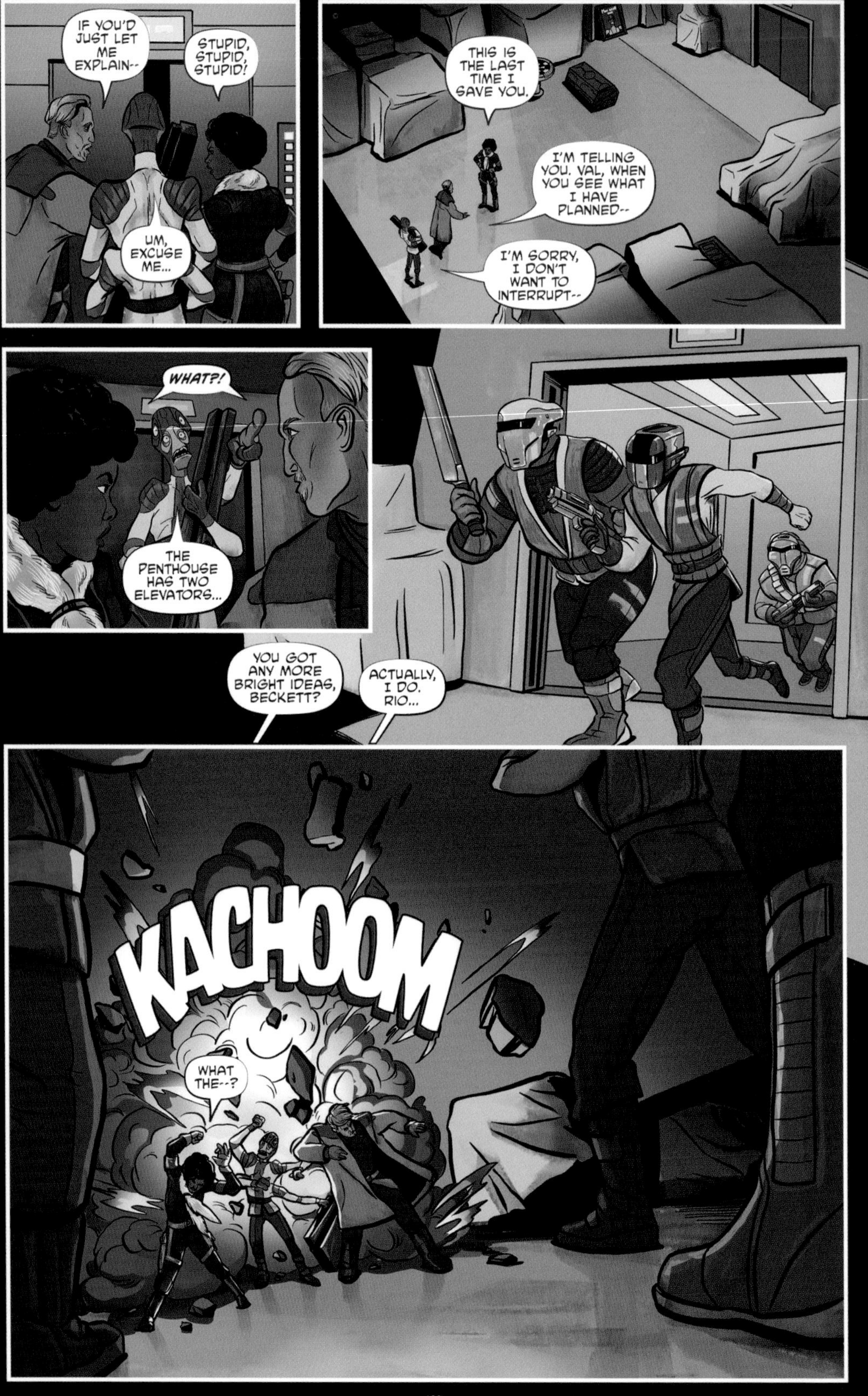
IF YOU'D JUST LET ME EXPLAIN--
STUPID, STUPID, STUPID!
UM, EXCUSE ME...
THIS IS THE LAST TIME I SAVE YOU.
I'M TELLING YOU. VAL, WHEN YOU SEE WHAT I HAVE PLANNED--
I'M SORRY, I DON'T WANT TO INTERRUPT--
WHAT?!
THE PENTHOUSE HAS TWO ELEVATORS...
YOU GOT ANY MORE BRIGHT IDEAS, BECKETT?
ACTUALLY, I DO. RIO...
KACHOOM
WHAT THE--?

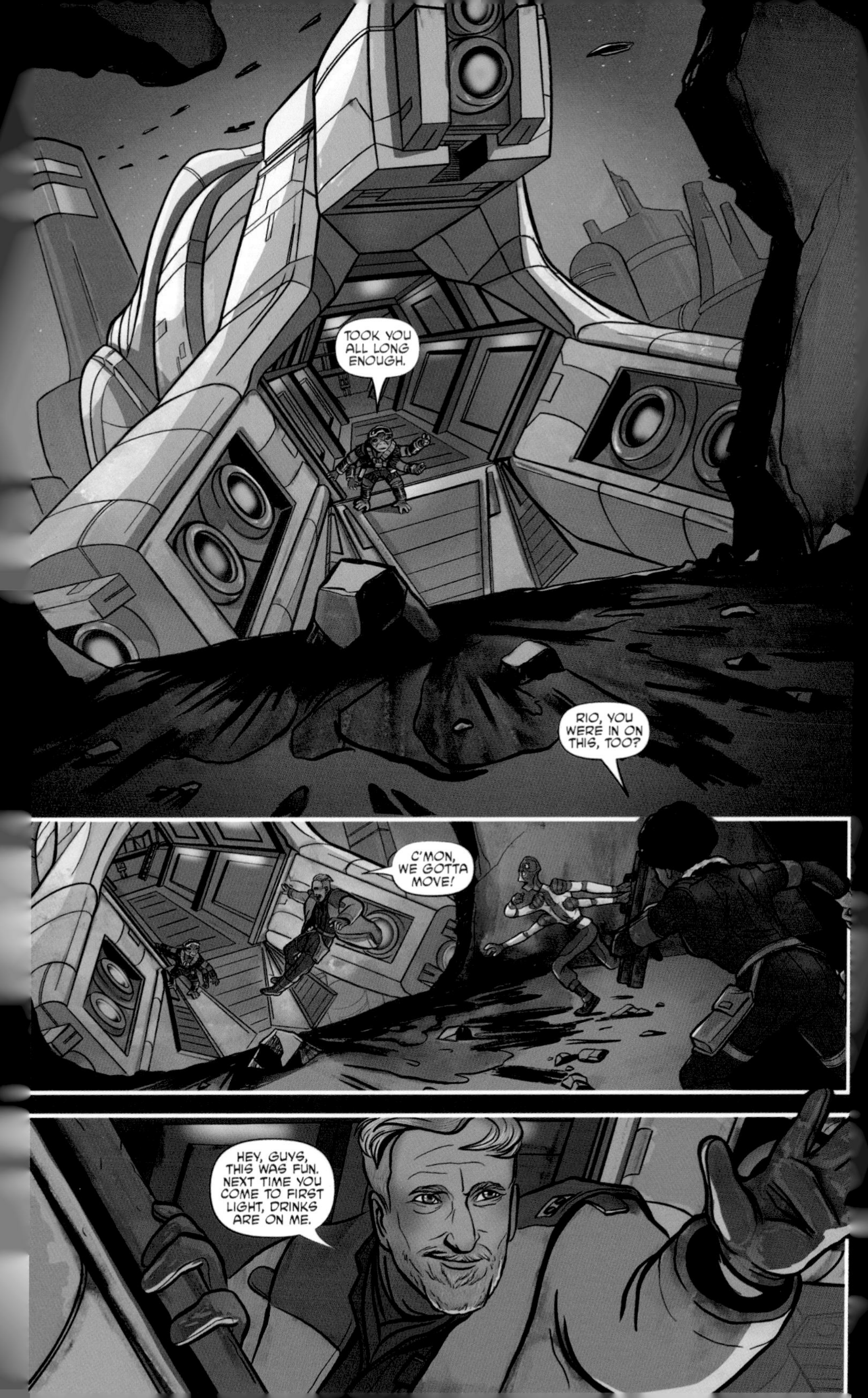
TOOK YOU ALL LONG ENOUGH.
RIO, YOU WERE IN ON THIS, TOO?
C'MON, WE GOTTA MOVE!
HEY, GUYS, THIS WAS FUN. NEXT TIME YOU COME TO FIRST LIGHT, DRINKS ARE ON ME.

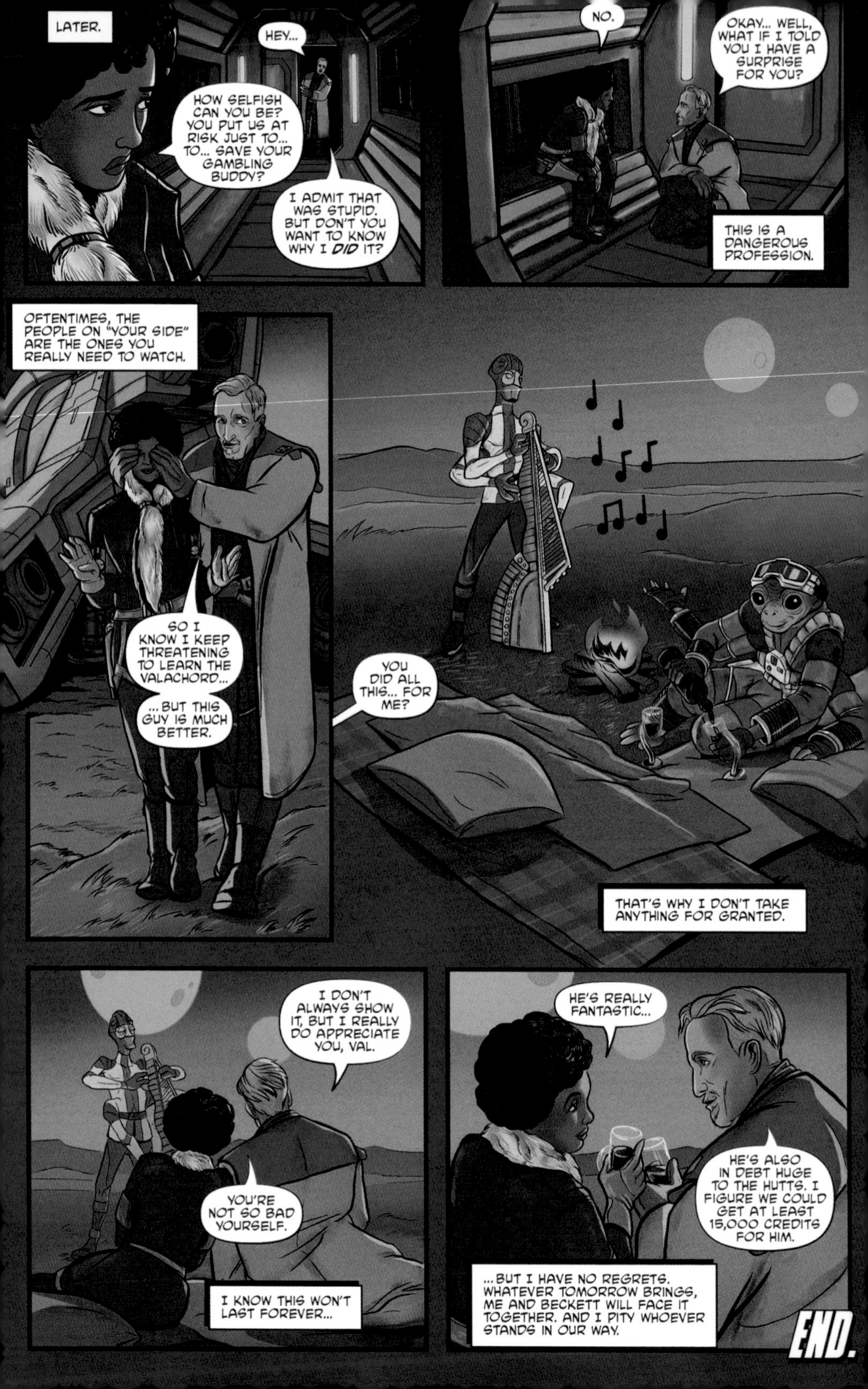
LATER.
HEY...
HOW SELFISH CAN YOU BE? YOU PUT US AT RISK JUST TO... TO... SAVE YOUR GAMBLING BUDDY?
I ADMIT THAT WAS STUPID. BUT DON'T YOU WANT TO KNOW WHY I DID IT?
NO.
OKAY... WELL, WHAT IF I TOLD YOU I HAVE A SURPRISE FOR YOU?
THIS IS A DANGEROUS PROFESSION.
OFTENTIMES, THE PEOPLE ON "YOUR SIDE" ARE THE ONES YOU REALLY NEED TO WATCH.
SO I KNOW I KEEP THREATENING TO LEARN THE VALACHORD...
...BUT THIS GUY IS MUCH BETTER.
YOU DID ALL THIS... FOR ME?
THAT'S WHY I DON'T TAKE ANYTHING FOR GRANTED.
I DON'T ALWAYS SHOW IT, BUT I REALLY DO APPRECIATE YOU, VAL.
YOU'RE NOT SO BAD YOURSELF.
I KNOW THIS WON'T LAST FOREVER...
HE'S REALLY FANTASTIC...
HE'S ALSO IN DEBT HUGE TO THE HUTTS. I FIGURE WE COULD GET AT LEAST 15,000 CREDITS FOR HIM.
...BUT I HAVE NO REGRETS. WHATEVER TOMORROW BRINGS, ME AND BECKETT WILL FACE IT TOGETHER. AND I PITY WHOEVER STANDS IN OUR WAY.
END.

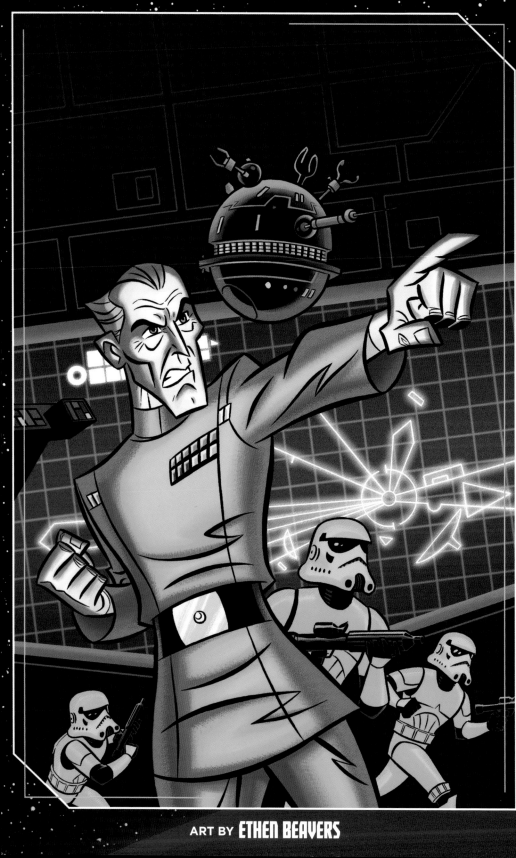

ART BY **ETHEN BEAVERS**

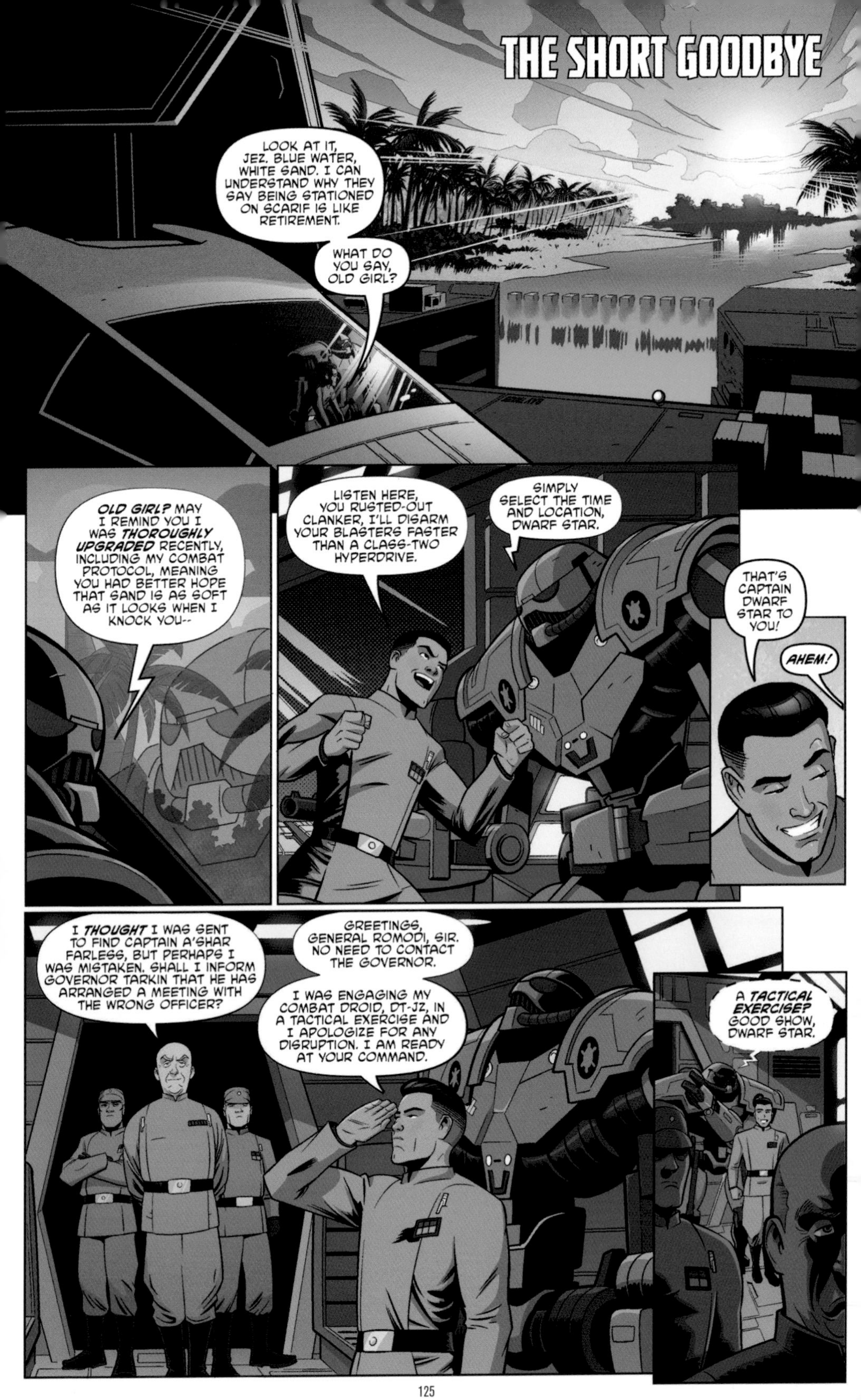
THE SHORT GOODBYE
LOOK AT IT, JEZ. BLUE WATER, WHITE SAND. I CAN UNDERSTAND WHY THEY SAY BEING STATIONED ON SCARIF IS LIKE RETIREMENT.
WHAT DO YOU SAY, OLD GIRL?
OLD GIRL? MAY I REMIND YOU I WAS THOROUGHLY UPGRADED RECENTLY, INCLUDING MY COMBAT PROTOCOL, MEANING YOU HAD BETTER HOPE THAT SAND IS AS SOFT AS IT LOOKS WHEN I KNOCK YOU--
LISTEN HERE, YOU RUSTED-OUT CLANKER, I'LL DISARM YOUR BLASTERS FASTER THAN A CLASS-TWO HYPERDRIVE.
SIMPLY SELECT THE TIME AND LOCATION, DWARF STAR.
THAT'S CAPTAIN DWARF STAR TO YOU!
AHEM!
I THOUGHT I WAS SENT TO FIND CAPTAIN A'SHAR FARLESS, BUT PERHAPS I WAS MISTAKEN. SHALL I INFORM GOVERNOR TARKIN THAT HE HAS ARRANGED A MEETING WITH THE WRONG OFFICER?
GREETINGS, GENERAL ROMODI, SIR. NO NEED TO CONTACT THE GOVERNOR.
I WAS ENGAGING MY COMBAT DROID, DT-JZ, IN A TACTICAL EXERCISE AND I APOLOGIZE FOR ANY DISRUPTION. I AM READY AT YOUR COMMAND.
A TACTICAL EXERCISE? GOOD SHOW, DWARF STAR.

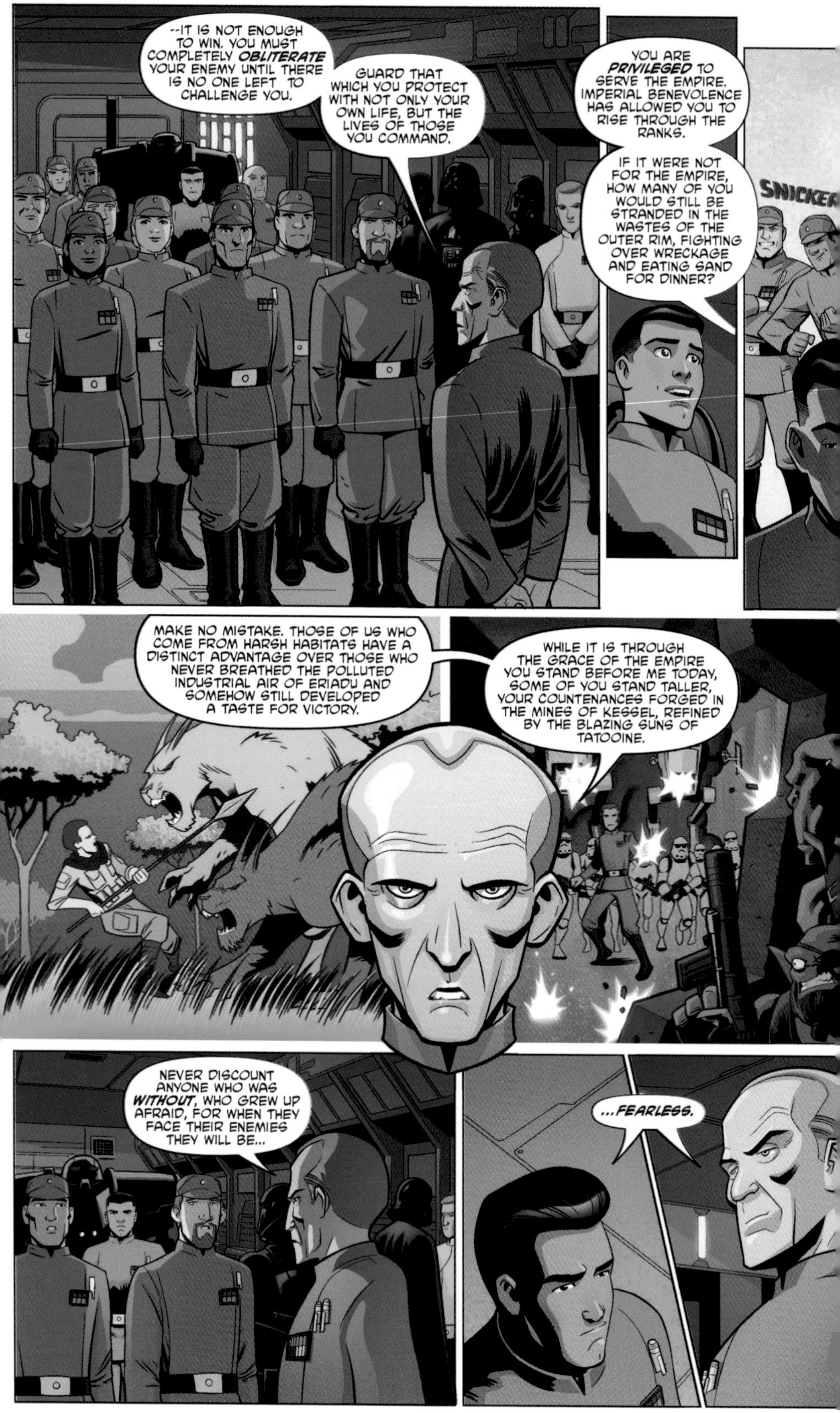
--IT IS NOT ENOUGH TO WIN. YOU MUST COMPLETELY OBLITERATE YOUR ENEMY UNTIL THERE IS NO ONE LEFT TO CHALLENGE YOU.
GUARD THAT WHICH YOU PROTECT WITH NOT ONLY YOUR OWN LIFE, BUT THE LIVES OF THOSE YOU COMMAND.
YOU ARE PRIVILEGED TO SERVE THE EMPIRE. IMPERIAL BENEVOLENCE HAS ALLOWED YOU TO RISE THROUGH THE RANKS.
IF IT WERE NOT FOR THE EMPIRE, HOW MANY OF YOU WOULD STILL BE STRANDED IN THE WASTES OF THE OUTER RIM, FIGHTING OVER WRECKAGE AND EATING SAND FOR DINNER?
SNICKER
MAKE NO MISTAKE. THOSE OF US WHO COME FROM HARSH HABITATS HAVE A DISTINCT ADVANTAGE OVER THOSE WHO NEVER BREATHED THE POLLUTED INDUSTRIAL AIR OF ERIADU AND SOMEHOW STILL DEVELOPED A TASTE FOR VICTORY.
WHILE IT IS THROUGH THE GRACE OF THE EMPIRE YOU STAND BEFORE ME TODAY, SOME OF YOU STAND TALLER, YOUR COUNTENANCES FORGED IN THE MINES OF KESSEL, REFINED BY THE BLAZING SUNS OF TATOOINE.
NEVER DISCOUNT ANYONE WHO WAS WITHOUT, WHO GREW UP AFRAID, FOR WHEN THEY FACE THEIR ENEMIES THEY WILL BE...
...FEARLESS.

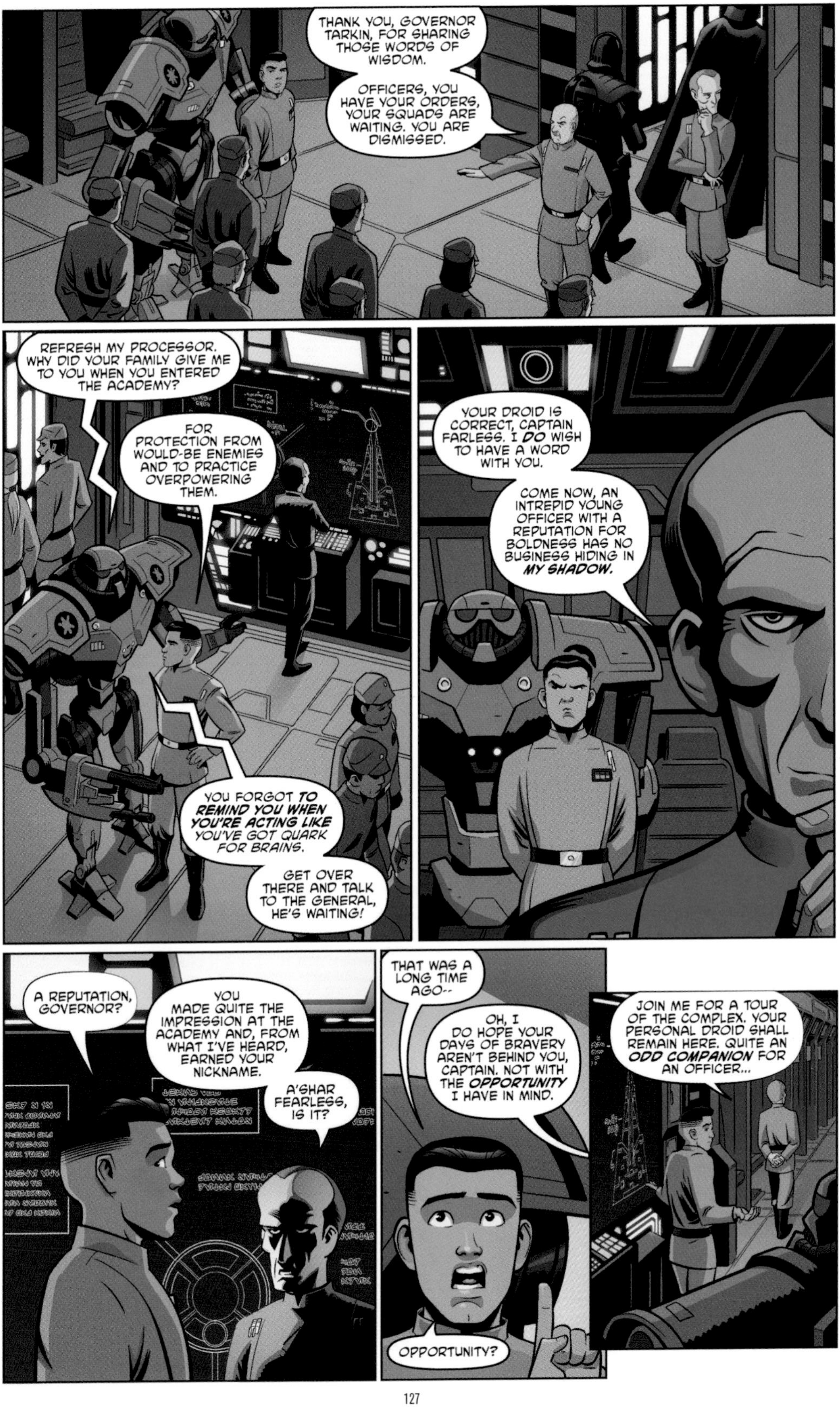
THANK YOU, GOVERNOR TARKIN, FOR SHARING THOSE WORDS OF WISDOM.
OFFICERS, YOU HAVE YOUR ORDERS, YOUR SQUADS ARE WAITING. YOU ARE DISMISSED.
REFRESH MY PROCESSOR. WHY DID YOUR FAMILY GIVE ME TO YOU WHEN YOU ENTERED THE ACADEMY?
FOR PROTECTION FROM WOULD-BE ENEMIES AND TO PRACTICE OVERPOWERING THEM.
YOU FORGOT TO REMIND YOU WHEN YOU'RE ACTING LIKE YOU'VE GOT QUARK FOR BRAINS.
GET OVER THERE AND TALK TO THE GENERAL, HE'S WAITING!
YOUR DROID IS CORRECT, CAPTAIN FARLESS. I DO WISH TO HAVE A WORD WITH YOU.
COME NOW, AN INTREPID YOUNG OFFICER WITH A REPUTATION FOR BOLDNESS HAS NO BUSINESS HIDING IN MY SHADOW.
A REPUTATION, GOVERNOR?
YOU MADE QUITE THE IMPRESSION AT THE ACADEMY AND, FROM WHAT I'VE HEARD, EARNED YOUR NICKNAME.
A'SHAR FEARLESS, IS IT?
THAT WAS A LONG TIME AGO--
OH, I DO HOPE YOUR DAYS OF BRAVERY AREN'T BEHIND YOU, CAPTAIN. NOT WITH THE OPPORTUNITY I HAVE IN MIND.
OPPORTUNITY?
JOIN ME FOR A TOUR OF THE COMPLEX. YOUR PERSONAL DROID SHALL REMAIN HERE. QUITE AN ODD COMPANION FOR AN OFFICER...

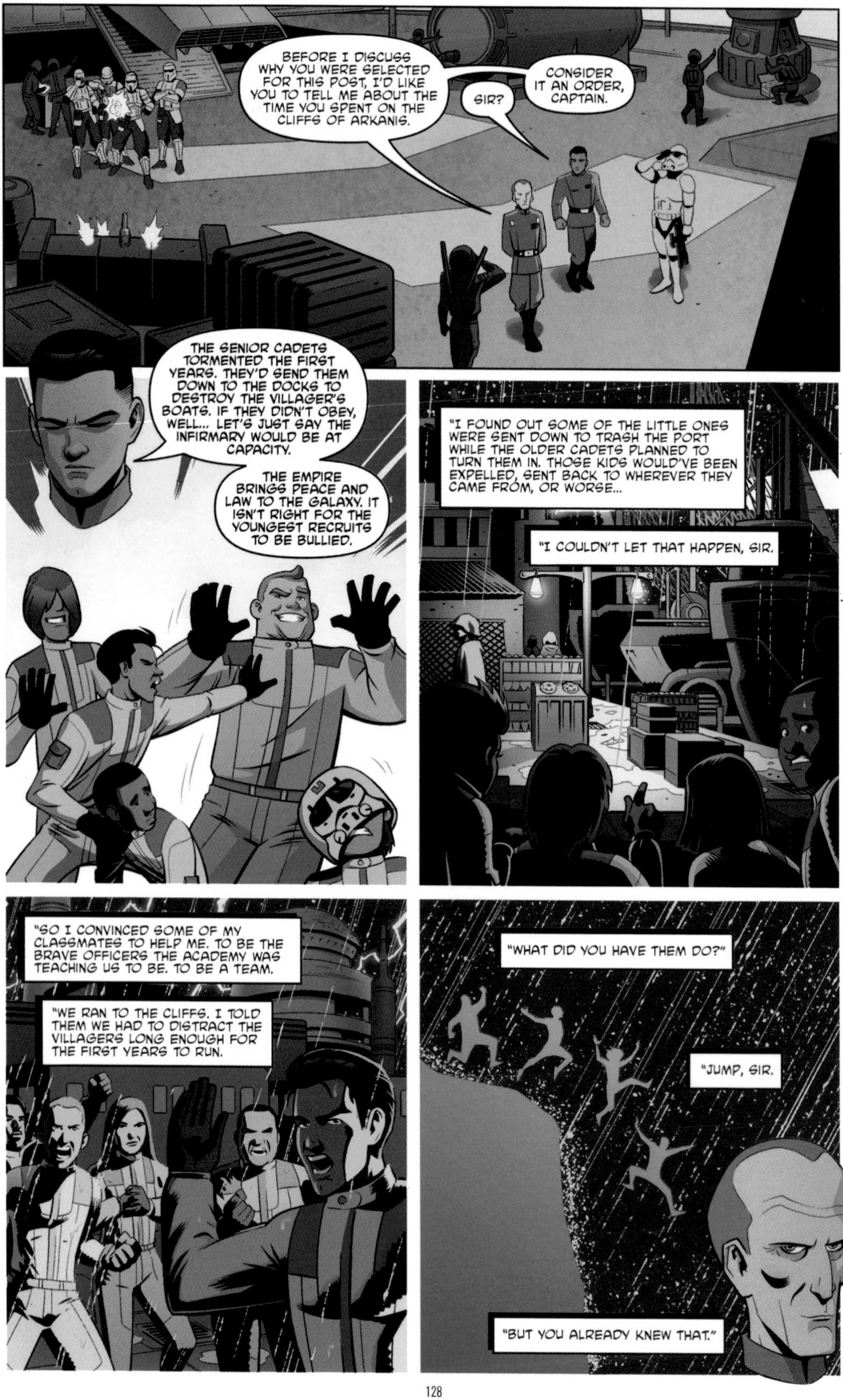
BEFORE I DISCUSS WHY YOU WERE SELECTED FOR THIS POST, I'D LIKE YOU TO TELL ME ABOUT THE TIME YOU SPENT ON THE CLIFFS OF ARKANIS.
SIR?
CONSIDER IT AN ORDER, CAPTAIN.
THE SENIOR CADETS TORMENTED THE FIRST YEARS. THEY'D SEND THEM DOWN TO THE DOCKS TO DESTROY THE VILLAGER'S BOATS. IF THEY DIDN'T OBEY, WELL... LET'S JUST SAY THE INFIRMARY WOULD BE AT CAPACITY.
THE EMPIRE BRINGS PEACE AND LAW TO THE GALAXY. IT ISN'T RIGHT FOR THE YOUNGEST RECRUITS TO BE BULLIED.
"I FOUND OUT SOME OF THE LITTLE ONES WERE SENT DOWN TO TRASH THE PORT WHILE THE OLDER CADETS PLANNED TO TURN THEM IN. THOSE KIDS WOULD'VE BEEN EXPELLED, SENT BACK TO WHEREVER THEY CAME FROM, OR WORSE...
"I COULDN'T LET THAT HAPPEN, SIR.
"SO I CONVINCED SOME OF MY CLASSMATES TO HELP ME. TO BE THE BRAVE OFFICERS THE ACADEMY WAS TEACHING US TO BE. TO BE A TEAM.
"WE RAN TO THE CLIFFS. I TOLD THEM WE HAD TO DISTRACT THE VILLAGERS LONG ENOUGH FOR THE FIRST YEARS TO RUN.
"WHAT DID YOU HAVE THEM DO?"
"JUMP, SIR.
"BUT YOU ALREADY KNEW THAT."

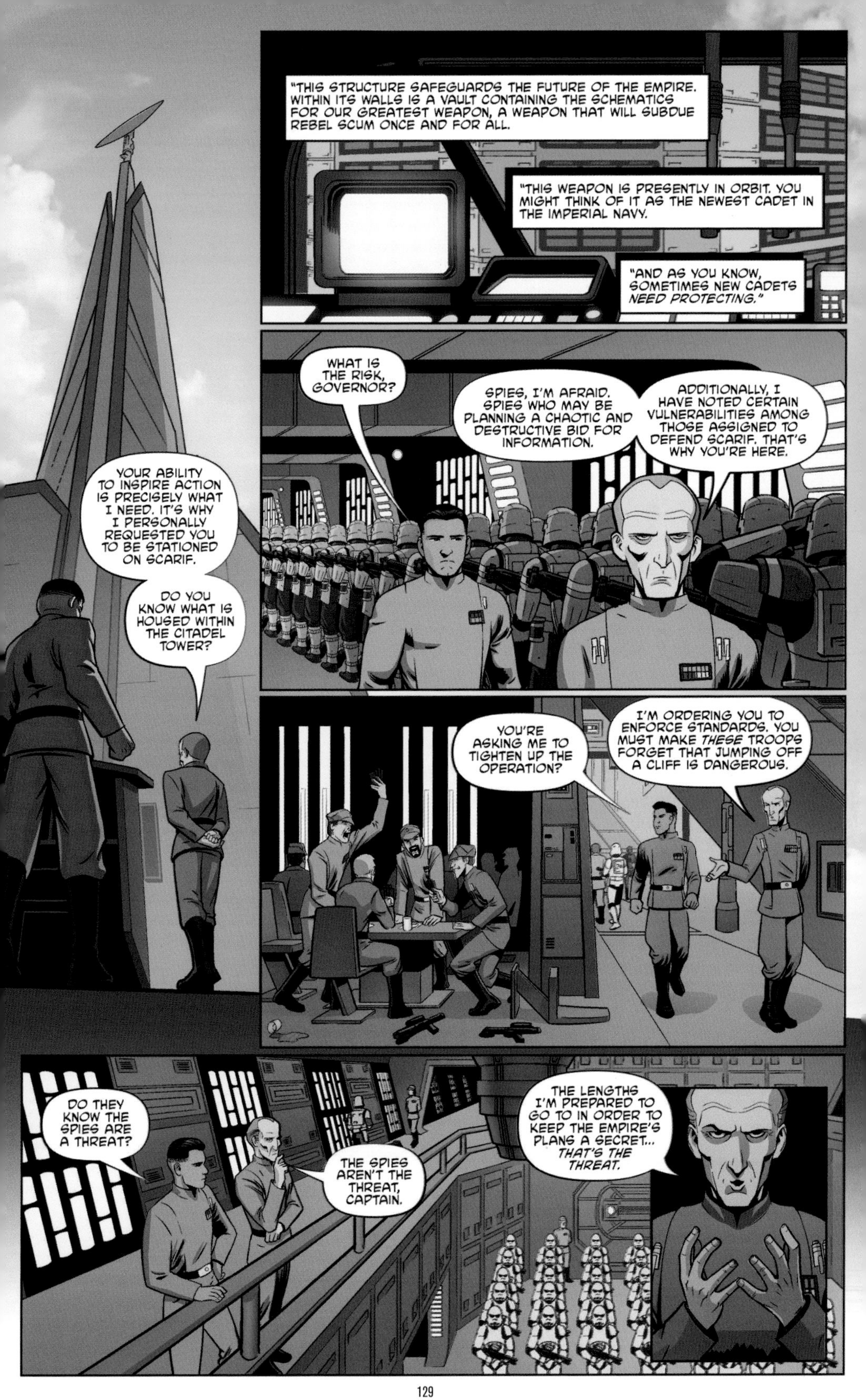
"THIS STRUCTURE SAFEGUARDS THE FUTURE OF THE EMPIRE. WITHIN ITS WALLS IS A VAULT CONTAINING THE SCHEMATICS FOR OUR GREATEST WEAPON, A WEAPON THAT WILL SUBDUE REBEL SCUM ONCE AND FOR ALL.
"THIS WEAPON IS PRESENTLY IN ORBIT. YOU MIGHT THINK OF IT AS THE NEWEST CADET IN THE IMPERIAL NAVY.
"AND AS YOU KNOW, SOMETIMES NEW CADETS *NEED PROTECTING.*"
YOUR ABILITY TO INSPIRE ACTION IS PRECISELY WHAT I NEED. IT'S WHY I PERSONALLY REQUESTED YOU TO BE STATIONED ON SCARIF.
DO YOU KNOW WHAT IS HOUSED WITHIN THE CITADEL TOWER?
WHAT IS THE RISK, GOVERNOR?
SPIES, I'M AFRAID. SPIES WHO MAY BE PLANNING A CHAOTIC AND DESTRUCTIVE BID FOR INFORMATION.
ADDITIONALLY, I HAVE NOTED CERTAIN VULNERABILITIES AMONG THOSE ASSIGNED TO DEFEND SCARIF. THAT'S WHY YOU'RE HERE.
YOU'RE ASKING ME TO TIGHTEN UP THE OPERATION?
I'M ORDERING YOU TO ENFORCE STANDARDS. YOU MUST MAKE *THESE* TROOPS FORGET THAT JUMPING OFF A CLIFF IS DANGEROUS.
DO THEY KNOW THE SPIES ARE A THREAT?
THE SPIES AREN'T THE THREAT, CAPTAIN.
THE LENGTHS I'M PREPARED TO GO TO IN ORDER TO KEEP THE EMPIRE'S PLANS A SECRET... *THAT'S THE THREAT.*

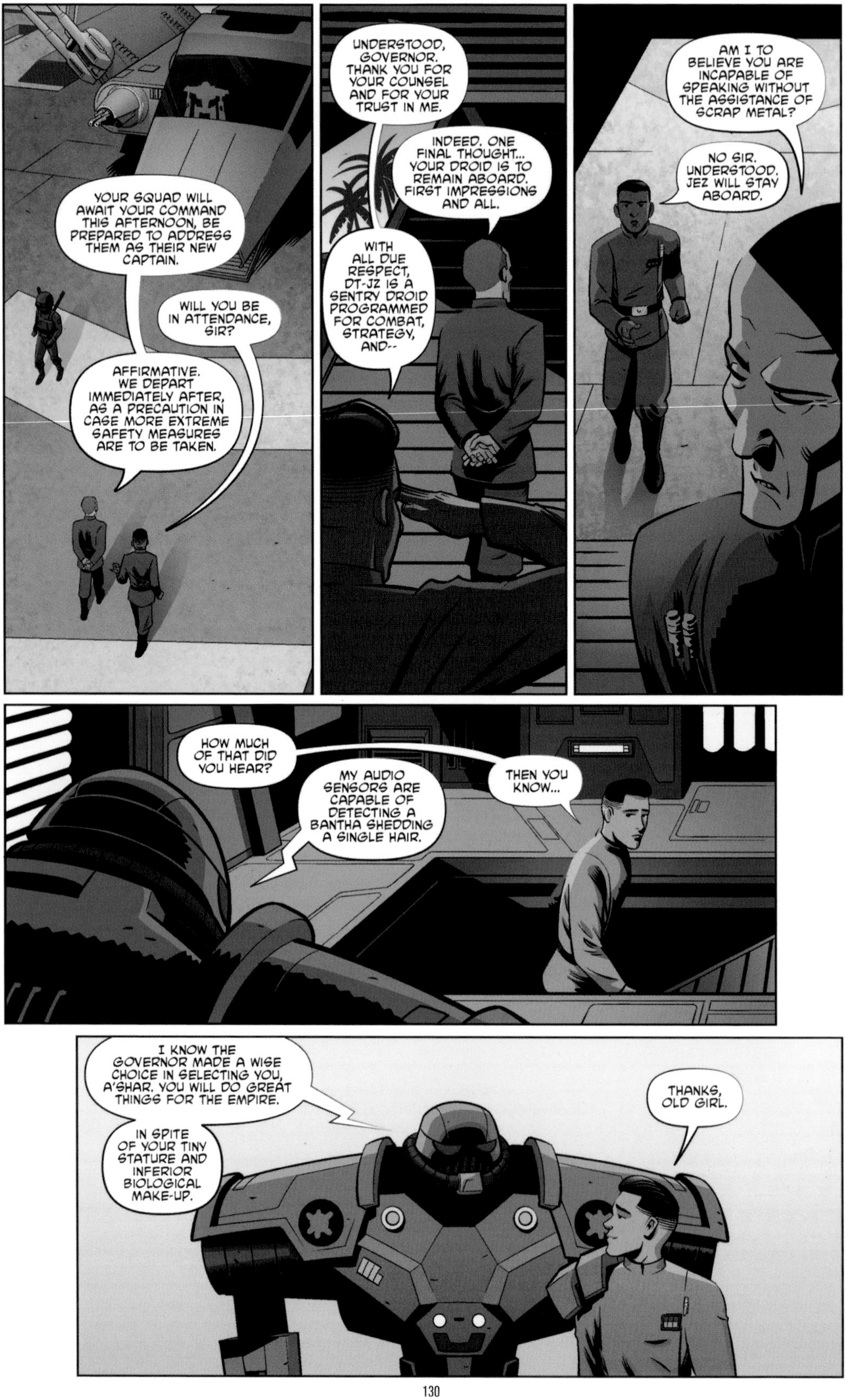
YOUR SQUAD WILL AWAIT YOUR COMMAND THIS AFTERNOON, BE PREPARED TO ADDRESS THEM AS THEIR NEW CAPTAIN.
WILL YOU BE IN ATTENDANCE, SIR?
AFFIRMATIVE. WE DEPART IMMEDIATELY AFTER, AS A PRECAUTION IN CASE MORE EXTREME SAFETY MEASURES ARE TO BE TAKEN.
UNDERSTOOD, GOVERNOR. THANK YOU FOR YOUR COUNSEL AND FOR YOUR TRUST IN ME.
INDEED. ONE FINAL THOUGHT... YOUR DROID IS TO REMAIN ABOARD. FIRST IMPRESSIONS AND ALL.
WITH ALL DUE RESPECT, DT-JZ IS A SENTRY DROID PROGRAMMED FOR COMBAT, STRATEGY, AND--
AM I TO BELIEVE YOU ARE INCAPABLE OF SPEAKING WITHOUT THE ASSISTANCE OF SCRAP METAL?
NO SIR. UNDERSTOOD. JEZ WILL STAY ABOARD.
HOW MUCH OF THAT DID YOU HEAR?
MY AUDIO SENSORS ARE CAPABLE OF DETECTING A BANTHA SHEDDING A SINGLE HAIR.
THEN YOU KNOW...
I KNOW THE GOVERNOR MADE A WISE CHOICE IN SELECTING YOU, A'SHAR. YOU WILL DO GREAT THINGS FOR THE EMPIRE.
IN SPITE OF YOUR TINY STATURE AND INFERIOR BIOLOGICAL MAKE-UP.
THANKS, OLD GIRL.

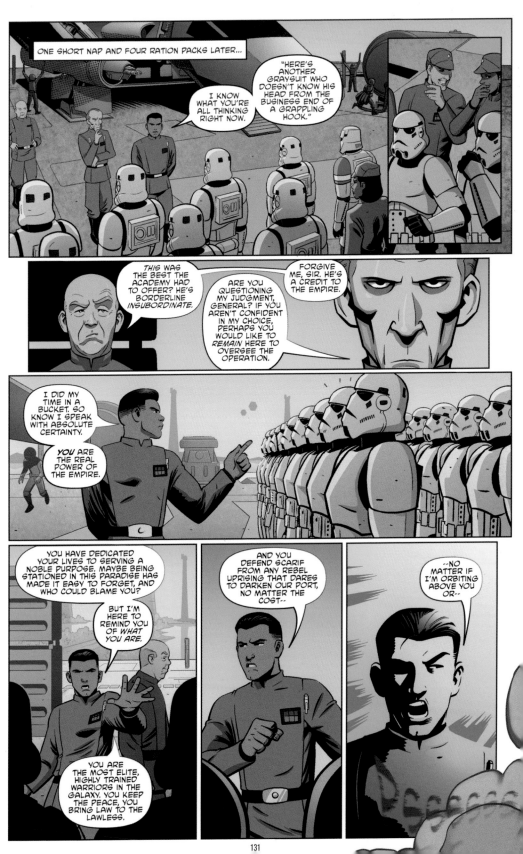

ONE SHORT NAP AND FOUR RATION PACKS LATER...

I KNOW WHAT YOU'RE ALL THINKING RIGHT NOW.

"HERE'S ANOTHER GRAYSUIT WHO DOESN'T KNOW HIS HEAD FROM THE BUSINESS END OF A GRAPPLING HOOK."

THIS WAS THE BEST THE ACADEMY HAD TO OFFER? HE'S BORDERLINE INSUBORDINATE.

ARE YOU QUESTIONING MY JUDGMENT, GENERAL? IF YOU AREN'T CONFIDENT IN MY CHOICE, PERHAPS YOU WOULD LIKE TO REMAIN HERE TO OVERSEE THE OPERATION.

FORGIVE ME, SIR. HE'S A CREDIT TO THE EMPIRE.

I DID MY TIME IN A BUCKET. SO KNOW I SPEAK WITH ABSOLUTE CERTAINTY.

YOU ARE THE REAL POWER OF THE EMPIRE.

YOU HAVE DEDICATED YOUR LIVES TO SERVING A NOBLE PURPOSE. MAYBE BEING STATIONED IN THIS PARADISE HAS MADE IT EASY TO FORGET, AND WHO COULD BLAME YOU?

BUT I'M HERE TO REMIND YOU OF WHAT YOU ARE.

YOU ARE THE MOST ELITE, HIGHLY TRAINED WARRIORS IN THE GALAXY. YOU KEEP THE PEACE, YOU BRING LAW TO THE LAWLESS.

AND YOU DEFEND SCARIF FROM ANY REBEL UPRISING THAT DARES TO DARKEN OUR PORT, NO MATTER THE COST--

--NO MATTER IF I'M ORBITING ABOVE YOU OR--

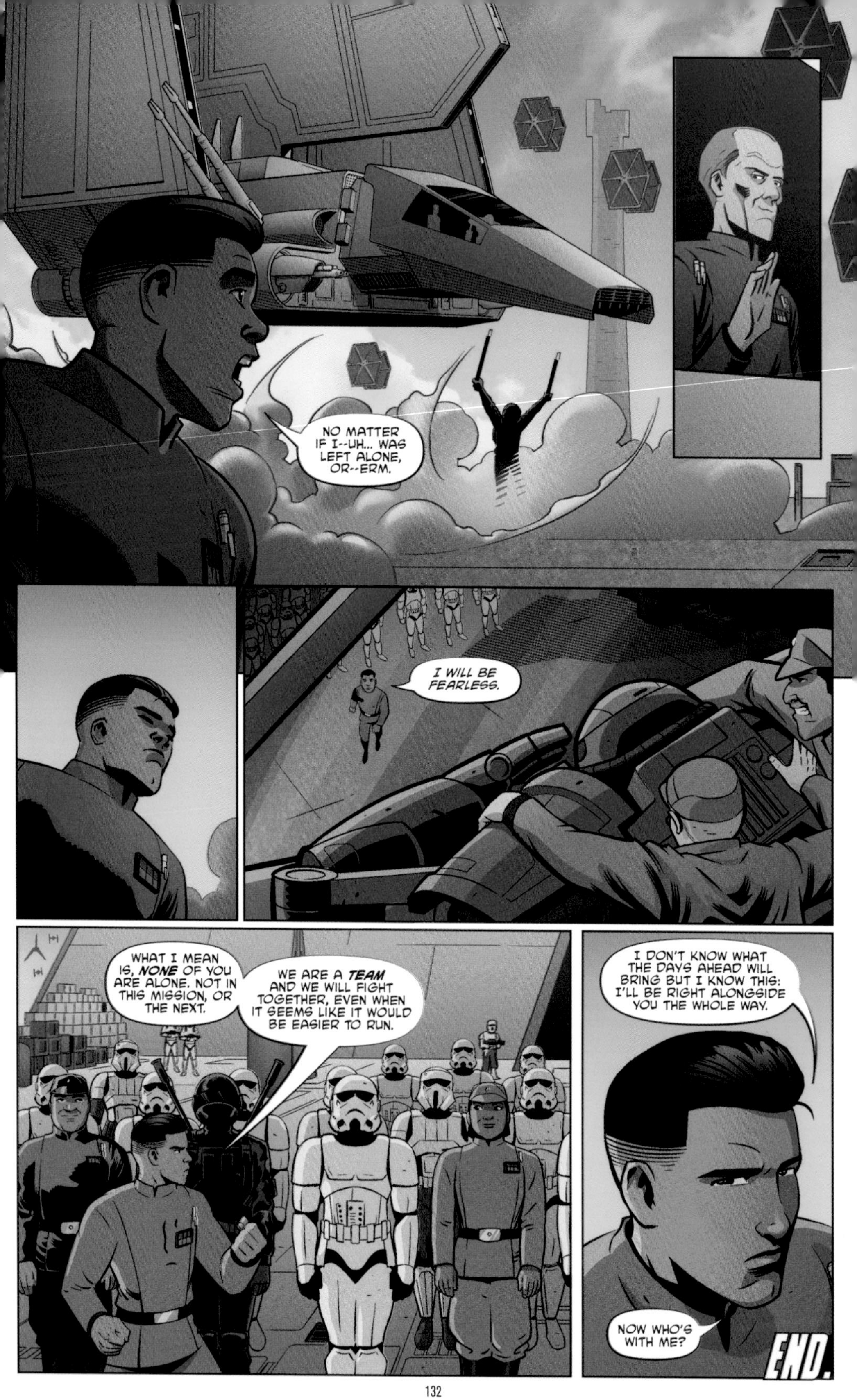
NO MATTER IF I--UH... WAS LEFT ALONE, OR--ERM.
I WILL BE FEARLESS.
WHAT I MEAN IS, NONE OF YOU ARE ALONE. NOT IN THIS MISSION, OR THE NEXT.
WE ARE A TEAM AND WE WILL FIGHT TOGETHER, EVEN WHEN IT SEEMS LIKE IT WOULD BE EASIER TO RUN.
I DON'T KNOW WHAT THE DAYS AHEAD WILL BRING BUT I KNOW THIS: I'LL BE RIGHT ALONGSIDE YOU THE WHOLE WAY.
NOW WHO'S WITH ME?
END.

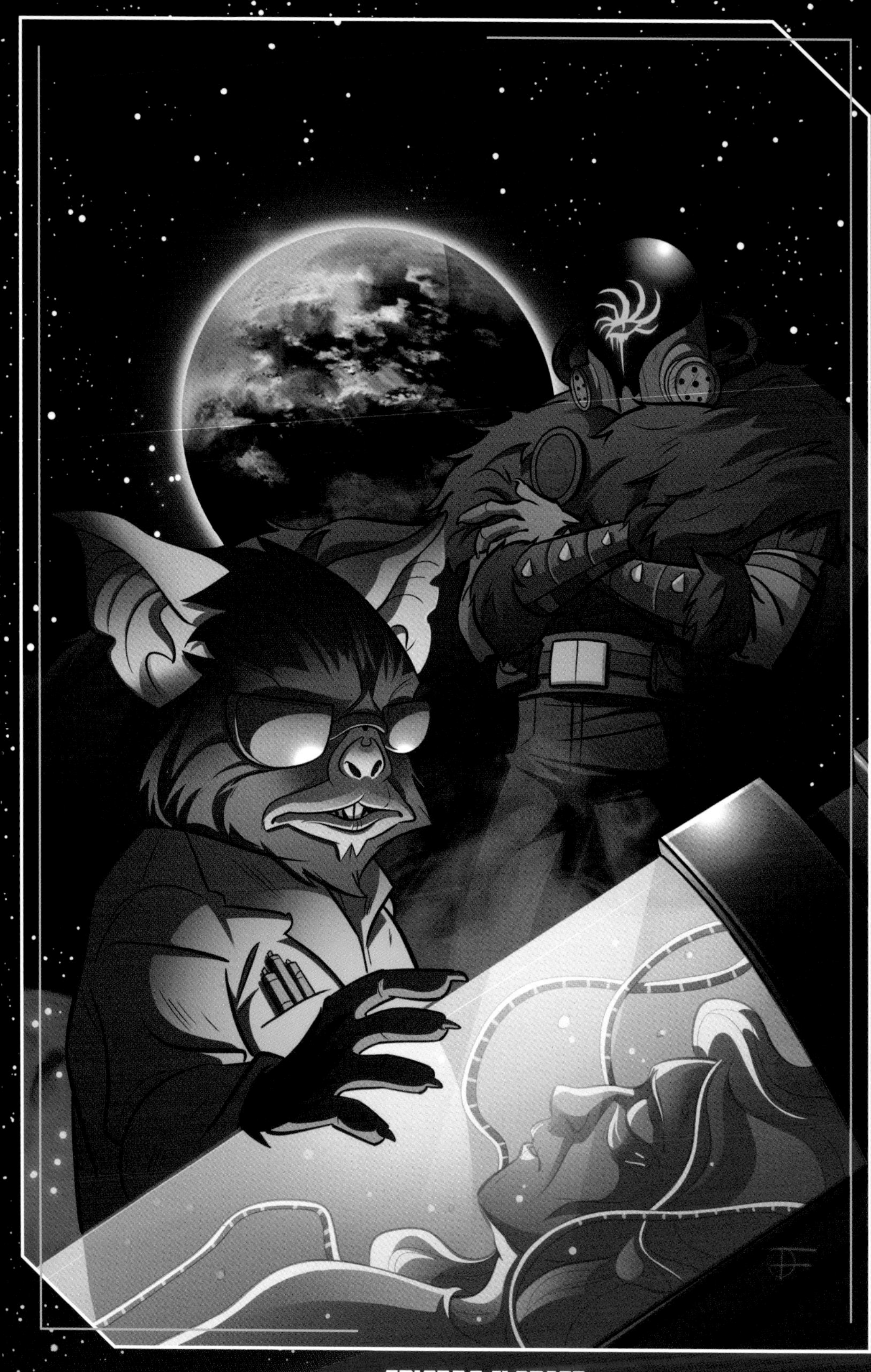

ART BY **ARIANNA FLOREAN**

# THE GAZE ELECTRIC

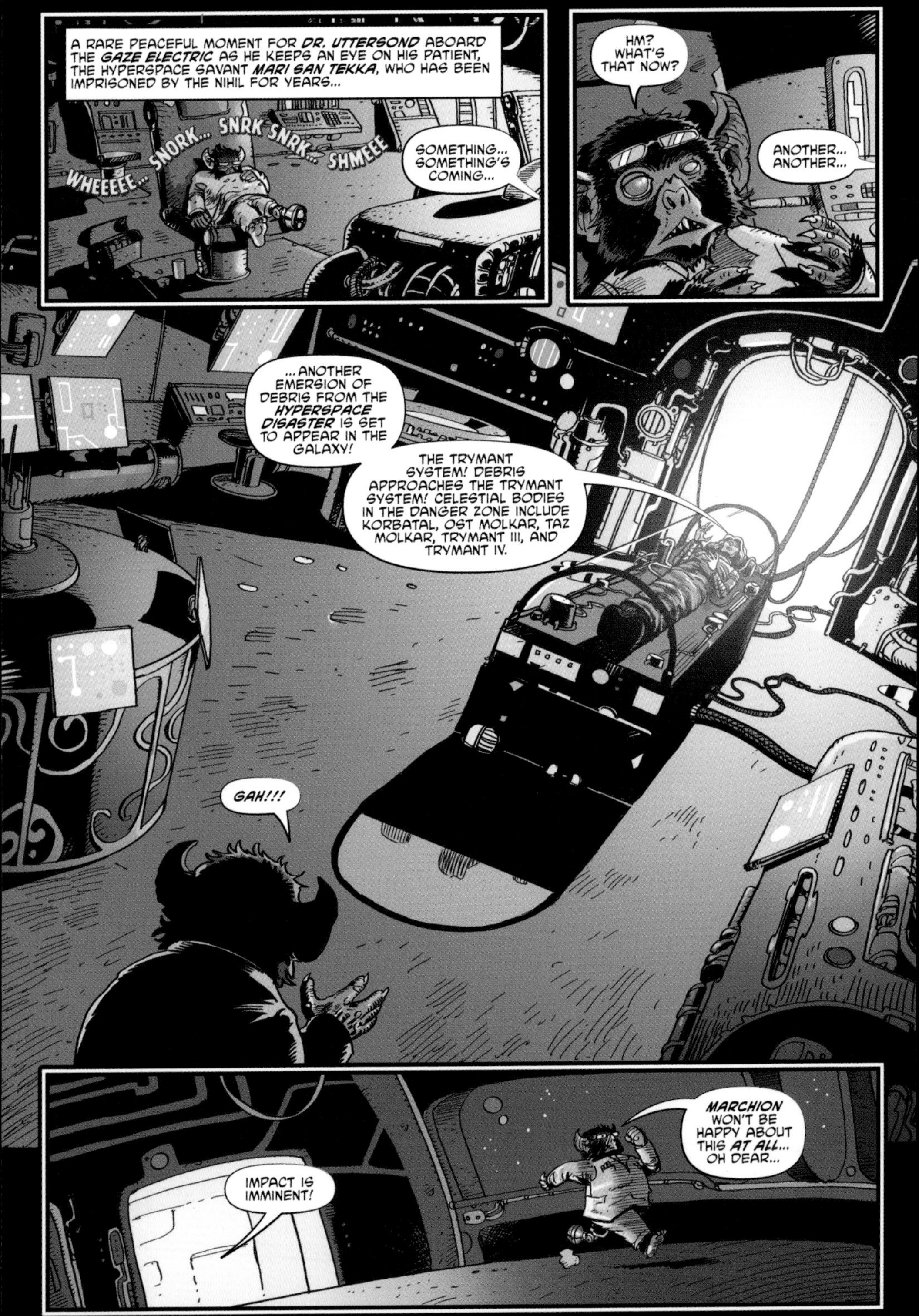
A RARE PEACEFUL MOMENT FOR DR. UTTERSOND ABOARD THE GAZE ELECTRIC AS HE KEEPS AN EYE ON HIS PATIENT, THE HYPERSPACE SAVANT MARI SAN TEKKA, WHO HAS BEEN IMPRISONED BY THE NIHIL FOR YEARS...
WHEEEEE... SNORK... SNRK SNRK... SHMEEE
SOMETHING... SOMETHING'S COMING...
HM? WHAT'S THAT NOW?
ANOTHER... ANOTHER...
...ANOTHER EMERSION OF DEBRIS FROM THE HYPERSPACE DISASTER IS SET TO APPEAR IN THE GALAXY!
THE TRYMANT SYSTEM! DEBRIS APPROACHES THE TRYMANT SYSTEM! CELESTIAL BODIES IN THE DANGER ZONE INCLUDE KORBATAL, OST MOLKAR, TAZ MOLKAR, TRYMANT III, AND TRYMANT IV.
GAH!!!
IMPACT IS IMMINENT!
MARCHION WON'T BE HAPPY ABOUT THIS AT ALL... OH DEAR...

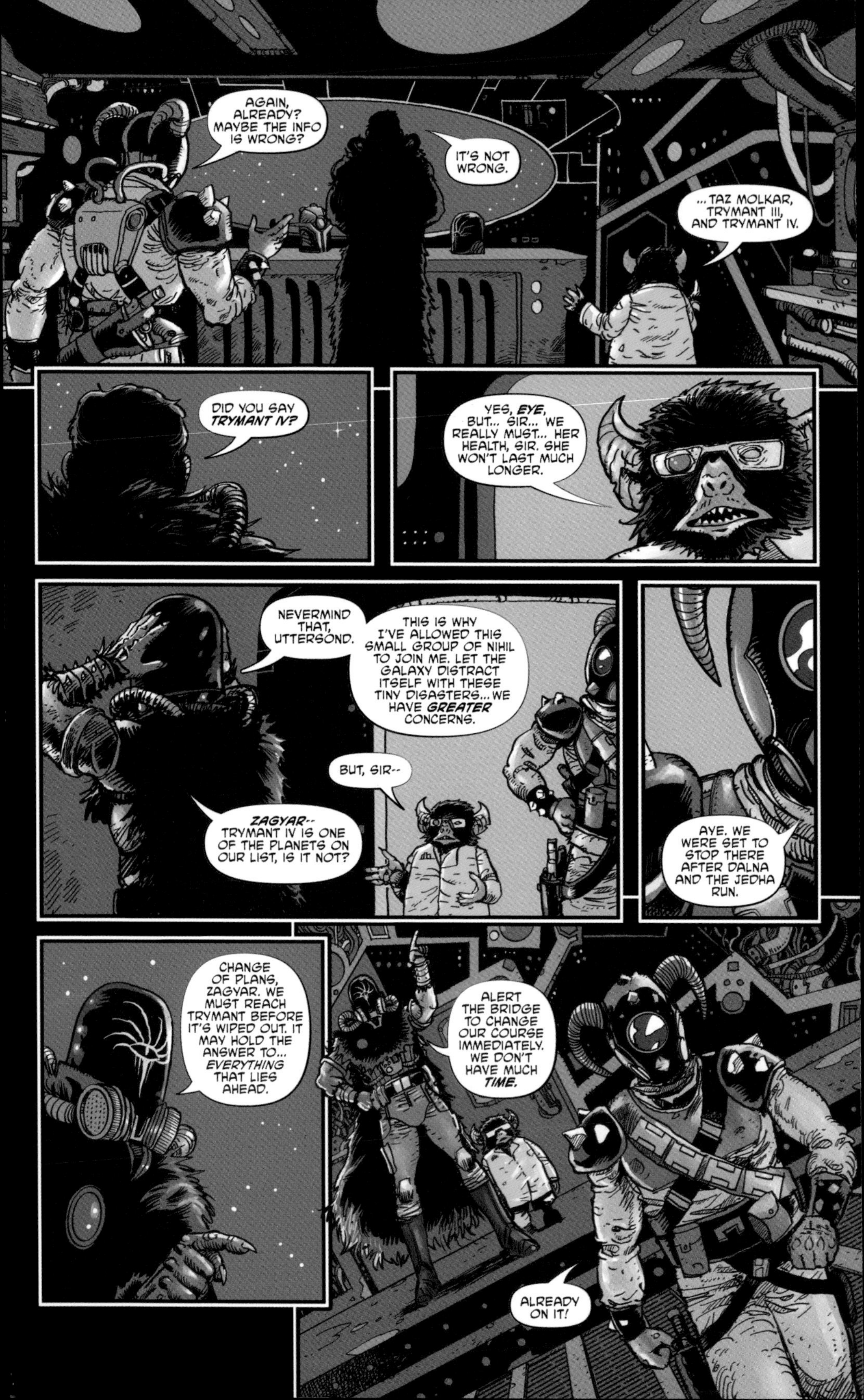
AGAIN, ALREADY? MAYBE THE INFO IS WRONG?
IT'S NOT WRONG.
...TAZ MOLKAR, TRYMANT III, AND TRYMANT IV.
DID YOU SAY *TRYMANT IV?*
YES, *EYE,* BUT... SIR... WE REALLY MUST... HER HEALTH, SIR. SHE WON'T LAST MUCH LONGER.
NEVERMIND THAT, UTTERSOND.
THIS IS WHY I'VE ALLOWED THIS SMALL GROUP OF NIHIL TO JOIN ME. LET THE GALAXY DISTRACT ITSELF WITH THESE TINY DISASTERS... WE HAVE *GREATER* CONCERNS.
BUT, SIR--
*ZAGYAR--* TRYMANT IV IS ONE OF THE PLANETS ON OUR LIST, IS IT NOT?
AYE. WE WERE SET TO STOP THERE AFTER DALNA AND THE JEDHA RUN.
CHANGE OF PLANS, ZAGYAR. WE MUST REACH TRYMANT BEFORE IT'S WIPED OUT. IT MAY HOLD THE ANSWER TO... *EVERYTHING* THAT LIES AHEAD.
ALERT THE BRIDGE TO CHANGE OUR COURSE IMMEDIATELY. WE DON'T HAVE MUCH *TIME.*
ALREADY ON IT!

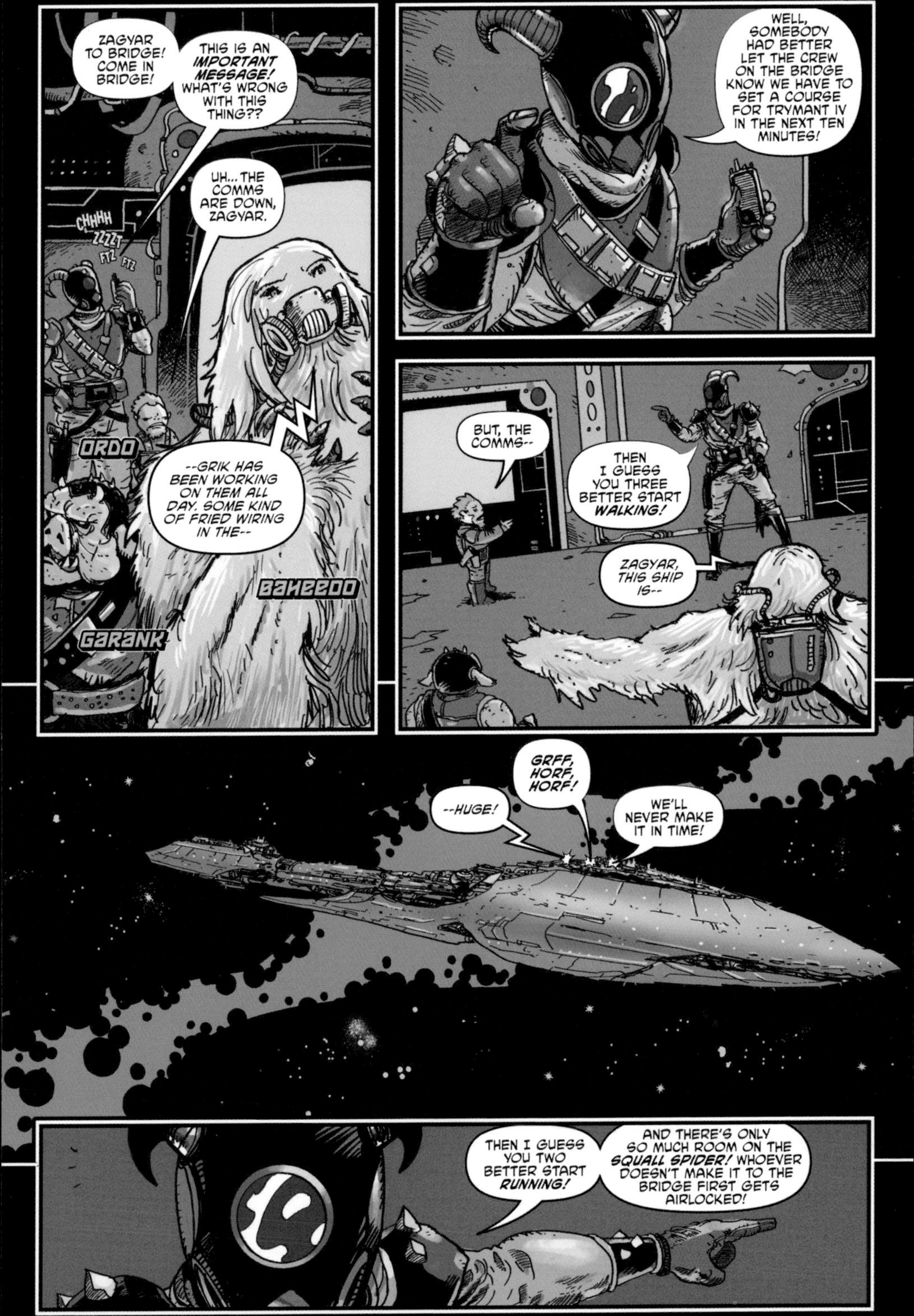
ZAGYAR TO BRIDGE! COME IN BRIDGE!
THIS IS AN *IMPORTANT MESSAGE!* WHAT'S WRONG WITH THIS THING??
CHHHH ZZZZT FTZ FTZ
UH... THE COMMS ARE DOWN, ZAGYAR.
ORDO
--GRIK HAS BEEN WORKING ON THEM ALL DAY. SOME KIND OF FRIED WIRING IN THE--
BAHEEDO
GARANK
WELL, SOMEBODY HAD BETTER LET THE CREW ON THE BRIDGE KNOW WE HAVE TO SET A COURSE FOR TRYMANT IV IN THE NEXT TEN MINUTES!
BUT, THE COMMS--
THEN I GUESS YOU THREE BETTER START *WALKING!*
*ZAGYAR, THIS SHIP IS--*
*--HUGE!*
*GRFF, HORF, HORF!*
WE'LL NEVER MAKE IT IN TIME!
THEN I GUESS YOU TWO BETTER START *RUNNING!*
AND THERE'S ONLY SO MUCH ROOM ON THE *SQUALL SPIDER!* WHOEVER DOESN'T MAKE IT TO THE BRIDGE FIRST GETS AIRLOCKED!

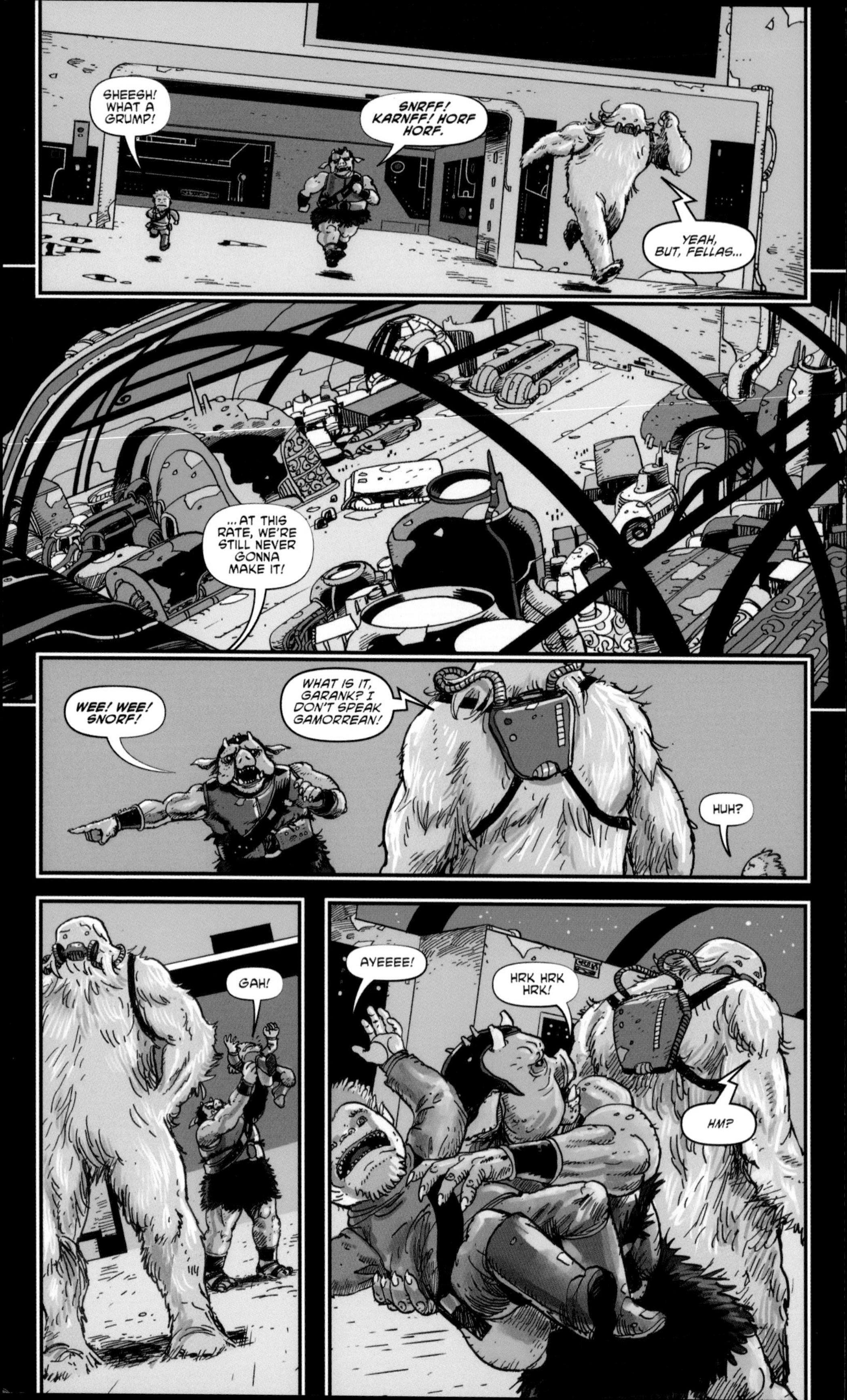
SHEESH! WHAT A GRUMP!
SNRFF! KARNFF! HORF HORF.
YEAH, BUT, FELLAS...
...AT THIS RATE, WE'RE STILL NEVER GONNA MAKE IT!
WEE! WEE! SNORF!
WHAT IS IT, GARANK? I DON'T SPEAK GAMORREAN!
HUH?
GAH!
AYEEEE!
HRK HRK HRK!
HM?

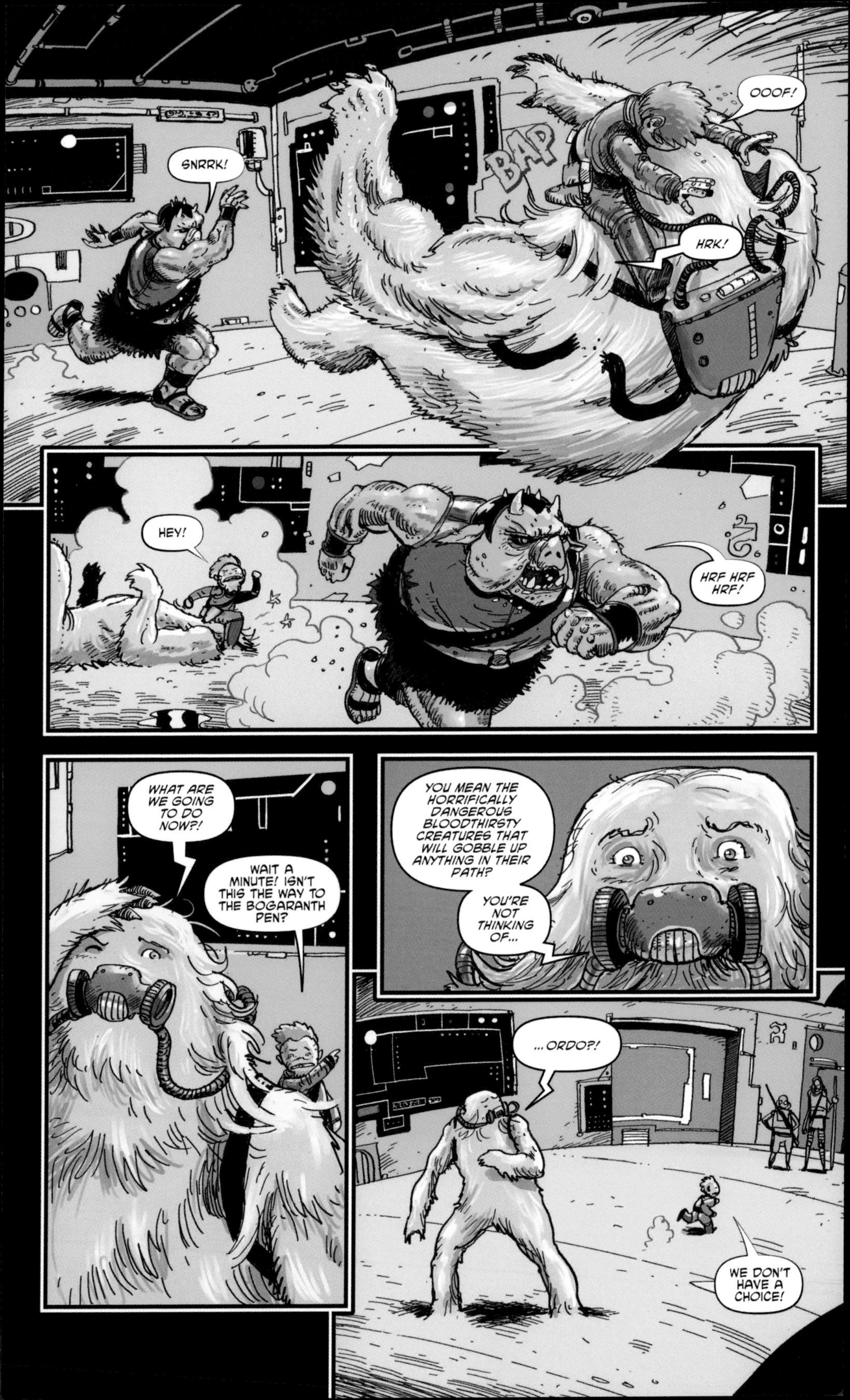
SNRRK!
BAP
OOOF!
HRK!
HEY!
HRF HRF HRF!
WHAT ARE WE GOING TO DO NOW?!
WAIT A MINUTE! ISN'T THIS THE WAY TO THE BOGARANTH PEN?
YOU MEAN THE HORRIFICALLY DANGEROUS BLOODTHIRSTY CREATURES THAT WILL GOBBLE UP ANYTHING IN THEIR PATH?
YOU'RE NOT THINKING OF...
...ORDO?!
WE DON'T HAVE A CHOICE!

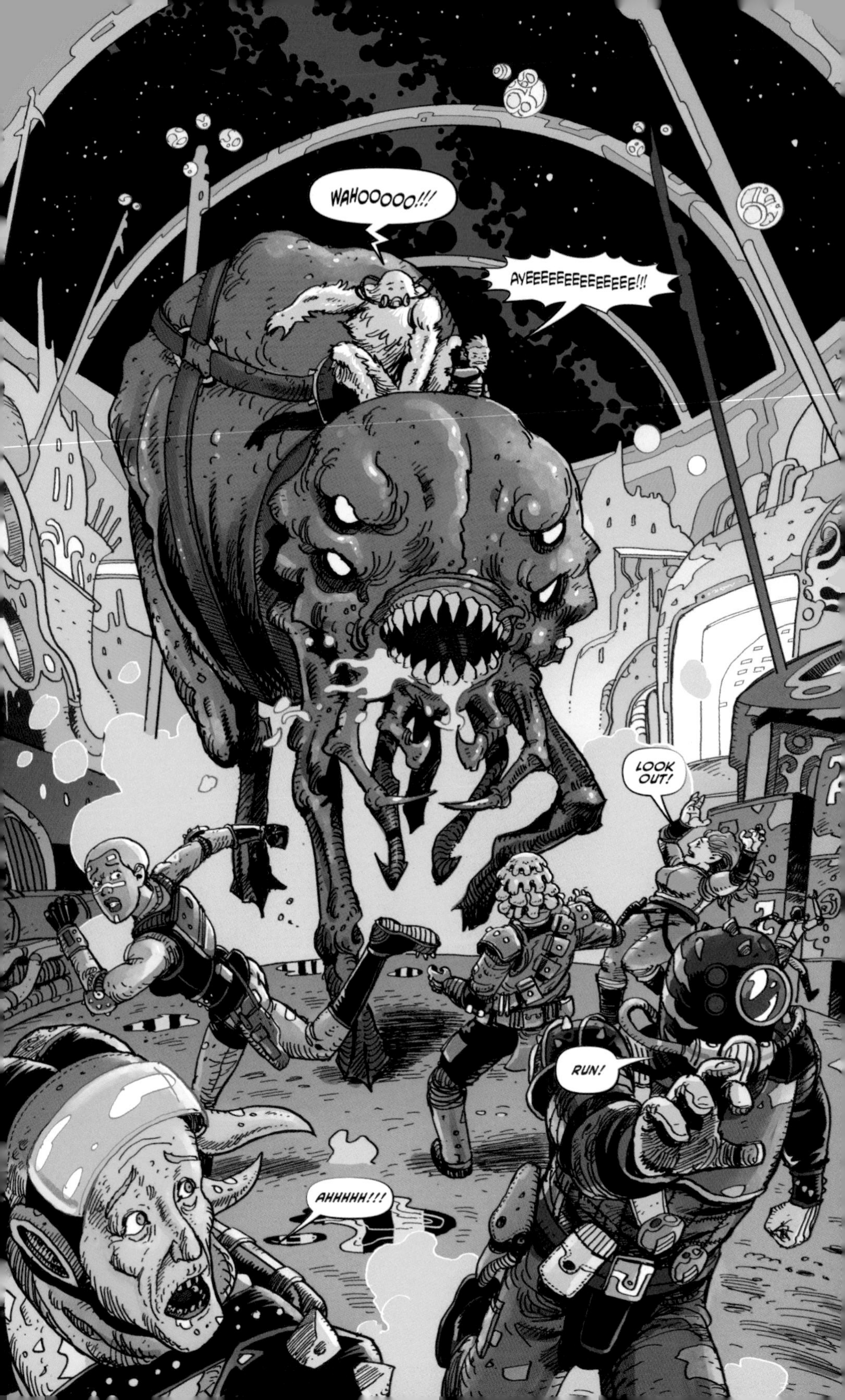
WAHOOOOO!!!
AYEEEEEEEEEEEEEEE!!!
LOOK OUT!
RUN!
AHHHHH!!!

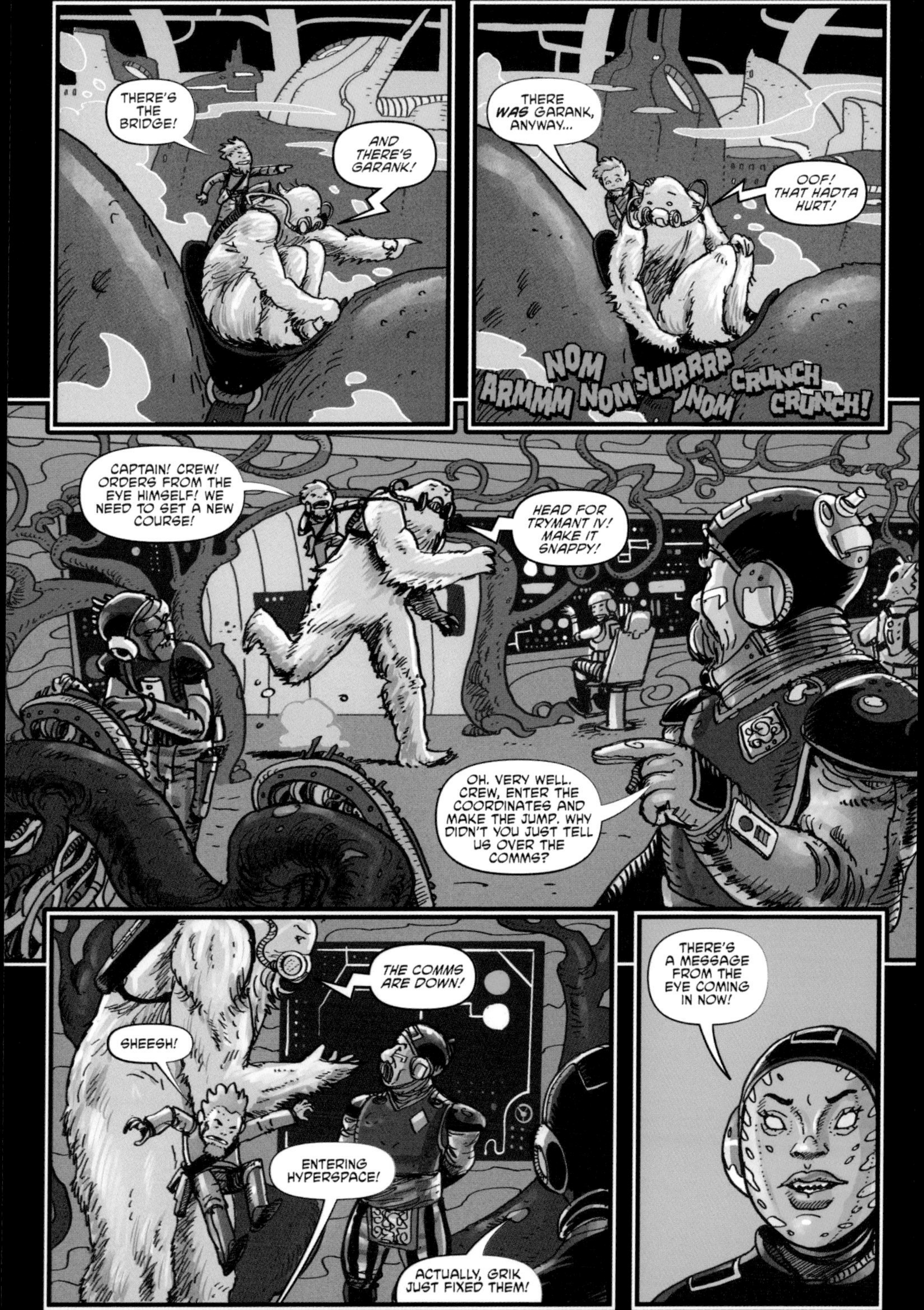
THERE'S THE BRIDGE!
AND THERE'S GARANK!
THERE WAS GARANK, ANYWAY...
OOF! THAT HADTA HURT!
NOM ARMMM NOM SLURRRP NOM CRUNCH CRUNCH!
CAPTAIN! CREW! ORDERS FROM THE EYE HIMSELF! WE NEED TO SET A NEW COURSE!
HEAD FOR TRYMANT IV! MAKE IT SNAPPY!
OH. VERY WELL. CREW, ENTER THE COORDINATES AND MAKE THE JUMP. WHY DIDN'T YOU JUST TELL US OVER THE COMMS?
THE COMMS ARE DOWN!
SHEESH!
ENTERING HYPERSPACE!
ACTUALLY, GRIK JUST FIXED THEM!
THERE'S A MESSAGE FROM THE EYE COMING IN NOW!

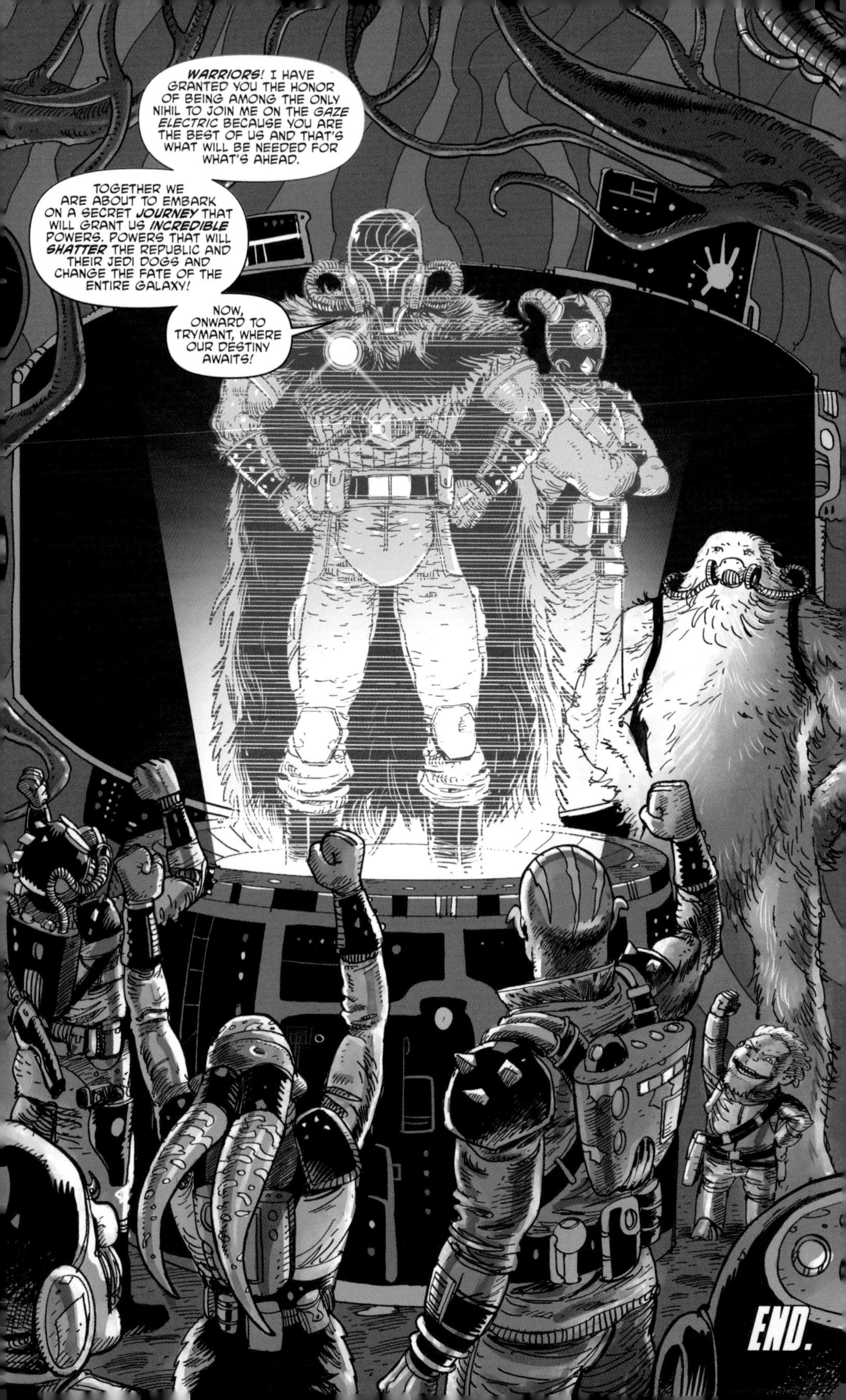
WARRIORS! I HAVE GRANTED YOU THE HONOR OF BEING AMONG THE ONLY NIHIL TO JOIN ME ON THE GAZE ELECTRIC BECAUSE YOU ARE THE BEST OF US AND THAT'S WHAT WILL BE NEEDED FOR WHAT'S AHEAD.
TOGETHER WE ARE ABOUT TO EMBARK ON A SECRET JOURNEY THAT WILL GRANT US INCREDIBLE POWERS. POWERS THAT WILL SHATTER THE REPUBLIC AND THEIR JEDI DOGS AND CHANGE THE FATE OF THE ENTIRE GALAXY!
NOW, ONWARD TO TRYMANT, WHERE OUR DESTINY AWAITS!
END.

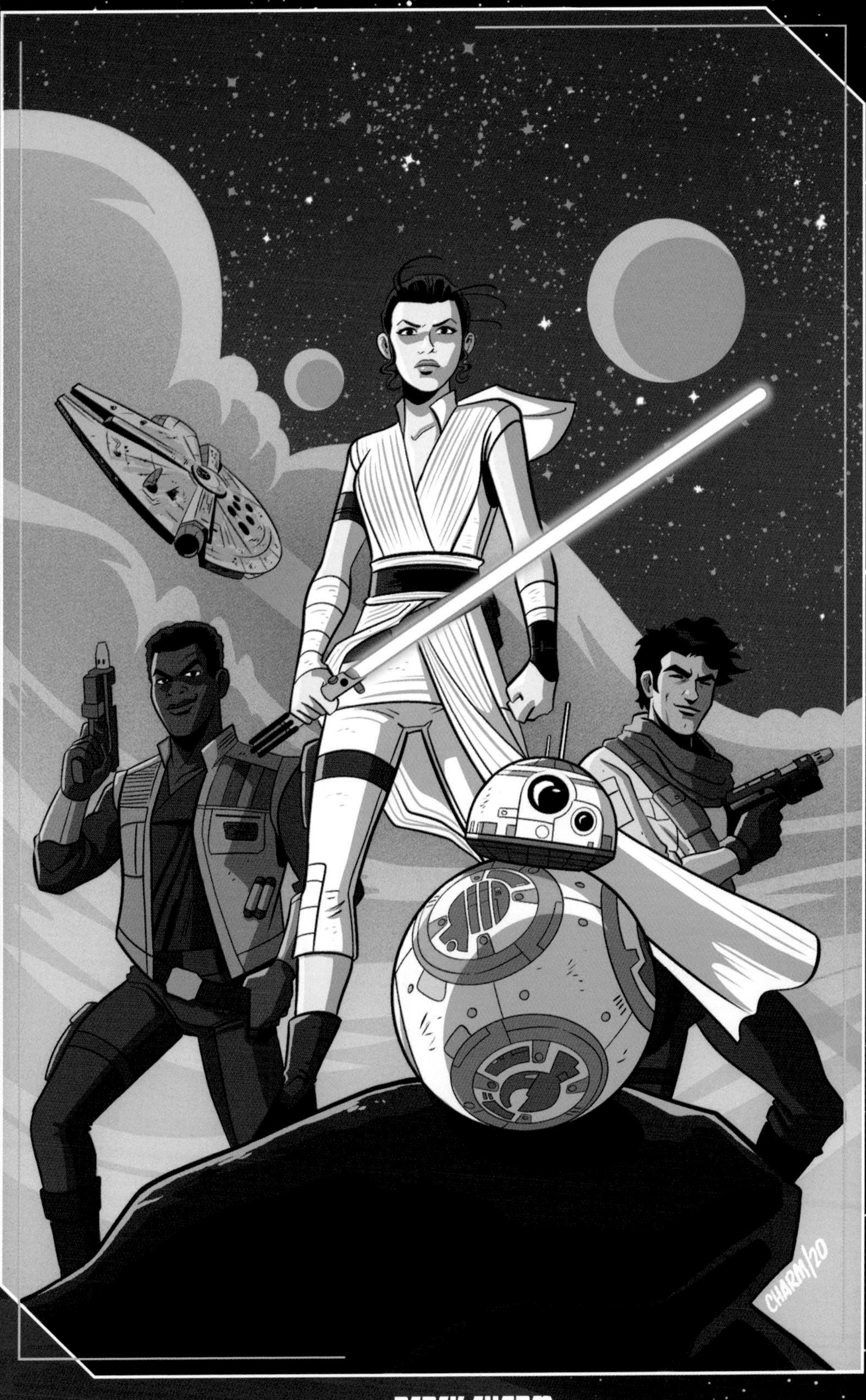
CHARM/20

ART BY DEREK CHARM

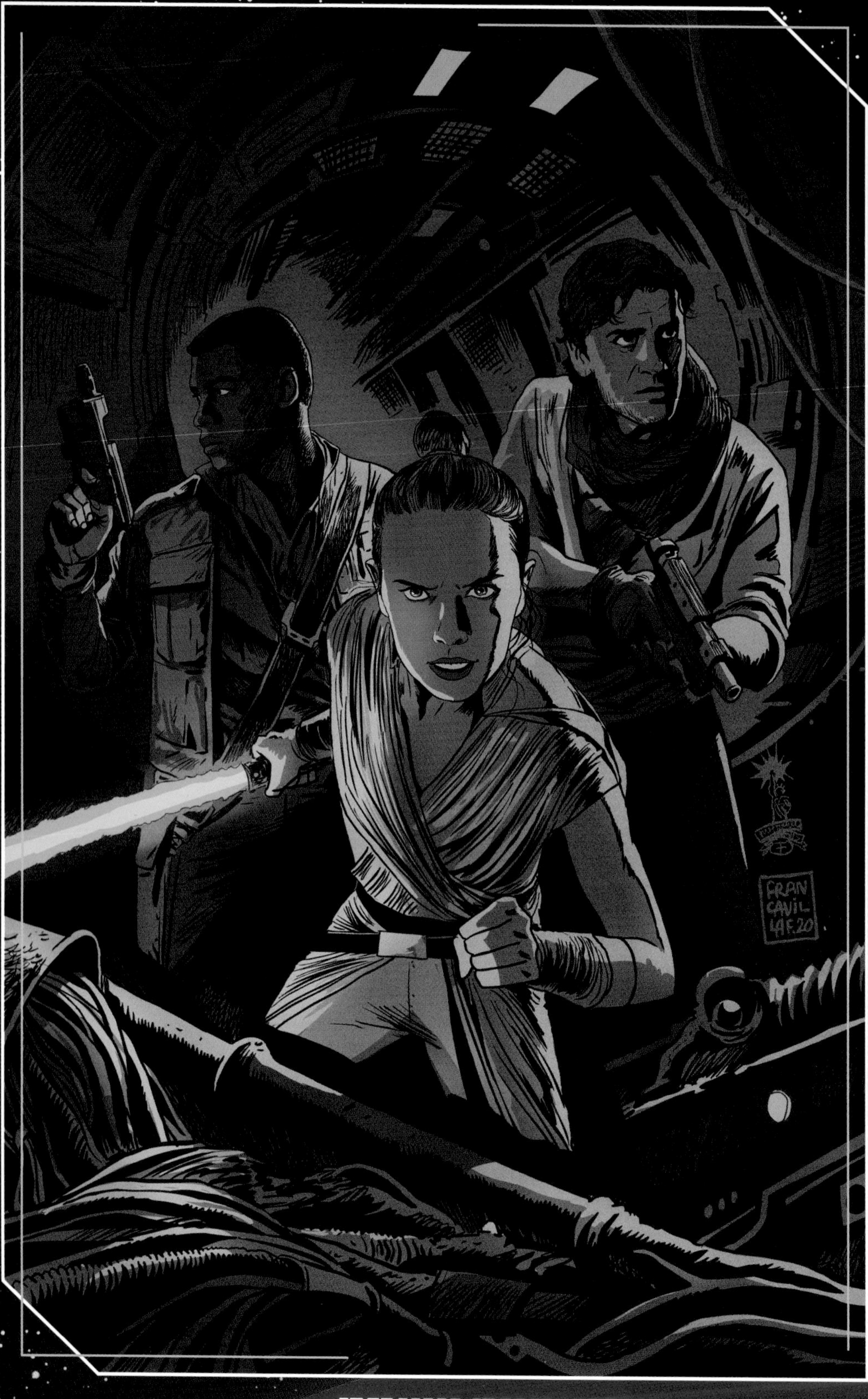

ART BY **FRANCESCO FRANCAVILLA**

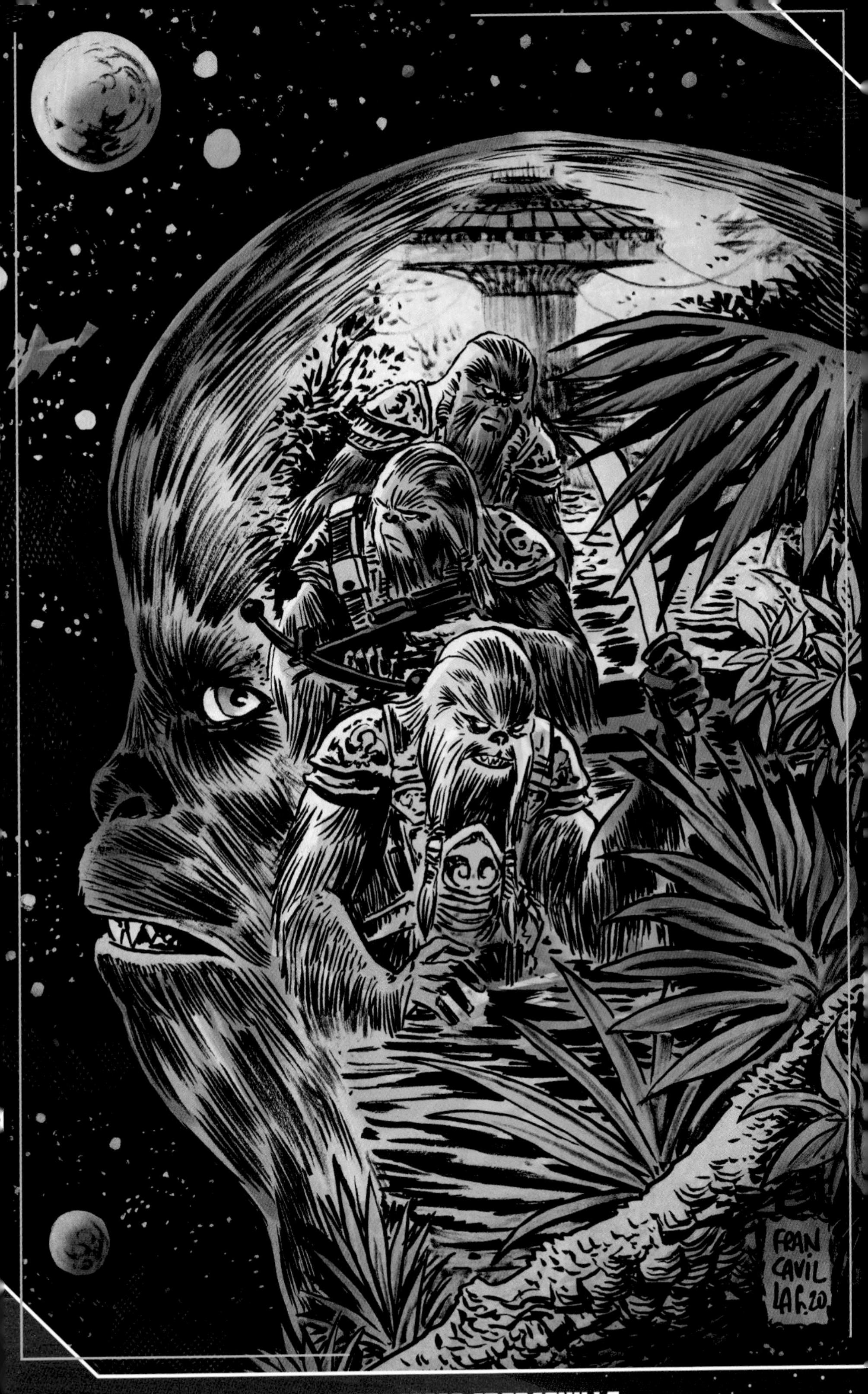
FRAN
CAVIL
LA f.20

ART BY FRANCESCO FRANCAVILLA

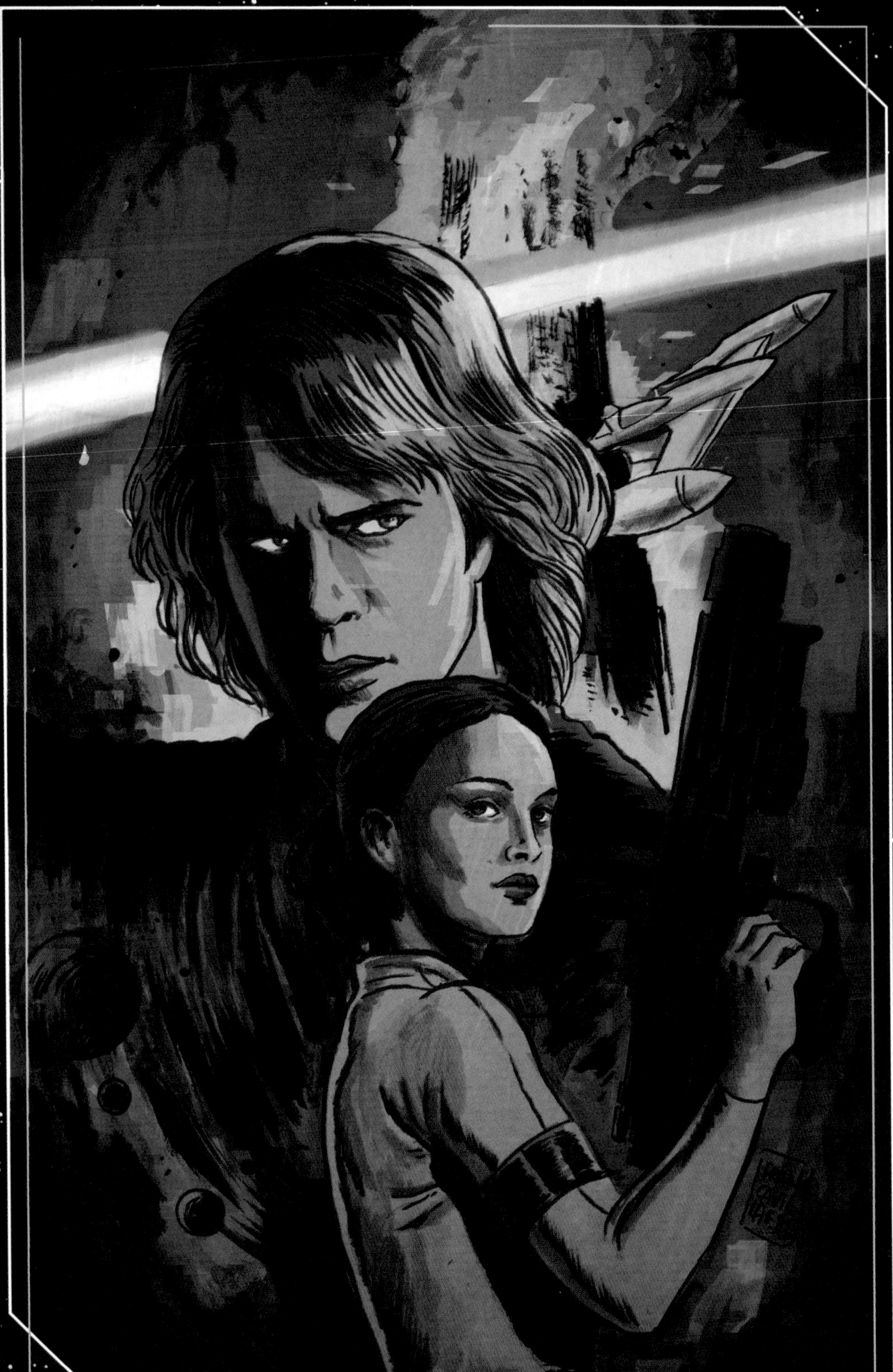

ART BY **FRANCESCO FRANCAVILLA**

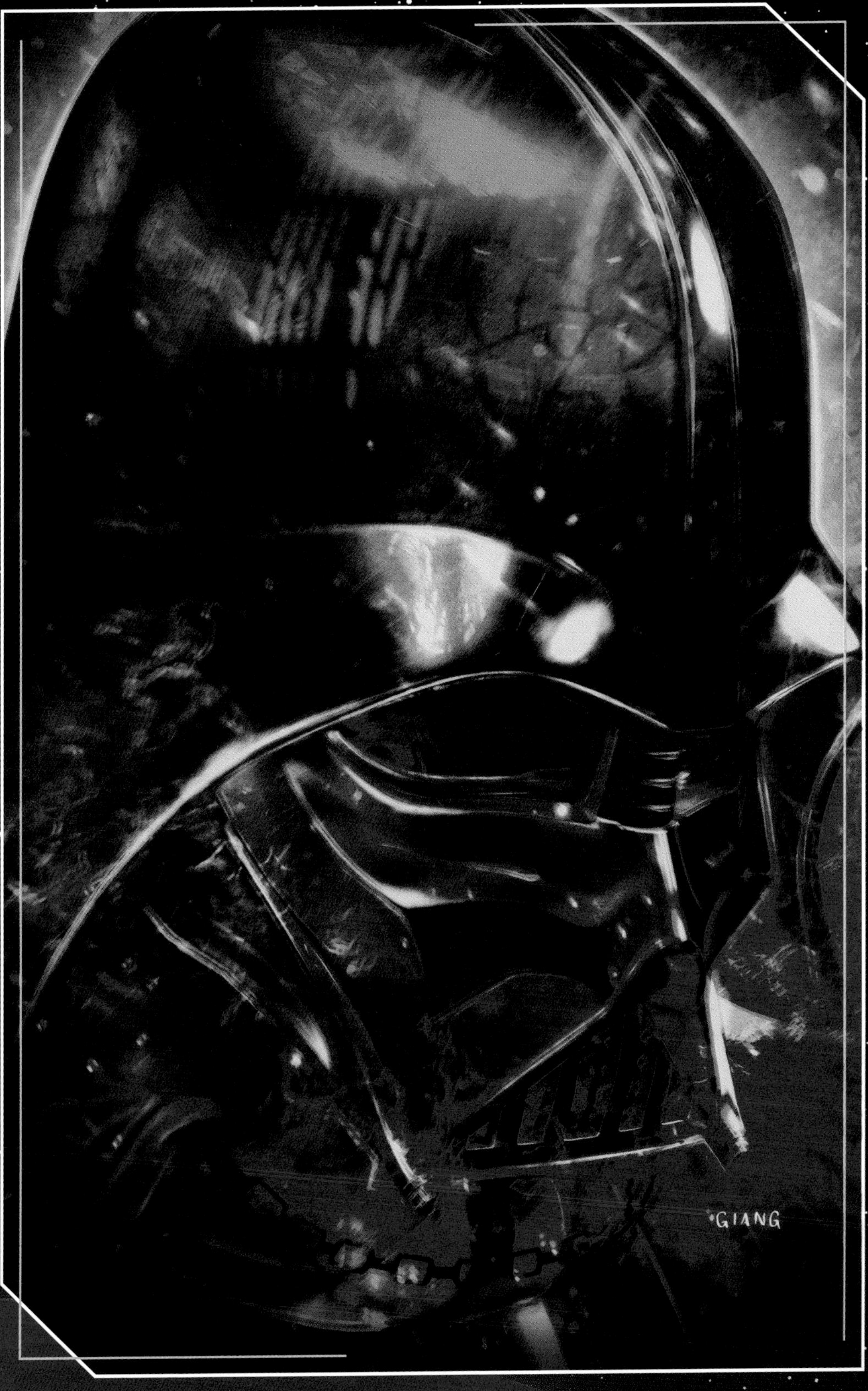
GIANG

ART BY **JOHN GIANG**

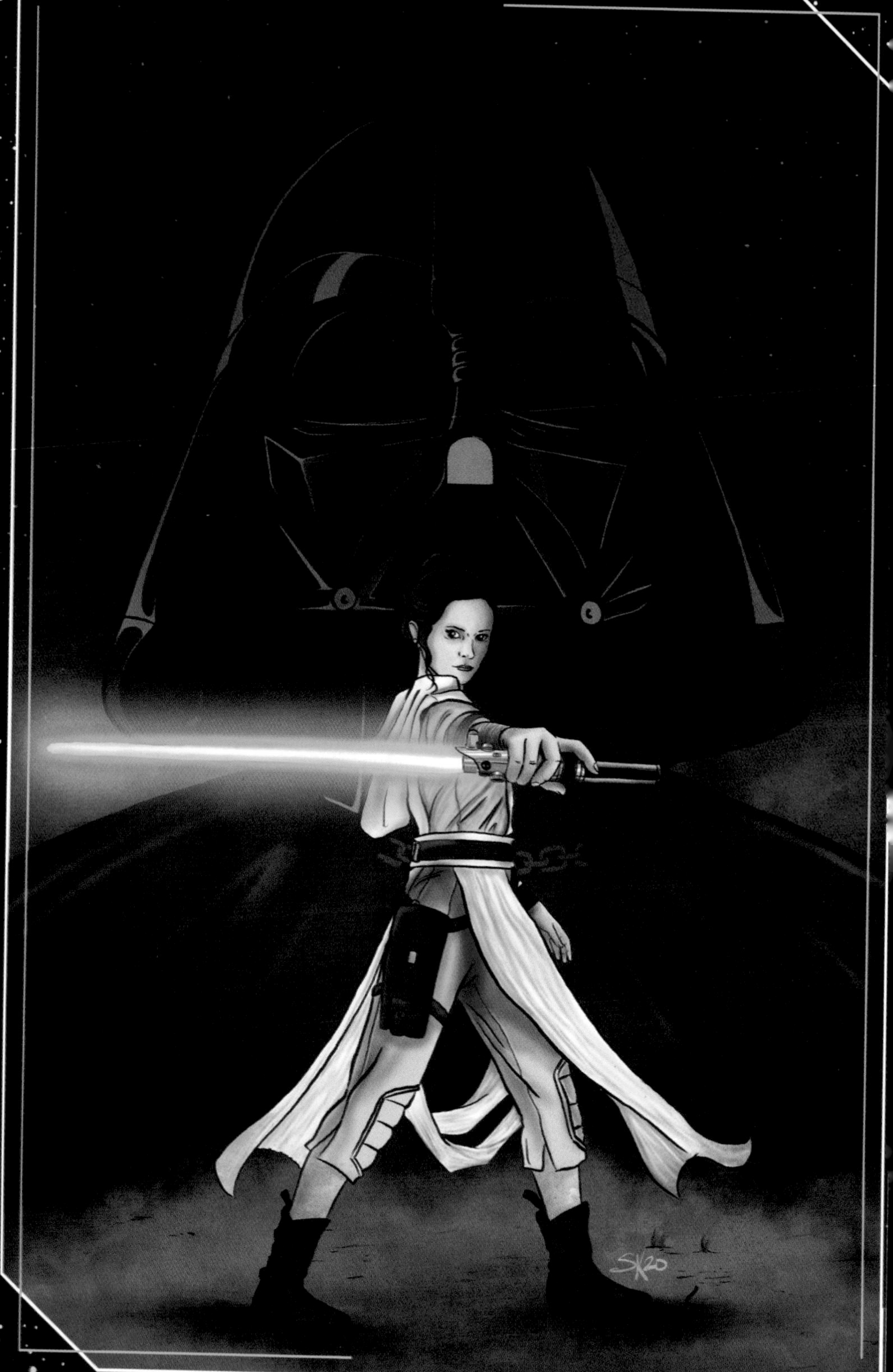
SK20

ART BY **SCOTT KRUGER**

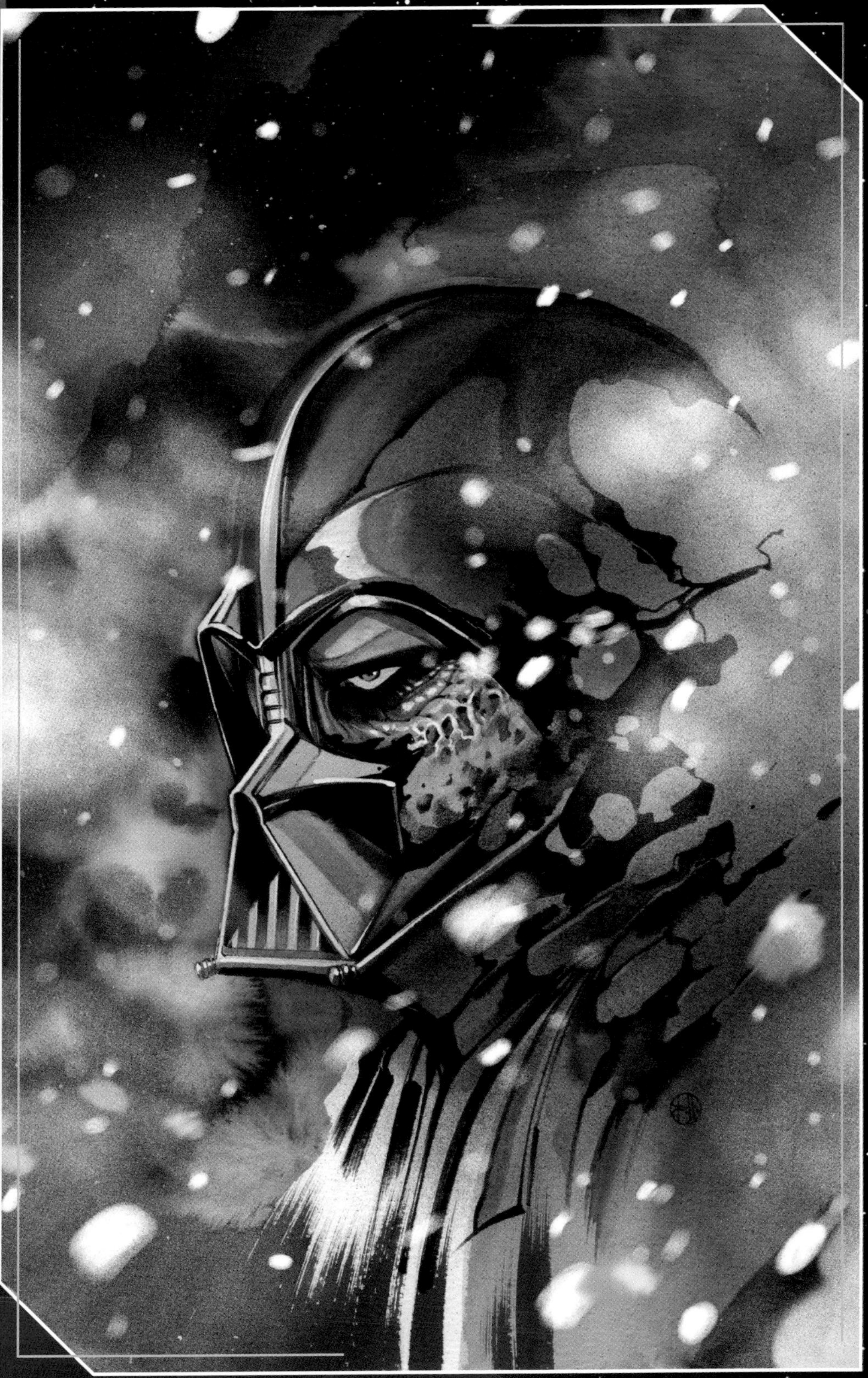

ART BY **PEACH MOMOKO**

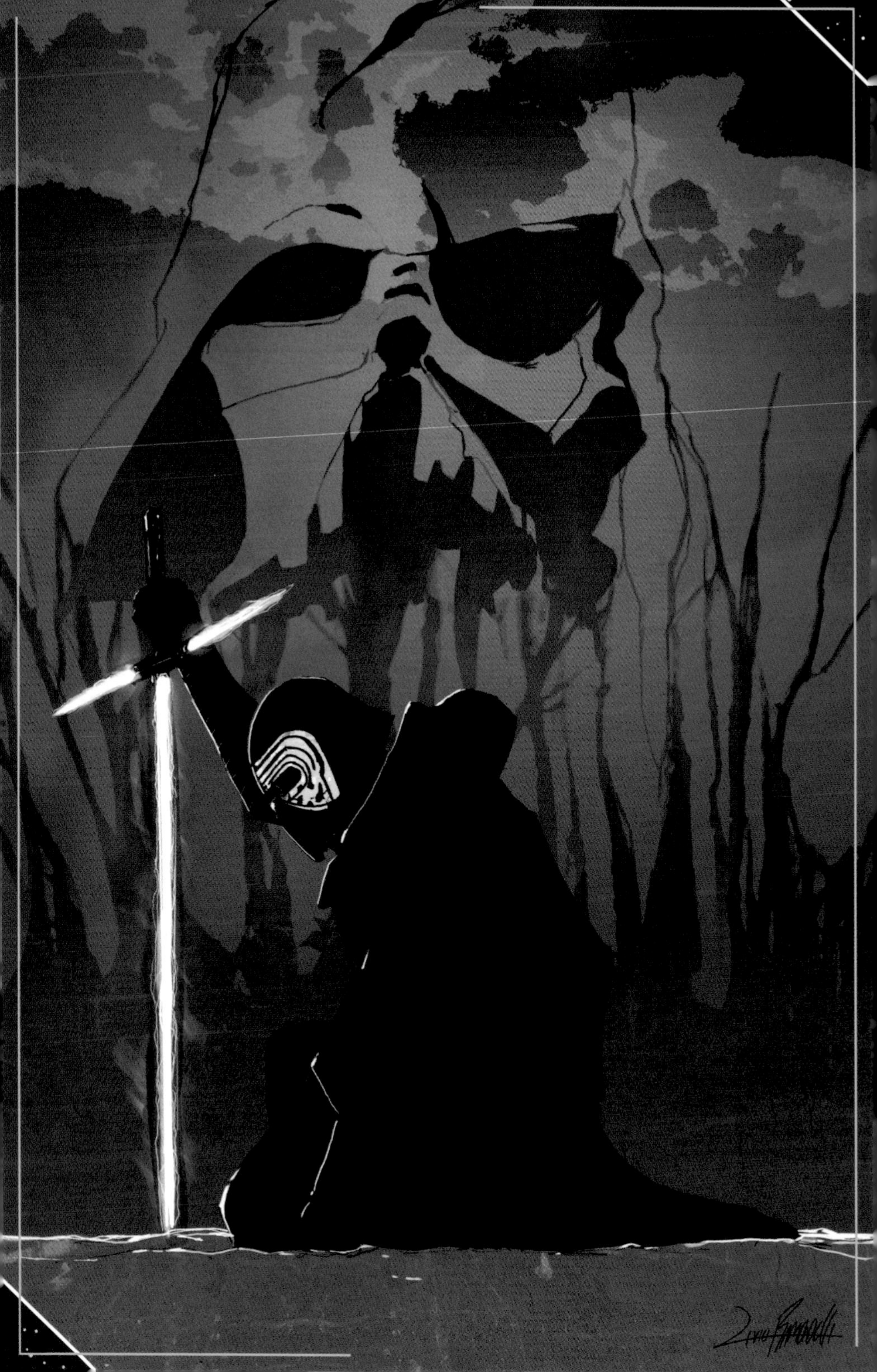

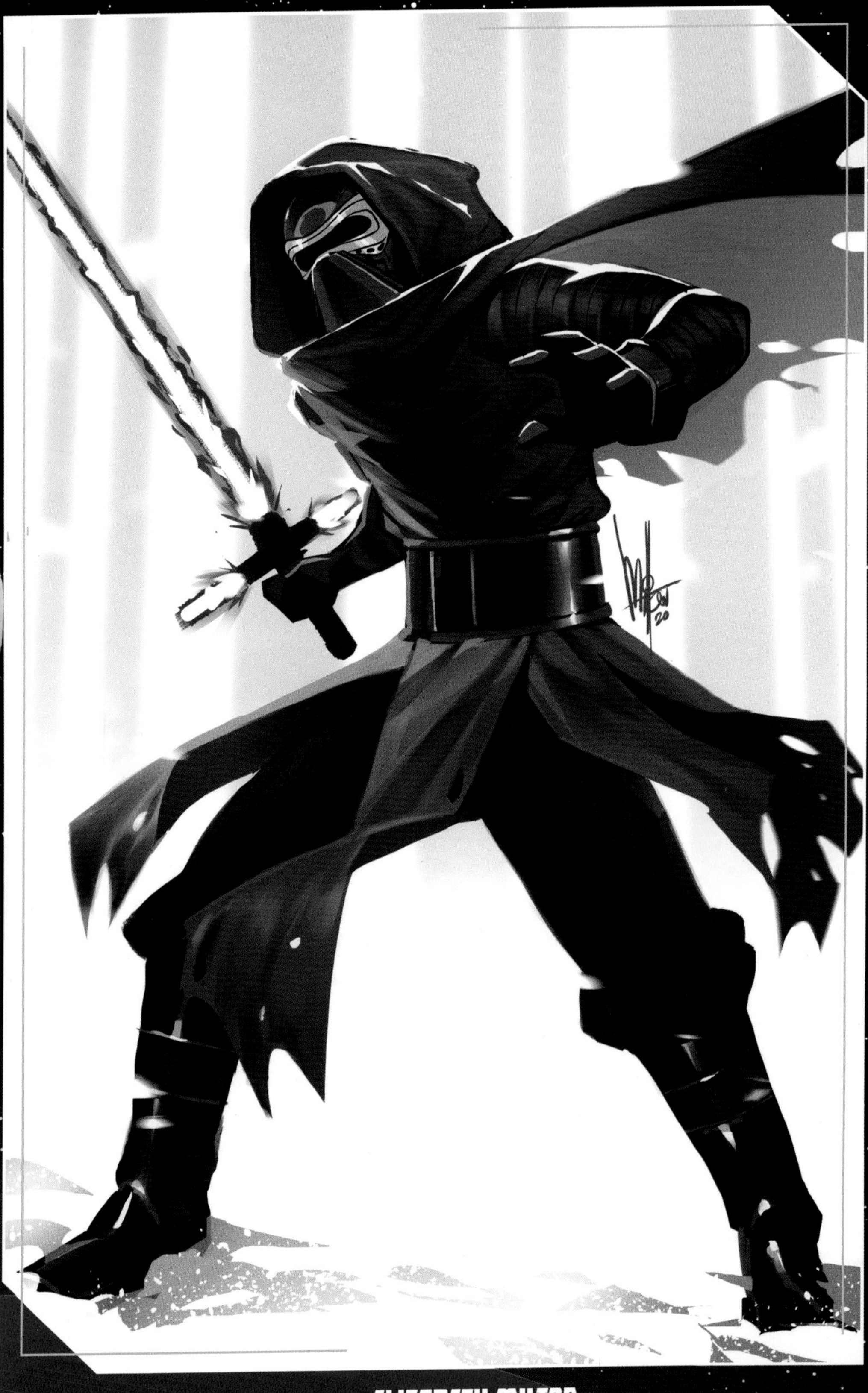

ART BY ELIZABETH MILTON